D1345364

THE FUGITIVES

Also by Jamal Mahjoub

Fiction
Travelling with Djinns
Nuban Indigo
The Drift Latitudes
The Carrier
In the Hour of Signs
Wings of Dust
Navigation of a Rainmaker

Non-fiction
A Line in the River

THE FUGITIVES

JAMAL MAHJOUB

CANONGATE

First published in Great Britain in 2021
by Canongate Books Ltd, 14 High Street, Edinburgh EH1 1TE

canongate.co.uk

1

British Library Cataloguing-in-Publication Data
A catalogue record for this book is available on
request from the British Library

ISBN 978 1 83885 082 1

Typeset in Centaur MT by
Palimpsest Book Production Ltd, Falkirk, Stirlingshire

Printed and bound in Great Britain by Clays Ltd, Elcograf S.p.A.

PART I

*   *   *

Raising the Dead

كثيرِ الغيومِ، قصيرِ العمرْ
'The clouds are many, and life is short'

Al Hussein al-Hassan
(Habibat Oumri)

Chapter 1

Learning to Write

This is a story about a band. A band that lived and flourished and then died its own natural death. At that point it should have disappeared from the pages of the history books for ever, and would have done so if an extraordinary miracle had not occurred and brought the Kamanga Kings back to life.

The only religion I have ever had any faith in is music.

I was brought up to respect tradition. I learned to say my prayers. In school we listened to an old teacher muttering on about the life and times of the Prophet. I did my best to picture it, but seventh-century Arabia felt as far away as Mars. In my heart I believed that if there was a heaven then it would be inhabited by saints who answered to the name of John Coltrane and Charlie Parker; to Monk, Louis Armstrong and Nina Simone. Some of our own would be up there too, seated alongside them. Hassan Attiyah and Al Balabil and, of course, our very own Kamanga Kings, the greatest of all.

Great music transcends all barriers. My father used to say that. He used to say a lot of things. He saw himself as something of a philosopher, when he wasn't being a musician. The way he told it, a nation is like a band waiting for a conductor to show up. Without a leader to guide them an orchestra is just a flock of lost sheep lacking direction. He was certainly right about the country. Our entire history was a list of men who claimed a divine right to lead us. Those who objected tended to fall by the wayside. By the time I was old enough to start asking questions of my own, he was already gone. And maybe that's just the way of things. He paid the price of living in an age when music was not simply frowned upon, but actively discouraged. Musicians had to flee for their lives. They were imprisoned and tortured, along with poets and writers, academics, journalists, anyone, in fact, who could voice an opinion. Musicians were objectionable because they could stir your soul and there were a lot of people who were scared of that.

At this point I should probably apologise. The last thing you expected when you picked up this book was a meditation on leadership and national politics. I beg for your patience just a little while longer. I'm new to this writing game. It's not easy. Whenever I get stuck, which is often, I ask myself, what makes this book worth writing? The answer I always find myself coming back to is simple: if I don't do it, nobody else will.

Were the Kings truly as great as people said? I don't know. I'm not sure how we define greatness. All I know is that when they played, back in their heyday, they did something extraordinary. And that when we reformed the band there were moments when we played, *really* played, when we stirred something in the fabric of the universe that could not be described or imitated, could not be repeated. It had to be lived in that moment. Because that's all it was, a moment. But that's what we did, and it's what we still do when we go out and play. Together we become something more than the sum of our parts. I don't know about you, but to me that sounds pretty close to a definition of greatness.

Like most little boys, I started out dreaming of becoming a superhero, a man possessed of extraordinary powers, who would devote himself to righting the world's wrongs, to saving people, leaping over tall buildings and flying to the rescue of beautiful women who were in distress. And like most children, I grew up to discover life doesn't exactly work like that. Instead of a superhero I became a teacher. I taught English and history to a bunch of ungrateful boys. I took my work seriously. I tried to instil in them a sense of appreciation and respect for the wonders of the world, and of literature. It was a thankless task. All they saw was a short-sighted man spouting nonsense that they could not put to any useful purpose.

It was a good school, or it had been. It was founded by an Italian priest who had left home a hundred and fifty years ago and risked his life travelling across the desert on a donkey to bring us news of Jesus. That's all ancient history now. He didn't manage to convert us all, but he did build this school. Nowadays it caters to the sons of low-ranking military officers and government officials. The high-ranking ones send their children to more fancy places abroad. My job was to try and teach them about *David Copperfield* and *A Tale of Two Cities*. Dickens was my hero, though there were times when I struggled to explain what the experience of a dead white man in nineteenth-century England had to offer a child growing up in Africa in the early twenty-first century. When I suggested we try to update the curriculum a little, the headmaster screwed up his face, as if I had suddenly started speaking another language.

'What are you saying?' he asked, when I explained my idea.

'Maybe it would help if they could identify with the writers.'

'Identify? How?' He cocked a wary eye at me.

'Modern classics, by African writers.'

'African writers, really?' He looked pained.

It was all academic anyway. The very notion of reading was itself alien to most of the boys. To them books were instruments of torture, inflicted upon them by a dying world. They rolled up the pages, scribbled obscene comments in the margins and drew moustaches and outsized genitalia over the illustrations.

Sometimes I felt like the old man who mistook windmills for giants. I was already twenty-six and, like many people my age, I saw no future for myself, nor the country I lived in.

When my father died, he left me two things: a rather battered trumpet and the legend of the Kamanga Kings. For as long as I could remember, the Kings were a part of a lost world, one I had just missed out on. The excitement that came over people when recounting the old stories made you wish you'd been born half a century earlier. Like all legends, that of the Kamanga Kings was a blessing and a curse. Their exploits were woven into the fabric of my life. They shaped the landscape and, of course, the soundtrack from which I had sprung. Their music was the only history I had, etched into my skin like the blue tattoo my grandmother wore on her lip.

A hot wind blows through this old house. Through the open doorway I can see it kicking up the dust in the open yard, tugging at the sheets hanging on the line. I found this typewriter at a stall in the market, its keys rusted into place. They stood out like bony fingers beckoning from the surrounding heap of junk, rusty saws, hammers and chisels, boxes of nails bent out of shape, car batteries, brass scales big enough to weigh a horse, bicycle wheels, wooden saddles and goodness knows what else. The old man who sold it to me confided that it had once belonged to a great writer, whose name had conveniently escaped him. I bargained with him half-heartedly. I knew I was going to buy it. We both knew it. We just had to go through the motions.

'Allah knows, we have need of good writers in these hard times,' he sighed, brushing his fingers fondly over the housing. As a salesman he could have sold sand to the Saudis.

Perhaps, if I had had a little more money, I might have considered getting a laptop, but once I had found it, I became fascinated by that machine. There was something noble about it. With its steel keys and chrome handles, it resembled a bizarre musical instrument. Embossed on the front plate in Arabic: أوليمبيا. Olympia. I had no idea what that meant, beyond some vague notion of a mountain where Greek gods and goddesses languished. He promised to have it cleaned up and oiled in a few days. He even produced a box of ribbons that looked as if they might have been used to wrap a mummy. 'Soak them in ink for a few days and they will be as good as new,' he assured me. I didn't care about the details. I didn't care about the ink. Certainly, I knew I could hardly afford the expense, but I also knew that I had no choice. It had fallen to me to tell this story and if I was going to tell it, then I had to do it now. If I didn't, nobody else ever would.

So now I sit and stare through the open door at the hosh, dazzlingly bright with sunlight. All I have to do is punch the keys to make letters, let the words build themselves into lines, the lines into pages. I can't think beyond that. I can't think that there is going to be an end to this. All I can do is press my fingers down onto the keys. One letter at a time.

Chapter 2

The Letter

It begins with a gentle swish; the sound of a wire brush being dragged across a snare drum. A stiff, ivory-coloured envelope sliding down a delivery chute to land in a post-office box. It was a hot and otherwise unremarkable day. Car horns croaked frantically as the midday traffic jostled past the old colonial building. Inside, a calm serenity reigned. Fan blades circled wearily overhead and nothing much was happening as the envelope in question slipped from the fingers of a distracted clerk going about his work. It's probably fair to say that this envelope was of no great significance to him, no more in fact than any of the hundreds of others that passed through his hands every day. There was nothing to suggest there was anything special about this particular letter that might cause him to pause, even for a second. The weight and quality of the paper, perhaps, or the unusual stamps covering one corner with a colourful spider's web (a work by the Abstract Expressionist Jackson Pollock of whom I had never heard until then). None of this distracted him from his task. In all likelihood he was already on his way long before the letter had flown down the final stretch of its journey, whistling over the polished metal, coming to rest when it hit the door at the end of the chute. He walked on with no idea of the role he had just played in bringing the Kamanga Kings back to life.

I was born in what my father, with his fondness for melodrama, used to call the Year of the Locusts. The year, as he put it, when they fell upon us from the sky like a plague, stripping away all that was good and green about this country and leaving it a decimated wasteland. He was referring to the coup d'état of June 1989. It changed everything. Well, not exactly everything. Some things it just accentuated. He was already drinking by then, awful stuff that could turn you blind. Like music, it was forbidden. The former president had stood proudly on the banks of the Nile to oversee the ceremonial dumping of thousands of bottles of alcohol into the river. It was a declaration of independence, of a return to old ways, and a rejection of Western influence.

It didn't stop people like my father, who would drink just to spite the pious ones. I'm not even sure he actually liked that raw spirit. You had to be desperate to drink the stuff. Toss a glass of it up in the air, they say, and it vaporises. People go blind, lose limbs and suffer terrible afflictions from drinking it. But what is all that against a cry of defiance?

When his body turned up one morning at the bottom of a dry ditch being pawed over by stray dogs, nobody could say they were really surprised. He had finally found the end he had been so keenly seeking. People assumed that it was the drink that had killed him, but that wasn't the whole story. There was no police investigation. No medical report. In those days musicians were an endangered species, as vulnerable as rare birds and ivory-bearing mammals. Saying bad things about the government didn't help your case. It marked you out. One day, shortly after he died, a man came up to me in the street and placed something in my hand. I ran home to show my mother. It was a bullet. He smiled before turning and walking away. I was nine years old.

After my father died, my mother and I moved into Uncle Maher's house. It made sense. He had been widowed for years and had no one to take care of him. My mother breathed new life into her brother's home. I knew my uncle only as a calm, courteous man. A tall, imposing figure who was generally to be found holding court in the street outside his shop every evening. That little corner shop was our only source of income. It was built into one side of the house and he would wander out there as the sun was setting to stand behind the lopsided wooden counter, grubby from years of elbows and greasy palms. He would chat with the customers who came in to buy the single cigarettes from the tin he kept on the counter, or a bowl of fava beans from the bubbling cauldron, a red brick of carbolic soap, a bottle of kerosene, or a handful of charcoal.

The rest of the time he lived like a recluse, locked away in his room. He never, ever talked about the old days when he and my father had formed and run the Kings between them. As far as he was concerned, that time was over and done with. Life moves on, he would say, if the subject ever happened to come up.

At that point, all I really knew about my father was sealed inside a battered greenish-brown trumpet case that had been kicked away under the only real piece of furniture we had – a large glass cupboard stacked with cups, plates and an ornamental teapot that we never used. The case was made of crocodile skin that had grown soft and smooth with time. As a child I would touch it cautiously, as if expecting it to turn around and bite me. When I lifted the lid, a warm glow lit up my face. I would gaze at the gleaming metal curves, the shiny flat brass cone in which my small face appeared, round and distorted like a fish. A fool gazing into a golden pool trying to divine his fate. I would stare and wonder at the mysteries it might contain. It was the only thing I inherited from him and for years I had no idea what on earth it was for.

When I wasn't daydreaming that I could see through walls and fly over the rooftops, that trumpet would hold me spellbound, filling my head with ideas and images that I could not understand. I would take it out and try to hold it, finding comfort in the feel of the worn-down brass valves. I always treated the instrument with a kind of reverence. Closing the case carefully and storing it away. Slowly I learned how to polish and clean it. One day I put it to my lips and blew. From then on, it seems to me, I have been struggling to learn how to play.

My mother helped me to read the piles of sheet music that were lying untouched inside that glass cupboard. She had learned from her father, who once led the police force's brass band. Alongside the music were stacks of vinyl records. CBS, EMI, Blue Note. They became my temple, the place I would go to worship. Their covers revealed another world, one inhabited by sharply dressed black men and women who resembled the people I saw around me. Familiar and at the same time alien. They were in New York and Paris. I wanted to know them, I wanted their walk, their throwaway smiles, elegance and wafting cigarettes. They had a radiance that I felt I could absorb through the pores of my skin just by studying them. I felt them watching over me as I picked my way unsteadily through the maze of notes.

I practised with a discipline that would have surprised anyone who knew me. I pushed the mute into the bowl and blew, alone in a dark room, until the sweat rolled down my brow and stung my eyes, and my fingers slipped on the valves. I played over and over, following the notes on paper as I listened to those records and the bootleg cassettes I bought at a record shop in town. I never played in public. Music was a means of escape, of losing myself, getting away from the troubles of everyday. I dreamed of growing up tall and handsome like Dexter Gordon, though the truth is I was probably more the Dizzy Gillespie type, small, chubby and short-sighted.

In time my dreams settled down. I grew up. I didn't wear a cape or fly through the sky. I cut my hair and stood in a classroom at a school across the river. It was an odd place. The headmaster, or warden, as he styled himself, was another Italian, but the students were a mix of Muslim and Christian. Once the best school in the country, now, like everything else, it was a dusty, worn-down shadow of its former self. My mother was happy. I brought home a salary each month, which meant that we weren't entirely in debt to my uncle. Every morning, as I jolted along on the ancient bus that carried me to and fro across the river, bouncing from side to side with the other passengers, all of us striving both to maintain some degree of dignity and avoid being crushed, I would dream that my life was about to change. How this was to occur I couldn't say. An unforeseen event. A falling meteor. A chance encounter. I was never sure. Whenever the bus stalled, sending up thick clouds of black smoke from beneath the exhausted chassis, I would sigh and tell myself that dreams were for the birds and that I needed to accept my fate. Things would never change and the sooner I accepted this the better.

On most days, my work consisted largely of trying to prevent a class of unruly boys from murdering one another. When I first began, I was driven by a noble sense of duty. I assumed that the point of teaching was to instil some feeling of possibility, some idea of the wonders the world contained, the lofty heights to which one might aspire. In the end, I stood at the board with a piece of chalk and scribbled page after page of notes for them to copy. I prayed only for the hour to pass without serious injury. With over fifty pupils per class it wasn't so much a classroom as a riot fenced in by green walls and battered wooden desks. My job was to keep them restrained for long enough to convey to their parents (who were paying their fees and thereby my salary) the idea that they were actually learning something.

In history class, I tried to give the boys an understanding of how we got to where we are today. They were not really interested, but I told them anyway, about independence in 1956, about the old world where everything was run by Englishmen wearing shorts and funny hats and that at its height the British Empire covered one fifth of the globe. I would explain how that came to an end with World War II, when people started to question the point of dying for somebody else's empire. As soon as it was over, everyone demanded their freedom.

12

I looked into their faces and asked them what they thought we had done with our hard-won independence. Nobody had an answer. It wasn't something they thought about, how we got here. We took our freedom, I would explain, and we began fighting amongst ourselves. This wasn't a country, I would say, it was a gigantic boxing ring. It was risky, talking politics. I had already been warned. Parents had complained. They didn't like that I was filling their children's innocent heads with ideas. As my students stared at me, I wondered if this was some part of my father's legacy, resurfacing from somewhere deep in my soul. Trying to change the world when nobody seemed to care. The point I am trying to make, I would tell them, is that we have to take responsibility for our future. If we don't, we will always be exploited by people for their own gain.

Of course, I didn't tell them the really important stuff, about how the Kamanga Kings brought the country together, about how one band managed what countless presidents had been unable to achieve: to turn us into a nation. Guitars hummed, Hammond organs buzzed, violins wailed and trumpets howled. In every corner of the land, people sat up and paid attention to their radios. For one brief moment the whole country was united. Most people don't remember that time and I knew of it only because of the stories my mother had told me. To my pupils the Kamanga Kings was a forgotten chapter. Their lack of knowledge of their own history was no accident. I didn't need to tell them that the music stopped when religion came in to replace politics, that the lights went out and darkness fell across the country, just as I didn't need to mention curfews, prisons, torture and war, because these were the things that had made their fathers wealthy. It was what had put them in this school to begin with.

'Literature is something you must learn to respect,' I told them one day. 'Modern man is deluded by the technical tools at his disposal. They give him the illusion of power over his physical environment.'

This confounded them. They gazed at me, mystified. There were a few giggles. They nudged one another. 'True improvement comes from within. You can buy a new watch,' I said, grabbing the hand of a nearby boy to demonstrate, ignoring his yelp of pain. 'But that doesn't mean you can speed up time. You can get into a shiny car and fly along the road, but you can't shorten the distance between two places. Literature, however, can achieve all of these things and more.

'Literature transports the mind. It allows you to become someone living in another century, on the other side of the world. An old man, say, or a beautiful girl.' (Bad move, this, as predictably it provoked a tirade of howls and cat calls.) 'Literature gives your imagination wings.'

But ustaz, they objected, if Allah had wanted us to have wings surely he would have given them to us, like the birds? This timeless logic was followed by a chorus of desk lids slamming and savage whoops as the bell marking the end of the lesson chimed, releasing all of us from this hopeless predicament.

In their eyes I represented everything they would never aspire to be. I had no money. I had no authority. Books were less a gateway to undiscovered universes than weapons for striking the boy in front of them on the head, or to hide behind when they wanted to whisper to a neighbour. They would sit there with a battered copy of the abridged version of *Oliver Twist* or *Lorna Doone* raised up to cover their faces, laughing and giggling like fools, thinking I could neither see nor hear them.

You cannot educate people who already know all the answers. I was the transmitter of useless facts, a clown for their entertainment. An amusement. These boys were the heirs to the oil boom that had come and gone. They were the sons of military officers, government functionaries, lawyers, entrepreneurs, businessmen who had built them-selves a fortress against the common man. Good things come not to those who wish to learn, but to those who seize what they want with both hands. The world of men with guns. The key to future prosperity lay not in what you knew, but who you knew. Making your way in the world was about having the right connections, and they already had those. School was just a way of passing the time until they were ready to go to work.

At the end of each day I wiped the chalk from my hands, packed my bag and walked out through the school gates to join the throngs jostling for space in a microbus, drawing a magical cape over me to cut out the noise and heat of the streets, the dust as rich and spicy as black pepper. I might glimpse a face looking at me through a speeding window as they growled by in their big cars, being sped home in air-conditioned comfort. It was a look of pity, before I was dismissed from their minds until tomorrow.

Chapter 3

Uncle Maher

U ncle Maher was probably the last person in the world who continued to use the old mailboxes at the central post office next to the presidential palace. Everyone else had forgotten all about them, which explained the abandoned state of the place; an old brick building left behind by the British. Letters had become a thing of the past. Nowadays everyone carried a phone in their pocket and could communicate with relatives abroad at the touch of a button. Who needed stamps and envelopes? Phones had gone from being sober instruments of communication to expensive, disposable toys. When they weren't chattering away people played games on them and listened to music. The old telephone exchange had been replaced by tea vendors sitting under neem trees around town. They would have a handful of cell phones draped around their necks so you could make a call while drinking your tea. Letters were as useful as hieroglyphics carved into stone.

But old habits die hard and for Uncle Maher collecting the mail remained a sacred ritual. Once a week he rode across the river, strode into the post office, pushed his key into the lock and opened the little green door to see if there was anything there. It was a duty he performed with all the solemnity of a state ceremony. Every Friday he would rise in the morning, take his tea and then proceed to dress carefully in a freshly ironed gellabiya, taking his time to roll and wind the long imma around his head so tightly you couldn't get a match-stick between the folds of cloth. Then he would reach for his ebony stick and walk out into the dirty streets like an apparition, floating in a swathe of white cotton. He would wander down to the main road and there the same battered yellow Hillman taxi would be parked on the corner waiting for him. It had a green stripe along the side and a black ostrich feather mounted on the front of the hood. The driver was a strange fellow with narrow eyes and a wreath of grey hair clinging to the sides of his skull. He was known to most of us as Wad Mazaj, due to his eternal grumbling. He'd been with the Kings in the old days and the weekly ritual of the post office visit was really an alibi for the two men to go on and eat breakfast at a café by the river and reminisce for hours.

Most weeks, of course, there was nothing in the little post box and my uncle would return home empty handed. Over the years, as other aspects of his life withered away, this ritual had acquired more importance than it perhaps deserved. He would peer into the empty box and ponder his fate. Not this time.

The first I knew of any of this was when I was summoned one afternoon to my uncle's room, a part of the house to which I was generally not invited. A wall separated the rest of us from Uncle Maher's little domain. Passing through the gap in the wall was always a little intimidating. I climbed the three brick steps and rapped cautiously on the door, only to have it fly open and Uncle Maher thrust his head out. He looked both ways to make sure there was no one else there before turning a wary eye on me.

'Well, boy, what have you got to say for yourself?'

'I'm fine, Ammu. I take it you are well?'

'Never mind how I am, I have something to show you.'

That room had not always been out of bounds. When I was younger, I would think nothing of sneaking in there when my uncle was out. There was a time, when I was very young, when he even invited me in to show me his collection. With a magnanimous sweep of his hand, he indicated the shelf weighed down with vinyl records and sheet music. The collection was once the envy of many. An extensive treasure trove that was surely one of the most comprehensive in the country. That afternoon it looked more dusty and dilapidated than ever. Dust filtered in beneath the doors, slipped through the wooden slats of the window shutters, building up in tiny ridges like miniature sand dunes between the racks of sleeves. Nowadays he refused to allow anyone in there without a fight – even my mother only managed to give it a dusting once or twice a year. The records were taken down too rarely and the intense heat of countless summers had in time caused a good few of them to become warped. The vinyl discs lost all plane sense. If placed on a turntable they would wobble like flying saucers visiting from another galaxy, the needle rising and falling over soft waves of black plastic.

'Half of these are rightfully yours,' he would often say. 'They belonged to your father.'

Maybe he was trying to tell me something. Either way, for a brief period I had enjoyed the privilege of being allowed to explore his collection, to sift through the row of albums at my leisure. I wasn't allowed to touch the record player myself, of course. We had to go through a lengthy ritual whereby my uncle would click the heavy round knob which brought the display panel to life. Raising the wooden lid he slipped the vinyl disc from the cover with great care to place it gently on the turntable. Then he would run a felt pad along the grooves to remove any dust or fluff, before engaging the arm and dropping the needle down on the revolving lamina. I would watch spellbound, waiting for the magical moment and even now, years later, I can recall the shock of that moment, hearing the sound of a trumpet (Miles Davis's 'Walkin'' from the 1954 album) coming so cleanly and loudly through the speakers it felt like brass wire drawn from thin air. It was as if the musicians were right there in the room with us.

In the company of my uncle every record had to be treated with reverence. Music was not a casual affair for playing in the background; it demanded one's full attention. During that time, we spent long afternoons shut into that airless room. Uncle Maher refused to open the windows because he said the dust got into the grooves. So we sweated away while we listened to one album after another. Jazz occupied a particular spot in his heart. The original source of inspiration for the Kings was Louis Armstrong, who had once played to a bemused audience in the football stadium here back in 1961. My father and uncle were in the audience. Uncle Maher preferred the more traditional sound of Duke Ellington, whom he regarded as nothing less than a genius, whereas my father, he claimed, had been more fond of the irreverence of Sonny Rollins or Mingus. His tastes ran in every direction, from bebop to cool to 1970s Ethiopian saxophonist Getatchew Mekurya, from mystical Hopi chants to Billie Holliday, he had it all covered. There were Morna singers from Cape Verde's creoles, Highlife bands from Ghana and dance music from Kinshasa alongside Mauritian Sega, classical Western music and even opera. There seemed to be no limits on what Uncle Maher felt he could learn from.

In my teenage years I summoned the courage to sneak into the room a couple of times when my uncle was out. I would even play some of the LPs at such a low volume, for fear of being caught, that I had to press my ear to the amplifier just to hear the strains of music drifting out. It was like listening to sounds of life from a distant planet. I was eventually caught, given a sound beating and warned never to enter the room unless expressly invited. Now, as I looked around, I felt like an exiled prince returning to a lost chapter of his childhood.

The old Blaupunkt Radiogram was still there in the corner, smaller and more fragile than I recalled, the records on the shelf looked more neglected than ever. And even the old man, standing behind the big desk at the far end of the room, resembled a relic that belonged in a museum. The shelves and table were cluttered with spiderwebs, dead beetles and heaps of brittle, yellowed newspaper. In the middle of this chaos I spied a single object. An ivory-coloured envelope covered in postage stamps and what looked like slivers of red onion. Uncle Maher handed it to me as he sank into his chair and cleared his throat.

'Well, boy, what do you make of that?'

'It looks like a letter,' I offered. Uncle Maher rolled his eyes.

'Of course it's a letter, boy. Any damn fool could have told me that!'

'Why does it have onion on it?'

He squinted. 'We took it with us to breakfast,' he shrugged, as if this was quite reasonable. He seemed unusually jittery. Whatever this letter was, its arrival had disturbed him in some profound way.

'Perhaps . . .?' I gestured. 'I mean, I could . . .'

Uncle Maher huffed and puffed, his cheeks expanding like an accordion as he sighed.

'Why else do you think I called you over?'

I picked up the envelope and brushed it off. 'Washington D.C.,' I read.

I pretended not to hear Uncle Maher's resigned sigh. I turned it over in my hands once again, feeling the quality and weight of the thick, sharply edged paper. It was certainly far superior to any envelope I had seen in my life. I looked up to see him lift a long slim dagger with a handle made of camel bone and point it directly at my heart.

'Ammu?' I asked, suddenly alarmed.

'Just get it over with,' he growled, handing me the knife.

Taking it carefully from him, I inserted the tip of the blade and slit the top of the envelope. Inside was a single sheet of thick paper which I unfolded and began to read while trying to ignore the nervous tattoo my uncle's fingers were drumming on the desktop.

My command of the English language is not perfect. I admit that.

Teaching a group of ignorant boys in Junior Secondary school does not encourage one to advance. In the land of the blind and so on. When I read the likes of Mr Defoe, or Miss Jane Austen, in abridged format, I am aware that I am only seeing a faint shadow of their great works. I read the same books every year and so I know them almost by heart. In other words, my understanding of the language is limited by my experience. Beyond that narrow band of illumination I know that the horizon stretches out far beyond my understanding. To put it simply, I was not too confident about what I was doing. Nevertheless, I couldn't let Uncle Maher down. So, I decided to take my time.

'It's from . . .' I mouthed the words carefully, aware even then of the significance of those embossed letters along the top of the paper. 'The John F. Kennedy Center for the Performing Arts, in Washington D.C.' I glanced up. 'In the United States.'

'Hmm,' he grunted.

'That would be Kennedy, as in President John Fitzgerald Kennedy?'

He eyed me wearily. 'He's no longer the president. He was shot, years ago, before you were born, by a communist, thank God, not a Muslim.'

I knew, of course, that Kennedy was no longer the president, that the post had been filled by a cartoon character worthy of the great Walt Disney himself. Nonetheless, I felt a touch of pride. The very notion of a direct link between that great man and the room we were standing in left me breathless and numb. I decided to keep my comments to myself for the moment as I carried on reading, picking my way along the lines cautiously, the syllables forcing my lips to move silently. I could hear Uncle Maher sighing.

'Get on with it, boy,' he growled.

I read through the letter slowly and understood almost nothing of its contents. But this was not the moment to admit defeat, so, with a glance at my uncle, I began reading it through again. The words swam before my eyes. I found it difficult to focus and could only pick out fragments here and there, gradually threading them together into some sort of coherent form.

'It's an invitation,' I said, as it finally dawned on me.

Uncle Maher scratched his nose. 'What kind of invitation?'

'On the occasion of the annual festival of world music,' I translated. Then I looked up. 'The Kamanga Kings.'

'They want . . . the Kamanga Kings . . . to play, in America?'

'It looks that way.'

'That's not possible.' His Adam's apple rose and sank like a toiling ship. 'I mean, how could they know about us? Is it a joke, do you think?'

'I . . . I don't know.'

'Please tell me this isn't one of your droll attempts at humour. I have precious few years left, so keep them for after I have gone.'

'No, Ammu, of course it's not a joke.'

He stared at me. 'Read it again.' He closed his eyes and sat forward in fierce concentration.

So I did, and this time, as I read it aloud, the significance of what I was reading began to dawn on me. I set the letter down and delivered my verdict.

'They want the Kamanga Kings to perform at a festival of world music in three months' time, in Washington D.C., America.'

'America?' he echoed, as if trying out the syllables in an unfamiliar word. 'America?'

'But this is wonderful news. It means . . .'

His white eyebrows shot up. 'What does it mean?'

'Well,' I hesitated. What did it actually mean? 'It means your reputation has arrived.'

Reaching for his ebony stick, he stamped it twice on the ground and growled. 'Your talents are wasted in trying to teach those boys anything. You would have more success with wild animals from the forest. At least they might teach you a thing or two about life.'

I was tempted to reply that this was in fact the case, but it didn't seem the time.

'We must write to them immediately,' I suggested. The letter was dated six months ago. There was no explanation for the delay, other than the obvious. The criss-crossed dates on the envelope indicated it had been sent to a number of places before it had finally arrived. Time appeared to be of the essence.

'It's impossible.' Uncle Maher shook his head.

'Sorry?'

'It's too late.' I saw his lips quivering.

'But surely . . .'

'Useless, I say,' he muttered, grinding the tip of his stick into the floor. 'The Kamanga Kings no longer exist.' His shoulders slumped as the breath went out of his lungs, indeed the essence of life itself seemed to escape him.

Chapter 4

Forgotten Kings

The old black and white photographs pinned inside the glass cupboard showed two skinny young men, their shirts tucked into high-waisted trousers. My father and Uncle Maher stood side by side against a painted backdrop in the photographer's studio, their trousers flared and their Afros high. Uncle Maher, the taller of the two, held his violin propped against his hip. My father, wearing a moustache that drooped down to his chin, held his trumpet against his chest with both hands as if it were a weapon.

Although people still talked of the Kings with reverence, the fact is that there were fewer and fewer who actually remembered them.

'Why now?' he murmured, resting his chin on the pommel of his stick. 'Where were they thirty years ago, twenty, even?'

'It's never too late, Ammu.'

His eyes lifted to find mine. I half expected him to reprimand me, but instead he smiled.

'It's kind of you to say so, boy, but no, I'm afraid you're wrong.'

'He misses your father,' said my mother when I recounted the story to her later. She was in the kitchen brewing tea, fanning the charcoal stove with a piece of cardboard. 'They built it all together. Now he's old and can barely see a sheet of paper if you hold it under his nose.'

'Wouldn't it be wonderful, though?'

The strip of cardboard she was flapping like a broken wing came to a halt. She gave me that look, the one that asked if she had really raised an idiot for a child.

'It's going to stir up all the old memories. All those things he has put away for ever. At his age it's enough to kill him. Listen to me, Rushdy, tear up that letter and forget about it.'

'Perhaps it would be good for him.'

She dismissed the idea with a click of her tongue. 'You're too young to remember, but in their heyday they were truly legendary. They lifted the spirits of the entire nation. Their music was played in every corner of the country. They shone. No one can ever take that away from him. But he's an old man now, and maybe it's better not to stir all that old dust up again.'

They shone.

The two men could not have been more different in character, she explained. Uncle Maher was the pragmatist, the one who believed that hard work and discipline were the route to success. My father, on the other hand, was the dreamer who thought that talent and sacrifice were mutually exclusive. The two of them were close, but that didn't mean that they always saw eye to eye.

'It wasn't always smooth sailing, but they needed one another,' she went on. 'They fought a lot because they loved playing. In the beginning they were the only two people in the world who really believed in what they were doing. Afterwards everyone claimed to love them, but it wasn't always like that.'

The sun set on the Kamanga Kings as an era came to a close. Piety and intolerance rolled in. Civil war broke out. More importantly, tastes changed. The Afro-Jazz they had pioneered gave way to tinny pop music. Two finger tunes tapped out on electronic synthesizers, apeing Western styles. The skills of the Kings went the way of flared trousers. Nobody really appreciated what they could do. My father and Uncle Maher watched the orchestra they had built up fall into decay. There were disagreements, the musicians drifted apart. My father's devotion to alcohol grew more serious. He became increasingly isolated, surrounded only by young writers and would-be poets who gathered around to hear him insult everyone, from the president on down.

'At a certain point, I remember thinking,' my mother said, her eyes growing moist, 'that he was determined to die. It was just a question of where and how. Your uncle never forgave him for losing faith in what they had had but the truth of the matter is that he had lost the will to go on.'

That night I lay in bed thinking about my father, how I had always believed that he had somehow been killed. Now I wondered if he could have simply drunk himself to death. What kind of despair could drive a man to that? Unable to sleep, I fancied I could hear the scratchy sound of the old gramophone records drifting across the yard from Uncle Maher's room. I hadn't heard him play anything for years. I wished my father had lived long enough for me to get to know him. I wondered what he had been like when he was my age, before he lost his way. I tried to imagine what it would be like to be able to talk to him now, to share this moment, to hear his thoughts.

When I finally fell asleep, I dreamed of the Kamanga Kings, all dressed up in fine clothes, standing on a stage resplendent with light, while below them the audience clapped and cheered every number. When I awoke the next morning, I could remember the whole dream, every moment of it. I couldn't really remember the music they had been playing. All I knew was that it was quite unlike anything I had ever heard in my entire life.

Chapter 5

Hisham's Garage

On most days, after the daily struggle with the savage boys and the subsequent battle to get home through the whirling inferno of traffic, dusty crowds and heat, I would arrive exhausted, eat lunch with my mother and then sleep for an hour or so. And when the day had burned itself out, I would drag the trumpet case from under the bed in my room and practice before heading over to Hisham's place.

We had been best friends for as long as I could remember. His father was an army officer, which was one of the oddest aspects of our friendship. Hisham's father and mine were essentially on opposite sides of the political fence. For years his father had been posted far away on the Red Sea coast and refused to return to the capital. Rumour had it that he had another wife and family out there, although Hisham never wanted to talk about that.

I say he was my best friend, but actually we were quite unlike one another. Even physically. Hisham being tall and slim, with a narrow beard that he cultivated thinking that it made him look more interesting. He was sharp, witty and impulsive while I was, well, not. Hisham lived with his mother, sisters and grandparents in a big, modern house that even had an upstairs floor. Since my house was smaller and seemed to have herds of people tramping through it day and night, we would usually wind up in his garage, which we liked to think of, rather grandly, as our studio.

The car had disappeared long ago, around the same time as Hisham's father. The garage behind the house had been turned into a storeroom, slowly filling up with cardboard boxes and packing cases, along with bits and pieces of broken furniture that had nowhere else to go but which somebody, for some inexplicable reason, thought worth keeping. Over the years we had made that space our own, clearing the junk to one side, making it habitable. It was far enough away from the main house for no one to mind the noise we made. By the time we were in secondary school, Hisham had managed to persuade his absent father to buy him an electric keyboard and we would practise together in the afternoons, playing along to all the old songs we had on cassette. We spent our time in the company of the greats. What we lacked in formal training we made up for in enthusiasm. Our collection of battered cassette tapes had been accumulated over the years. Some had been recorded from vinyl LPs ages ago, in someone's home, or in one of the shops downtown where they provided this service as the only means of getting hold of recorded music. Often, we had no idea how we had even come by them. Many of the tapes bore no marking to show what they contained. In some cases, it wasn't until years later that we discovered we had been playing along to a renowned classic.

Included in our collection were most of the known recordings of the Kamanga Kings. The two albums they had recorded in the studio, along with a handful of live performances taped informally at wedding parties and the like. Legendary stuff. We listened to them over and over, despite the poor quality. We would smile at the background noises, the sound of people having fun, and fall into a reverent silence when an instrument came in that we recognised; my father on trumpet, or Uncle Maher's distinctive kamanga, the violin that gave the group their name.

My uncle had sworn me to secrecy regarding the letter but three days had gone by during which I had done nothing but think about

America and what it might be like to travel there. The idea obsessed me. It made sleep impossible and left me tossing from side to side all night. On the bus ride into town every morning, what was usually an unendurable torture of heat, discomfort and noise passed in a fleeting blur. I was so lost in my thoughts that I missed my stop on the way home and had to walk back along the road in the dust. It was as if a door had opened, dangling a world full of possibility before me.

And so the inevitable happened. I poured out the whole story in one long, rambling, incoherent flood. As I spoke, I became aware that Hisham had stopped working on the joint he was rolling. His face was going through some form of transformation. His jaw dropped and his eyes widened.

'Amreeka? You're going to Amreeka?'

'No, no.' I held up my hand to stem the tide. 'That's what I'm trying to tell you, no one is going anywhere.'

'You're crazy,' he said. He ran his tongue along the paper and twisted it into shape.

'The Kamanga Kings are history.'

'Who says?' Hisham struck a match and held the flame up to his creation. He puffed away for a moment or two before handing it over.

'Who says?' I echoed. A part of me felt that this was none of his business. This was a family matter. We were just talking. I champed my teeth down on the joint and filled my lungs. I waited for my thoughts to clear.

'Look, I mean, you know, Ammu Maher is getting on and besides, he hasn't played for years. As for the rest of them, well, they're long gone.'

'What is the matter with you?' Hisham stared at me. 'They're not history, they're a legend. They're alive.'

'What are you talking about?' I asked, handing back the joint. 'Most of the original line-up are dead.' Including my father, I wanted to add, but didn't.

'In our hearts, they will live for ever.' He thumped a fist into his chest to emphasise the point.

'Okay, this was a mistake. I should never have said anything.'

But Hisham was no longer listening. He paced up and down, puffing away agitatedly. 'Do you have any idea what this means?'

'Hold on a second. You talk as if it was you who was invited.' I picked up my horn and fiddled with the valves. 'Come on, let's play something.' Hisham pushed the trumpet aside and rapped his knuckles on my head.

'Wake up, sleepy head! We can't let an opportunity like this pass us by.'

'Who is we?' I could feel myself growing angry. 'When did you enter the debate?'

'This is part of us, part of who we are.' He handed me the joint again.

I laughed. 'You and I?' I took a puff. It was ridiculous. We were not even part of the band. It was over before we were old enough to walk.

'What are you saying, that we just accept it?' Hisham snatched the joint from my lips. 'The Kamanga Kings are part of us. They're in our DNA. If there is anyone in this wide world who has a right to consider themselves direct heirs, it's you and me. We grew up playing their music.'

'Our DNA?' I giggled. The whole thing was absurd. 'You're taking this much too seriously.'

'I can't believe you don't see what this is.'

'Well, maybe you should enlighten me.'

'All right,' he said. 'I will. We're going to reform the band.'

'What?'

'You heard me.'

'You're not serious?' But he had an odd stare in his eyes that told me he was.

'Who else is there? Like you said, most of them are dead, and the ones that aren't are as good as.'

'We can't just reform the band.'

'Why not? Give me one good reason.'

'How about, because we weren't in the band to begin with?'

Hisham lifted his shoulders. 'I don't see that as a problem.'

'You don't see . . .' I had feared something like this. 'I should never have mentioned it.'

'Look, Rushdy.' He grabbed me by the shoulders and shook me so hard my eyeballs rattled. 'This is it, our one chance. Our only chance. The best chance we will ever have. The chance to start a new life in America.' He twirled away, spinning on his toes, tapping his feet to a tune in his head.

I held up the joint. 'Did you smoke one of these before I arrived?'

Hisham lurched back towards me. I pulled away warily.

'We'll persuade them. All of them. We'll put a band together, a great band, a legendary band. A mix of the old and some of the new.'

He was talking so fast I could barely catch it all.

'They'll jump at it. Come on, it's what they've always dreamed of.'

'Yeah,' I pointed out, 'but it's their dream, not ours.'

'You've said it yourself, plenty of times. The Kings symbolised all of our dreams. They made us what we are. Think about that.'

'This is crazy. You're crazy.' I started to get to my feet. Hisham pushed me down again.

'What if all they've lost is their *faith* in the dream. What if it's our responsibility, our destiny, to bring that dream back to life?'

'Faith? Destiny? Hisham, pull yourself together. You're making no sense.'

'No, no, I'm making perfect sense, and you know it. They still have the dream, but they've been crushed.' He clenched his fist in front of my face. 'Crushed by time, despair, hopelessness, by a world where the answer is always no, never.' His eyes were wide with some kind of madness. 'You know what I'm talking about. It's been crushing you for years.'

I stared at him. His wild gaze scared me. Not just because I thought he was wrong, but because I knew that a part of me wanted to believe that he was right.

31

Chapter 6

Broken Dreams

The next day I went straight to see Uncle Maher after work. I had spent the whole night thinking about what Hisham had said. That morning, as the screaming boys leapt like monkeys between the aisles, across the desks, thumping one another's heads against the walls, throwing flaming balls of newspaper across the room, I had wished I was anywhere in the world but there.

I approached Uncle Maher's room with newfound purpose. Once I reached the door, however, I hesitated, the old fears returning. I called his name a couple of times. When there was no reply, I pushed the door. It creaked gently open to reveal him stretched out on the bed, staring at the ceiling. He was unshaven and did not appear to have changed his clothes since the previous day. A glance around the room told me it was more chaotic than usual. Records and album covers were strewn about, scattered across the table and chairs, even the floor. The old gramophone player, which had been buried underneath a mountain of old newspapers, stood open, the turntable revolving slowly.

I had assumed he was asleep, but as I drew closer I saw that his eyes were open. I edged up to him slowly, then noticed that he didn't appear to be breathing.

'Ammu?'

I jumped back in surprise when he drew a deep, slow breath.

'It's all over, boy,' he murmured in a deep, low rumble. 'The Kings are ancient history and there is nothing anyone can do about it.'

I realised then that over the years we had all allowed this room to become a tomb in which the old man had been slowly burying himself. On the floor beside him lay his old violin case. Uncle Maher had not played in a very long time. I lifted it up gently and carried it over to the desk. The leather case was split in several places. I blew the dust off it before undoing the catches and opening the lid. Inside, on a threadbare red velvet lining, rested the old kamanga. The varnish was worn down to bare wood where his chin had rested. It was many years since he had used it. There was something terribly sad about the way it sat there on the faded lining, neglected, forgotten. I reached into the case and lifted the instrument delicately with both hands, holding it up towards the light. I turned towards him and held it out. He straightened up slowly but said nothing, just stared at me. After a long time, he reached out to take it from me. I watched his long, slender fingers as they stretched and folded around the lacquered wood, remembering the shape of it, the way it fitted to his body. He turned it this way and that, squinting along the neck, looking for signs of distortion. Then his despair returned and he rested the instrument on his knees. It looked so fragile, for a moment I thought he was going to smash it with his bare hands. He plucked at a string and it snapped with a loud ping.

With a sigh, he handed back the violin and reached for his walking stick. He struggled to stand and then gave up, his fingers opening and closing, as if he had forgotten what he was planning to do. I followed his line of sight and it led me to that old black and white photograph. The glass was broken and the frame tilted at a lopsided angle. We both stared at it in silence. The two young men full of hope and dreams. He was tall and slim, proud in his sharp clothes. His eyes, reflecting the fierce lights of the photographer's studio, gleamed with hope. In his hand he held the same violin I was now holding.

Uncle Maher's shoulders arched like a bow. His long, thin legs made him resemble a stork. On the rare occasions when I had seen him play that violin he seemed able to transform it, to bring it to life, to make it melt into any shape he wanted it to be, bending and contorting it to play as sweetly as if it was a living, breathing creature.

'I am a foolish old man,' he muttered, peering at the photograph. 'That letter brought back all the old memories.'

'It's never too late, Ammu.'

'You're being kind, boy.' He shook his head. 'If they had invited us back then . . . we could have shown them a thing or two.' He stared at the floor. 'But now? You think the Americans would fly us around the world just to watch us expire in front of them?'

'No, no please . . . don't say that. Of course you can do it.'

'It was good of you to try and cheer up an old man.' Carefully, he replaced the instrument in its case and closed the lid. His hands lingered for a moment after he had clicked the clasps shut. 'Kindly destroy that letter before anyone else sees it.'

'But Ammu . . .'

'Please,' he said softly. 'You cannot play a concert with ghosts. Most of the old line-up has gone to their grave, including your dear father. We must face the facts.'

He turned away, mumbling to himself as he left the room, with the same dignified hobble that I had come to know in recent years. It was true he was getting older, but it wasn't a physical ailment that was weighing him down, it was his spirit. He paused, then looked back at me and I saw, for the first time in as long as I could remember, something approaching compassion in his eyes.

'Thank you for trying, my boy.'

Maybe he was right. Maybe there was no longer a place in this world for his kind. It made it seem much sadder somehow, as if we had just lost something we never knew we had.

✻ ✻ ✻

The next morning the class was again in uproar and I found myself numb with inertia. What was I doing with my life? I stared helplessly as the boys hopped up and down, slamming the desk lids, hurling sandwiches across the room. As silence spread, I turned to see Ustaz Awad standing in the doorway, summoned no doubt by the noise.

Ustaz Awad was a pale-skinned Egyptian maths teacher who always wore immaculately pressed white shirts and trousers that looked as though they had been ironed five minutes ago. He had a high forehead and a stony gaze. On his forehead he had a zebiba, the dark blemish that pious men wore as a badge of their devotion. It was to signify how frequently and fervently they bowed to touch the prayer mat. I had heard stories that he beat the pupils, that he twisted their nipples and slapped the ends of their fingertips with a wire-edged ruler. His reputation was so fearsome that if ever his shadow crossed the threshold of a classroom every boy would turn to stone.

He said nothing, just stood there and glared. The boys tumbled over one another in their haste to return to their seats. They picked up their books and sat in silence. He looked at me for a second before spinning on his heels and walking away without a word. Later that morning a boy ran up to tell me I was wanted in the warden's office. I went down to explain myself. The office was dark and lined with wood. He sat behind the desk. A dour man with a pallid complexion and prominent eye teeth that had earned him the nickname Dracula among the pupils and even some of the staff. He gestured at the seat opposite him. He wore a spotless white soutane, which made him look even more pale.

'I warned you about talking politics to the boys,' he said, tapping his fingers on the desk.

'I wasn't.'

He glared at me. 'Several boys have complained to their parents.'

'About what?'

'They say you are teaching evolution. Darwin and all that.' The warden gave an irritated flap of the hand. '*Ev-o-lu-zione.*'

'But I don't teach Darwin.'

'This is a very serious accusation. We could be shut down.'

'Whatever they said, it's not true. I haven't . . .' I stopped talking when I saw his hand held up.

'Frankly, I don't care if it's true or not. With you, it's always . . .' He wrinkled up his nose as he fished for the right word in English. 'Trouble.'

I passed Ustaz Awad on the stairs. He didn't say a word. He didn't have to; the look was enough.

That afternoon for some reason I was unable to find a ride home. There seemed to be twice as many people as usual, or half as many minibuses. From snatches of conversation around me I understood there was a shortage of fuel. Queues of vehicles tailing out from petrol stations confirmed this. Drivers settled down, dozing in their cars, waiting for the diesel to arrive and the pumps to start working again.

By the time I got home I was exhausted, too tired even to eat the lunch which my mother reminded me she had spent hours preparing. It was the end of an incredibly hot afternoon and I had struggled through one of the worst days of my life. I felt as though everything was conspiring against me. All I wanted to do was to shut my eyes and lie down in a dark room. I managed to close my eyes for what felt like a minute when there was a furious knocking at the door. It was Hisham, at his most infuriating. Literally hopping from one foot to the other.

'Go away,' I said. 'I'm tired.'

'You are familiar with the Hegelian concept of thesis, antithesis and synthesis?'

'You've been reading a book again,' I said, wearily turning to go back to bed. He ignored me, of course. It was that kind of a day. He pushed past me.

'Hegel argues that progress is spiral.'

'Spiral?' I sat down on the bed and watched him. He was buzzing around so fast the room seemed to have shrunk. It made me dizzy just to watch him.

'Change is constant. We begin with a thesis, counter it and then rise above it. This is called synthesis.'

'This is called madness and you need to go away and let me sleep.'

'Don't you see, I've solved it.'

'Solved what?'

'I've found a way to make this work.'

'Make *what* work?'

As Hisham paced up and down – two steps up, an about-turn at the cupboard and then two more back – he was also smoking, filling the air with a nauseating cloud of tobacco fumes with quick, urgent puffs, which meant that more of it ended up in the room than ever came near his lungs.

'Come on, I'll show you. Get up. Get up!'

He dragged me by one arm, which left me hanging reluctantly out of bed, half on the floor. I followed him, still in my teaching clothes, out through the narrow doorway into the yard. It was almost sunset and the light was dipping wistfully down through languid shades of tangerine and indigo. Hisham led on, out through the front door into the street. The old one-eyed man who kept goats called a greeting across the street.

'Where are you young men going then, out chasing girls, are we?'

I ignored his chuckles as he writhed against the wall on the twisted frame of a chair that had three legs and no back. Hisham clutched my arm.

'Where are you taking me?' I asked.

'The Kamanga Kings are alive and well, and I am going to take you to see them right now.'

'What?' I asked, lifting the hems of my trousers up to skirt around a pool of green mud.

'Will you stop saying that?'

'At least tell me where we are going?'

'To see the Golden Bird herself, Alkanary.'

I let my trouser legs drop. 'She's dead,' I said. Hisham was beginning to worry me.

'No, no,' he assured me. A gust of dusty wind blew Hisham's hair from side to side like a bush in a sandstorm. 'She's not dead. She is alive and well in Shambat.'

I drew to a halt. 'What is this?' Hisham was climbing into a raksha. These motorised rickshaws were notoriously dangerous contraptions at the best of times. Driven by a lunatic spouting nonsense they were indistinguishable from death traps.

'What does it look like?'

'I mean, where did you get it?'

'What does it matter where I got it? I borrowed it. You hop in the back.'

'I'm not getting into that.'

'Stop being such an old woman.' He got into the front and kicked the starter a few times until it sputtered angrily into life. 'Come on.'

'Are you sure about this?' He was hanging onto the brakes as if the thing threatened to run away with him.

'Will you for once in your life stop thinking of all the things you *have* to do and try doing something that you *want* to do.'

I stared at him, then slowly climbed into the passenger seat only to be thrown back as he twisted the throttle and sent us shooting off with a high-pitched whine. I clung on.

Darkness had fallen and headlights now swirled around us as the evening traffic bumped and hooted its way by. I began to worry that we might actually hurt someone other than ourselves. People leapt out of our path as we rattled towards the stream of headlights up ahead. Hisham kept up his monologue as he drove.

'Take a good look,' he yelled over his shoulder. 'This is it. This is all our lives will ever add up to. These streets.'

I knew what he meant. We'd talked about it enough times. This was home. Everything we had known for as long as either of us could remember. The dusty streets, the flooding water, the crumbling houses. I couldn't say that I was unhappy about living there. It was all I had ever known, but I also knew that it had its limitations.

'One day we won't have a choice,' he was saying. 'Nobody stays young for ever. We'll just wake up one morning and realise that we've wasted away our lives.'

Hisham made it sound like a prison sentence. He broke off to steer with one hand as he fished a cigarette out of his pocket, which he miraculously managed to light without losing control. The small wheels bounced over the potholes and dust swirled through the open sides as I rolled about in the back, trying to hang on and not fall out. These things tipped over easily – there were fatal accidents every day of the week. I feared we were about to become a bad statistic. Hisham was making it worse by turning to yell against the slipstream.

'Think of your pupils. Every year you watch them go off to lead their lives, but what about you? Where are you going?'

'I don't think of it like that,' I yelled back. He didn't hear me, and besides, there was no point in arguing when he was like this. My heart was beating and my throat was dry. He was right. It was almost certain I would still be living the way I was now in ten, or twenty years' time. I was going nowhere. The boys in my class had a life mapped out for them. They laughed in my face. Their fathers were running this country and they knew it. For people like us there were no chances ahead. No great jobs waiting for us, no fat bank accounts, no houses to buy. We would live and die in the exact same situation we were in now.

'We must seize this moment and hang on, hang on for all we are worth.'

I could have pointed out that I was, at that moment, clinging on for dear life. I was being flung around like a bird whose cage was being rattled. I had placed my life in Hisham's hands and now I was beginning to wonder if I would ever get it back in one piece. He drove the rickshaw as if it were a donkey, twisting the throttle with his wrist and whipping us through narrow gaps in the traffic.

Eventually, we settled down to speed along a dark road. I could see nothing but shadows creeping in on us. Where were we going? It occurred to me that even if Alkanary was not already dead she must have been close enough to need medical aid to keep her alive. Finally, we slowed and turned off the road to bump along yet another uneven, unsurfaced track, this time thankfully at a slower speed. A dog barked somewhere in the distance and the sound of a television threw a peal of foolish laughter at us over a wall. There were no lights around us when we came to a halt. I climbed out of the raksha on shaky legs.

'Maybe I'll drive on the way back.'

'I thought you didn't know how to drive.'

'I don't.' The house we were standing in front of didn't look like much and I had no idea how Hisham had ever found it. 'What is this place again?'

'This is where she lives.' Hisham had that gleam in his eye again. He seized me by the shoulders and shook me until my teeth rattled and my glasses slipped down my nose.

'For the rest of your life you will ask yourself, what if we had done it? What if we had really tried?' Hisham fell silent for a moment and then stared at me. 'Things don't always have to make sense,' he ended.

Chapter 7

The Golden Bird

The legend of Alkanary, or Al Asfoura al-Dhabiya, the Golden Bird, stretched back down the dusty arcades of our collective memory, across the decades to a warm evening in 1966, when a barefoot (itself a source of scandal) young girl stepped quietly across a recording studio at Radio Omdurman, raising herself on her toes to reach the microphone that the technician had set too high and opened her mouth to capture the heart of the nation. Everyone who heard her sing fell instantly under a spell of collective bewitchment.

It was a time when the world's social order was in flux, when Patrice Lumumba, Che Guevara, the Black Panthers, Stokely Carmichael, Malcolm X and Martin Luther King were not names in history books, but real-life people struggling to change the world. There had been riots on the streets of Paris. Students protesting the war in Vietnam had been shot down in American universities. Our own brief socialist revolt came in the youthful form of Gaafar Nimeiri, who had seized power a couple of years before in a coup d'état.

Television was black and white and only broadcast for a few hours every evening after the sun had set. There was no cable, no satellite receivers, no internet. Everyone had to watch the same thing at the same time or miss it for ever. So when she stepped up to sing, the

41

whole world, well, the part of the country that was lucky enough to be in the vicinity of a TV set, were there with her.

She was then no more than a child of sixteen. A skinny girl who swayed her shoulders from side to side awkwardly as she stood in the background of a trio of women who sang harmonies. Al-Sununu, they were called, the Swallows. They began as backing singers, but they didn't stay that way for long. The sight of them emerging from the infernal grey fog of a cathode ray tube provoked cries of delight all over the country. A joyous chorus would rise over the walls of houses and spread across weary neighbourhoods. She didn't look like much, but her singing seemed to cause the world to alter shape (I have heard versions of this story my entire life). People chattering away in backyards, on buses, crowded into taxi cabs, standing by the side of the road sipping tea, all would fall instantly under a silent spell. Jaws would drop and food would go unchewed. Babies ceased their wailing, children stopped tugging at their parents' clothes. When Alkanary began to sing she held the whole nation hanging by the ear. She could have done with them what she wanted, marched the whole band of us into the river, and nobody would have raised a finger in objection.

Not quite true. There was some old-fashioned parochial resistance. Many singers did not enjoy being upstaged by a girl half their size and age. As a result, she often wound up being placed somewhere towards the back of the line-up behind the brass section and the violins. As far out of sight as possible. Eventually, unhappy with how she was being treated, she joined the Kings: at the time, a small, upcoming group of youngsters who had yet to find their own style.

The truth is that with a voice like that it didn't matter where you put her, she was going to find her way to the front. As soon as she opened her mouth, no one had time for anything else. The Kamanga Kings were fresh and new. They played with verve, and certainly more enthusiasm than skill in those early days. But the energy was what distinguished them, making music that was so good it left the rest of the competition hobbling along in their wake.

42

Alkanary brought a touch of pathos as well as charm, a harmony and romanticism that countered the more jubilant tone of the band's male members. Together they achieved an ecstatic, heightened state akin to that of those mad dervishes who spin in dusty circles wailing their Sufi chants in search of enlightenment and oneness with God. They were outlaws together, going against tradition. The two albums they managed to record are said to be among the finest ever produced not just in the country, but the entire continent.

It wasn't an easy partnership. She was a wild child who circulated among the bohemian classes; artists, painters, writers. There were countless suitors vying for her affections and she was romantically linked with a string of men. All of this emotional turmoil fed into her music. You could hear it in her voice. When she sang of heartbreak, she wasn't pretending. You could feel her pain. And when she sang of the wonders of love, you understood that she had known the highs as well as the lows. Then, almost overnight, she disappeared, withdrew from public life without explanation. Perhaps she sensed that her time was over. By then musicians had become a threatened species. That in the face of the new conservativism ruling the country her presence was no longer welcome.

And now, here I was, nearly three decades later, standing outside a high-walled house wondering what we were doing there. I, at least, was wondering. What Hisham was thinking, I had no idea. He knocked furiously for what felt like ages.

'Maybe it's the wrong house,' I offered. 'Maybe they moved.'

Hisham glared at me before knocking again more loudly. After what felt like forever, we finally heard the shuffling of feet and the tall metal door creaked open to reveal an ancient and very small Ethiopian woman, her eyes vacant and her back bent almost double. She didn't even raise her head to see who we were, but simply turned away leaving the door ajar. Hisham and I looked at one another and decided to take this as an invitation to enter.

It was a simple house, with a rectangular front yard of bare earth

surrounded by a few split oil drums along the walls containing withered plants. We wandered round the side, along a narrow passage
behind the rapidly disappearing maid to find ourselves in a small but
not unpleasant garden. It had a secluded feel to it. A fig tree grew
like a twisted hand out of the earth in one corner and an explosion
of red and white bougainvillea covered the rear wall. On a patio of
broken tiles two narrow beds covered with pink sheets faced one
another. The space between them was occupied by a low table. We
stood there awkwardly, unsure how to proceed, when a diminutive
figure appeared in the shadows on the veranda.

'Who is it? Who's there?'

'Visitors, madam,' said the maid.

'Visitors? I don't have visitors.' She stepped forward into the light.
She was wearing a traditional tobe, which she pulled up over her hair.
Despite the darkness she was wearing large sunglasses that had been
bent somehow and sat lopsided on her face.

It was hard to reconcile the rather scary, shrunken figure before
us with the girl whose features had graced the album covers I had
studied for years. She wasn't even that old, but she carried herself as
though her bones were made of glass. The years of hard living had
left their toll. What surprised me as she drew nearer was how beautiful she still was. Her skin seemed to glow as if possessed by an
inner force. Rumours of her death had been fuelled by accounts that
she was drinking herself into an early grave, despite the ban on
alcohol. No one had seen her for years. Regardless of the passing of
time, there was no mistaking her. Strands of grey hair hung down
the sides of her face. She pushed these angrily under the loose cloth
draped over her head. The lines were still strong and firm, and the
gaze fierce enough to render us both speechless.

'Who are you?' she asked, peering at our faces in the watery light
from the naked bulb high on the wall behind us. It was a wonder
she could see anything through those dark glasses.

'We are two of your biggest fans,' Hisham began boldly, launching into his prepared speech. It came out as a high pitched skitter, so quick he even made me nervous. I wanted to reach out and throw a halter around him, but it was too late. He was gushing from the throat like a slaughtered lamb. 'We know every song you have ever recorded by heart. The arrangements and everything.'

'Good for you,' she said drily. 'That still doesn't answer my question.'

'You used to know my uncle,' I offered, thinking to break Hisham's flow.

'Who is your uncle?' When I told her a slow smile spread on her face. 'We used to argue all the time, about everything.' She paused. 'Of course, I knew your father, also.' She fell silent for a moment, lowering her face. 'You don't look anything like him,' she pronounced, bringing her face so close to mine her nose was almost touching my chin. 'Your flame is weak.'

That silenced me and for once I was happy to let Hisham talk.

'Your music is timeless,' he chattered away. He had clearly spent days preparing it. He held his palms together as if in prayer. A gesture that looked as if it had been lifted from a Hindi film. He would be wagging his head in a minute. 'All we ask is that you grant us permission to spend a little time in your presence. Is that too much to ask?'

'Does he always talk like this?' she asked, turning to me.

'Only when he's nervous.'

'Oh well,' she sighed. 'I don't know what you are doing here, but I suppose you'd better sit down.' So saying, she sat herself on the bed against the wall. Hisham and I sat on the bed opposite. 'How did you find me?'

'How we found you is less important than why.'

I looked across at Hisham. Even I was beginning to feel suspicious of our motives.

'Perhaps we should have some tea.' She clapped her hands and the maid shuffled off in the direction of a small kitchen across the yard from which various clanking and banging sounds issued. The three of us sat in silence.

'What a lovely garden you have here,' I ventured. She stared blankly at me. I could read her thoughts. Two maniacs loose in her house. I was beginning to take this personally. What was Hisham thinking and how was it that I was never able to persuade him to listen to sense? This was such a bad idea. Now we were committed to drinking tea. I wanted to take one sip and then make our excuses and leave. I prayed that Hisham would follow my lead.

The maid took forever. She seemed to move in slow motion, coming over from the kitchen, as if her limbs were trapped in molasses. Porcelain cups, a sugar bowl and not one but two tea pots slid about the tray as if it was the deck of a ship caught in a storm. By some miracle she managed to make it without losing anything overboard. I noticed that she poured for Alkanary from a separate pot to the one she served us from.

'We have come to tell you that the world is waiting for you,' beamed Hisham. I stared into my teacup. Let him do his worst, I thought, this farce will soon be over. Alkanary, however, seemed to chirp up a little and now sat nursing her cup carefully in both hands, rocking back and forth meditatively.

'Waiting for me, you say?'

'The entire world,' confirmed Hisham with a brief glance at me. I said nothing. I wasn't planning to encourage him. The old lady reached over to pour herself another cup of tea for herself. She took a long gulp before noticing us watching her.

'The doctor says it's good for my rheumatism.'

We both nodded in time. Hisham opened his mouth again, but before he could speak, he was interrupted.

'I can't tell you how it lifts my heart that you came to visit an old lady like me,' she smiled. 'You're still young, but when you get to my age, I can tell you,' she shook her head wistfully, 'there are days when I think that everything we achieved has been forgotten. When that happens, the burden of life is just unbearable.' I thought she was about to burst into tears. Just when I thought we were getting ready to leave, Hisham, of course, leapt straight back in.

'Well, the fact of the matter is that we are here on an urgent mission.'

'Oh, yes?'

'A request has arrived from Amreeka. From the president himself, in Washington.'

I took a deep breath and gazed into my cup. I could easily have strangled him at this point. But already I was too late, she was studying him with renewed interest. Her chin lifted a notch.

'The president, you say?'

'In Washington D.C.'

'And what did this president say . . . exactly,' she purred, 'about me?'

Hisham nudged me. I glared at him angrily before realising I had no choice. I turned my attention to the woman sitting opposite. The shawl covering her head had fallen away, leaving her face exposed in the harsh light from the wall opposite. A straggle of hair, loosely braided and threaded with grey, hung down over her shoulder. Between the lines etched into her face I fancied I could make out the traces of the young woman who had once captured the hearts of the nation. She was still there inside that ageing body. I felt ashamed. We were offering her the impossible, and we had no right to do so. Underneath the fire and the fury, I saw a vulnerable soul yearning to be young again, to play in the light, to shine one last time. But I also saw defiance. I tried to speak and choked. I cleared my throat, then began again.

'The President of the United States of America asks whether there is any possibility of you returning to the stage.'

'Me?' she fluttered, one hand to her breast.

'Naturally, it would mean reforming the group for one final, legendary performance for the whole world to see.'

Her eyes had glazed over and in the watery glow from the bare lightbulb I saw a single tear slip from beneath the frame of her glasses. She put a hand up to wipe it away. For a moment nobody spoke. Reaching for her cup and finding it empty, she refilled it, draining it in deep, thirsty draughts.

'Legendary,' she repeated, soft as a cat. She sat like that for a long time, head bowed, hands clasped together, deep in thought, then she reached up and removed her dark glasses. 'You are both too young to remember, but when we were at our height, we played some wonderful music. It was a great honour to be among musicians who were so dedicated that they knew every change, every single note by heart. We played as if our lives depended on it.' Something about her voice had changed. There was a rough, husky grit to her now. Her eyes were grey, glazed over with cataracts, but she held my gaze. 'We created a kind of sorcery. I don't know where it went, but it must be there yet, up in the air somewhere . . .'

We all took a moment to gaze up at the stars in silence.

'Surely it can be found again,' whispered Hisham.

She clucked her tongue. 'Something like that doesn't come twice in a lifetime. I was lucky to have been a part of it then, but to recreate what we had again . . . No, it's quite impossible.'

'But why?' I demanded, perhaps a little too insistently. 'I mean . . .?'

'Because it can't be done,' she said angrily. 'It just can't.' The glasses went back into place, shutting her off from us. Her voice had acquired a slur to it and she was unsteady getting to her feet and rearranging her shawl. She smiled in a sad, wistful way. 'It was nice of you to come and visit me. I thank you both for trying.' She rested a hand on my shoulder as she went by, perhaps for balance, and belched quietly, filling the air with the reek of raw alcohol. 'You've stirred the heart of an old lady and brought back many sweet memories. For that there is no reward sufficient.'

We watched her totter off a little unsteadily and disappear up the steps and through the doorway to the interior. Hisham and I stood there for a time in silence. Neither of us could think of anything to say. Then came what sounded like a crashing and banging from within followed by a sob and a long drawn-out wail of despair. The maid hobbled over.

'I think it's better if you go,' she said as she began to clear up the tea things.

Chapter 8

Hard Truths

On the way back I was too preoccupied to attempt driving, despite my concerns about safety. I felt guilty about breaking my promise to Uncle Maher, for mentioning the letter to Hisham, and now this, breaking an old woman's heart into the bargain. At the same time, however, in a strange way everything had become real. Seeing Alkanary formed a connection between us and that old world of legend. I sat lost in my thoughts as Hisham steered the auto-rickshaw carefully round the potholes and cracks in the road. He too seemed affected and was no longer as reckless as he had been earlier.

Through a tear in the canvas awning above my head I gazed skywards, watching the stars turning as we plotted our little course across the dark face of the planet. How often had I reminded myself of the foolishness of looking up and thinking there is something more to the heavens than a vast, cold, empty void.

Hisham and I exchanged hardly a word as we parted. There wasn't much to say. I stood on the street corner and watched the little red lights stuttering off into the darkness.

The house was silent. I crawled into bed and shut my eyes. I couldn't sleep. All my life I had listened to tales of the glory days of the Kamanga Kings. My mother had filled my head with them, perhaps to remind herself, but also to give me something to be proud of. But the truth is the Kamanga Kings were largely an untold mystery to me. A handful of anecdotes and a pile of dusty records that seemed to belong to a long distant century. Deep down inside me I had always believed, unconsciously, that one day I too might achieve great things to rival my father's. Yet what did I have to found that belief on? Not a lot. No real experience, no formal training, no opportunity, until now.

Listening to Alkanary, her voice alive with passion, I realised it was real to her in a way that was different to Uncle Maher. Maybe it was because in his heart he had truly consigned the Kings to history whereas she had managed to keep a tiny spark alive inside her for all these years. Locked away in her room, drinking herself into oblivion, somehow she had never really given up on her dreams.

I saw what my father and the Kings had achieved all those years ago and it scared me. It wasn't about fame or the adulation of audiences, or about making lots of money; it was more than that. It was about doing something extraordinary, creating something that was immortal, that could touch people long after you have gone. The Kings hadn't sat around in a garage playing to old cassettes that unravelled and knotted themselves up like shoelaces whenever you took them out of the machine. They had gone out and faced the world. They stood up proud. This is who we are, they said. They had achieved greatness because they hadn't been afraid to fail. They had dared to believe in themselves.

*　*　*

The next day proceeded in grimly predictable fashion. As a result of my restless night I could barely open my eyes in the morning. I stumbled to work half asleep, arriving in time to find my class in pandemonium. The monitor was valiantly trying to bring the boys to heel. Books and bits of chalk flew back and forth, along with all manner of strange objects, some edible, others not. Two boys crouched in the corner. One rolled sheets of newspaper into balls while the other held a match to them. They shot across the room like comets. I stood in the doorway, surveying the mayhem, unable to move.

The boys started to laugh as they noticed me standing there. 'Sir, you have forgotten to dress properly this morning,' one of them called out, to a chorus of laughter. I turned to find the warden standing next to me with his arms folded. He didn't look happy.

'You are setting a bad example for the boys.' He stared at me. 'Is there something wrong? Are you sick?'

'No, no, nothing like that,' I assured him.

'Then please explain yourself.' He brought his finger up to somewhere close to my nose. 'First the politics, then evolution. You are testing my patience. I don't want to fire you, but if there is any more of your insolence . . .'

'Let me make it easy for you,' I said. 'I quit.'

Without waiting for a response, I began to walk away. It's hard to describe what I felt on that long journey down the stairs and out across the open yard. I heard the catcalls from the upstairs veranda, but I never looked back. I didn't need to turn my head to see the boys celebrating, or to know that the other teachers had come out of the staff room to observe the show. They nodded and chuckled amongst themselves, pleased to see that their predictions had at last come to pass. I didn't belong here.

I walked out through the school gates in a daze. I can't explain what was going through my head. I was feverish and could not think straight. What had I done? I carried on past the bus stop, my feet stumbling over the dusty, broken ground, the sweat pouring down my face. How was I going to live? My mother and my uncle and so many others depended on me. I was the only one with a decent, well-paying job. I marched straight across busy streets, oblivious to blaring horns, curses, even the shrill persistence of a police whistle. None of it could penetrate the cloud that had settled over me.

At some point I found myself in the middle of the bridge. The sun was hot on my head. I came to a halt. My old school bag fell from my numb fingers as I leaned over the railings and gazed down at the glittering blue-green water. What was to prevent me from throwing myself in? I would surely break my neck or perhaps be knocked unconscious in the fall and drown. In either case it would be a swift end. I would sink into darkness and never rise again. It wouldn't be so bad, I told myself. Suicide, I knew, would mean spending all of eternity in Hell, as punishment for casting aside the gift of life that Allah had bestowed upon me, but at that particular moment in time it felt like a fair exchange for my current existence.

The water below me sparkled with light. I moved on, lost in thought. I had reached the far side of the bridge when I realised that I no longer had my bag with me. I turned and started back, only to spy two young boys picking it up and going through it. I called out to them and turned to go back. They looked at me and then, without ceremony, tossed it over the side before running off. I leaned over the side and saw my old bag hit the water with a splash. It floated there for a moment before sinking out of sight into the green depths. It seemed like a fitting end to the day.

By the time I got home I was tired, hungry and thirsty. Certainly in no mood for company, but my mother was waiting anxiously. Almost beside herself, her eyes widened when she caught sight of me.

'Al Hamdoulilah! Where have you been?' she asked, pressing her hands to her face.

'Why? What's happened?'

All I wanted was to be left alone, to lie down in a dark room and close my eyes. Instead, she trailed behind me as I prepared to change out of my city clothes. I waited for her to leave but she seemed to have made up her mind not to.

'What is it?'

'Your uncle,' she whispered, biting the corner of her scarf.

'Is he ill?' I imagined it had all been too much. A heart attack, a stroke? 'What happened?'

'No, no, nothing like that.' Her voice dropped. 'He has a visitor.'

'A visitor? That's why you're like this? That's nice for him. It's not often he has visitors.'

'It's a woman!'

'A woman?'

'Yes, a woman. And all morning they have been locked up inside his room getting up to Allah-knows-what.'

'Please, don't excite yourself. Think about what the doctor said, about your blood pressure.'

'My blood pressure is not the point. You're giving me blood pressure!' She ran a nervous hand over her hair, straightening her scarf. 'Oh, what mischief is this?'

'I am sure there is an explanation.' The very idea of my uncle getting up to anything that could be described as mischief was so absurd it was amusing.

'It's not funny,' my mother said, catching sight of my smile. 'They are playing music.'

I turned to stare at her. 'What did you say?'

'Music! They have been playing music all day on that dreadful machine of his.'

I wrenched her out of the way without, I am ashamed to say, much ceremony or tact, and threw open the doors. My mother was hot on my heels as I rushed across the yard and through the gap in the wall. I approached the long room and put my ear to the door. I could hear muted voices from within and, yes, the sound of a record playing in the background. Duke Ellington's 'Black and Tan Fantasy'. A roar of laughter sent a shudder down my spine, or up it.

'They're laughing,' I said, incredulous.

'What did I tell you?' My mother slapped the back of my head, just the way she did when I was a child. 'Do something.'

Do what though? I stepped upwards and knocked on the door.

There was no response. I glanced at my mother, who flapped her hand at me. I tried again, more loudly this time. Finally, the door opened and I found myself staring into my uncle's face. He was barely recognisable as the grey figure I had seen the previous day. He was grinning so broadly he had dimples in his cheeks such as I had never seen before. A cigarette was clamped tightly between his teeth. My mother and I stared at him in stunned silence before she recovered herself and brushed me aside.

'What are you up to?' she hissed. 'At your age? Haram alayk.'

Uncle Maher waved her away. 'Stop your fussing, woman.' Then he grabbed my arm and pulled me forward. 'Come along, boy, come inside. We were just talking about you.'

'Me?' I stuttered, stumbling up the step and into the threshold, ignoring my mother's protests that were lost as the door shut behind me.

The room was dark and cool. Beyond the floundering outline of my exhilarated uncle padding away I glimpsed a figure sitting in the long armchair beside the big desk. I thought at first I was looking at a stranger, for Alkanary had transformed herself from the shuffling old woman of the previous evening into an altogether more alluring figure. Gold twinkled at her ears, and her face was radiant. The tobe wrapped around her dress was shot through with silver thread and gave off flashes of colour, so that the gloomy old room seemed to swirl around her like a kaleidoscope in a dust storm. The record came to an end, the arm lifted and swung through the air ushering in silence.

'I should give you a good telling off, boy, for going behind my back like that.' Uncle Maher was chuckling, wagging a long finger at me as he went behind his desk.

'But you're not going to, are you, Mahi?' she purred softly.

'No,' he smiled at her. 'No, I am not.'

My head went back and forth between the two like an idiot. She had a pet name for him? My uncle was smiling like a besotted teenager. I would have found it embarrassing, if it wasn't for the fact that I was completely bewildered.

'Now, where were we?' said Uncle Maher, returning to his chair behind the desk and shuffling some papers. 'Ah, yes, we were talking about the piano.'

'Yes, of course.' She stared at the ceiling. 'Well, we have to get Mohammed Sani, there's no doubt he's the best there is.'

'Old Sani . . . yes, of course.' My uncle began noting this name down, then stopped and set down the pen. 'No good, I'm afraid. That's not going to work. He had a stroke three years ago, poor man. He still can't lift his left hand without using his right.' He demonstrated what he meant.

'Oh no!' Alkanary exclaimed. 'How sad. I must go and see him. I have lost touch with so many people. Time is a cruel master!'

'Yes, indeed, but that still leaves us without a keyboard player.'

They went through more names, all of whom they finally concluded were incapacitated in one way or another, or had gone to an early grave. Others had departed for foreign parts and never returned from exile. Each name in turn provoked a new bout of reminiscing. Nostalgic memories, many of them humorous, some of them tragic, were exchanged. I stood by unable to do anything more than watch and listen. By the end of it they had no one.

'Never mind,' said Uncle Maher, undeterred, picking up his fountain pen again. 'Perhaps we should leave that for the moment and move on to the brass section. Now who do we have there?'

I cleared my throat and they both turned to look at me.

'What is it?' asked Uncle Maher. 'Do you know someone?'

'This is never going to work,' I muttered.

'Don't be silly.' Her laugh trickled lightly across the room. 'You were the one who came to try and persuade me to come back, remember?'

'Yes, I know. And I think it is wonderful that this . . . that you . . .'

'Spit it out, boy.' Uncle Maher rolled his eyes.

I gathered myself. 'What I mean is that it is not going to be possible to bring back the old orchestra.'

'Not possible?' echoed my uncle, his eyebrows clouded together.

'Not in this way.' I cast around me, trying to think of a way of putting it. 'They're all too old, or they've passed away, or they can no longer play.' I watched their faces as I spoke. It was heart-breaking to hear the words spoken out loud, but I knew it had to be said. They stared at me.

'He's right,' Alkanary sighed. 'Of course, the boy's right, Mahi. How foolish of us. We can't bring the dead back to life.'

'But . . .' You could see the breath going out of him, you could almost count the years piling back onto his shoulders. She shook her head adamantly.

'No. The Kamanga Kings are gone,' she said quietly.

An awful silence flooded the room. My uncle set down his pen and sat back, his big hands coming up to meet under his chin. He gave a long sigh. Without another word, Alkanary got to her feet, slowly rewinding her wrap about her. My uncle, too, then struggled to stand.

'Thank you both for bringing back the memories,' she said softly. 'I suppose I wanted to believe it was possible to turn the clock back.'

'Wait a minute,' I said. 'Don't you see?'

Alkanary smiled. She lifted a hand to touch my shoulder. 'You're too kind,' she said. 'But I think you have done your best. We have had a lovely morning reminiscing, but you are right, we cannot bring the Kamanga Kings back from the dead.'

'No, no, listen.' I was gesturing wildly. 'We can't reunite the old orchestra, but that doesn't mean we can't re-form the orchestra.'

'What are you talking about, boy?' demanded my uncle, who had returned to his old grouchy self in a matter of minutes. I had no idea what I was talking about. It had only just occurred to me. I was making this up as I went along. But the more I spoke the more obvious it seemed.

'I mean, rebuild the orchestra. Recreate the Kings.'

They looked at one another and then to my astonishment they began to laugh, rocking back and forth, she covering her mouth with a hand and he clutching his side.

'I'm sorry, my dear,' he apologised. 'My nephew, you understand, is a teacher,' as if this explained everything. The two of them chuckled away at this misfortune for a while. Then I took a deep breath and tried again.

'What I am saying is we need a new line-up.'

'A new line-up?' frowned Uncle Maher, shaking his head.

'All the great bands did it. The Miles Davis Quartet. Duke Ellington's Band. Louis Armstrong's Hot Fives, Hot Sevens. They carried on with different players.'

'It can't be done,' said my uncle with a firm shake of the head. 'What we had back then was unique. It has never been matched before or since. You can't recreate something like that.'

'Why not? What difference is there?'

They stared at me as if I was mad. Alkanary actually looked offended at the idea.

'We had something special,' she said. 'Unrepeatable.'

'I understand that. What I am asking is why can it not be done a second time by replacing the missing pieces?'

'Replace them?' Uncle Maher looked appalled. 'That's impossible.'

I held up my hands for patience. 'Surely, what matters is not who the Kings were, but what they were.' It took a while. They stared at me, then at one another. Finally, Alkanary spoke.

'Maybe . . .' she murmured, 'maybe the boy has something.'

'Not the original line-up, you say?' My uncle's eyes studied me, then the floor. There was another long silence. One of them tried to speak and then fell silent. Then the other. Then both together. Then both gave up. They couldn't see it. They were still tied to that old world, that line-up. It was real to them. To me it was just a story, a fairy tale from another age. But then, as I was about to make my excuses and leave them alone, he made a puffing sound like a train.

'It wouldn't be easy.' Alkanary lifted her chin slightly.

'Even if it could be done, it would take . . . years.' Uncle Maher tilted his head to one side and tugged at his earlobe.

'Not to mention luck.'

'No,' he decided finally. 'You could never find people like that any more.'

'I agree,' she said.

'The quality.'

'Impossible.'

'Nowadays . . . I mean the last twenty years. There are no musicians.'

'Even if there were, how would you find them?'

'Exactly,' he agreed, turning to me. 'How would you find them?'

'Listen to yourselves,' I said. 'You sound like a couple of old people.'

'Watch yourself, boy,' Uncle Maher growled.

'Let him speak, Maher.'

'I don't know how we can do it,' I admitted. 'All I know is that a moment ago I felt something in this room, something I have never experienced before.' I turned on my uncle. 'Look at you, both of you. You've come alive. I've never seen anything like it.' Uncle Maher sniffed, but remained silent, which I took as a good sign. I still had no idea what I was talking about, but I felt obliged to press ahead. 'This is a once in a lifetime opportunity. It will never come again.'

'Well, that's true enough,' murmured Uncle Maher, 'but that's no excuse for doing it badly.'

'Our reputation is at stake,' she said.

'Better to leave things as they are than tamper with that.'

'What are you talking about?' I could hear my voice rising. I saw the startled look in their faces. 'The world out there hasn't heard of you. And they never will. And all of this . . .' I gestured around us, not quite sure what I was saying. 'It will just die . . . with you.'

They were stunned, staring at me with their jaws hanging. For some reason I decided that since I had started, it would be better to carry on.

'Do you think anyone out there in the world cares about past glory? No, and you know why? Because they have never heard of the Kamanga Kings. This is real. An opportunity to bring the Kings back from the dead. To make the world dance to those old tunes.' Some part of me was wondering if I had overdone it, another part told me to press on. 'You owe it to yourselves. You owe it to their memory. What would the others say? My father and all the others? If they had a chance to speak now, what do you think they would say?'

The last bit was a little underhand, but it seemed to work. They muttered and mumbled. They looked at one another again. They looked at me, and then, very quietly, they sank back down into their seats. Neither of them spoke for a moment. Finally, after what felt like a very long time, they started to speak, each of them, independently. It began as a murmur. Sounds, not really words, spoken between them and muttered to themselves. Little sighs and gasps, the beginnings or endings of words that would have taken a trained linguist to interpret. It was as if they were reaching for some common sentiment neither of them could express on their own. As if they couldn't trust themselves to speak as individuals. The murmurs grew in duration and intensity, humming back and forth between them gaining strength and conviction. Gradually it crystallised into phrases.

'A new line-up. New players replacing the old ones.'

'If we did it once . . .'

'We had no idea what we were doing then.'

'Exactly, we didn't care.'

'We had faith in the music, in ourselves.'

'It's all we had. It's all we ever had. Our instincts told us what was right and wrong.'

Then they were on their feet again, laughing and crying and we were all hugging one another. I stared at them, at once terribly proud and at the same time scared of what I had unleashed.

For the next eight hours we did not move from that room, save to answer the call of nature. My mother kept us supplied with a steady flow of tea and coffee and trays laden with biscuits and snacks. We talked about the records, the instruments that would be needed. How many in the brass section, how many guitars, ouds, tambours, etc. More than anything we played music. The old recordings, albums, anything that occurred to us, as if we were trying to rope in a definition of the sound we were looking for.

Our plans suddenly had no limits. This would be the greatest band the world had ever seen. The list of players was growing, but each decision was drawn out, dragged out of the ground like precious ore. Someone would suggest a name and another would launch into a long summary of the qualities of such and such a player. Then the other one would weigh in and it would go back and forth, with me offering the occasional observation. At times I just sat back and thought to myself, where did this come from? Where had this been buried all these years? We all have it within us and yet we haul ourselves from day to day unable to think beyond the simple demands of keeping body and limb together, putting food on the table, eating, sleeping, taking care of our loved ones. And yet it is there all the time, buried down in some hidden crevice of the soul. This thing. This spirit. This freedom. This passion.

As midnight drew near the three of us, suddenly starving, sat around a tray laden with a fine supper. My mother had the kitchen running like one of those old train engines at full steam. She laid out small omelettes and thick slices of crumbly white cheese along with hot pastries and a bowl of fava beans drenched in olive oil and cumin and fried ta'amiya that sat on the plate like warm brown eggs. We talked with our mouths full, unable to halt our minds from working.

At some point Alkanary made a discreet phone call and twenty minutes later there was a knock at the door. I answered it to find a nervous fellow with a large black mole on his nose, carrying a package wrapped in newspaper. This transpired to be a bottle of dubious-looking clear liquid, which was to remain discreetly placed beside the Golden Bird's chair. Neither my uncle nor I mentioned the matter. From time to time she would pour liberal gouts of the fiery spirit into her glass and down it as though it were water, which of course it wasn't. It filled the room with a fierce, satanic whiff.

By three in the morning everyone was beginning to grow quiet. I was stretched out on the bed, my eyes fluttering closed, unable to understand how I could still be awake when I had been exhausted twelve hours earlier. My uncle was sitting at the desk resting his head on the table. Alkanary was in the armchair, her head lolling back, murmuring to herself. From time to time a snore would escape her and then she would give a start and sit up again. My eyes were all but closed. I recall the flutter of her wrap as she got to her feet and left. I heard the whisper of their voices at the door. I felt like a child again, comfortable and safe in the embrace of adult conversation, then thankfully I fell into profound and undisturbed slumber.

Chapter 9

Auditions

The next day was Friday. I didn't have to make excuses for not going to work. I lay in bed and thought about everything I had said the night before. I could not, for the life of me, explain what had got into me. I pulled the sheet over my head and tried desperately to keep the world at bay. When I finally decided I could no longer put it off any longer, I managed to get myself out of bed and stumble out into the midday heat, where, naturally, my mother was waiting.

'What kind of time do you call this? Shouldn't you be in school?'

'It's Friday.'

'What about sports? Usually you do sports on Friday.'

I mumbled something about not being needed. To my surprise, she seemed to accept my explanation. It turned out she had something else on her mind. I realised this when she began pushing me towards the front door.

'Get out there and find out what they want.'

'What who wants?'

I had no choice. The door leading onto the alleyway beside the house was always open. I stepped outside and immediately saw that something was very wrong. I walked down the alley towards the street. At first I thought there had been an accident, but on that quiet street it seemed unlikely. The crowd milling around the corner had formed itself into a line that stretched along the side of the house towards Uncle Maher's entrance. I wandered along, still rubbing the sleep out of my eyes. Young and old, they ranged from those who were well dressed in clean clothes to barefoot, ragged men whose clothes were more holes than fabric. Who were they? I had never seen any of them in my life. As I reached the head of the queue and the pale blue door, someone called out to me.

'Hey, where do you think you are going?'

'I live here.'

'A likely story. Get to the back of the line like everyone else.'

'What is going on?' I asked.

'Auditions,' said the one who had spoken. 'Some of us have been here for hours. Go to the back of the queue.'

'I'm not here for an audition,' I said, indignantly. 'This is my home.'

The man clicked his tongue. 'People will say anything to get ahead,' he remarked to the person standing behind him.

When I finally made it back inside, I found my mother in the kitchen, busy preparing tea and coffee while shooing away uninvited visitors who wandered in like stray goats.

'How did this happen?'

'It's that woman,' she said, pointing at the transistor radio that sat on the counter. 'It was on first thing this morning. She announced that the Kings were reforming for an American tour.' I had never seen my mother looking so distressed. 'She said they would be holding auditions. The first ones started arriving about ten minutes after that. Not more, I swear, ten minutes.'

I took the tray from her hands. 'Go and lie down,' I said. 'Have a rest.'

'Rest? How can I rest when the house is overrun by strangers?'

I didn't have an answer to that one, but when I had made sure she was inside her room and the door was closed, I proceeded at high speed across the yard to my uncle's room. The door was closed. There was drumming coming from within and I had to knock for several minutes before it was opened.

'What are you doing here?'

'Helping out,' Hisham grinned. 'Where've you been?'

Before I could reply, the door was wrenched wide and my uncle stood there, looking agitated and distracted.

'Ah, there you are, boy, and about time too. Where have you been?'

'Why does everyone keep asking me that?'

I stepped inside. The room was crowded. Three old men in traditional clothes were holding up big round delouka drums which they were beating in time.

'We are going to need your help,' Uncle Maher shouted into my ear. 'The response has been overwhelming. It's lucky your friend came around, or I don't know what I would have done.'

Hisham rocked on his heels, a smug look on his face. I resisted the temptation to pour the coffee over him.

'Thank you, brothers, you will hear from us.'

The three drummers took their leave, shaking hands with each of us in turn, declaring earnestly that if we wanted the best players in the world they would be honoured to serve. Finally, the three of us were left alone. Uncle Maher made some notes on the sheet of paper he was using to make his selections.

'Where is Alkanary?'

'Oh, she's resting,' said Uncle Maher, looking over his reading glasses. 'We need her to be in her best form for when we begin rehearsals.'

'Rehearsals?' I set down the tray and looked at both of them.

'Why so surprised?' Uncle Maher asked.

'I just feel, maybe we need to plan this a little bit.'

'You were in fine form last night. I mean that. I never thought you had it in you.'

'I'm sorry,' I mumbled. 'I got a little carried away. I shouldn't have shouted.'

'Don't apologise, boy. Sometimes, we all need to be put in our place. Now, where was I . . .?' As he began to pace once more my concerns were dismissed. 'The main problem is that we shall not have time to rehearse properly, which is why we cannot afford to waste a single minute. By tonight we must have a rough outline of the shape of this new orchestra. It took years for us to find the sound in the old days and here we have a matter of weeks. Three months is nothing.'

'I'm sure you will manage, Ammu,' said Hisham.

'Thank you, my boy,' said Uncle Maher, patting him on the shoulder. I clenched the tray tightly. 'Oh, and one other thing, we have to draft a reply to the Americans, to let them know we're coming. Then there are travel arrangements to be made, and visas will be needed. It all takes time.'

Hisham's euphoria got the better of him and he gave a whoop of excitement. 'I can't believe it! Washington! Amreeka! Can you believe it?'

'You sound as if you were going,' I said.

'Well, I am, aren't I, Ammu?'

Uncle Maher explained. 'Hisham has kindly volunteered to be our keyboard man and for the moment, until these things are settled, I have accepted. It's one less thing to worry about.'

'One less thing . . . Uncle, please, a word.' I steered him out of the room onto the steps and pulled the door to behind us. 'I thought we were going to select only the best?'

Uncle Maher frowned. 'What's the matter with you, I thought he was your friend?'

'He is, but this isn't about me, or anyone else. These auditions have to be impartial. We can't be seen to be doing favours.'

'You're getting ahead of yourself, boy.'

'I'm trying to stop you making a fool of yourself.'

Uncle Maher loomed over me. 'I'm old enough to make a fool of myself if I want to,' he growled. 'Now why don't you do something useful instead of putting stones in our way.'

He turned and went back inside without another word. I heard him telling Hisham to go out and look for some more drummers. I could hear the clamour from over the wall. A car or something with amplifiers had arrived and was rolling ever closer, the music deafening. It sounded like a street party was taking off.

'And tell those people to shut that noise up, we have work to do!' Uncle Maher yelled from inside the room.

Hisham and I met face to face on the steps. We stared at one another for a moment and then he turned and ran off without another word. I went back inside.

'Is there any chance of getting your mother to make some more tea?' Uncle Maher asked.

'She made coffee,' I indicated the tray. I read the look on his face. 'I'll make tea.'

'That's very good of you, we're going to need all our strength, and Rushdy . . .'

'Yes.'

'This is not going to be easy for any of us, but if we are going to do it then we have to put our personal differences aside. What matters is the Kamanga Kings. Nothing else.'

I realised that for the first time I was seeing him in a different light. I had only known him as a rather grumpy old uncle who was never satisfied with anything. But now I caught a glimpse of the steely old band leader.

Outside, Hisham was wandering along the queue calling out for drummers.

'Please, brother,' I heard someone plead. 'I really need this job.'

'Look around you, brother. Everyone needs it. You just have to wait your turn.'

'I'm sorry about before,' I said when I caught up with him. 'It's not that I don't want you along.'

'Forget it.' Hisham sniffed, fishing a cigarette from his pocket. He jerked a thumb over his shoulder. 'Looks like we've really started something.'

'Yeah, it looks that way.'

I wondered what exactly we had started. And whether we would ever be able to finish it. Looking at this quiet little street crowded with people, I had to ask where they had come from? How did they all respond so quickly? Not all of them were musicians out of work. A good number of them were just taking a chance. By the end of the day we would hear all manner of excuses. People who didn't know one end of an instrument from another.

'So, what can you play?'

'I can cook,' one of them said. By the size of him he certainly looked as though he knew how to eat.

'How about driving?' offered another. 'You must need a driver.'

'I will carry your bags, master. I will be your very slave.'

'I don't think so,' I told him. He was tall and muscular and looked just a little threatening. In the end he left, to be replaced by a strange little man who claimed to be a sorcerer.

'I will protect you on your journey, ensure your mission is a success and bring you home safely.' He spoke with a lisp, which somehow made his offer sound more menacing. He grew incensed when we asked him to leave. 'If you don't take me with you, I shall curse you.'

By the second day there were even more. A radio car with speakers mounted in the back roamed up and down, blasting out music. Hawkers worked the line steadily, selling roasted melon seeds, peanuts, brightly coloured lumps of iced drinks in plastic bags, along with Brazilian football shirts, running shoes, clothes hangers, alarm clocks shaped like the Kaaba in Mecca, electric fans, purple monkeys with wagging heads, and all manner of paraphernalia. An air of anarchy hung over proceedings. People were hungry for opportunity, any opportunity. They flocked to us like flies to water.

The auditions went on throughout that day and into the next. I don't know how we kept going. I seemed to be constantly standing in the kitchen waiting for coffee to boil.

As the sun set and the light in the yard grew soft and grey, a crowd of strangers remained, at least thirty of them. Hisham leafed through until he came to a list Uncle Maher had given him and read aloud.

'He wants four violins, a brass section with three trumpets and a saxophone. Then there are the drummers, flute players, bass players and keyboards. This isn't an orchestra; this is an army.'

Over by the door I spotted a little boy of about eight squatting patiently against the wall. He appeared to be holding a violin case on his knees, clutching it to him.

I nudged Hisham. 'What's his story?'

'I don't know,' he muttered. 'I don't think he's on the list.'

Just then my uncle appeared, beaming with excitement, despite the obvious fatigue. He stretched his arms wide.

'Isn't it wonderful? This is going to be historic. Do you have the list?'

'Yes, Uncle. I have a question.'

'Yes?' He was looking down the list, using a biro to make amendments. 'Three trumpets for the brass section and maybe two saxophones. Or one sax and one clarinet, I'm not sure yet.'

'I was just wondering,' I began. 'I mean. Do I . . . should I . . . must I audition as well?'

'Everyone must audition,' he said without looking up. 'No exceptions. I'm sorry, Rushdy. We can't compromise, not for anyone. You do understand, don't you?'

'Of course, no problem.' I looked at Hisham, who held up his hands in defence.

'I'm just standing in.'

It was long after midnight before people drifted away and the house began to settle down. To get away from it all I walked over to Hisham's house with him. The night air was cool and calming.

In the garage, Hisham put on the tape of his latest hip hop discovery. I wasn't particularly keen on the music, but he loved it. He played it himself with a couple of like-minded people. Despite the heat, they walked around with woollen hats on their heads and baggy trousers falling off their behinds. He had even recorded a couple of songs with them. There was a table pushed up against the far wall. He dug through the heaps of sheet music and old vinyl records, boxes of cassette tapes, headphones, cables and goodness knows what else to find his stash of bhango and proceeded to roll a fat joint. When he had got it started he passed it to me. I took it from him and inhaled deeply.

'Wait, there's something I have to show you,' he said. He reached into the drawer again. This time he produced a photograph, which he solemnly held out.

'Who's that?' I asked, trying to focus on the blurred image of what looked like a girl of about twelve.

'It's Zeina. Don't you remember her?'

'No.' I handed the picture back. 'I've never seen her before in my life.'

'Sure you have.' He held the picture under my nose. It looked blurry.

'That's too close.'

He pulled the picture back a little. I took another drag.

'Now that you mention it, maybe I have seen her before.'

'She's not a child any longer.'

'That's exactly what I wanted to say. She's a child.'

'You're not listening.' Hisham rolled his eyes. 'She was a child. She used to live here, remember, in one of those big houses over in Safia.'

'When we were small.' Gradually, it was coming back to me. 'Why am I looking at this again?'

'She left. Her father died, remember? Her mother took her to live in America, in New York City.'

'New York City,' I repeated, taking the joint back from him. I was exhausted. I felt like a condemned man who has nothing more to lose. I squinted through the smoke. 'Wait, why are you telling me all this?'

'Try and get a grip, will you?' He plucked the joint from my fingers, sucked on it a couple of times and blew smoke into my face as he leaned closer.

Her mother was crazy as I recalled. She used to walk around the streets barefoot as if the dust was a bed of roses. The father was a mean little man who drank a lot and lost every friend he ever had. Hisham was still gazing at the picture.

'They went back to America when Zeina was only a young girl.'

'You said that. I never liked her father.'

'Nobody did.' Hisham was stroking the picture wistfully.

'That's weird.'

'What's weird?' He looked up at me.

'What you're doing with that picture.'

'She's beautiful, isn't she?'

'She's a child. You just said so.'

'*Was* a child.' Hisham looked me in the eye. 'Was. I'm going to ask her to marry me.'

'To marry . . . you?'

I began to giggle. I couldn't stop. It went on and on until I had to clutch my sides. It hurt almost as bad as the time I had appendicitis and my whole body was doubled up in pain. I went into convulsions. It started somewhere down near my toes and it curled my whole body up. I tipped over and lay on the big wooden crate with my drawn knees up to my chest, then I toppled onto the floor. By now I had a pain in my side and was having trouble breathing. I began to get scared, but still it wouldn't subside. Hisham stood over me. The serious expression on his face made me laugh all the more.

'It's not that funny.'

'No, no, it's not funny,' I managed between fits.

'I'm serious.'

'I know,' I whimpered. 'I know.' I lay on the floor. The room was spinning and I was beginning to feel nauseous. 'I'm okay. Really. I just need to lie here for a moment.'

He sat there looking at me.

'You can't be serious.' I started then, clamped my mouth shut. 'Marry her?' I broke off as it started again.

'I don't see why you find this so funny.'

'You haven't seen her for years. She was just a little girl. And besides, why?'

'Why what?'

'Why would anyone in their right minds want to marry you?'

Hisham glared hard at me. He sucked deeply on the joint and said nothing. I gasped for breath and slowly settled down. I could see he was offended.

'This is about this afternoon, right?'

'How do you mean?'

'I mean, the fact that your uncle chose me to join the line-up, while you have to audition.'

'That's just temporary.' I sniffed and sat up, suddenly sober again. 'You'll see. You'll have to audition later.'

'Maybe, maybe not. Your uncle didn't seem too bothered.'

'That's not true.'

'Admit it, you're jealous.'

'No. That's not it.'

We both fell silent. Neither of us really wanted this to become a problem.

'Okay,' I sighed finally. 'Tell me about her.'

'It's not important.' He was sulking now.

I pressed him more, but I could see I wasn't going to get anywhere. Once he dug his heels in there was no budging him. I picked myself up and started towards the door. When I got there I turned and looked back at him.

'Do you really think this is going to happen?'

Hisham lifted up his hands. Either he didn't know, or he no longer cared.

'All I know is that this is it,' he said. 'This is our one chance to get out.'

'Get out of what?'

'Everything.' He gestured at the room around us. 'This whole dead-end life.' Hisham stared at me for a long time. 'I know that for you this is all some dream about reforming the Kings and taking them out into the world. The whole thing with your father. Maybe this is your chance to be him, right?'

'I didn't say that.'

'You don't have to say it. The point is you're just about the only person who sees it that way. You and Uncle Maher and Alkanary.' He was shaking his head. 'You saw those people lined up in the street. You think they all share that dream of yours? No, what they see is a way out of this mess, a way to leave this country. A ticket to the land of dreams.'

'That's what all this is about, the story of the girl?'

Hisham fixed me with a stare. 'If I get out of this place I'm not coming back. You'd have to drug me and drag me back screaming. No way.'

'So, what? She's your ticket to a new life?'

'Whatever,' he shrugged. 'I'll do whatever is necessary. There are no second chances in life. I'll find her and I'll make it true. You just wait and see.'

Chapter 10

The Ministry of Disapproval

The following weeks flew by in a blur. The house became sanctuary to a tribe of strangers who came and went with increasing rapidity. The names and faces jumbled in my head. They appeared out of nowhere and popped up sleeping in all kinds of strange corners. They camped in the yard, curled up in the straw beside the three goats we kept behind the kitchen. My mother would emit a wild scream as she opened the bathroom door to find it occupied by a man she had never seen in her life, his modesty covered only by a layer of soapsuds. And, of course, they played music at all hours of the day and night. At first this was an interesting development, but in time we grew tired of their improvisations. They did their best to impress us, myself, my mother, but most of all Uncle Maher and Alkanary. The list of who was in and who was out changed from one day to the next, even from hour to hour. This part of the process none of us could really understand, as it seemed completely random. Uncle Maher knew what he was looking for. The best musicians, sure, but they also had to be moulded tightly together. They had to fit. The separate pieces of the orchestra had to complement one another, to grow organically. A collection of virtuosos who would leave no space for the others to play in was no use to anyone.

Weeks went by with no word back from Washington. We didn't

even know if they had received our letter accepting their invitation. It began to seem as though all our efforts might eventually prove pointless. We couldn't really be sure anyone was going anywhere. Yet on we went, vetting players, trying to put together an ensemble that would bear some approximation to the original group.

People continued to turn up, although in smaller numbers than at the beginning. They blew in like dried leaves from some forgotten corner, begging for a chance to prove themselves. I wanted to believe that it was because they wanted to honour the memory of the Kings, but Hisham's words stuck in my mind and now I always wondered how sincere they were and whether they just saw this as an opportunity to travel abroad.

Some were talented, others brought more enthusiasm than skill, but it was fair to say that few of them had any real experience of playing before an audience. Musicians had been under siege for so long, it was as if they were trying to find their way back to something they had lost, banging drums, strumming lutes, tuning guitars.

In the midst of this chaos, Uncle Maher seemed in his element. No longer a bowed old man but reborn. What did he use to do with his life, I wondered? Where had all this energy come from? In the face of that euphoria I often found myself in the role of the inquisitor, probing, dismissing, raising doubts. Some days we struggled to agree on anything. Tempers would flare. My uncle would choose someone only to have Alkanary dismiss him outright, with no room for negotiation. It got to the point where we were all going mad from lack of sleep. Just feeding the uninvited guests was digging into our savings, and the shop storeroom was being steadily drained.

'What are we going to do?' my mother implored. 'We have to tell him we can no longer afford this. They are eating us out of house and home.'

She too was beginning to show signs of strain. When I went to say goodnight to her she pulled me into her room and made me sit beside her.

'You know, I think it's wonderful what you are doing. Your father would be proud.'

'But?'

She looked pained. I had never really thought about it for some reason, but of course she had been a part of what happened back then. I was thinking maybe it was about time I told her that I had lost my job.

'It wasn't always laughter and smiles.' She glanced up at me, then her eyes moved to the picture of my father that hung from a nail on the wall. The frame was cracked and the glass had been repaired by a piece of Sellotape that was now yellowed and curling. 'Your father was a wild spirit. He followed his instincts, wherever they took him.'

I began to feel uncomfortable. 'Are you saying there were other women?'

'I never asked and I never pointed a finger. Perhaps I should have. Perhaps that was what he needed; a line drawn in the sand.' She took my hand in hers. 'You're older now. We can talk about these things. Your father wasn't the hero you like to think he was. He had bad sides too. He was human, after all, like the rest of us.'

I stared at the picture and wondered if I had ever really known him.

'Mama, there's something I should tell you,' I began, but she cut me off. She wasn't finished.

'If you do this thing,' she said. 'You must do it for yourself. Not for him.' She dug her fingers into my hand. 'I don't ask much from this life, but you're my only child. All I pray for is to see you settled, with a wife of your own and maybe the sound of children in the house once more.' Her stare grew fixed.

'What?'

'You do like women, don't you?'

'Mama!'

'It's okay, I just wondered. It's not so strange. Every family has them.'

*   *   *

On top of all our other problems we had to deal with the press, who were making a meal out of the whole thing. Journalists lay in wait behind every wall. Cameras poked through the doorway without warning. Microphones would be thrust into your face at any time of the day or night. They would leap out at you and ask how preparations were going. The newspapers were full of stories – some true, but most of them false. The reforming of the legendary Kamanga Kings had now become a focal point for political dissent. 'Revolution Always Begins in the Mind' one headline ran. It was enough to get the newspaper shut down for a week.

All of this meant that our activities had come to the attention of the authorities. And so it was inevitable that sooner or later we would be approached by the Ministry of Culture. The president no less had made reference to us in one of his long, rambling, incoherent speeches. Nobody understood if he was saying we were the cause of the country's problems, or that we offered a solution. One day soon after we found ourselves in a little anteroom at the ministry waiting for an audience. There had been much debate amongst us as to whether we should even go.

'The fact of the matter is that we cannot leave the country without their permission,' Uncle Maher pointed out.

'They can't stop us,' Alkanary said.

'Actually,' I said. 'They can.'

'The point is we need their approval,' Uncle Maher insisted. 'Also, they are offering financial support. We need that, for outfits and instruments.'

'We can manage. I'm happy to perform naked if I have to,' she said.

'Well, let's hope it doesn't come to that,' muttered Uncle Maher.

'Let us at least listen to what they have to say,' I suggested.

'The voice of reason,' sighed Alkanary. 'Your father would never have given in so easily.'

I let that one go. I was the one who had been up against the bureaucracy. There were a thousand and one formalities to be completed. Permission that had to be sought from here and there. Forms had to be filled out and taken to nine different places for twenty-seven lethargic civil servants to pick up their respective stamps and press them to the paper and scratch a mark with a pen. At every bend in the road a little money was expected to smooth the passage. On top of this we still had not heard back from the Kennedy Center.

So the three of us found ourselves sitting in a long anteroom fitted with a worn red carpet. A large and rather moth-eaten stuffed gazelle stood in one corner. A row of chairs was set out along the wall underneath a huge photograph of the president smiling and trying to look presidential. A frail-looking old man dressed in what appeared to be ceremonial robes sat at one end, his head down, snoring quietly to himself. When we sat down, he jerked upwards in his seat and cocked a rheumy eye at us. We waited. Half an hour went by, then a door at the far end opened and a young man in a grey suit rushed in with great importance. He bowed and wrung his hands. When he spoke he appeared to be addressing the carpet.

'The Minister has unfortunately been delayed, but he will be with you as soon as possible.'

'You'd better tell him how old we are,' Alkanary quipped. 'If he keeps us waiting too long, we might not be around to meet him at all.'

The building's general state of decay was a reflection of how little importance was assigned to cultural matters. The minister was himself a dopey-looking character who had clearly missed out on more important positions. The key ministries were those which dealt with selling off our petroleum and other mineral and natural resources. To make up for it he gave a lengthy account of just how pious he was, underlining the fact that national culture was synonymous with the tenets of Islam. Beyond that there was, to this mindset, nothing but wild tribal drumbeats and dances involving spears and blood sacrifice. The pictures of pilgrims in Mecca, the large model of the

Kaaba that stood on a table to one side, even the little dark spot on his forehead. All emphasised the oneness of our national culture with God.

This explained, at least in part, his visible discomfort. Here he was, after all, sitting with a woman whose famous song 'This Sharia Law Drives You on the Road to Drink' was still officially banned. He folded his hands together as he embarked on his prepared speech.

'Naturally, we are greatly honoured that you have been chosen to represent our country in such a prestigious international affair.' A derisory snigger escaped Alkanary. The minister made a point of not looking in her direction. 'It is a great opportunity,' he resumed, 'to display our great cultural heritage to the world.'

Alkanary sat scrunched up, eyes fixed beadily on the minister with unmistakable malice.

'Why don't you just tell us what you have in mind?'

'We are poorly represented in the West. Take this travel ban, designed purely to humiliate Muslims.'

'Maybe it has something to do with the fact that they keep flying aeroplanes into buildings.'

The minister refused to look at her. His face was contorted, although whether with anger or fear, it wasn't clear. It looked as though he might just have an apoplectic fit. Uncle Maher cleared his throat.

'As I'm sure you can appreciate, we wish to make the best impression we can. For that we need funds, along with all the necessary permits and so forth.'

'But of course, it goes without question. This is a great honour for our country.' The minister smiled his greasy smile. 'And we are very interested in working with the Americans. For so many years we have been isolated for political reasons. Listing us as supporters of terror. Unfair sanctions that have crippled our economy.'

'You make it sound as if you've done nothing wrong,' interjected Alkanary. 'Poor you!'

He managed to squeeze out a thin smile in her direction, while carrying on with his speech.

'In short, friends, we are completely behind you. Why, the president himself mentioned you in a speech he made just yesterday.'

'Listen to me, you snake. You're not going to turn this into an opportunity for yourself or that crook of a president.' Alkanary leaned over the desk. 'You may not approve of what we do, or how we do it, but the world is offering us a stage and we are going to play for them. Just try and stop us.'

'I can assure you, sister, we have no intention of stopping you.' There was a steely edge to his voice. 'However, I shall be obliged to consult before a decision is made.'

'Consult with whom? God?'

He ignored this. There was no avoiding the fact that we had not come out of this meeting with the kind of assurances for which we had hoped.

'They are toying with us,' she muttered as she marched off. 'They will stall and stall, and in the end they will give us nothing.'

As we came out, the old man leapt to his feet, looking hopeful. His hopes faded as we marched past him and out of the building. We came to a halt beside a fancy new fountain built of steel or chrome. A symbol of official bad taste, it looked like an instrument a dentist might use, or a torturer. When you chase the best artists out of the country, you're left with schoolchildren and engineers with no imagination and little technical know-how. Things had been so bad for so long we had forgotten they could be different, that we could be different.

'We're not taking a drop of their blood money,' growled Alkanary, stalking towards the gate.

Uncle Maher gave a sigh as he watched her go. 'When she is right, she is right.'

Chapter 11

Moving Shadows

In rare quiet moments I would find myself recalling my life just a few weeks earlier. By some trick of the mind I managed to forget the pain and humiliation, and all that remained was the memory of walking through the school gates every morning towards a day rich with hope and possibility. Order. Routine. Now, instead, I was running about all day trying to revive the ghost of a dead orchestra. My mother took it badly, when I finally screwed up the courage to tell her I no longer had a job.

'Allah preserve us. We're going to wind up destitute. Is that what you want, for me to lose my mind and wander the streets?'

'No, of course not,' I said. I tried to alleviate the damage. 'It's only temporary. I mean, I can have my job back any time I want.'

'Really?' She looked at me as if she wasn't sure whether to believe me or not and I wondered to myself if there was a special level in hell reserved for people who lied to their mothers.

Recreating the Kamanga Kings was like trying to throw a net over a moving shadow. The work of bringing so many musicians into line, steering them together, instilling a sense of discipline and dedication, identifying what worked and what didn't, cutting out the loafers, the time-wasters, the chancers, making them understand what we were trying to do when, if truth be told, we had no idea ourselves. I read once of those ancient armies that marched into the desert never to be seen again. That is how I thought of us in those weeks. We had no idea where we were going, or who we were supposed to fight when we got there. We just struggled on, day by day, in the hope that we would not be swallowed up.

I slept odd hours during the day and stayed awake long into the night. I no longer ate regularly, nor shaved, nor took much care of my clothes or appearance. I didn't have an official title, but simply ran around trying to solve every problem as it showed its face. I stood in to play when I was needed and gradually I felt my place in the band was becoming more assured. When I stopped running for a moment I would be seized by fierce anxiety at the thought of what would become of me without a steady job. I lay in bed with a blanket over my head, thinking dark thoughts.

The old cassettes of informal recordings made at wedding parties that we had played along to so joyfully only a few weeks ago now filled me with dread. Trying to match that style, that verve, that was what we had to do, and yet there were days when it felt impossible.

The Kings had learned by practice, playing together, over and over, night after night, for years. They followed one another until each member became a moving part within the same machine. You can't recreate something like that overnight, not with all the goodwill in the world. The ability to improvise, to communicate without words, to sense one another's mood, where the changes came, to follow one another into dark corners and emerge again in complete harmony.

More often than not our rehearsals would collapse into chaotic free-for-alls. Improvisation sessions in which no one agreed on anything, least of all who should be playing what and when. There were too many musicians trying to prove themselves, dragging us in different directions. It was like trying to rearrange large, cumbersome pieces of furniture in a small room; you kept banging into the walls. Nobody could provide the centre of gravity needed to pull the whole thing together. Even old timers like Wad Mazaj, who had lost none of his dexterity on the oud and tambour finally conceded to joining us. He had the patience of a sphinx, but even he would shake his head and roll his eyes. It wasn't enough. I had a feeling we were going to need more than prayers to get this thing off the ground.

It was into this happy ship that another letter landed. Uncle Maher returned from the post office full of excitement. Another crisp ivory envelope had appeared bearing the American eagle. He was out of the car before it came to a standstill and was running by the time he reached the yard, waving the missive in the air and demanding I read it aloud. Which, of course, I did, with everyone gathered around. When I had finished my uncle sank down to the ground, staring at the earth like a man condemned, his head shaking from side to side, unable to absorb the facts.

'Are you sure you've understood it properly?' In his voice I detected an echo of the weary man of old. I had read it aloud three times already. There was no room for doubt. I knew the offending section almost by heart:

'Regarding travel arrangements, please note that we can only cover the costs of the seven original members of the Kamanga Kings Orchestra. Due to budget restrictions we cannot assume any further undertakings such as spouses, family members, etc. Please ensure that you give us the correct particulars of the individual members as soon as possible.'

'Seven . . .' repeated Uncle Maher. 'It actually says seven?'

I folded the letter carefully and slid it back into its creamy envelope. I thought of the individual who had typed those words, in an office thousands of miles away on the other side of the world. Were he or she aware that their fingertips carried the power of life and death, I wondered? Did they even realise that a simple digit could decide the fate of countless individuals whom they had never set eyes on?

'We cannot do it,' muttered Uncle Maher. The heavy ebony stick tapped the earthen floor. 'It simply cannot be done.'

'Perhaps, Uncle, perhaps there is a way.'

'Way? What way, boy?' He screwed his eyes closed with pain. 'The sound of the Kamanga Kings is made of layers. The orchestra needs breadth. It needs depth. To create that we need players, lots of them. Seven musicians is not an orchestra, it's a . . . pop group.'

'Except that it is true. There were only seven of you in the original line-up.'

He looked up sharply, but then conceded I had a point. 'Yes, yes, but that was when we were starting out. That was nothing.' He got to his feet solemnly. 'I must go and talk to her, explain that we must cancel the whole thing. Then you must begin to draft a letter to these . . . Americans. Tell them we are an orchestra. We cannot possibly perform under these circumstances. There is nothing more to be done. We must gather all the musicians together and give them the news.'

The others who had been standing around us in the yard now drifted away without a word. I stood there long after he had left the room, wondering how we could have come so far thinking it was going to be easy. We were like creatures starved of light. So fragile are we, knowing that we hold so little of our own fate in our hands.

* * *

Meanwhile, the solution to our financial problems arrived from an unexpected quarter. One afternoon there was a loud banging at the front door. We were just sitting down to eat lunch. As usual there were about five or six uninvited guests who had stayed on to eat. The atmosphere that day was particularly sombre. News of the limit to our group was still sinking in. People spoke in whispers. Uncle Maher was silent at the head of the table. He had lost his appetite and didn't even react to the banging. I realised it was going to be up to me to go and answer the door. I had to climb over several people until I could squeeze out of the little room and cross the yard.

Outside the front door, standing poised between muddy runnels and potholes in the unpaved alley, I found a tall, thin man with dark lips and eyes that glittered like wet stones. He wore a beige checked suit and his hair gleamed unnaturally. He looked me up and down.

'Your father is home, boy?'

'My father passed away,' I said and resisted slamming the door in his face.

That produced a grunt. He glanced left and right down the street as if he might have the wrong address. 'I am looking for the Kamanga Kings.'

'Are you a musician?' From his clothes, it seemed doubtful.

He waved aside the question. 'Tell the master of the house that Suleiman Gandoury has arrived.'

I watched as he placed a cigarette in an amber holder and lit it. I wasn't sure what to make of him.

'There's someone to see you,' I said, when I got back inside. My uncle was sitting there with his mouth open.

'Who is it?'

'A man named Suleiman Gandoury.'

My uncle leapt up, scattering food all over the table in front of him. 'Here? Now? Why didn't you say so, boy?'

Who is this Suleiman Gandoury, I wondered? Meanwhile Uncle Maher was busy throwing off his clothes, oblivious of the fact that we were all still there. He was standing there in his vest and shorts. The room in which we ate also doubled as a bedroom. I opened the wardrobe and managed to find a clean and pressed garment while he wiped his hands and mouth.

'Where is he?'

'Outside in the yard.'

'You left him standing in the sun?' He gave me a pained look, then rushed past me, straightening his clothes as he went. I followed at a distance.

'My dear Suleiman, what an honour to see you here. I'm sorry the boy left you out here. Why didn't you call and tell me you were coming?'

'Oh, Maher, yes, I'm sorry. I've been meaning to drop by. I was in the area.'

'This is my nephew, by the way, he is taking care of all the practical arrangements. It would make sense for him to sit with us.'

The glittering eyes appraised me all over again until seemingly satisfied that I presented no threat. Uncle Maher led our guest off to his room, saying over his shoulder, 'Do you think you could bring us some tea?'

I bit my tongue but said nothing. When I arrived with a tray and some glasses, they were chatting about mutual friends and acquaintances. Gandoury turned to my uncle.

'Now, Maher, my old friend, I come to you with a proposal. The entire country has heard the news that you are on the verge of a historic tour of the United States of America.'

'Well, yes, that does seem to be the case.' Uncle Maher couldn't prevent a beaming smile from playing on his lips. He said nothing about the crisis we were in the midst of.

'Please, don't be modest. This is a great honour for all of us, for the country as a whole.'

'Well, let's see how it turns out.'

'The Kamanga Kings will restore our national pride.'

'Ah, well, that's a matter of opinion.' Uncle Maher flashed me a wary glance. He seemed to know that all of this praise was a little embarrassing.

'I am here to offer my services.'

'Well, that's very kind of you, but I don't see . . .' Uncle Maher stopped when he saw Gandoury's upraised hand.

'I am sure you have had many offers already, but I urge you to consider mine.' Suleiman set down his glass of tea. 'Travelling to the United States of America is no small undertaking. Have you agreed terms yet with your hosts?'

'Terms . . .?' Uncle Maher looked over at me. 'I'm not sure I follow . . .'

Gandoury leaned forward, his eyes glittering. 'This is an opportunity of a lifetime. Matters cannot be left to chance.'

'Oh, of course not. We wouldn't . . .'

'All I ask is that you hear me out,' Gandoury purred. 'I am prepared
to underwrite all your costs: outfits, equipment, instruments, what
have you. Whatever you need. No expense spared.'

'That's too much of you, we cannot possibly accept.'

'Far from it.' He stretched out his arm to grasp Uncle Maher's
hand. 'All I am doing is helping an old friend in need.'

'What do you get in return?' I asked.

'Ha ha ha,' Gandoury chuckled as if I had said something hilari-
ously funny. Naturally, he had an answer prepared. 'This is an honour.
I seek no reward, only a chance to help in raising this worthy endeavour
to the skies.'

'Sounds too good to be true,' I said, drawing a glare from Uncle
Maher, who went on.

'That's very generous of you, Suleiman.'

'Generosity doesn't come into it.'

'I'm sorry, but I still don't see what your reward is,' I said.

'Please, Rushdy,' Uncle Maher urged.

'No, no, the boy is right.' Gandoury's smile did not falter. 'I am a
businessman. It's what I do. I came here to offer my services, it's true.
And I seek no reward for that. All I ask is that you consider the
possibility of expanding your program.'

'Expanding it how?' Uncle Maher was frowning.

Gandoury threw out his chest. 'Once we have crossed the great
ocean to the United States, we must leave no avenue unexplored. You
are an artist, Maher. You must not worry yourself about the details.
Leave it to me. I shall take care of everything. I shall arrange everything.
Leave it in my capable hands.'

Uncle Maher was entranced. His eyes followed Gandoury's hands
as they sketched an imaginary billboard in the air.

'The Legendary Kamanga Kings,' he announced, placing each word somewhere over our heads with thumb and forefinger. 'One night only, direct from the heart of Africa. The ancient Kingdom of Kush, home of pyramids and the dawn of civilisation. I propose a tour that will take in all the major cities of the East Coast of the United States. From New York to Philadelphia to Boston to Chicago and Baltimore, perhaps even Las Vegas.'

'A tour?' I queried. 'Can we really manage that?'

'My nephew is a teacher,' said Uncle Maher, by way of apology.

'Not of geography, obviously,' he said, adding another well-rehearsed chuckle, echoed, I was dismayed to hear, by Uncle Maher. 'America is a country of wide, open spaces. Unlike this country of ours they have major roads from one city to the next, as well as aircraft that cross the distance in a matter of minutes.' Gandoury pulled out a roll of cash, spreading the notes across the desk. 'Costumes, instruments. You will undoubtedly need supplies, repairs, strings and what have you. Am I right? All of these items cost money.'

'Suleiman,' said my uncle, a little breathlessly. 'This is very kind of you, but I'm afraid we could never manage such a complicated agenda. We would however like to take you up on the offer of funding.'

'As you wish, Maher. I will always respect your wishes. I have already taken the liberty of sketching out a proposal for you. At least consider it.'

He handed Uncle Maher a sheet of paper. He looked at it and then passed it on to me.

'This is very kind of you, Suleiman. To be honest we were in a bit of a bind. Please, come inside, let us drink a glass of tea.'

I left them to it. Hisham was waiting when I came out of the room.

'What's going on?'

'Ah, that creep wanted to make some money off us. Luckily, Uncle Maher saw right through him.'

'Make money how?'

'Oh, he wanted to arrange some kind of tour across America.' I rolled my eyes. 'People like that, all they think about is lining their pockets.'

'Maybe, but maybe we should consider it.'

I stared at him. 'Are you serious? We are going to struggle to pull off one concert, let alone a string of them.'

Hisham held up his hands in defence. 'Hey, take it easy, I was just voicing my thoughts.'

'Well, do us all a favour and keep them to yourself next time.'

I don't know why I was so annoyed. It just seemed to be adding to our problems instead of solving them. Maybe I should have listened more carefully to what he was saying.

Chapter 12

Kadugli

A few days later I was awoken in the middle of the night by a strange sound. A curious, nagging moan that dug its claws into my skull, refusing to let me get back to sleep. I turned over in my bed but I couldn't shake it free. It was a golden wire sawing through my head. Hypnotic and beguiling, I couldn't tell whether it was real or imagined. I pressed my head under the pillow, struggling against the inevitable until I realised it wasn't going to go away. I opened my eyes and lay there staring at the stars.

'Rushdy?' I heard my mother whispering from across the yard. 'Are you awake?'

'Yes, go back to sleep.'

'Can you hear it too?'

In my dazed state I had assumed that I was the only person in the world capable of hearing the music. Some delirium that afflicted only me. I groaned, realising that I would have to get up. Yet another aspiring musician, no doubt, come to serenade us, thinking this was a novel way of getting our attention.

At that particular point in time I had had enough of musicians. I would have been happy never to have to set eyes on another aspiring guitarist, drummer or one-fingered flute player again. I rolled over on my side and buried my head beneath the pillow. After a few minutes I realised this was not going to be enough. Our mystery player was certainly persistent. He wasn't going to give up and go away. The odd thing was that this music had a way of digging into your thoughts. It wouldn't leave you alone. Despite my fatigue and my irritation, I actually quite liked it. A slipper flew through the air to hit the bed frame next to my head. My mother was growing more agitated.

'Go and find out what it is!' she hissed. 'Tell them to go away.'

As I sat up and scrabbled around for my sandals, Uncle Maher wandered in from his side of the house like a sleepwalker.

'It's all right, Uncle,' I said. 'I'll deal with this.'

'No . . . wait.' He raised a finger towards the stars as the notes undulated up over one another tracing their course skywards. 'Listen to that . . .' he whispered.

This surprised me. In all the weeks of listening to one player after the other, not one single solitary time had I seen him so moved.

'I can't put my finger on it,' he muttered. He grabbed my arm. 'Find out who he is before you get rid of him.'

When I got out into the street, I was confronted by an extraordinary sight. There in the middle of the road, lit only by a crescent moon high above his head, stood a striking figure. He was a big man, broad shouldered and tall, the alto saxophone a silver wand in his hands. Dressed in loose white clothes, he appeared to be suspended in mid-air. Up and down the street there was not a doorway or window in which a captive audience was not present. They all stood to watch him play. Sleepy children pushed their heads under their parents' elbows, rubbing their eyes. Other faces could be glimpsed peering over the tops of walls here and there. A stray dog cocked its head.

It seemed a crime to interrupt his playing. When the music reached a lull and he lowered the sax, it was like being released from a spell. I had intended to be quite harsh with him, but now as I approached I found myself apologising.

'I'm sorry,' I began, 'but I am afraid your efforts are in vain.'

'In vain?' He smiled, his voice a low whisper, so deep it sounded like an instrument itself.

'We are not looking for any more musicians.'

'You already have a sax player?'

'Well, no.' I was already beginning to feel muddle-headed. 'But that's not the point. I mean, obviously you're a brilliant player.'

'Thank you.' He gave a short bow and attended to his instrument.

'Where did you learn to play like that?'

'Oh, here and there.'

I looked him up and down, not sure what to make of him. He was older than I had first thought and his broad face was slashed by tribal scars. I became aware that the whole street was watching and decided I couldn't just turn him away.

'You'd better come inside.'

'Did you get rid of him?' asked my uncle anxiously, shuffling out of the shadows as we came into the yard. His voice tailed off as he realised I was not alone. 'Didn't you tell him?'

'I tried.'

With a heavy sigh, Uncle Maher beckoned the big man in.

'It's all right,' he said. 'You'd better come in. I'm afraid my nephew didn't explain clearly.'

'I came to lend my services to the great Kamanga Kings.'

Right from the start, there was something old fashioned about him. Noble even. Physically, he was rather an imposing figure. Dark skinned and with a calm serenity about him. The disconcerting effect he had was obviously troubling my uncle too, because he seemed to have difficulty finding the words he needed.

'Would you like something to eat? Do you need somewhere to sleep for tonight? Have you come a long way?'

'Not at all. I am not hungry.' He cleared his throat. 'I came because I had a dream.'

'A dream?' My uncle's gaze flickered towards me. I rolled my eyes.

He was obviously mad. I didn't have to be a mind reader to see who was going to get the blame for this. 'What kind of dream?'

'A dream that told me to come and speak to you, to urge you not to give up.'

The two of us stared at one another and then at him, not sure whether to laugh or cry.

'I travelled for six days to get here.'

'Where from?' I asked, sceptically.

'The Nuba Mountains. I was born in Kadugli, which is what people call me.'

Uncle Maher smiled. 'You're not going to tell me you learnt to play like that in Kadugli.'

'No,' he conceded. 'I have been abroad for a long season,' he said. 'Many years of travelling. I admit that when I came back I thought my musical life was over. But then I heard the Kamanga Kings were reforming.'

Despite his obvious talent, I was convinced that we had a lunatic on our hands and getting rid of him was not going to be easy. Uncle Maher drew himself up to his full height and fastened his hands behind his back, which he always did when he tried to convince people of his authority.

'Now, listen to me, young man, dreams are all very well, but the fact of the matter is that we are limited in the number of people we can take with us.'

The man simply smiled. 'Conditions. Circumstances. You sound a lot like a politician, if you don't mind my saying so.'

Uncle Maher let that one go. 'They will only allow seven of us to travel, when clearly we need at least twice that number.'

'But, correct me if I am wrong, the original number of the Kings was in fact only seven?'

'Yes,' sighed Uncle Maher. 'That's true.'

'Yet you managed to create the spirit of the band with only seven players.'

'Well, that's true . . .' Uncle Maher was slightly taken aback. It was, after all, the middle of the night and he was not expecting to have to go into the technical details. 'But that was a long time ago. We were . . . young. We didn't know any better.'

'I know all the stories.'

'I'm sure,' said Uncle Maher. 'But I was there, you see?'

'My brother played with you.' He held up the saxophone. 'I inherited this from him.'

'Your brother?' Uncle Maher scratched his head. 'You're related to Adam?'

'He was much older than me. Same father, different mother. Same name,' he added finally.

'Ahh,' said my uncle, the fog lifting from his face like a veil. 'Adam, poor Adam. We lost him much too early on. I thought there was something familiar . . . Well' – he turned to me – 'your father played some wonderful solos with Adam. A duo made in heaven. My god, they could play.' There was a hint of a smile on his face as he turned back to our visitor. 'And your playing just now was wonderful. I mean, we were transfixed by it, weren't we?' He turned to my mother and me for confirmation and we dutifully murmured our agreement. 'I'm only sorry things couldn't have been different.'

'Is that it?'

We all turned in the direction of my mother.

'What?' My uncle stared at her.

My mother, more astute than any of us, had seen what we couldn't see.

'Look at the boy, Maher. Listen to him! He's the solution to your problems.'

'Solution . . .' Uncle Maher's face twisted in turmoil. 'What solution?'

'He just said, you don't need more than seven musicians,' she explained slowly.

Uncle Maher and I turned to look at the newcomer once more.

Could she be right? Was the answer to our problems standing right in front of us? My mother, realising this was going to take time, withdrew with a sigh towards the kitchen to prepare tea while the three of us sat down on two parallel beds facing one another.

'Perhaps you would care to explain,' I started.

'It is very simple,' Kadugli said, glancing at Uncle Maher. 'And please don't take this the wrong way, but in their later years the Kings may have been bigger and had a larger audience, but technically they were nothing compared to their early years.'

Uncle Maher muttered something to himself, then fell silent.

'Go on,' I urged.

'Well, the real uniqueness of the Kings was created in their early years, before the group got too big, when the rapport between the instruments built itself into a harmony that comes only when the musicians are in such close proximity that they truly work together.' He clenched the fingers of his right hand into a fist. 'From that intimacy and trust comes the confidence, the audacity to strive for greatness. That's what they had.'

'But you're forgetting,' Uncle Maher interrupted. 'We had years back then. We have months, even weeks now.'

'Are you familiar with George Russell and modality?'

Uncle Maher and I looked at one another in puzzlement. Kadugli turned to me.

'What is the greatest jazz record of all time?'

I shrugged. '*Kind of Blue*?'

Kadugli nodded. 'Miles Davis, 1959. Recorded over two days with a group of six.' He leaned forwards, his elbows on his knees. The two of us did the same, all of us crouched as if about to spring into the dark.

'Davis was turning away from the complex chord changes of bebop. He wanted something simpler, more spare. He heard about the ideas of George Russell and totally changed his approach. He went back to melody.'

I wondered if Kadugli could be right. Whether there was a way of recovering the old sound of the Kamanga Kings. I had to admit, I was beginning to believe he might just be what we needed.

'So, you're saying we can modernise the Kings by going back to their origins,' I heard myself say.

'Exactly,' Kadugli smiled. 'That's it.'

We both leaned forward as Kadugli went into detail. He outlined how he envisaged recreating the sound of the Kamanga Kings with fewer instruments. The way he talked he made it sound simple, which of course it wouldn't be. I didn't have the experience to argue with him. I wasn't sure I believed it could work, but it sounded real. He had brought a sheaf of papers with him, wrapped in a thick folder held with an elastic band. These were his arrangements. We went on talking for the rest of the night, until the sky began to grow light. At one point, my uncle pulled me aside.

'Tell me honestly, do you really think he knows what he's on about?'

We were standing in the kitchen. Through the open doorway, I could see Kadugli sitting in the yard extracting papers from the bag he carried.

'I don't know. I have a feeling he knows as much about it as anyone. If he can see a way of making this work maybe we should give it a try?'

'Maybe,' he mused.

We went back out and Kadugli went through the group in detail, taking one number after another to explain his idea. He already had a handful of arrangements that he had been through before he arrived. Clearly he had been thinking about this for some time. It began to seem possible, to arrive at a lighter, simpler means of expressing what we had wanted to do originally.

When it was all over, Uncle Maher's head dropped for a moment and he sat so still I wondered if he had fallen asleep. But then he lifted his head and I had never seen an expression of such tenderness in his eyes. He stood up, a hand to his aching back and he patted

Kadugli on the shoulder. 'Thank you, my boy, thank you.' Then he turned and walked away, not so much because he was exhausted, but because he did not want to break down in front of us. Both of us got to our feet. As we parted, I stopped. There was something that bothered me.

'How did you know we were about to give up?'

'I told you,' he shrugged. 'I had a dream.'

'Right.' I was still curious. 'What else did you see in this dream?'

He yawned, rubbing a hand over his eyes. 'We were playing on an enormous stage. I was there, and you, and several others whom I do not know. All of us were dressed in fine clothes of a very dark material, like blue silk.'

'You saw me?' I felt my doubts about him come flooding back.

'Oh, yes, very clearly.' He was smiling broadly now. 'You were at the front of the stage. It was an old theatre, full of people. And the audience were holding lights up in their hands.'

He was either a very good storyteller or he truly had some kind of gift. I couldn't decide which, but my cautious nature told me to watch this one. I didn't really believe him. I didn't know what to make of him. When I turned and looked back he was still standing there in the doorway, every bit the stranger he had been a few hours ago when we had met him for the first time, just as if he had fallen through a hole in the sky.

Chapter 13

Finding the Centre

With eight weeks left to prepare, an old friend of Uncle Maher's who was a supervisor on the riverside docks allowed us to use an old steamer as a rehearsal hall. And so people wandering across the bridge would stop and lean over the railings wondering where those strange sounds were coming from.

Kadugli's arrival was a turning point. He blew into our band so easily it was as if the notes from his saxophone were a kind of charm. Everybody was under his spell. While Uncle Maher remained, in name at least, the leader of the Kings, it was Kadugli who directed us as if he was an arrow fixed on a target. His vision was disconcertingly clear. And we needed it. The room felt suddenly empty. We looked around at ourselves and wondered how we were supposed to fill it.

Some days it was hot and dusty, but most of the time there was a nice breeze blowing across the water to keep us cool. The interior had been stripped down, leaving no furnishings of any kind save for a few old chairs and packing cases we carried up there by ourselves. Weaver birds flew in and out of the airy room through cracks where the window shutters were broken, adding their song to the mix. The days went by in a blur as we descended deeper and deeper, digging down into the essence of the music itself.

Kadugli was a hard taskmaster, and he would leave no melody

unchallenged, no bar unquestioned. He took the old arrangements and stripped them down so as to build them up again. The result was a sound none of us had ever really heard before. In the beginning, I have to admit, I had my doubts. And there was resistance, particularly from the older folk, like Uncle Maher, Wad Mazaj, and even Alkanary. But as time went by and the weeks rolled into one another, their objections grew softer as we grew together. My uncle had not known how to condense the orchestra into this new ensemble. Even he had to admit that without our latest addition we would have been lost. Kadugli had the vitality and range to find solutions to every problem that presented itself. He would march up and down, back and forth across the deck like a general planning an attack. His shirt unbuttoned at the neck, sweat pouring from his brow. Then he would turn and add a few short scribblings to his sheet notes and we would go back and try it again. He was a man possessed, driven by a need for excellence, and his enthusiasm was as contagious as any disease.

By the end of our rehearsals each day I was too exhausted to think of anything but crawling into bed and closing my eyes. Even then I would not be left in peace and instead find myself dreaming of miraculous notes and phrases that spiralled into the air above my head, shimmering in starlight. In my sleep I gave performances where the horn seemed to come apart in my hands as if made of rubber or smelting gold.

We went through the entire repertoire of the Kamanga Kings from start to finish, their complete history, sifting through the catalogue to find what was suitable, which songs we were capable of adapting to our new style and which had to be abandoned. We had settled on our final line-up by now. After all our efforts to put together a larger orchestra, we now shrunk back to where we had started, almost. The horn section was myself on trumpet and Kadugli on sax. We had Hisham on keyboards, Uncle Maher on violin and Wad Mazaj on the oud. Alkanary was our front singer. The last member of our ensemble was a bass guitarist in the long tall form of John Wau, who hailed originally from the South and had started out with the Skylarks back in the 1980s and later played with the legendary Yousif Fataki. John was not only tall, he was also impossibly thin. He had a deep, low voice that he rarely used, but when he spoke the room reverberated. He could play anything under the sun and when he got together with Wad Mazaj they played as though they were in a duel, their fingers racing nimbly up and down the frets as they recalled songs they had learned to love over the years.

There were moments like that when I had the sense that this was no longer about us, the seven of us cooped up in that place hour after hour, day after day. It wasn't about the honour of being invited to play in America. It was about the music, about excavating a spirit that had been buried for decades, something we had each carried within us all these years as a longing. And we couldn't achieve it alone. It was bigger than any one individual, and greater than all of us put together. We were learning that we needed each other. It was an act of re-incarnation. A form of sorcery that should never have worked, but nonetheless came alive in those weeks of rehearsal. It was something that none of us could have planned for or predicted; it just happened.

Which is not to say that we didn't experience problems. It would be astonishing if we hadn't. Everyone had an opinion. We had never played together before, didn't know or trust one another. But a strange thing happened. Without the crowded line-up, each of us stood alone, naked you might say, in our separate corner. That brought extra responsibility. We could not afford to make a mistake and expect it to be swallowed up by the storm of noise swirling around us. Where there had been chaos now there was a stark clarity. We had to slip in and out of the arrangements with precision, knowing exactly where we belonged and the limits of what we could do. It was as if we were striving to become one instrument. One that could flex and bend, sway and fold with the different components each covering one another, flowing like water into a space that was not filled, or ebbing away to leave room for another to move in.

And it was fun. There were moments I would not exchange for all the money in the world, when an old number would be taken up and the whole ensemble would join in, no longer serious musicians, but joyfully, almost like children playing together. A song we had heard individually, far away from this place, from one another, but whose memory brought us together instantly.

None of this could have been achieved without the help of Kadugli, who seemed to have an instinctive understanding of where we should be aiming. His years abroad had equipped him with a tremendous breadth of experience. He knew the old songs, but he was also familiar with jazz standards, with fusion and improvisation. He had played on 52nd Street in New York, at the Village Vanguard, at jazz festivals in Copenhagen, Amsterdam and Montreux. He had toured with legends like Art Blakey and Herbie Hancock. There was a spiritual side to him too. He'd worked with Sufi masters and knew trances and spells and all kinds of things about which I had no clue. He had his difficult side. He could be evasive and didn't like answering questions. This added to the uncomfortable feeling of mystery that enveloped his past life. Hisham and the others shrugged it off, and so I too tried to put it out of my mind. One thing is certain, we all played harder than we ever had in our lives, trying to keep up with him. He was world class and we had to become the same.

Even Hisham managed to put his usual cynicism aside and truly play. No more wandering around or breaking off in the middle to tell a joke. I think he, like the rest of us, realised that we were on the verge of something great. It was a challenge and he was playing better than I had ever heard him play. And as for me, well, I played as if I had a jinn inside me, fighting to get out. I played until the sweat poured from my brow and I could barely hold on to the trumpet.

'What's got into you, boy?' my uncle asked, shaking his head in amazement.

'I don't know,' was all I could say.

But I did know. In those few short weeks I had begun to feel as though my life had started along a new plane. I began to experience a newfound conviction about the way I was playing. I was no longer trying to channel that part of my father I always felt I had inside. I was beginning to find the confidence to play the way I wanted to, the way I had always known I could. Whatever happened in America, I knew I would never be the same again.

PART II

*   *   *

The Kamanga Kings Fly!

'Don't play what's there, play what's not there.'

Adam Kadugli

Chapter 14

Night Flight

Then, all of a sudden, our time was up and we were on our way to the airport. I was a little nervous, I must admit. I'd been by it enough times, but I'd never actually been on an aeroplane before. As we drove there that evening we went past the old football stadium. That felt like a good omen to me, remembering that, in a sense, it had all started there when my father and Uncle Maher had seen Louis Armstrong play. My mother used to tease me that I was nearly named Satchmo, but she managed to talk my father out of the idea. It felt almost as if this was my father's way of giving us his blessing.

The rest of the evening passed in a blur as we shuffled through the whole business of checking in, fighting through the crowds (Where was everyone going?), having our papers scrutinised by security officers. Every step of the way I was expecting us to be turned back. So much so that when finally we stood on the tarmac looking up at the enormous aircraft, I couldn't quite believe it.

Hisham nudged me and I turned to see him grinning as usual.

'This is it,' he said. 'No turning back now.'

No turning back? I looked up at the long flight of stairs and the darkness above and asked myself if this was really what I wanted. Why was I doing this? A part of me longed for my old life, the steady routine of catching the bus every morning with a bag full of worn-out copies of books that I had read so often I knew whole passages by heart. That was who I was. This just wasn't me.

I think if the others hadn't been there behind me, waiting for me to move, I might just have turned around right then and walked away. What did we know of America? True, we had grown up with its music. We had memorised its love songs. We knew its tempos and chord changes. We knew its moods. Sometimes I felt I had been listening to the sound of America's joy and pain my whole life. Yet what was the use of all that theory compared to the real thing? All I saw was the mystery of this huge machine before me. How could anything that big ever leave the ground? But this was no longer about me, it was about something bigger than me, bigger than all of us. I was, as Mr Micawber might say, but a straw on the surface of the deep.

The sound of beating drums and singing filled the night air. On the other side of the perimeter fence a crowd had gathered to give us a send-off. A procession of hooting cars had followed us from the house, with people sitting half out of the windows waving branches along with the old green, blue and yellow flag from the first days of independence. It was two in the morning and there was an air of celebration. They cheered and sang as if they might never see us again. They might have a point, I thought, as I gazed up the stairs again and saw a great, black hole in the sky that was about to swallow us up.

At the top of the stairs a woman wearing a little round hat and a red uniform beckoned. I heard a chuckle and turned to see Alkanary's niece standing behind me trying not to laugh. I wasn't happy about her coming along. She had not earned her place in the band. As far as I was concerned, she was an intruder in our midst, a stowaway who had no business being there. She was even costing us money, since the Kennedy Center had made it clear they were only paying for seven of us. But I had no choice in the matter. I had been overruled by the old bird herself. She needed the girl to help her apparently.

I managed to find my seat alongside John Wau, whose long legs were folded like bows. I was surprised to discover that this wasn't his first time to fly. He chuckled, shaking his head.

'Typical. You think we spend our time wandering about naked, tending our cattle, right?' He didn't wait for me to reply, just lifted up his headphones and clamped them over his ears, which effectively put an end to any conversation between us.

'They are always so sensitive. You can't say anything.'

I turned to find Wad Mazaj across the aisle on my other side. Sweat was rolling freely down his forehead. I was glad of the slight distance between us. His oversized suit and sweater reeked of mothballs.

'We were never equals,' he said with a shrug. 'We ruled them, after all. We traded them as slaves. They never forget that.'

'That was a long time ago,' I pointed out. 'Centuries, in fact.'

'There are some things time cannot change. They're never going to forgive us. That's why the South voted for secession.'

I suddenly felt guilty about my behaviour towards John Wau. He didn't deserve it. Nobody did. But it was a fact. We northeners had treated our brothers and sisters of the south as inferiors. We had ruled over them and sold them as slaves. In the end we had been unable to persuade them to remain with us as a nation. There was something deeply disheartening about the fact that we were carrying our old prejudices with us, even now, as we embarked on such a noble mission.

Wad Mazaj shifted nervously in his seat. 'I hear these things are like tubes filled with petrol. We might as well be swimming in the stuff. Sometimes they just catch fire and you burn in your seat like a kebab.'

I had heard enough. I sat back clutching the armrests. I heard people around me, talking, laughing, behaving as if all of this was normal, that we were not sitting inside this enormous exploding fireball. I wished I was safely on the ground, in my little room, lying in my bed on firm and solid ground, rather than rumbling and rattling along a runway that seemed to be full of holes. The noise was deafening and everything around me was shaking. A locker above me snapped open releasing a heap of coats onto my head. The table in front of me dropped down. I could not move. I was pushed back into my seat as we rushed forwards towards our fate. Someone let out a cry like a man being thrown into a dark void, and I realised it was me. Then we were rising up and I was falling back, back, back. My eyes closed.

I must have blacked out, because when I came to, we were floating in mid-air. Wad Mazaj was snoring gently and John Wau was still bobbing rhythmically to the sounds coming through his headphones, his long fingers tapping the armrest. We were not dead, nor burning in hell. Everything was calm. After a time, I sat up and straightened my clothes. The coats had been returned and the locker closed. A glass of orange juice now sat on the table in front of me. I felt a little ashamed. I sipped my drink and looked cautiously around.

Far down towards the front of the plane I caught a glimpse of Suleiman Gandoury in one of his cheap suits. He had booked himself into Business Class, of course. He was paying for himself, but still, I really didn't like the man. It was true that his support had been a help. It had paid for all the little costs we had run up, instruments and stage outfits and so forth. We couldn't have done it without him, but he didn't belong here. I tried to put him out of my mind.

Hisham meanwhile was sauntering up and down, waving greetings here and there, stopping to chat like he was back home on the street. He was always at ease with the world wherever he went. Across the aisle, Kadugli was framed in a cone of white light, buried deep in a book. He had a bag full of them, on all manner of subjects. The only intellectual among us. Uncle Maher slept with a blanket over his head for the entire journey, no doubt relieved to be on the way finally, exhausted by all the preparations. Further down I saw Alkanary with her niece. The old lady was working her way steadily through the plane's supply of Johnnie Walker miniatures. Some people sail, others swim, but the old bird seemed determined to drink her way across the Atlantic. The stewardesses got so tired of her demands, tugging at their skirts every time they passed, that they got into the habit of simply dropping off a handful of the little bottles whenever they went by. Eventually, she succumbed and snored her way through the rest of the flight, even more loudly than Wad Mazaj.

I took a moment to study her niece slyly. Officially, Shadia was Alkanary's personal assistant, and also doubled as a backing singer. I didn't really know her but my aversion towards her had shot up with that laugh as we came aboard. Now she was glued to the little screen in front of her, smiling to herself as she watched some ridiculous American film, the blue light reflecting off her spectacles. Perhaps she was trying to improve her English before she arrived.

Settling back into my seat I began to allow myself to feel the excitement of what was happening. Nothing could detract from the idea that this was going to be the greatest adventure of our lives. It didn't matter what happened afterwards, whether I got my job back or found something else. None of that seemed to matter any more. What mattered was the unknown that lay ahead of us. I felt like a pioneer, a navigator of the great oceans, the Arab sailors who had charted the seas.

It was dark when we landed in Cairo. There was another routine to go through. We stood in lines and sat in uncomfortable chairs. This flying business seemed to involve a lot of waiting. Finally, another plane took us west to Spain, where it was grey and raining. By now it felt as if I was in a dream I could not wake up from. I went where I was told. I sat where they told me. I ate when they brought food. In Madrid we sat in a crowded corridor and waited for another plane to take us across the ocean. All around us people were chattering away excitedly in what I assumed was Spanish. I began to enjoy this feeling of seeing the world. Already, I felt as though home was a long way behind me.

As soon as we boarded the next plane I fell into a deep sleep. When I opened my eyes, we were skimming over treetops. Leaning over the sleeping John Wau, I rubbed my eyes and wondered where I was. Somehow, I had expected to see glass towers rising towards the sky, gleaming steel arches and sculpted pinnacles. But that was New York and this was Virginia. Instead of buildings there were forests, trees, rivers, leaves of all different colours, yellow, brown, deep red.

A big glass box with tall legs rolled us to the terminal building on huge wheels. We might have been arriving from another planet. As we shuffled along through the arrivals hall I tried to push forward, nervously anticipating problems. There was still a chance we would be refused entry. Not so long ago their president had ordered that nobody from our country be allowed in, since we were considered high risk. Hisham had only just heard about it.

'How can you ban a country? I mean, the whole country is made up of terrorists?'

I was urging him to be quiet when a large man stepped in front of me, holding up a hand covered in a white plastic glove.

'Step back, sir.'

'Yes, but . . .'

'Sir, I'm not going to ask you again, sir. If you refuse to cooperate you will be removed from the line.'

'Just shut up,' a voice hissed behind me. I turned to find Alkanary's niece glaring at me. 'Just do what you're told.'

Needless to say, I found this a little annoying. Who was she to tell me what to do?

'I'm worried about my uncle,' I explained.

'He's doing fine without your help.'

I looked and saw she had a point. Uncle Maher was smiling and appeared to be joking with the young lady who was checking his documentation.

'Why don't you just relax?' she said, rolling her eyes.

I turned to Hisham for support, but he just stared at the ceiling.

'I'd like to know who put her in charge,' I whispered as we shuffled along.

'Shadia,' he said. 'Her name is Shadia.'

'Americans never trust anyone who is not one of them.' Behind me Wad Mazaj was blowing his nose into an enormous handkerchief. 'You're holding the line up,' he nodded.

I hurried forward. The woman behind the counter studied my face and then the photograph in my passport. She seemed to have trouble reconciling the two.

'What is the purpose of your visit, Mr Hassan?'

'Oh, we are here to perform at the Kennedy Center in Washington, District of Columbia.'

'And what is your profession?'

'My profession?'

'Your job, what do you do?'

'My job, yes, well until recently I was a teacher of English language.'

Her eyes lifted a fraction. 'Until recently? Does that mean you are no longer employed?'

I glanced over at the next aisle and saw Shadia, Alkanary's niece staring at me. It finally dawned on me what I had to say.

'No, no, I am a musician.'

'That's your profession?' She made it sound doubtful, but I stuck with my story and put on a big smile. Over the shoulder of the officer I could see Shadia rolling her eyes again. It seemed I could do nothing right in the presence of that woman.

Finally we stumbled out of the building and stood there blinking in the bright sunlight. The air was so cold it hurt your chest. The sky was a brilliant blue colour and the sun winked on icy patches on the ground. We shivered and looked at one another, amazed to find ourselves in this strange place. A broad-shouldered man in a dark suit and a peaked cap was holding up a sign with Kamanga Kings printed in large letters.

'Welcome to the United States, ladies and gentlemen,' he declared.

None of us had ever set eyes on him before but he greeted us as if he had known us for years. 'My name is Ezekiel, but you can call me Easy. I shall be your guide and driver for the duration of your stay.'

Easy led the way over to something he called a 'people carrier', which was really just a van like a microbus. Soon we were seated inside and speeding down the ramp and away into America. Hisham grabbed my arm.

'Can you believe we are here?'

I wasn't really listening. I was staring around, trying to take it all in. It didn't seem real. It looked like the America I knew from television, but it was different somehow. The people, their clothes, big thick coats that turned them into unrecognisable creatures, and the signs everywhere telling you where to go and what to do. It all looked strange. As we drove away, I pressed my nose to the window of the van. Beyond the lanes of neatly divided vehicles, I saw wide open tracts of forest. There was a gentle sprinkling of white across the landscape and a golden blade of sunlight arched back sharply from a river. Easy lifted his head to address us over his shoulder, watching us in the mirror as he drove.

'If you *need* anything, you just *axe* me and I'll take care of it.' He spoke with slow, deliberate emphasis, as if addressing people who were hard of hearing or mentally deficient, watching us in the mirror to check that we understood. 'Right now, I am *taking* you to the *hotel* . . .?' He waited to see if this word meant anything to us. 'You can rest for a while and then this *afternoon* I shall *personally* transport you to the Kennedy Center.'

'Somebody told him we were arriving from Africa.' Hisham winked at me. I didn't reply. I was reminded of John Wau's comment on the plane. You make assumptions one minute and the next someone is making them about you.

'So, Easy,' Hisham said, 'America is a great country, no?'

Easy was around fifty years old. His hair was black and shiny and threaded with the odd strand of grey. He studied Hisham cautiously in the mirror. 'We have our problems.'

'Sure, but you're living the dream, right? In America everyone's a winner, right?'

'That's the American way.' Easy nodded.

'Everyone can become rich and famous, yes?'

'That's right.'

'And then you become president, right? Can I become president?'

'No, you have to be born in this country to become president.' Easy seemed a little uncertain about what he was dealing with. 'But your son can become president.'

'My son? Okay.' Hisham slapped my back. 'Easy, we are very excited to be here with you in America.'

'How come you speak such good English?' Easy asked, his face a puzzle of confusion.

'My friend here . . .' Hisham jerked a thumb at me. 'He's an English teacher, or he used to be.'

'Really?' said Ezekiel, glancing at me in the mirror. 'And what books do you teach?'

'Oh, don't ask him that. Very boring. Lots of books by white men who died hundreds of years ago.'

'Is that so?' Easy's look turned to one of pity.

'But it doesn't matter, because now he's a world-famous musician in America.'

'I hear ya,' nodded Easy.

'Amazing!' Hisham gave a howl, throwing his head back and slapping his thigh. 'I'm speaking American,' he laughed.

'Unbelievable,' said Shadia, rolling her eyes.

At the hotel, I noticed how Easy carried himself with great confidence, smiling at the woman on reception as if he had known her all her life, which he might well have done for all I knew. Apparently, this was how things worked in America.

'How you doing today?' Easy beamed at her.

'I'm fine.' The woman smiled back. 'How are you?'

'Just fine, thank you.'

She looked at me and I got a smile, too. America, the land of smiles.

'Now . . .' Easy held up a clipboard. 'I have a list of names for you. I'm not even going to attempt to pronounce them.'

As they chuckled their way through the list and assigned us rooms, I moved away to find Shadia standing in my path, arms folded. I braced myself for trouble.

'Why are you two determined to make us all look like fools?'

'Relax, sister, give the cat a break,' Hisham said in English as he hooked his arm through mine and led me away. 'This is America. Chill.'

'Why does she hate me so much?'

'Forget her,' Hisham said.

'She's only here because of who her aunt is.'

He looked at me. 'So that makes her the same as us, right?'

'What?' I was incredulous. 'How could you compare us?'

'Forget it,' he said, with a dismissive wave.

We were sharing a room. Hisham immediately went around pressing every switch or button he could find, while I lay on my bed and stared at the ceiling.

'Not bad, eh?' he said, coming back from the bathroom. 'What's the other toilet for?'

'What other toilet?'

I had a feeling it was going to be a long week. I followed him into the bathroom to take another look. He was right, there was a second toilet, only it looked more like a washbasin, set very close to the ground.

'Maybe it's for short people to wash,' I suggested. Hisham gave me a leery look.

'You know what I think? I think it's like a bath, for people who travel with pets. Americans love animals, treat them better than people.'

114

I wasn't convinced. 'And how exactly do you know this?'

'It's just one of those things.' Hisham shrugged, always pleased to show off his knowledge was greater than that of your average teacher, or ex-teacher in this case. Still, it seemed an odd thing to have. I studied the object again, determined to prove him wrong.

'Maybe it's for washing your feet. Before prayers, for example. And that's another thing,' I went on. 'How come there isn't a tap to wash . . . you know.'

'That's what the paper is for,' said Hisham confidently.

'Paper?'

He pointed to the roll hanging from a dispenser on the wall. 'For after you've finished your business.'

'Paper?' I echoed. 'How paper?'

'They don't use water for that.'

It sounded not only impractical, but also uncomfortable. Coming to terms with this new world was not going to be easy. Over the next few days I was to experiment, sometimes with disastrous results, to discover how one was meant to clean oneself properly after going to the toilet. Compared to water, paper seemed like an incredibly ineffective, not to say painful method of getting the job done. In no time at all I was sore in places I cannot mention. I kept finding little scraps of paper attached to my body. I washed my feet in the little foot basin every night before going to bed. I felt that I was entering a new stage in my life, that I was growing into a man of the world, a globetrotter capable of adapting to foreign customs like a bird whose wings know only open skies.

Chapter 15

Talking American

That first afternoon we all assembled in the lobby to find Easy waiting to take us over to the Kennedy Center. A tall, elegant woman wearing a grey suit came striding towards us down the red carpet of the entrance hall with her hand outstretched.

'Please, call me Cerise,' she announced. None of us ever did, of course, apart from Hisham, in his usual irreverent manner. 'Sir-ease,' he purred, with a wink at me. The rest of us settled for Ms DeHaviland.

Uncle Maher loomed like a crumbling pillar of dignity and cleared his throat.

'Madame, on behalf of all of us, indeed, on behalf of our country, we thank you for this opportunity. We only hope that we are worthy of your faith in us.' He attempted a small bow.

I was impressed. It was the first time I had heard him speak English.

'I've no doubt you will exceed all expectations,' she beamed. 'We are honoured to receive you and I am sure it will be a wonderful concert.' She talked a little about the programme we fitted in to. Musicians were coming from across the world to take part over a three-month period. 'We shall do our best to make your stay here in Washington as comfortable as possible.'

After that, she took us on a tour of the centre. This involved a lot of walking. The place seemed to be made up of vast halls and long corridors that went on and on. The more I learned about the centre and the illustrious names alongside ours the more I realised what an honour it was to be here. We stopped to look at a huge bust of President John F. Kennedy, the one who was killed by a communist. At the end we finally arrived at the concert hall where we were to play. A silence came over us that was awe and reverence along with a good dose of pure fear. We were speechless. It seemed enormous. Certainly it was bigger than anything any of us had imagined. None of us had ever played a venue that size, with the possible exception of Kadugli, of course. We stood in the middle of the stage and contemplated the cavern before us. I am pretty sure the same question was going through each of our minds: How could we possibly fill this space? Uncle Maher tried to put our minds at rest; the concert was sold out. It would look and feel very different when the audience were in and seated.

That didn't really reassure us. The same look of dread was painted on all of our faces. Then I caught sight of Kadugli, who stood apart from the rest of us. He seemed to be pacing the stage from left to right, walking about as if measuring it, getting a feel for it, flexing his knees like a boxer preparing for a fight, checking the spring of the floorboards. Gradually, we all gravitated in his direction until we stood around him.

'It's good,' he pronounced finally. 'It feels good.'

We waited for more, but there was none.

'A stage is a stage,' sighed Alkanary with a twirl of her hand. 'An empty space. What matters is how you fill it.'

She looked tired and I suspected she wanted to get all of this over with as fast as possible and get back to the hotel. I looked out one last time at the rows of seats rising up to the ceiling and felt a sense of panic. Could we really pull this off?

We all turned in early, exhausted from the journey and the time difference. The following morning our education in all things

117

American continued over the breakfast buffet. A man in a tall white hat greeted Hisham and me with a smile.

'Good morning, gentlemen, and how are we this fine day?'

'I am very fine, thank you very much,' replied Hisham, without missing a beat.

I nudged him and pointed at the tables running around the end of the room. 'What's the idea?'

'It's a buffet,' he explained. 'Don't tell me you don't know what a buffet is?'

'Sure, of course I know.'

Hisham was appalled at my ignorance. 'A buffet means you can eat anything you want and as much as you want.'

'Really? Are you sure?'

'I thought you knew?'

I ignored him. It was no longer important. I went over for a closer look. I didn't know where to begin. There were mountains of pastries, fruit, cereals, there were wheels of cheese, there were eggs and cold meats, some of which I knew were haram, but when you are travelling, as they say, all is permitted (and besides, the others were not around). Hisham and I heaped our plates high. I ate until I couldn't eat any more. Our table looked like a maniac had been let loose. I sat back and felt faintly sick.

'What's the matter?' Hisham asked.

'I can't eat any more.'

Hisham laughed. 'I get it. You're worried about your weight, right?'

'Why would I be worried about my weight?'

'You have to admit you're a little sensitive on the subject.'

'I'm not sensitive.'

'You've always been sensitive. Ever since we were in school and people called you fat.'

'I'm not fat.' I glanced sideways and saw my reflection in a mirror. 'I'm just big.' Hisham was chuckling into his scrambled eggs. 'What?'

'Nothing. I'm just saying, maybe you're trying to impress a certain lady?'

'Don't be ridiculous.' I had no idea where all this was coming from. 'You realise that's pork you're eating?'

'Hmm, I thought it tasted funny.' Hisham examined his plate. 'I don't know what all the fuss is about. I mean, it's okay, but not worth going to hell for.' He pushed his plate away and reached for his cigarettes. A waiter came over to quietly explain that smoking was not permitted anywhere in the building. He got to his feet. 'Coming?'

I could do with some fresh air, so I followed him out of the dining room and through the lobby. Our path crossed that of a man walking by carrying bags in from the street. Hisham remembered him from the day before.

'How you are doing today?'

'Fine, sir, how about yourself?'

'Great. I'm just great.' Hisham chuckled, shaking his head in wonder. 'Hey, how about this day, eh?' he said, continuing his spree. A woman dragging a mop across the floor looked up sharply and glared at us.

'Why do you keep asking people how they are?'

'Relax, will you? It's expected. Everyone does it.'

'I don't think they mean it.'

'It doesn't matter if they mean it. It's how they do things. We have to adapt to the American lifestyle.'

As if to prove his point the doorman greeted us.

'How are we doing today gentlemen?'

'Oh, we're just fine,' I said. 'We just had breakfast.'

'Well, I'm sure glad to hear that,' he said, touching the peak of his cap.

Hisham turned to stare at me. 'You really don't get it, do you?'

I would have asked him to elaborate when Shadia stepped out of nowhere. I nearly didn't recognise her. For one thing she had hair. What I mean is that up until that moment she had always worn her

119

hair covered. She looked entirely different. Almost as if she was another person.

'What doesn't he get?'

'Ah, it's just the professor here,' Hisham said, leaning forwards to light her cigarette. 'He keeps going around telling his life story to anyone who speaks to him.'

Shadia's eyes narrowed. 'Are you staring at me?'

'Me? No, no . . . I just. I didn't know you smoked.' The look on her face said it wasn't very convincing. 'What happened to your hair?'

'What *happened* to it? Do you think I grew it overnight?'

I tried to think of some kind of response, but the words were caught somewhere down in my throat. Hisham had turned away, clutching his sides, trying not to burst out laughing. Shadia tossed her head and looked away with a shiver of disgust. I decided the best thing was to leave them to it. I went back inside and sat in the lobby reading a newspaper until Easy turned up in the van.

We had been allocated a practice room in the basement of the Kennedy Center and spent the morning rehearsing. That first session was frankly awful, with everybody playing off key. Our timing was terrible. The instruments seemed to have become alien to us. They no longer responded to our touch the way they had back home. After the first couple of numbers we sat staring into space, utterly lost.

'Maybe it's the change in climate,' pondered Wad Mazaj, his eyebrows drooping with dismay. John Wau plucked his guitar in frustration only to be rewarded with the twang of a broken string. He looked down in horror. The curse seemed to have affected all of us. Even Kadugli was rattled. He wandered away into a corner on his own where he huddled with his saxophone facing the wall. He played so low it was like a hoarse whisper running round the room. The same phrase over and over again. When he paused I went over to him.

'"My Favorite Things"?' I asked.

'Do you know it?' I nodded as he went on. 'Coltrane's music has a spirituality. It calms me.'

'Maybe we could try it together?' I suggested. He smiled.

'Sure. Let's try that. Slow.'

So we stood there, our backs to the others, with me following him through the chord changes. We played it over and over, until gradually something strange began to happen. I started to feel the notes coming from somewhere else, as if it was no longer me playing the trumpet, but the instrument somehow leading me.

The others wandered over slowly, gathering around us. Gradually, they started to join in, with Kadugli and me at the centre, like the hub of a wheel somehow. I couldn't explain it. When we came to the end of it we all knew we had found something. I looked up and realised I was grinning like an idiot. The next hour or so went by in a blur.

Just before lunch it all broke down again. An argument flared between John Wau and Wad Mazaj, who had missed his cue. Alkanary snapped that both of them were off. Into the midst of this Hisham threw his opinion into the mix, in his usual subtle way, and before you knew it everyone was shouting at everyone. A concerned assistant stuck her head round the door and blinked in fear before ducking out again. Uncle Maher called for calm. He looked at his watch.

'Let's take an hour's break and come back fresh.'

I wandered around the centre hoping to avoid the others and spend some time alone. I needed to clear my head. So much had happened and yet it seemed we were ready to tear one another apart at the slightest provocation. I found a cafeteria that none of the others appeared to have discovered. There was a huge poster of us on the wall. The Fabulous Kamanga Kings, it read. It was a picture taken when we were in rehearsals. It seemed like a long time ago. I had just sat down when Hisham dropped into the seat opposite me.

'She was here.'

I squinted at him. '*Who* was here?'

'Zeina. She was *here.*'

I said nothing. I just stared at the idiotic smile on his face. We have more important things to think about right now, I wanted to tell him, but he was not listening. He had this weird electric light in his eyes. Our behaviour was starting to draw attention. A girl in a uniform who was clearing the next table glanced in our direction. I tried smiling but succeeded only in scaring her away.

'You have to stop this,' I said, leaning over the table. 'You make people nervous when you behave like that. You make me nervous.'

'You're not listening to me. She's close. I can feel it.' Hisham slid a pamphlet across the table and tapped it, reciting – he already knew the words by heart. '"The Wings of the Sun. A lyrical exploration of Nubian heritage in verse, by world-renowned performance poet, Zenobia."'

'Zenobia?'

'It's a stage name. Look at the picture. It's *her*.'

I peered at the shiny paper. I had to look long and hard to connect that face to the girl I had once known. She looked like a modern-day Nefertiti, with her long slim nose and her slanted eyes. There was no question she was attractive. Despite the fact that he was my best friend, I honestly couldn't see that Hisham had much hope with a woman like that.

'What? What is it?'

'Nothing,' I said, pushing the pamphlet back across to him. 'She's just, you know . . .'

'She's *Am-er-ican*.' He pronounced the English word slowly, rolling it off his tongue. 'I know what you're thinking, you're thinking that she's way out of my league.'

'I didn't say that.' I took a moment to consider the matter seriously. 'Are you really willing to give everything up for her?'

'What's to give up?' He grinned. 'The way I see it I have everything to win.'

'At least wait until this is over. Until we've played the concert.'

'Sure, sure.' Hisham looked down at the flyer before folding it and putting it into his pocket. 'It's going to be all right,' he said, leaning over the table. 'I just know it.'

I looked at him but said nothing. I went outside for a walk after that. The air was sharp and clear. I watched three dark helicopters whirring across the sky with great urgency. We were in a strange country. I had the sense that things were happening around me that I didn't quite comprehend. When I got back to the rehearsal room, everyone was waiting.

'Ah, finally, he graces us with his presence,' said Uncle Maher, who was rolling up his shirtsleeves.

'Sorry,' I muttered, aware of everyone's eyes on me as I took my place.

Despite everything, the afternoon session went a lot better and by the end of the day the collective mood had improved. We emerged into an icy wind; I had never felt cold like it before.

On the way to the hotel the mood was subdued. Everyone was tired and perhaps the time difference was making itself felt. Once back at the hotel we went our separate ways. Hisham disappeared without a word. I ate a sandwich in the bar alone and then, since no one else was around, I decided there was nothing else to do but get some much-needed sleep. On my way down the corridor I spotted Kadugli through the open door of his room. I knocked and he waved me in.

'How are you doing?' he asked.

'I'm okay, I think. It's a big thing, being here. Maybe not to you, but you played with so many of the greats.'

'Sure.' He looked at me. 'Listen, it's always a challenge. You never know when you go out there how it's going to pan out. You just have to trust yourself.' He was sitting in a chair by the window polishing the sax with a soft cloth. 'If you don't believe in yourself, nobody else will.'

'Did you always know?' I asked, sitting down on the edge of the bed. 'Did you always know you were going to be a musician?'

He stopped his polishing. 'We're all born with something. Inside. I believe that. Some of us are lucky enough to find it. Others never do. We just have to make the most of what we've got.' He gave the instrument a final wipe before placing it gently back into its case. It was an old case, battered and covered in stickers. Miles Davis World Tour 1987. Herbie Hancock. Cassandra Wilson. Alicia Keyes.

'You played with all these people?' I pointed at the names.

'It's not as big as it sounds,' he said with a dismissive shrug.

'I don't understand. Why give that up and come home?'

From the little I had learned of Kadugli's story I knew that for the last few years he had been living in his family home in the Nuba Mountains. I had never been there, but I imagined it as remote a place as you could get to.

'Sometimes you have to travel far to discover where you belong.'

'Are you saying it was difficult for you to come back here?'

He smiled. 'You're a smart kid, and a good player. You just need to learn to believe that, to trust yourself.'

'I'm not sure I know what that means.'

'It means you have to stop trying to be your father.' He gave another shrug as he got to his feet. 'He did his thing. Now you have to do yours.'

'You always make it sound easy.'

'Just let go. Be yourself.'

I closed the door behind me and stood there in the corridor for a long time, thinking about what he had said. I'm not sure how long it was. It felt like a long time. I couldn't move. I didn't want to. I had the feeling I finally understood, that I could see myself the way he was describing. I wanted to keep to that, to internalise it, fix it in place, make it mine. If I could just stick to that thought, if I could just hold on.

Chapter 16

Stagefright

Early next morning Uncle Maher knocked at the door to inform me that my services as interpreter were required. There was an administrative matter to be taken care of. As Easy hadn't turned up yet, we were to take a taxi to the Kennedy Center. Suleiman Gandoury was waiting for us outside the hotel smoking a cigarette. He smiled as we approached.

'Do we need the boy?' he asked.

'I'd prefer it,' said Uncle Maher. 'If you don't mind.'

It was a bitterly cold day and the sky was a pale grey colour I had never seen before. Everything sounded strangely soft and muted, as if we were wrapped inside a heavy cloud. As we drove, odd specks of white drifted across our path, slapping the windscreen from time to time.

'You know what that is, boy?' grinned my uncle. 'That's snow! Now you'll have something else to tell them when we get home.'

I wound down the window to watch the people hurrying by with their heads down. I stuck my hand out. The flakes were like little white moths that melted as soon as they touched my skin. I felt disoriented. It wasn't that I longed to go back. It was more as though something had been dislodged inside me. I was no longer certain of the world around me or my place in it. Everything here seemed new and yet somehow familiar. The people, the streets, the cars. All was the same, yet different. It was like a language that I couldn't quite understand. The snow in the air blurred the line between sky and earth as if the ground was dissolving beneath me. I was floating, with no real sense of direction.

We were early and had to wait in the hallway until a young man appeared, his eyes blinking behind round spectacles as he brushed snow off the lapels of his coat.

'Not the kind of weather you are used to, I suppose. Can I get you something? Tea, coffee?'

Uncle Maher and I both declined. Gandoury, of course, wanted a coffee. I was nervous. I wanted to get this out of the way quickly so we could get on with rehearsals. When we were settled in his office, I explained this to the man. He seemed unconcerned.

'Actually,' he said, adjusting his glasses. 'We have a slight problem.'

'What kind of a problem?' asked Gandoury.

His face took on a tortured expression. 'Well, your home country is no longer under economic sanctions but it is still officially on the list of state sponsors of terrorism.'

'Terrorism?' I replied. 'We're not terrorists.'

The man hastened to explain. 'No, no, of course not. We're not suggesting that. It's just that this means bank transactions are complicated. We can't transfer the money we owe you to a bank in your country.'

'This is not a problem,' said Suleiman Gandoury.

'Ah, you have a solution?' The man leaned on his desk, eager to hear. I too wanted to hear what Gandoury had in mind.

'I conduct a lot of business in this country, despite the political situation. I can transfer the money easily through unofficial channels.'

'You mean, some kind of informal system?'

'Yes, exactly.' Gandoury was beaming now. 'It has worked for centuries, long before your banks existed.'

I was translating for Uncle Maher, since he wasn't clear what Gandoury was talking about.

'This is quite a substantial amount of money,' the man said as he settled himself behind his desk.

'That is not a problem. We simply need the payment to be ready in cash.'

'In cash? Is that advisable?' The man seemed unsure and I shared his concerns, but there wasn't much I could do. Uncle Maher waved me down.

'It'll be fine,' he said.

Gandoury was all smiles. 'Leave it to me, Maher,' he said. 'That's why I'm here, after all, to take care of this petty stuff so that you can focus on the important business of playing.'

'I don't know what you've got against him, boy,' Uncle Maher said, as we made our way back through the maze of corridors trying to find our rehearsal room. 'Without Suleiman we would never have been able to do this. He's been a great help.'

I wasn't convinced, but I could see that the matter distressed Uncle Maher, so I dropped the subject. The others were waiting for us, impatient to get started. We worked steadily through the morning. It was beginning to feel as if we were making progress, coming together again. It was still hard work, but now at least we were listening to one another. Around midday we hit a wall and everyone collapsed, exhausted, onto whatever chairs were available, some even sprawled on the floor. Lunch had been brought in for us but no one even had the strength the eat. As I looked around I felt a strange warmth flow through me.

'What are you smiling at?' Hisham asked, as he threw himself down beside me and passed me a sandwich wrapped in plastic. I turned it over. This American food was already beginning to depress me. Everything tasted the same. You might as well eat the plastic it came in. I longed for my mother's cooking.

'I don't know, it just seems pretty amazing to me that we made it, that we got this far.'

He nodded as he chewed. 'Just remember, if it had been up to you we'd still be back home in my garage.'

I couldn't argue with that. 'Well, we did it together,' I said, but he wasn't having that either.

'Things don't just happen. You have to make them happen. You have to fight.' With that he got to his feet and walked out of the room. I could feel a gap opening up between us. Hisham was still determined to stay here and chase his dream of a new life with a girl he hadn't seen since we were kids. It was a crazy idea, but I couldn't help but feel a little envious of him, of his conviction.

When we finished eating everybody quietly began putting aside their cups of coffee and half-finished sandwiches and brushing the crumbs off their laps. Slowly they got to their feet to take up their positions. They began adjusting reeds and tightening strings. Without anyone saying a word, we all prepared ourselves to play. There was a solemnity hanging over us now. Kadugli counted us in and we began slowly building again, gathering pace, until we were gliding together towards some common goal. It crept up on us slowly but it was as if we had tapped into a new well of pure energy. It didn't come easily, or in a rush, but piece by piece, as if we were each working in a separate mine, trying to link up to one another. There were flashes when the music seemed to snap around the room like electricity only to fade again. Then suddenly we were playing together, rather than each of us going through the motions on our own. A new element had been incorporated, something indefinable and intangible. You couldn't exactly say what it was, but you could feel it. It lasted through two numbers, then three, then four. Then we hit a rough spot and the whole thing began to wobble before coming apart. Accusations flew across the room. In a matter of seconds we were at each other's throats again and Uncle Maher declared the session over.

'Go away, all of you. Think about something else.'

I watched him carefully replacing his violin in its case, his shoulders bowed in resignation. I wanted to say something, but somehow couldn't think what.

I had grown up listening to the stories of the Kings and their amazing feats. It was a weight I had been born with, holding me down. For as long as I could remember I had known that whatever I did with my life it would never compare to those great, glorious days of old. But now we were on the cusp of something of which my father had never even dreamed. I think all of us found that a little scary. When we went out there we would be playing not just for us, but for all the others, the ones who couldn't make it. The ones we had left behind. The ones who had never had an opportunity like this and never would. The ones who paid for their musical talent with their lives. That's who we were playing for. We owed it to them. When we walked out onto that stage tomorrow night they would all be with us.

'Are you all right, Rushdy?' Uncle Maher asked.

'Yes, fine. Just thinking.'

'Well, stop it. We need you to be alert, not with your head in some daydream, boy!'

Chapter 17

Sightseeing

Outside, the December wind was so cold it cut through my clothes as if they were made of paper. We hurried along, Hisham and me, having agreed to spend the afternoon sightseeing. The first place we came to was a museum. We spent half an hour or so wandering through huge halls examining musty paintings of French ladies wearing heavy gowns and diamond necklaces, bald-headed Spanish saints, their eyes raised to the heavens, or plump white babies floating in the air with golden wings. We were staring at a picture of two dead rabbits lying on a table wondering what it might possibly mean when Hisham leaned over and whispered.

'What are we doing here?'

'I have no idea.'

So we decided to brave the Washington winds again and stepped outside to find that conditions had improved. The snow had stopped and the sun even came out as we climbed the steps of the Memorial towards the statue of Abraham Lincoln, calm and resplendent on his white marble altar. He gazed into the distance. We sat on the steps and looked up towards the white dome of the Capitol.

'Tell me again, who is he exactly?' Hisham asked.

'Lincoln. The president who won the civil war. He abolished slavery.'

'Right, I knew it was something like that. Okay, I have a question for you.' Tugging his cigarettes from his jacket pocket, he sat down on the steps. 'Ever hear of Sitting Bull?'

'Of course, but what does that have to do with anything?'

'The Battle of Little Big Horn.' Hisham puffed confidently. 'That's what this country is founded on, white people killing those who lived here before them.'

'Do you have any idea what you're talking about?'

'Sure, I saw a documentary on television last night.'

'I thought you were watching those girls doing . . . you know.' Sharing a room with Hisham meant getting used to the fact that he stayed up half the night staring at the flashing screen.

'I have to improve my English.'

'Yeah? Well, those girls have a very limited vocabulary.'

'I'm serious, by the time I find Zenobia I'll be fluent.'

'Don't start that again, please.'

For a time we sat in silence, staring down at the long strip of water. It stretched away towards the tall spike of the Washington monument that jutted against the sky.

'I'm serious about staying,' Hisham said quietly. 'I'm not going back.'

I looked over at him. 'Think about what you are saying. You would be here illegally. You would never be able to go home.'

'So what? What have I got to lose? Tell me that. What is there at home for me? A job, the chance to build a family?' He turned towards me. 'We both know that there is no hope there. You know that as well as I do.'

'It's home. It's where we belong. And if there's no hope, it's because we, people like you and me, have stopped believing it's possible.'

'Come on, do you really believe that we can make a difference?'

'Of course I do.'

'No,' he said, shaking his head. 'You *want* to believe it. That's not the same thing.'

'Look at this, at us. Look at what happened when we announced the Kings were reforming. People came to us.'

131

'They came because there was a chance to go abroad. You're a dreamer, Rushdy. You can't see what's right in front of you.' He stared off into the distance before turning to me. 'Come with me. Let's do this thing together.'

'Look, Hisham, you're my best friend,' I began, but he already knew what I was going to say. He pushed himself to his feet and started down the steps. I caught up with him at the bottom.

'It's just not that easy for me.'

'It's okay,' he said, turning to me. 'You don't have to explain.'

I read the coldness in his eyes. I'd seen it before. This was his way of cutting me out. I wasn't ready to let go.

'So tell me, how are you and your bride going to live?'

'It's the land of opportunity, remember?'

'Think of the scandal it will cause. We're guests in this country. We were invited here.'

'What difference does that make?'

'It'll reflect badly on all of us. Don't you care what people think of us?'

'For all you know they are all planning to do the same thing. Only an idiot would go back to what we had.'

'Meaning me? Thanks.' I paused, realising that somehow I needed to make this argument properly. 'Look, you can't even be sure that this Zenia, or Zenobia, or whatever she calls herself, wants to have anything to do with you. You haven't even spoken to her.'

'That's where you're wrong.'

I stared at him. 'Seriously? Are you in touch with her? Do you know where she is?'

'All I know is that nothing comes if you're not willing to take a chance.' Hisham stared off into the distance like a moody actor. 'If I'm going to get her, I have to do it now.'

'You've already planned this, haven't you?' I couldn't believe it. 'All that stuff in the cafeteria was just for show, wasn't it? That was you trying to get me to come along on this crazy scheme of yours.'

'She wants to meet. We have plans.'

'Plans, what plans?'

'Big plans.' Hisham puffed away on his cigarette as he spoke. 'I can't tell you any more.'

'What are you talking about?'

'*This* is what I want. All of it. America.' His arms went out, taking in the park, the people, the boys and girls strolling together, the joggers and cyclists, the roller-skaters and baby carriages, the stone finger of the obelisk rising in the distance like an arrow. When he turned to me, his eyes glistened in the grey winter light. 'I can't live there any more, Rushdy. I can't do it. The old ways. The rules and traditions. I feel like I'm being buried alive. Here, I can have a life, not there.'

'You can't just walk away.'

'Why not?' He sank back down onto the steps and I sat down beside him, finally stunned into silence. 'Go on, tell me why not?' I'd seen that stubborn look on his face all too often and I knew I wasn't going to get through to him. Still, I had to try.

'At least, you can't leave us now, not before we play.'

'No, of course not.' Hisham looked offended. 'I wouldn't leave before the concert. But afterwards, when it's all over and done with, I'll quietly exit.'

'We can't just turn away and leave.'

'Why not? What are we holding on for? The best years of our lives are slipping away. I've been dying a slow death for years. I need to get out.'

'What about your family?'

'They'll be fine. They barely know I exist anyway, and the way the country is going they will be glad that someone is earning money for them somewhere.'

'We don't belong here and we never will.'

'So what?' he laughed. He gestured at the people passing us by. 'Look around you. Look at these people. You think they belong here any more than we do?'

'Just tell me, what makes any of this better than what we have at home?'

'Look at them, Rushdy. They're free. They can earn money, buy houses and cars. They can live how they like. They're not like us, trapped in time. They live in the present, while we live in the past.'

'Is that all this whole thing has been to you, a chance to change your life?'

'No, of course not.' He looked hurt.

'Because that's what it's going to be. If you do this, that's how we're going to be remembered. Not for the music, not the history, not the performance. We'll be remembered as the group that broke the trust that was placed in us.'

'Come on,' he scoffed. 'Nobody cares about that stuff any more. Honour, tradition, are you serious?'

'I am serious. I think it's the stupidest thing I've ever heard.'

'Now there's a surprise. A man who's never taken a risk in his life.'

'Not to mention criminal and insane.'

'What is criminal and insane?'

We both looked round to see Shadia standing on the step behind us.

'Shit.' I looked off into the distance.

'Where did you spring from?' Hisham asked. 'Were you following us?'

'No, of course not. I just wanted to take a walk.' Her eyes darted from one to the other. I wondered how much she had actually heard. 'What were you talking about just now?'

'Nothing,' I said. 'We were just talking.'

'Oh, good, then you don't mind me joining you?' And without another word she sat herself down between us. I decided she was probably the most irritating person I had ever met.

Hisham was busy trying to light another cigarette. His fingers were shaking, whether from the cold or from the plans he had just confessed to me I couldn't say. I must have been staring because she plucked the cigarette from Hisham's fingers and turned to me.

'Something wrong?'

'No, no, not at all.' I shrugged.

'Maalish, it's okay, I get it.' She smiled knowingly. 'You don't approve of women smoking.'

'I didn't say that.'

Hisham flicked the lighter and she coughed as the smoke caught in her throat. She stared at me, as if daring me to comment. I watched her blowing smoke into the air.

'So, tell me, what were you two talking about when I came along.'

'Nothing,' both of us said simultaneously.

'Yaa? Now I know it was something important.'

We sat there for a time watching people wandering by. The way they paused to look at the monument before moving on again, it had the grace and respect of a ritual. Some looked like tourists, others I imagined were perhaps newly arrived migrants. Couples stood holding hands as they gazed up at the monument with an expectant look of hope on their faces. They looked as though they had stopped by to pay homage to the father of the dream they had just bought into. I couldn't really stop thinking about what Hisham had just told me. I tried to imagine him in a similar posture. I had known him for as long as I could remember. A part of me told me he would never be at home here. But then again, what did I know? Another part of me knew he would make it. He would always make it somehow, but the thought made me sad. I tried to imagine what it would be like to belong to this country. America was like a language that made itself up as it went along, and it was a conversation that excluded us. To move here would be to barely be able to follow what was being said. I don't mean the language, I mean the whole thing, how the country works, how people think, what they care about. Hisham would become a part of it. There are still things for us to do, I wanted to say, things that have to be sorted out at home. If we don't do them, who will?

I watched a young couple as they made their way down the steps. They could have been from anywhere, I realised. The Middle East,

South America. Now they were Americans. You could tell by their clothing, by the confidence in the way they walked. A small child, a little girl with a red jacket and her hair in plaits, swung between them, clutching their hands in each of her own. She trusted them completely, throwing her legs in the air as they held her weight and she flew down, two, three steps at a time. All three were laughing as they went by. Maybe Hisham had a point and we were stuck in our own history. For half a century we had been at war with ourselves and where had that got us? Didn't it make sense to forget the past and get on with the present?

We were all freezing by now so when Shadia suggested we get a cup of coffee we jumped at the idea. She led the way to a place with heavy wooden floorboards and high tables. A man who might have been Chinese brought us coffee laden with clouds of frothy cream and we sat for a time and watched the world go by. Americans came and went, ordering their coffee on the run before rushing out into the street again. Everyone in a hurry. I was fascinated.

They finished talking and we decided our next stop was a department store, which Shadia thought might be a good place to buy presents for friends and family back home. She wasn't actually going to buy anything, she explained, she just wanted to get an idea. It made no sense to me, but inside the shops it would at least be warm.

Soon I was lost in a human kaleidoscope of colour, shape and form, light and movement. Figures rushing by me, men and women whose features seemed to blur. They dug their way through tables piled high with shirts and trousers, jeans and skirts, shorts, caps, vests, underwear, tossing them into the air as they waded through, struggling to find some item they wished to purchase. Women hauled baskets behind them like legless beasts as they draped jackets over reluctant husbands. I dodged back and forth out of their way, trying to find a place to stand. At some point we became separated and I remained there with my back to the wall until Shadia and Hisham came to rescue me.

Chapter 18

Nerves

At breakfast early the next morning, I sat glumly staring at the heap of food I had piled enthusiastically onto my plate. Today was the big day. Whether it was nerves, or what, I don't know. It seemed like a crime to leave all that food untouched, but I couldn't help it, I had no appetite. I apologised to the chef in the high hat as I left. He smiled and wished me a good day.

I felt miserable and wondered if I was ill. None of the others were around. I had left Hisham sound asleep in his bed. I wandered through the lobby, unable to sit still for more than five minutes at a time. Then I went out for a walk. The air was thin and icy. The light was dull on the cars that swept past me. The general mood had changed, or maybe it was just my nerves. People seemed angry. I heard two drivers yelling at one another. A bundle of newspapers tossed from a passing van almost hit me as it landed on the pavement. I hurried back to the hotel. Just walking along the street today felt dangerous.

No one said a word as we drove over to our last rehearsal. We played until lunchtime with a strange, listless unease. Then there was a sound check in the actual theatre. This took a long time as each instrument and microphone had to be balanced with all the others. The sight of the vast stage brought the nerves rushing back. My stomach was in turmoil. In a few hours it would be full of people gathered to hear us play. I began to feel sick.

'Cheer up,' said a voice and I turned to find Kadugli. 'Everyone's nervous. It's natural.'

'That doesn't make it any easier.'

'It'll be fine.' He smiled. 'You'll see.' I watched him walk away and wondered why I couldn't be more like that.

The silence in the van on the way back to the hotel felt ominous. We each sat buried in our own private thoughts. The excitement of being here was now swamped by our fear of having to perform. Uncle Maher, Alkanary, Wad Mazaj: all of them wore rigid, distant expressions on their faces. Every time Hisham disappeared from sight I was afraid that he might have deserted us. Part of me wanted to kill him. The other part wished I had the courage to go with him. I went to the room and lay down to close my eyes for a minute. The prospect of failure was so acute I could hardly breathe. When I looked at my watch again, I realised an hour had gone by and I still wasn't dressed. I quickly showered and changed into my outfit. A midnight blue tuxedo with a stripe down the side. When I had the whole thing on I looked in the mirror and thought I looked like a clown. Whose idea had this been, I asked myself, and then remembered it was mine.

By the time I got downstairs they were all in the van waiting.

'The last one, as usual,' said Shadia, tapping Easy on the shoulder to indicate he could leave. I was beginning to think of her as an evil force whose presence was jinxing our entire trip. As we sped down the ramp into the street I looked out of the window. It was trying to snow again, and quick, nervous flurries of white blew past us, so that it felt as though we were underwater. The sight no longer filled me with wonder but rather with dread.

After that everything went by in a blur. The Kennedy Center was illuminated with bright lights as we rolled up the ramp and came to a halt in front of the entrance. It felt like a completely different place to the one we had come to know. A man was waiting to lead us through the various levels of security, down access tunnels and up stairs, pressing codes and swiping his security pass to open doors. As we were shepherded along, various members of the staff who had become familiar with us over the previous days nodded and called out encouragement. One or two even clapped. There was no time to stop and look round. We were led into a room where we had to wait for what felt like an eternity. We sat staring at one another, all dressed up. Alkanary was resplendent in a bright yellow wrap with orange flowers over a green dress while Shadia was quite unrecognisable. I had to look twice to be sure it was actually her. She was wearing some kind of shimmering dress that came down to her feet and swept up her body. It had some kind of peacock feather design that made it look as if the colours were floating around her. Her head was covered by a matching wrap. In comparison, the men looked like shabby doormen on a tea break, despite, or perhaps because of, the suits we'd had made at Gandoury's expense. Wad Mazaj's tie was askew, John Wau's trousers ended halfway down his shins. We looked like a joke. A sad collection of jesters brought in from an exotic place far away for the amusement of kings and queens who were indifferent to our existence. I couldn't break off the thought that everything had gone horribly wrong. Technical staff wandered in and out to make sure that our instruments were fitted with microphones for the amplification. Kadugli stood in the corner doing his Coltrane thing with the murmuring sax. Even that sight didn't calm me. I paced up and down, trying to shake off the negative energy. Where had it come from? Here we were, on the verge of what was the most important performance of our lives and I simply couldn't lose the idea that we were about to make complete fools of ourselves.

'Relax, will you,' Hisham hissed at me. 'You're making everyone nervous.'

I wanted to confess to Hisham that I was grateful to him, that I wished I had been more understanding about his plans, but I couldn't speak. I was paralysed by my own inability to act.

Then Ms DeHaviland shimmered into sight, looking elegant in her evening gown. She put me in mind of the portraits we had seen hanging on the walls of the museum that afternoon.

'I've come to wish you all luck,' she said with a smile. 'I'm sure you won't need it. We have a full house tonight. I'm positive it will be a wonderful success.'

A door opened behind her and a short, stumpy woman wearing glasses and a headset announced that she was the stage manager and that they were ready for us.

'Good luck.' Ms DeHaviland waved cheerily as she swept from the room. Then we were being led into a dark space at the foot of a small flight of stairs. For some reason they put me in mind of the steps up to the gallows. I heard a low hum like the sound of a dusty wind scuttling about outside the walls of a house.

'What's that noise?'

'That's the audience,' whispered Hisham behind me. I could feel the palms of my hands itching. Tiny lights illuminated each step but we were feeling our way like a train of blind people, one hand on the coat tails of the person in front. At the top was a heavy black curtain that you had to wrestle your way through – the stage manager was holding it but when I stepped up she was distracted by a voice in her headphones and let it fall back in my face. I panicked then. It felt like I was smothering. I tore it aside and stumbled out into the light.

Chapter 19

Showtime

I was floating on a sea of humanity. Hundreds of faces stared up at me. I felt as naked as the day I was born. Strangers were ranged across every available surface. I recovered enough to give a little bow that I had been rehearsing for weeks and moved across the stage, which seemed to have grown in the short time since I had last seen it. It was now three times as wide. The gentle humming was rising into a deafening roar as they clapped enthusiastically in anticipation. I suddenly found myself resenting them. Who were these people? Where did they come from and why had they come to hear us play? Why couldn't they leave us alone? They were whistling and cheering and we hadn't played a note yet. It was so overwhelming I bumped into a microphone and forgot where I was supposed to stand. I saw the others staring at me. Uncle Maher stood centre stage, bowing and smiling in all directions, gesturing to the others as they came on. Wad Mazaj settled on a high stool making the final adjustments to his oud, running the plectrum up and down the strings. Behind him stood John Wau, tall and silent, plugging in his guitar and running his long fingers up and down the frets to warm up. Hisham sat behind his electric keyboard cracking his knuckles, tapping his feet to some nervous rhythm in his head. Everybody seemed to be digging them-selves in. My terror increased with every breath I took. I felt dizzy.

Alkanary was over to Uncle Maher's left with Shadia just behind her. Kadugli and I were on the right side of the stage, just back from Uncle Maher.

My uncle held the violin above his head and bowed. At least he seemed to know what he was doing. Then he turned round to see if everyone was in place. As he looked at us a silence fell. A stunning, deep silence that spread itself over the auditorium. Then Uncle Maher gave a slight nod and Wad Mazaj launched into the opening bars of 'Nubian Indigo'. The strings hummed and trembled, making the air crackle with their vibrations. Each touch of his fingers stood out against the wall of silence. He was a miserable old fool most of the time, but I had to admit that when he played he was close to sublime. Uncle Maher tucked the kamanga under his chin, lifted the bow and we were off.

The next hour and a half went by in a fever. I can recall only flashes of it. The spotlights blinded me, knocking sparks out of the air. Somehow, and I cannot explain this, we managed to reach down into some place in our souls of whose existence we were hardly aware normally. Whether it was fear or the sense of occasion, I cannot say, but there were moments that evening when we managed to surpass anything we had achieved in our rehearsals. Something magical came over us.

At one point Alkanary raised a hand and stepped over to the microphone to surprise us all by speaking in English.

'Ladies and gentlemen, it is wonderful to see you here in all your fine clothes.' She paused for a smattering of appreciation. 'Fifty years ago we made our country dance to this next song. Tonight we are going to make you dance also, in your fine clothes.'

I glanced over at Shadia as she was speaking and found she was smiling. We all were. To my surprise she didn't turn away or pull a face. Then Uncle Maher lifted his bow and we launched off into a rousing version of 'Angareeb!'.

Maybe it was the presence of an audience that made us all try that little bit harder, or maybe it was the realisation that this was all we had; all we would ever have. This was our moment in the spotlight and we wanted to make it count.

In any case, the audience loved it. They refused to let us go. Round after round of applause rained down on us. Then suddenly it was over and we were stumbling off stage to stand in the gloom of the backstage area, dripping with sweat, looking round at one another in amazement, stunned, laughing with delight, unable to speak. No words were necessary though. The stage manager signalled and held aside the curtain for us to bounce back out. The house lights were up now and some of the audience stood and cheered. It was a mixed crowd. Young and old, mostly white, but also not. I felt moved and tremendously grateful. We stood together in a row at the front of the stage and bowed before taking our positions.

Then we launched into another number. This time one of Kadugli's more adventurous compositions, 'Kandaka Sunset'. A blend of his love of jazz with a rhythm that bent and swayed in sinuous time. The atmosphere grew even more frenzied. The entire audience was on their feet by now, clapping along in tune. Then John Wau stepped up, whipping into a kicking bassline that took us straight back to the heart of Africa for 'Ya Zoul, Ya Zoul'. Alkanary clapped her way to the microphone, bringing the audience to their feet as she started to sing. Uncle Maher sawed away as if the violin he held was in flames.

Shadia moved forward to join Alkanary at the front of the stage, getting the audience to clap along. I can remember Kadugli standing next to me and it was as if we were feeding each other phrases to pick up and play with. He played, I replied, and on it went, back and forth. By now some of the younger people were dancing down the aisles towards the stage.

When we finally staggered off, I felt like crying and found myself shaking hands warmly with the crew, the stage manager, people I had never seen in my life before. Then Ms DeHaviland was there, beside herself with joy.

143

'That was so wonderful! I can't thank you enough.'

Everything was a blur. We were led through along a corridor to a large reception room where we were greeted by a spontaneous round of applause. More were coming in through the door at the far end. I found myself shaking hands with an awful lot of people I had never seen before, their grasping my hands as if I were a long lost relative.

'Wonderful.'

'Magnificent!'

'We so much wanted to buy the album.'

'Alas, the albums are impossible to come by.' Uncle Maher wiped sweat from his brow.

'Is that true?' asked one man. He looked like a cowboy, tall, with shoulder-length straggly grey hair and a shaggy beard that was braided at the tip. He wore a jacket with fringes hanging from the sleeves and cowboy boots with steel toecaps. 'That strikes me as a real tragedy.'

'Rushdy, please.' Uncle Maher thrust me forward. 'My English is not strong.'

'Waldo Tucker, at your service,' the man beamed. I watched Uncle Maher's retreating back. 'I love what you guys did out there tonight.'

'Thank you, that's very kind.'

'No, really. Actually, I'm a record producer,' he went on, handing me a business card. 'We have to get you guys into the studio.'

'Mr Tucker, the Kamanga Kings have not recorded before in our current form.'

'Well, I know, because that's kind of the idea of this festival, you know, to bring back some of the old artists that never got properly heard in their day.'

'I see.' I really hadn't paid much attention to the rest of the festival programme. I had been too worried about our own contribution.

A waiter appeared carrying a tray on which were arranged a circle of tall slim glasses containing a bubbly golden liquid.

'Champagne?' Waldo Tucker helped himself to two glasses and handed one to me. I looked into the long narrow glass and wondered how to drink it without getting my nose stuck. I held it in my hand and smiled as he went on.

'As I said, it's a crying shame. What's the recording business like back home . . . you know, where you come from?'

'Oh, it doesn't exist,' I nodded confidently, watching how he tilted his head back to sip his drink. 'We have religion instead.' I tried the same and managed to get some of the liquid into my mouth; the rest dribbled onto my shirt.

'Is that a fact?' Waldo Tucker handed me a napkin and then waved another waiter over to select a piece of some kind of pastry that he popped into his mouth, grinning at me as he chewed. 'Actually, we have something of the same problem over here.'

'Is that true?'

'Oh, sure, man.' Waldo Tucker waved a hand expansively. 'The White House is run by religious nutjobs planning the apocalypse, safe in the knowledge that they will be the only ones to survive. Funny, huh, the way things work out?'

I looked at the piece of food I was holding, trying to work out what it was. Finally, I put it in my mouth and began to chew. It tasted of fish and had the strange consistency of melted plastic. It confirmed my conviction that all food in America tasted the same.

'We think we're still an empire, but look at the Chinese, man.' Waldo Tucker paused and leaned forward. 'You wanna . . . you know, the tail? It's shrimp. You don't want to eat the tail. They just leave that on for decoration.'

I nodded and put my fingers in my mouth to remove the offending piece. As I did so I caught sight of Shadia watching me from across the room. Why did she always have to catch me when I looked like a fool? She was talking to a tall man who resembled Michael Jordan. People moved between us and I strained to look around them. I wondered if he could be the real Michael Jordan.

I was still trying to make my escape when I became aware of someone standing next to me. She had appeared so silently and was

145

standing so still that I stared at her for a moment or two before I accepted she was not a figment of my imagination.

'I am . . . sorry,' I stammered. 'I didn't notice you.'

'That's quite all right.' She smiled. I must have looked like an idiot because Waldo Tucker laughed lightly.

'Maybe I should give your ears a rest. I'll leave you two together.' He squeezed my arm and winked in a gesture of complicity. 'Let's talk again, man.'

He sauntered away, greeting people left and right. My head was buzzing. An elderly couple dressed in fine clothes paused to smile and nod their heads at me. She seemed to be showered in diamonds, and they flashed as she moved her head.

'Lovely concert. We adored it.'

'Thank you.'

I turned back to the woman next to me. 'I'm sorry, all this is a little overwhelming.'

'Well, you deserve it,' she smiled. 'You were extraordinary.'

'Thank you.'

She had a wonderful smile. She was on the whole pretty wonderful full-stop. I felt hot and dizzy all at the same time. 'I was hoping I might be able to get an interview?' she asked.

'An interview?' I was confused. Her hair glistened in the white light. Her blue eyes glittered. I found myself suddenly tongue-tied. 'Who would you like to interview?'

'Why you, of course!' She burst out laughing, covering her mouth as she did so.

'Of course.' I was relieved she thought that I was trying to make a joke. 'Interview me? About what?'

She reeled off her answers without hesitation. 'About the group. How you met. What your relationship is. Life back home. You must have lots of fans.' She seemed to sense that I was ill at ease. 'Look,' she whispered, leaning close, 'why don't we get out of here, find a quiet corner where we can talk?'

As we made our way through the crowd, John Wau clapped me on the shoulder, his eyes were wide and shining.

'My brother,' he said, leaning down, 'we did it.'

I put my arms around him and honestly felt closer to him than I had ever done before. I was proud of him, of all of them. Beyond him, I saw Wad Mazaj deep in conversation with a group of gloomy-looking Arabs. An intense Kadugli was addressing a group of studious and well-dressed young bearded men wearing spectacles.

It was as if the whole world had been condensed to fit into that room and the magic lamp around which they were assembled was the Kamanga Kings. It was a marvellous feeling. Alkanary appeared more glamorous than I had ever seen her, as if restored to her former self. Beside her, Shadia looked oddly radiant. Perhaps it was the effect of the champagne, which I was not used to, or the euphoria, but she seemed oddly beautiful, which was a little confusing. By the door my uncle was chatting away, throwing his head back and laughing. He looked younger than I had ever seen him.

Chapter 20

The Interview

After the lights and excitement of the reception room it was a surprise to discover that the rest of the building was quite dark and deserted. The rush of the concert and the celebrations had left my head buzzing, so it felt calming to walk in silence down towards the main hall. People we passed along the way nodded and greeted me. Suddenly I was a celebrity. I was walking on air. Vanessa, that was the blonde woman's name, led the way to a bench in the front lobby, which she straddled, in a very unladylike fashion, as if riding a horse. She carried on talking as she began unloading items from the bag she carried over her shoulder.

'So, I think it's safe to say that you guys were the revelation of this festival. We've seen all kinds of groups, some really extraordinary artists from across the world, but they all had some kind of following. You guys came out of nowhere. Nobody had ever heard of you.' Vanessa said as she set a little egg thing down like the one they had at the airport and angled it upwards towards my face.

I had been thinking of my life a couple of months ago. The misery of my days in school now seemed to have taken place on a distant planet far away on another galaxy. Now I was being interviewed. What did I have to say? I decided it was best to begin with a question of my own.

'Please,' I said. 'Can you tell me about yourself?'

'About me?' She seemed surprised by the question. 'Well, there's not so much to tell, I'm afraid. I'm studying politics and journalism at Georgetown university.'

'And what do you hope to do, when you graduate?'

'Oh, I don't know. I mean there is so much in the world that seems wrong, don't you think? I would like to do something good, to make a contribution.' She flapped a hand in front of her face. 'Listen to me. Anyone would think it was me who was being interviewed.'

'You live in a world of possibility. It is our duty to make the most of our opportunities.'

She tilted her head to one side. 'Is that what you have done? Have you made the most of your opportunities?'

I had made the remark without really thinking, now I was forced to consider my words. Had I made the most of my opportunities? I had spent my life up until very recently doing whatever came easiest. The truth was that I had never really tried to do anything before this. I couldn't exactly say that, though, could I? I was beginning to realise that this interview business was more complicated than I had imagined.

'It was all decided for me before I was born.'

Her face grew sober. 'Oh, you mean some kind of tribal ritual?'

'No, no. I mean . . . my father was a musician.'

'Right.' She was no longer looking at me, but rather addressing her laptop. 'And he wanted you to carry on the family tradition.' That was another thing about Vanessa, she was good at finishing my sentences for me. I waited while she tapped away, her face oddly pale in the blue glow.

'What do you do?' she asked.

'What do I do?'

'Yes, I mean, you know, apart from being a musician? I mean do you have a job?'

What do I do? What did I do? As far as I knew there was no job waiting for me on my return.

'I teach,' I said. 'I used to teach.'

'You were fired? You lost your job?'

'No, well, actually, yes,' I corrected myself. Vanessa was tapping busily at the keys again.

'You were fired because you were a musician. Was it a religious school?'

'Yes, actually, but not in the way you are thinking.' I was having trouble making sense of my own answers. Vanessa, on the other hand, seemed to understand everything I was saying.

'You were persecuted. Were you arrested? Thrown in prison? Tortured?' Her eyes widened with each beat. I had to smile.

'No, nothing like that.' I saw the frown on her face and changed my tone. 'Which is not to say that people are not arrested and persecuted.'

'Musicians?'

'Yes, musicians. All the time. Many have suffered.'

'That's very noble of you.' She placed her hand on mine, which further confused my thoughts. 'I understand what you are trying to do.'

'You do?'

'Of course. You don't want to draw the attention away from more deserving cases. I get it. It's very honourable. Do you think Bashir should be delivered to the international court in the Hague?' I hesitated and she looked up. 'Don't worry, you're doing fine. I understand. All of this must be overwhelming for you.' She was nodding and smiling all the while. 'Tell me, why are you the Kamanga *Kings?* I mean, is that like a political statement? Are you saying the country should go back to the ancient kingdoms that existed prior to British imperialism?'

'It's just a name,' I shrugged. But was it, really? Was that something I should have asked myself? Was it possible that my father, all those years ago, had been thinking along those lines? A political statement in the name of the orchestra? A cry of defiance in the face of repression? Why had I never considered these things before?

'Okay, why don't you just tell me about the Kamanga Kings? Where did they begin?'

'Oh, that's a long story.'

'Well, take your time. There's no hurry.'

How long I talked, I don't know. There seemed to be so much to tell, so much to explain before you could begin to talk about the band.

'The Kamanga Kings represent the diverse nature of our country's cultural heritage. Our broad heritage mixes traditional elements with modern influences, from jazz and blues, African beat music and so on.'

'Where does that idea come from?'

'Where?' I had no clue. I racked my brains. I sensed that Vanessa preferred my answers to be simple, without ambiguity or doubt. 'It comes from being nomads,' I said firmly. 'When you are constantly moving, adapting to new places, you have to learn to improvise.' As I am doing now, I might have added.

'Great,' she nodded. 'This is great.'

I had no idea where any of this was coming from, but I kept going because, well, that seemed to be what she wanted.

'We find ourselves caught between the old ways and the new. We live in the modern world, but the message we are trying to transmit is from ancient times.'

'I totally get it,' she cooed. 'The Kings are a celebration of diversity and that is in direct opposition to the political hegemony of the current regime.'

'I'm sorry?' I wasn't sure I fully understood. Vanessa, on the other hand, seemed to understand all too well.

'That's what you're saying, right? You're challenging the existing political order.'

'I'm not sure I expressed myself clearly.'

'Oh, but you did. You're doing great.' She rested her hand on mine again, and again my heart began to flutter. I felt emboldened.

'We are musicians. We challenge the very nature of the universe. Our music will change not only our country. It will free us. Music is a tool of liberation. It can free the world.'

'That's wonderful. Let's end there. I can't thank you enough.' She began packing up her things. I began to get to my feet.

'When will your newspaper be printed?'

'Oh,' she laughed brightly. 'We don't print things any more. It's bad for the environment? Save the trees?' She held up two fingers in a bad imitation of a tree. 'It goes straight onto the internet. It'll be out as soon as I finish this.' She handed me a card.

'*The Wasteland Chronicles*?' I read.

'The United States uses eighty-six per cent of the world's natural resources and produces seventy-five per cent of the world's waste,' she explained. 'And our current president has basically declared war on the environment. People are very upset.'

I watched her walk away, not quite sure what had just happened. By now the hallway lights were dimmed and the lobby was deserted. I wondered how long we had been talking and where everyone had gone. Wandering the unlit halls, I felt as though I was trapped in a mausoleum. Light filtering through the high windows from outside painted the room in layers of orange and black. The huge gleaming bronze bust of John F. Kennedy loomed out of the darkness, floating in mid-air like the ghost of another age.

I stepped outside into the cold night air to clear my head. In the distance I could see the dark river gleaming with mystery. Laughter drew my attention to two figures standing in the shadows at the far end of the building.

Waldo Tucker and Hisham were sharing a joint. Hisham, as usual under such circumstances, was explaining one of his crackpot theories.

'The thing about the Reformation is that it took like a thousand years from the fall of the Roman Empire for people to realise that the church was obsessed with materialism, right?'

'Uh huh,' nodded Waldo.

'I mean, it was all about the money, right? In Islam, okay, there is no priest between you and Allah. So nobody has the right to speak and everyone has the right.'

'So nobody has the right to judge others. Cool.' Waldo passed the joint to me. I declined.

'We don't need a Reformation to get back to the true essence of the religion. It's right there.'

'You sound like a man who knows his Hegel.'

'Big fan,' nodded Hisham, puffing away like a Turkish pasha.

'Hegel? Seriously?' I asked.

'Sorry, brother, but some things just never come up in our conversations,' he shrugged.

'Intellectuals.' Waldo tilted his head back to blow a ring of smoke at the sky. 'Everybody hates 'em, right?'

The icy wind blowing up from the river whipped around the building. The two of them were hopping up and down and rubbing their arms to keep warm. Hisham was grinning at me.

'So, how did your interview go, brother?'

'I told her we were nomads.'

Hisham doubled over with laughter.

'The press is like an ex-wife.' Waldo paused to inhale deeply. 'You can't stand them, but you can never get rid of them, either. Have to learn to love it, man.' He held out the joint. 'This stuff is great, man. I can taste the desert.' Both of them started giggling at that. 'I'm serious,' Waldo insisted. 'I can't believe you brought this stuff in through the airport. They have dogs and shit.'

'We have our mysterious desert ways,' giggled Hisham, and again they broke into laughter.

Waldo Tucker clapped me on the back. 'I really like your friend here, hell, I like both of you! But what we really need to do is compare this with the best this country can offer. Either of you boys ever tried California's finest?'

'Where we gonna get some shit this time of night?' Hisham asked. He seemed to be already acquiring an American accent.

'Don't worry about it.' Waldo tapped his nose. 'I just happen to know a place.'

'Your place? You have a place here?' Hisham asked. 'Washington D.C.?' I wondered how stoned he was.

'I have a place everywhere I go,' Waldo said mysteriously. 'Follow me.'

With a twirl of his hand he turned and led us down a narrow path to a spot protected by trees and there, under the bowl of a streetlight, stood a long silver wall with wheels, lots of wheels. It had a kind of bulbous shape at the front and back and resembled a large fat worm or a spaceship, a submarine, or perhaps an enormous groundnut.

'This is where you live?' I asked. Hisham was giggling, either at me, or the vehicle, I couldn't tell.

'Gentlemen, welcome to my humble abode.' So saying, Waldo produced a key and opened a door in the side. 'When I'm on the road, which is most of the time, this is how I roll.'

Both Hisham and I were speechless as we climbed the steps and peered inside. The interior consisted of an open space like a salon. On one side was a kitchen with a small table and a bench. Next to this a couple of armchairs that swivelled. Beyond that lay the driver and passenger seats, both of them big, padded chairs. Every available surface was cluttered with objects: books, magazines, boxes full of compact discs, clothes, bags of food, cups filled with some kind of green substance that might once have been coffee, crushed beer cans and bowls of snacks. Everything looked really old and rather shabby. All the fittings were the same tan colour, from the wood panelling to the fake leather and the carpet with its pattern of burn marks.

The dashboard had enough instruments to get you to Mars. The top of it was covered in little plastic figures. I could see Elvis Presley, dancers with grass skirts, a bear wearing a hat, a golden cat, along with guitar players and dogs of various sizes, all with moveable parts.

'Look,' laughed Hisham. 'It's ET, and that's Luke Skywalker.'

A narrow corridor led through to the back, where an unmade bed could be glimpsed. Waldo was busy throwing things into boxes and

154

cupboards, shutting doors and generally trying to make the place more presentable. Seeing him in this space put him in a different light somehow. He cut a less impressive figure than he had at the reception. A little sad, even.

'Sorry about the mess. Sit down, make yourselves at home.'

I settled myself in one of the swivel chairs while Hisham slid in behind the table. Waldo bent down to snap open a little hidden compartment from which he produced a plastic bag full weed. Hisham's eyes widened. As he started rolling a joint, Waldo gave us a brief account of his life.

'I left home in 1977, I was sixteen years old. Basically, I've been on the road ever since. I've been living in this thing since my divorce.'

'Waldo is a record producer,' Hisham said.

'Yes, I heard that,' I said. 'He wants to record us.'

'Look,' he said, splaying his hands out. 'I'll be honest with you. I run a small and somewhat obscure company. I'm known as a maverick. Stuff like the Ton Ton Zombies, from Haiti. That kind of stuff. The Rhinestone Underground? They were a kind of black Tex-Mex combo? No? Well, it was something of an acquired taste. Guacamole Exit? Death rock meets Trini Lopez is how we marketed them. They were from Nicaragua. No, Guatemala. Well, one of those places.' He handed the joint to Hisham.

'You see, the thing you have to understand,' Waldo continued, 'is that we're an empire in decline. We cling to the relics of a dying culture. The only kind of culture that we respect, apart from our own, is a dead culture. We make the death machines.'

'Death machines?' I wasn't sure I was hearing right.

'Sure. Our instruments of war are named after the peoples we have destroyed. The Apache helicopter, the Tomahawk missile. You know? We turn their annihilation into our death machines.'

'Cool, right?' Hisham murmured, as he took a long drag. 'Waldo, what kind of car is this?'

'This isn't a car, man.' Waldo laughed. 'This is a piece of American history. A 1976 GMC Birchaven. A modern classic.' He spoke as if this might mean something to us.

'This country is built on motion. Our entire history is that of a people on the move. From the pilgrims landing on Plymouth Rock to the Pioneers going out west in their wagons.' He was busy rolling another fat joint between his fingers as if it was a fine cigar. Hisham and I were still busy with the first one. 'Ever read *On The Road*? Jack Kerouac?' We hadn't. 'Anyway, Sal Paradise travels across the continent in search of himself, of people who were mad to live, to burn out like roman candles.' There was something endearing about Waldo sharing his youthful memories so openly. 'When I read those words, I knew what I wanted to do with my life and, well, here I am.'

Clouds of white smoke filled the confined space as he lit the joint and took a couple of long, intense puffs before handing it over.

'This is a little more mellow. More of your Indica rich blend.'

Hisham grinned at me and then tried it. Waldo was watching closely, raising his eyebrows in attendance.

'So, what do you think?'

'Smooth,' puffed Hisham, handing it on to me. 'Not bad at all.'

'I need to get out of here,' I said, struggling to my feet.

'Hey, what's the rush?'

I didn't know where to begin. I looked at them both. I felt I no longer knew who they were.

'I have to go.'

'Wait!'

Hisham stumbled out of the door and fell on his face. He remained there, giggling to himself until I helped him up. For a moment I had no idea where we were or how we had got there. My head was spinning and I was convinced we were lost, deep in a forest.

'Take it easy, man,' Waldo waved from the doorway. 'I'm here if you need me.'

We waved back and then somehow made our way, rather unsteadily, up the road and back across town.

Chapter 21

Gandoury's Game

The lobby of the hotel had been taken over by an impromptu party that was in full swing. The bartender, a small man in his forties with thinning hair and a drooping moustache that made him look like a bandit, had kindly agreed to stay open beyond his usual hour in our honour. He was cheerfully and rather enthusiastically pouring drinks for everybody. The place was reeling. It looked as if half the audience had come back with us. Ties had been loosened and jackets thrown off.

Hisham didn't waste any time, vanishing across the room where he was soon surrounded by what looked like a new group of friends he must have made earlier, young men and women dressed in sweat-shirts and headscarves. They resembled a militia who were looking for a cause. His hip-hop friends, no doubt. All part of his new world. I felt a sadness, knowing that soon I was about to lose my best friend.

I spotted Uncle Maher and made my way over to him.

'My boy, I was worried about you,' he smiled, throwing his arm around my shoulders. 'Where have you been? Have a drink.' He himself had clearly had a few glasses of wine, which he tended to lap up rather like a cat licking milk. Ruby droplets bobbed in the air on the whiskers of his moustache. 'Not bad, eh? I have to thank you, and Hisham, wherever he is. If you hadn't talked us into this, we would never have been here. Your father would be proud.' His chin quivered and he patted me on the shoulder before turning back to the conversation he was in.

'Why the long face?'

I turned to see Shadia standing behind me.

'Oh, nothing,' I muttered. 'I'm just tired.' I couldn't explain without telling her about Hisham's plans, and that would have been unfair. Instead, I tried to move by her. She blocked my progress.

'Everyone is having a good time except you. Why? What's going on?'

'Look, it's nothing, really.'

Shadia rolled her eyes. 'Okay, I get it. Because I'm a woman, I wouldn't understand.'

'I didn't say that. Why do you always assume that I think badly of you?'

'Don't you?'

'No,' I said. 'No, I don't. As a matter of fact, I think . . .' I was running out of words the way the Road Runner ran out of road. 'I think you've been a great help.'

Shadia gave a snort. 'A help? You make it sound like I am here to do your laundry.'

'No, no, I didn't mean that. I only meant . . .'

'Forget it.' She held up a hand. 'It's all right, you don't need to say something nice. It's over. We had a great concert and my aunt is happier than I've seen her in years. I was getting worried about her. Some people just don't like getting old, and she was very unhappy. Now she looks twenty years younger. You've given her her life back.'

I turned to follow her gaze. Alkanary was surrounded by admirers, many of whom looked like our fellow countrymen, people who knew her history.

'Yes,' I agreed. 'She does look happy. What I wanted to say, is that without you this wouldn't have been the same.' But when I turned to her, Shadia had already gone.

I stayed in the lobby for a little longer, but my heart wasn't in it.

I wanted simply to sit and remember the evening. I wished I could commit the whole concert to memory, so that I could give all the details to the people back home. After a time, I set down my glass and slipped quietly away. I felt exhausted. The work and worry of the last few weeks seemed suddenly to have caught up with me. As I waited for the lift, Hisham appeared, coming from the direction of the bathrooms at the far end of the lobby.

'Hey, where are you going?'

'I'm tired. I need to sleep.'

'Come on, man, this is the one night when we deserve to party.'

'I know,' I said. 'I just can't keep my eyes open.'

'Well, we did it!' He clapped me on the shoulder and then put his arms around me. 'Whatever happens, nobody can say we didn't pull it off, eh?'

I freed myself and looked at him. 'You're not . . . you know?'

'Tonight, I'm just going to have fun.' He nodded towards the party. 'A lot of very friendly young ladies in there that I intend to get to know a little better.' He winked and slapped me on the shoulder once more. I watched him walking back through to the lounge. I was half tempted to go back and join him, but I knew I wouldn't last five minutes. The lift doors slid open and I stepped inside.

I was awoken much too soon the next morning by an insistent knocking on the door. I stumbled out of bed and staggered out to find Uncle Maher looking the worse for wear. He was still clad in his concert clothes. His tie was askew, his shirt collar stuck up on one side.

'Shouldn't you be asleep, Uncle?'

'Yes, yes. It's just that there's been some kind of misunderstanding. I need you to get dressed and come with me.'

'What kind of misunderstanding?'

Uncle Maher leaned on the doorframe. 'I'm so tired. I should be asleep. I'm afraid I overdid it a little last night. I got carried away.' He put a hand to his head. 'I feel terrible.'

'What kind of misunderstanding?' I repeated.

'Oh, yes. The man, you know, the one we spoke to, the administrator? He called me first thing this morning. I had literally only just put my head on the pillow.' Uncle Maher tried to pull the sleeve of his jacket back to look at his watch. 'What time is it anyway?'

I pulled his wrist gently towards me and spun the watch round so that I could see the face.

'It's just gone midday.'

'That late? It can't be,' he gasped. I reared back from the gust of alcohol-laden breath.

'Go back to your room and get some rest. I'll sort this out.'

I had no idea how exactly I was going to do that, but it felt like the right thing to say. I watched him shuffle away towards his room. I went back inside to dress, confirming what I had noticed earlier, that Hisham's bed had not been slept in.

I tried calling the Kennedy Center but couldn't remember the name of the person we had spoken to. Instead, I dressed and went downstairs, asked a taxi to take me there. I had enough American money to get me there but would have to walk back. When I arrived I discovered that nobody remembered me and it took some time before I found someone who would take me to the administration office where the same man in spectacles that we had seen met me. He wore a pained expression on his face.

'I'm afraid this is simply a misunderstanding,' he began. 'I called your uncle because I was not sure I'd done the right thing.'

We were standing in the reception area outside his office.

'He's an old man and his English is rusty. Perhaps you could explain the whole thing again.'

'Sure, well, the point is that when your colleague showed up I sort of was surprised, because we hadn't agreed a time.' He shrugged to himself. 'But since he was with your group I assumed it was all right. It was only afterwards . . .'

'Hold on,' I said. 'I'm confused. What colleague? Who are you talking about?'

'The man who was with you the other day. Your business manager?'

'Suleiman Gandoury? What about him?'

'Well, when he turned up, I assumed it was as we had agreed, but then I realised that I had forgotten to get him to sign an insurance form. I tried to reach him at the hotel.'

I held up a hand. 'Hold on, one second. Are you telling me that you gave Gandoury our money?'

'Exactly. That's what I'm trying to tell you.' The man's face took on an expression of sheepishness. 'I assumed, you know, that he was just a bit eager. I mean, this was before you had played and normally we don't pay until after the event.'

'When was this exactly?'

'Yesterday morning.'

'And you said you tried to reach him at the hotel?'

'Yes, but they said he'd checked out. Which can't be right, right?'

I looked at him. I was trying to remember the last time I'd seen Gandoury. I couldn't remember him at the concert, or at the party last night.

'I'm sure it's a simple misunderstanding,' I said.

'Yes, exactly.' The man looked relieved.

'I should get back to the hotel, to sort this out.'

'That would be best.'

Twenty minutes later I was at the reception desk in the hotel. The same woman who was always smiling and asking how you were doing was there.

'I need to check something. One of our group, Mr Gandoury.'

I waited while she studied the screen in front of her. She clicked her way through this and that. It seemed to take forever.

'Mr Gandoury checked out yesterday morning,' she said. 'There seems to have been a problem with the minibar?'

'The minibar?'

'Costs of the minibar are not covered by the Kennedy Center.'

'I don't care about the minibar. I want to see Mr Gandoury.'

There must have been something about the tone of my voice but her manner changed. She stepped back from the counter and signalled to a man further down the reception area.

'Carl, this gentleman is with the group from the Kennedy Center. I was just explaining to him that items taken from the minibar have to be paid for.'

Carl was a big man with broad shoulders. He was smiling, but he meant business.

'What seems to be the problem, sir?'

'Look, I don't care about the minibar. The minibar is not the issue.'

'Well, we have strict rules that we have to enforce.'

'I know, I understand. It's just that . . .' I tried to think how I could explain. Suddenly all of this, the polite language, the smiles, felt suffocating. 'Look, I just need to find this man.'

Carl consulted the screen. 'I'm afraid that won't be possible.'

'But it can't be. I mean, he has our money.'

A frown crossed Carl's face. 'I'm sorry, sir?'

But I was already gone, moving away towards the lifts on the far side of the room. I had to speak to Uncle Maher.

'Sir!' I heard Carl calling from behind me. 'Sir!'

I ignored him. I pressed the buttons frantically. One set of doors opened and there, by some miracle, was Uncle Maher. He looked me up and down.

'What's the matter, boy? Did you sort out that business?'

Before I could answer a man stepped up to us. He was a big man, rather overweight and wearing a suit so creased it looked as though he might have slept in it. He looked rather angry. As we tried to pass by, he blocked our way.

'Excuse me, but we are in a hurry,' I said.

'Would you mind walking this way?' he asked, gesturing towards the dining room. I was about to speak but had a feeling there was no point. Uncle Maher and I looked at one another. What choice did we have? We followed the man as he led the way. The interior of the dining room was dark, unlit by natural light. In the middle of the room, under the glow of a blue lamp over the table sat Ms DeHaviland. She got to her feet as we came towards her.

'Ms DeHaviland,' I said. 'What is going on? And who are these people?'

'These are FBI agents Baumgarten and Blanco who will be co-ordinating with Homeland Security and ICE.'

'ICE?' I asked. 'What is ICE.'

'It's the immigration service,' said Ms DeHaviland.

'Immigration?' I could feel my heart start to beat faster. I was convinced they had caught Hisham somewhere. 'Sorry, Uncle,' I began. 'I should have told you.'

'Told me what?' Uncle Maher was as confused as I was.

At first glance I had thought the two agents were both men, but now I saw that one was in fact a woman. Her hair was pulled back from her rather square face in a fierce ponytail. She wore a man's suit and had legs that seemed to bow outwards under her weight. The one who had walked us from the lift was tall and heavily built, dark skinned with a pockmarked face and thinning curls that were combed back across his forehead.

'I'm sorry that this has to be so formal, but the regulations are quite strict. The Center cannot afford to be seen to act inappropriately. These are difficult times. Politically, I mean. I hope you understand.'

I didn't frankly understand a word of this, but I was beginning to get a very bad feeling.

'This is now a national security matter and I am obliged to act. I'm sorry, Rushdy, but I have no choice in the matter. Agent Baumgarten.'

The woman agent stepped forward. Her pale grey eyes narrowed as she addressed me.

'At approximately eight forty-five this morning an anonymous phone call was made to our emergency line. We do not know who made that call, obviously, otherwise it would not be anonymous.'

I couldn't tell if she was trying to be funny. Her face, however, remained impassive and showed no trace of amusement. She went on.

'The caller, who spoke English, was identified as female with an accent identified as possibly being Latino. The information she gave our operator was that a certain visiting ensemble invited to play at the Kennedy Center tonight was planning to seek political asylum in the United States.'

'Seek what?' I echoed. Uncle Maher clutched my arm.

'But how?' he asked, his lip quivering. 'Never.'

Agent Baumgarten went on, speaking in the same flat and lifeless tone.

'Obviously we would like to avoid any unpleasantness but we would be failing in our duty if we did not make it clear that any member of this group failing to depart this country according to the conditions under which entry was permitted will be designated an undesirable alien. Do I make myself clear?'

'Undesirable alien,' I repeated dully.

'What did she say?' Uncle Maher asked.

I turned to Ms DeHaviland. 'I don't understand any of this. Nobody in our group is claiming asylum.' Even as I spoke, I was thinking of Hisham. Where was he?

Ms DeHaviland sighed. 'This is not easy for me,' she began, lowering her voice. She led me to one side, out of earshot of the two immigration officers. 'We're in a tough position, Rushdy. This administration has made immigration one of its cornerstones. As an institution we are very vulnerable. If we are found to be aiding and abetting asylum seekers we will be in a very tough position.'

'You have nothing to worry about,' I said. 'Believe me.'

'I want to believe you, Rushdy, I really do.' She stared at me. 'We invited you here in good faith.' She shook her head in despair. 'This is such a disaster.'

'An anonymous phone call. It could be anything.' I shrugged, trying to make light. 'Somebody didn't like the look of us and decided to stir up trouble.'

'I truly hope that is the case.' Her eyes were shining. 'The concert was a huge success. The audience loved you. The press is all over it. There are countless requests for interviews. I would hate for that achievement to be overshadowed by unpleasantness.'

Uncle Maher stepped forward and took her hand. 'Please, Madame, we are honourable people. We would not do such a thing.'

'I appreciate that,' she said, withdrawing her hand gently. I had come to like Ms DeHaviland. I liked her style and grace, her elegance. I felt there was something special between us. An understanding.

'All we need is a roll call. If you can get everyone together and show that nobody is missing, that would be a start. But Homeland Security have insisted that nobody leaves the hotel. I know it's a lot to ask and I shall do my best to get it lifted. If you can prove that nobody here is planning to run away that would be a great help.'

Over her shoulder I saw the two agents. They were standing back, arms folded. The woman shifted her weight from one foot to the other, while the tall man scratched his nose. If they were here to scare us, they were doing a fine job of it.

'I'm glad we have an understanding.' Ms DeHaviland turned to the agents and they huddled together to talk in low voices before she came back to us.

'A car will be posted outside the hotel for the rest of your stay. It's just a formality.'

There was more handwringing and apologies and forced smiles before Ms DeHaviland and the ICE agents withdrew to leave us alone. Uncle Maher sank slowly into one of the chairs.

'Well, at least that was not so serious. These Americans, eh?' he chuckled. 'Everything is a movie to them. Now, what was it you wanted to tell me about Hisham?'

'I think perhaps we should get the rest of the group together.'

'As you wish. Let's call a meeting in my room.'

Chapter 22

Decision Time

Half an hour later we were all crowded into Uncle Maher's room. All, that is, except Hisham. Uncle Maher began by telling everyone what had just happened.

Wad Mazaj gave a dismissive grunt. 'These people think that everyone in the world dreams only of becoming Americans. As if it's so great here.'

There was agreement and general disbelief that our hosts could possibly think we were capable of such a thing.

'It's always the poor African who comes begging to the rich man's table,' said John Wau.

Uncle Maher chimed in, 'Whatever the case may be, we are guests in this country and we must respect their way of doing things. We must make it clear to them that we didn't come to America to beg them to take us in.'

I cleared my throat. Everyone turned towards me slowly.

'There's something I have to tell you.' I looked around at them. 'It's about Hisham.'

Shadia's hand flew up to her mouth. 'Ya Allah, that's what you were talking about in the park, isn't it?'

'What were you talking about?' Uncle Maher asked. 'Spit it out, boy!'

So, I did. When I had finished, they all looked at me blankly for a moment.

'Are you telling me,' Uncle Maher began, his voice rising. He was furious and for a moment couldn't speak. He pointed blankly at the door. 'Are you telling me, that we, that I just gave that woman my word that we had no such ideas in our heads. In other words, I lied. Is that what you are saying?'

'I didn't think he would go through with it,' I said softly. There were moans and groans all round.

'And the money, our money, did he take that as well?'

'No,' I said. 'That's the other thing.'

'What other thing?' Shadia asked.

Everyone stared at me. I took a deep breath and started at the beginning. When I'd finished there was a long silence. Nobody seemed to really understand what I had just said.

'Why would he do that?' Uncle Maher asked. 'It makes no sense.'

'He took the money and checked out of the hotel?' said John Wau.

'He stole our money,' said Wad Mazaj.

'We don't know that,' reasoned Uncle Maher. 'There might be a perfectly good explanation.'

The rest of them were silent. 'I'm afraid I agree with Wad Mazaj. It looks as though Gandoury has taken our money and gone.'

'But that's crazy!' said Shadia. 'He's supposed to be our manager.'

'They do it all the time,' said Alkanary wearily. 'What can you do?'

'I can't believe he would do something like that,' I said, even though I had never liked Suleiman Gandoury.

'Gandoury is not important.' Kadugli was leaning on the window-sill with his arms folded. Now he straightened up. 'Whatever reason Hisham has for doing this, he should have discussed it with us. This was not his decision to make. It affects everyone. And you,' he pointed at me, 'you should have come to us earlier.'

I knew he was right. Everyone agreed, but somehow, coming from him, made it hurt all the more.

'He's brought shame upon us all,' Uncle Maher concluded. 'Not just us, the band, but our country.'

'What was he thinking?' John Wau asked.

'That's obvious,' said Wad Mazaj. 'He was thinking of himself. He doesn't care about us. After all the work we've put in, this is our reward, and now he takes it all for himself.'

'You don't think they could be in this together, do you?' Uncle Maher asked, speaking my thoughts aloud.

'No,' I said. 'I can't believe that. Hisham and Gandoury?'

'Whatever it is, this has brought shame on us all,' Uncle Maher said quietly. 'The money is not important, but we have deceived our hosts. They invited us here in good faith and this is how they are rewarded. I'm just thankful your father is not around to see it.'

The others joined in but nobody had anything new to say. They went over the whole thing time and again, with everyone airing their grievances. We weren't getting anywhere. I held up my hands for silence.

'Look, mistakes aside, the point is we have to decide what to do.'

'What can we do?' Wad Mazaj asked. 'We have to do as they say. We wait here like criminals until it is time for us to leave the country.'

'It's humiliating,' said John Wau.

'He's looking for the woman of his dreams,' said Alkanary, taking a philosophical line. 'How are you going to tempt him back? Let him go, is what I say. Good luck to him.'

It was hard to argue with that. Everyone else seemed to agree. There was some further discussion but eventually everyone filed out and went back to their rooms.

I walked back along the corridor, lost in my thoughts. We seemed to have fallen a long way from our moment of triumph the previous evening. Everything was sullied by the news. All I wanted now was for it to be over and we could get on the plane and go home. However, when I got back to my room there was a surprise waiting for me.

I was lost in my thoughts. There was so much to think about. I wish that I had acted earlier. Maybe if all of us had intervened Hisham might have seen reason. At the end of the day he was my friend and if I hadn't known him, he would never have been brought into the group.

I shut the door and went into the bathroom. I was standing there, looking at my reflection in the mirror when I heard it. I wasn't sure at first what it was or whether my mind was playing tricks, but I could definitely hear something strange. I had left the door open, which I would normally never do unless I was alone. Now, suddenly, I was no longer sure this was the case.

Fixing my clothes, I stepped out and walked the two steps to the main room. There, lying on his bed fully dressed was Hisham. He had his head back with his mouth open and was snoring gently, which was the sound I had heard. I was shocked. I stared at him for a second, unable to move.

'Wake up! Wake up!' I shook him hard.

'What? What happened?' Hisham sat up and looked around him. 'Is it the police?'

'It's worse than that.'

'What is wrong with you?' He pushed my hands off him and I stepped back. I still couldn't believe it.

'What are you doing here?'

Propped up on one elbow he rubbed his eyes. 'This is my room, isn't it? I mean, you're in it, so it must be.'

'No, I mean, I thought you'd gone. You know, for good.'

'Oh . . . yeah.' He lay back and closed his eyes. 'Something else came up.' He had a strange smile on his face.

'Where were you last night?'

'You remember that girl, the one with the afro?'

'No. I mean, what girl?'

'She was at the thing last night. There was a group of them.' Hisham was chuckling to himself as he spoke. 'Anyway, they took me along to another party and afterwards . . .'

'You and this girl?'

'Aha,' he nodded. He looked very pleased with himself.

'But you hardly know her.'

Hisham frowned at me as though I was mad. 'You know that you don't have to marry someone first, right?'

'Okay, okay.' I was having trouble taking everything in. I began pacing along the front of the two beds, from the entry hall to the window and back again. 'Listen, a lot has happened.' I started to explain, and then I stopped again. 'Wait, how did you get into the hotel?'

'The back stairs, remember? I didn't want to bump into anyone in the lobby.'

Hisham had shown me the way out using the fire escape at the back of the building. Because there was no smoking anywhere in the hotel, he had used it several times to go outside for a cigarette. He wasn't the only one – apparently the staff regularly used it for the same purpose. There was even a wedge that could be used to stop it locking itself when it shut.

'Okay, well, that explains why you weren't picked up by ICE.'

'ICE? What are you talking about?'

I watched his face as the gravity of the situation sunk into his face as I explained.

'You mean, they're watching us? We can't leave the hotel? But this is a disaster!'

'Wait, there's more,' I said, and told him about the money. He listened and then took a moment to work it out.

'So, you're saying everyone thinks I stole the money and ran away?'

'Well, that's sort of how it looked.'

'With Gandoury?' Hisham started swearing. 'I can't believe it. You're supposed to be my friend. How could you think I would do something like that?'

'I don't know. It was confusing. There's no explanation.'

'Except that your best friend is a thief?'

He was angry and I suppose that was understandable. We both settled down and sat in silence for a moment before there was a knock at the door. We looked at each other.

'We should hide,' Hisham whispered. There was another knock.

'Don't be silly,' I said, getting up. 'Where are you going to hide?'

I pulled open the door to find Shadia standing there with her hand raised as if about to knock again.

'Can I come in?' she asked.

'In here? You mean, in my room?'

She looked up and down the corridor. 'That's where we are, right?'

'Yes, of course. Okay.' I looked over my shoulder.

'Oh,' she said, as if she understood. 'You have someone in there?'

'No, I mean, yes.' I didn't know what I meant.

'Okay, well, it doesn't matter. It can wait.' She made to turn away. Impulsively, I grabbed her arm and pulled her in.

'Hey! What are you doing?'

I let go of her, holding up both hands in a show of innocent intent. 'There's something you have to see.'

'What's got into you?' she frowned. I led her into the main room and showed her Hisham. Shadia looked at me before turning to him.

'I thought you'd run away with our money?'

'You too? How could you think I would do something like that?'

'Okay,' Shadia said, turning to me. 'If he didn't run away and he didn't take the money, then what's going on?'

'Gandoury is definitely gone. And he's taken our money.'

'Well, it's just money.' Shadia sat down on the chair by the television and turned to Hisham. 'So, where were you last night?'

'Don't ask,' I said.

She read the look on my face. 'Okay, well, that explains one thing.'

'Why are you here?' I asked.

'Some of us were talking, after you left. This whole thing is not good. I mean, I know it's not about the money but a lot of the group were depending on getting something back. People have put in months of work, they've made sacrifices. It's just a little unfair to end like this.' She paused, looking down at her hands. 'And Uncle Maher keeps talking about honour and so forth. I don't really care about that, or I thought I didn't.' She looked up. 'But actually, I do. I mean, it's not good that this is how we will be remembered. Dishonest. Like all the stereotypes they have of us. We should be proud of what we achieved, coming here, playing for an international audience. Nothing should detract from that.'

Hisham and I looked at each other. Neither of us had anything to add really. Shadia got to her feet.

'Anyway, I just wanted to tell you, I suppose.' She looked at me and then at Hisham. 'I'm glad you're back, anyway. And now you'll have to forget about running away to this woman. They are watching the hotel.'

Hisham was silent. I walked Shadia to the door.

'Maybe it's not so bad,' she said, as she stepped out into the corridor. 'I mean, we had a good time. We saw America.'

'The Kamanga Kings had their moment of triumph on the world stage,' I said. 'That's still something.'

'I suppose we'll all go back to being what we were before.'

'I suppose so.' I looked up at her and noticed that her hair had come loose and hung in long, soft tresses down the side of her face. I wasn't sure I wanted to go back to how things were. 'In time,' I said, 'we won't even remember whether it actually happened, or we just dreamed it.'

'I'll remember.' She looked at me and seemed to be waiting for me to say more. Only I couldn't find the words.

'Somehow that makes me feel sad.'

'Endings are always sad.' She smiled.

I watched her walk away down the corridor and wondered why I always found it so hard to say what was on my mind. Then I told myself to stop being foolish. There were more important things to worry about.

Chapter 23

A Change of Plans

Hisham was asleep again. I sat on the bed and tried to think. There was something that I had missed. Why would Suleiman Gandoury steal our money? There had to be something more to it. And the phone call, warning that we were about to run off. Was that what Gandoury was planning? I couldn't see him stealing our money and going home. That made no sense.

So Gandoury was planning a new life in America. Good luck to him. Frustrated, I turned to the television that was set on a table in a corner of the room. I pressed the buttons and continued pressing, unable to settle on anything that made any sense to me. I was staring at the screen but my thoughts were elsewhere.

'Turn it off,' groaned Hisham from over by the wall. 'I'm trying to sleep.'

As I was about to do so my eyes went back to the screen where I saw a young girl chasing a puppy around a big house. The dog was wrapped in paper that was unwinding from a roll in the toilet. Funny ideas these Americans have. Then it struck me.

'Wake up!'

There was a mumbled plea for me to shut up and go to sleep. By now I was on my feet going through the pile of clothes lying on the floor in the wardrobe. Then I went through my bag. I was sure I had it.

'Where is it?'

'Where is what?' mumbled Hisham.

I finally remembered and went back to the bedside table. 'Get up,' I said to Hisham. 'Pack your things, we're leaving.'

'What? Are you mad? Leaving, now?'

'Just the essentials,' I said. I dragged my suitcase out of the closet and began throwing clothes into it. It didn't take me long to realise that this was never going to work. I shut the bag. My eye fell on my trumpet case. No way I was leaving that behind.

'Could you please explain to me what's got into you?'

'I know where he's going.'

'Where who's going?'

'Gandoury.' I did my best to explain. Hisham didn't look entirely convinced, but he was game.

'We only take what we can carry.'

'Hold on a second.' Hisham was on his feet, blocking my way. 'We can't just walk out without telling the others.'

I considered the point. He was right, of course. It would be unfair to just leave. On the other hand, I couldn't bear the idea of another long discussion with the whole group.

'We'll tell Shadia,' I decided. 'She can tell them.'

Hisham agreed. 'Good thinking. I'm still not sure I understand.' He was fighting his suitcase out of the closet. I stopped him.

'Just take the rucksack. I'll explain in Shadia's room.' I grabbed him by the shoulders. 'Once we do this there's no turning back.'

'Okay,' he said, shaking me off. I thought he was about to say something else, and then he stopped himself. When we got into the corridor, I turned to him. 'You're not going to disappear on me, are you?'

'Me? No, of course not.'

'Promise? Not until we find him.'

'I promise. After we find him . . .'

'After we find him you can do what you like. Deal?'

'Deal.'

Two minutes later we were knocking on Shadia's door.

'It's Gandoury,' I said, pushing past her, not waiting to be invited in. 'I think I know where he's going.'

I was surprised to see that her room was as messy as ours, if not worse. There were clothes everywhere. I was momentarily thrown.

'Would you care to explain what's going on?' Shadia demanded, hands on her hips.

'Yes, please explain,' said Hisham, sinking down onto the big double bed. I made an effort to gather my thoughts.

'The whole thing with the phone call and the ICE or whatever they are called, it's all a ruse.'

'A ruse?' echoed Shadia.

'It's perfect,' I said. 'Look at us, now we're stuck in this hotel. We can't move until they take us to the airport to leave.'

'Why is that perfect?' Hisham was lying on his back with his eyes closed.

'Because it means we can't follow him.'

'Follow who?' asked Shadia.

'Suleiman Gandoury. He's not finished.'

I explained my theory. Shadia wasn't convinced.

'But he's a businessman. Surely he has lots of money. Why would he come all the way here to America to steal our money?'

'Because he's in some kind of trouble. He's not planning to go home. He's going to set himself up here.'

The two of them looked at me, waiting for an explanation. I held up my copy of *David Copperfield*.

'Charles Dickens?' Shadia frowned. 'How is that going to help us?'

I pulled out the sheet of paper I had tucked inside the book. 'I put it away after our first meeting but then forgot about it.' I unfolded it carefully.

'What is it?' asked Shadia.

'This is the proposal Gandoury gave us back home. It's a list of places, venues, arrangements that he wanted to set up for us to play.'

'I thought you turned him down?'

'We did,' I said. 'But supposing he went ahead and made deals with these places anyway?'

'So, you're saying that he's not just going to cheat us out of our money, he's also going to collect money from all these people in our name?' Shadia grabbed the paper from my hand and began to read down the list. 'Paradise Pavilions, West Egg Hall, The Buttercup Center?'

'I think he booked us to play in them all.'

'But how do you know he's going to go there?'

'He has to collect the money and I'm betting that he's going to tell the same story about needing the cash. That way the payments can't be traced.'

Both Shadia and Hisham sat quietly, taking it all in.

'And you want to go after him?' Shadia asked finally.

'We find him, get him to come back and explain himself, and make him repay the money, of course.'

'You're mad,' she said. 'I mean, can you hear what you are saying? You know nothing about America, about these places. How are you going to find them? And aren't you forgetting something? They have a car outside watching the hotel.'

I had to admit that hearing her spell it out like that did make me wonder for a moment if perhaps it was a crazy idea.

'We have to try. I mean, it's like you said, if we do nothing then this is how we will be remembered. There will always be a shadow hanging over our name.'

'Maybe we should just tell Ms DeHaviland and they can pick him up.'

I dismissed the idea. 'Why would they believe us? A list of scribblings in Arabic? They'd say we were just making excuses.'

Hisham nodded. 'We have to do this ourselves.'

'Okay,' Shadia said. 'But exactly how are you going to do this? I mean, you have no means of transport.'

'Maybe we have.' Hisham looked at me. 'Our cowboy friend.'

'That might work,' I said.

'Then we should get moving before he leaves. No time to waste. God, I could kill for a cigarette.'

I picked up my case. 'You can have one on the way.'

'Hold on a second!' Shadia yelled. 'Stop it, both of you. I can't understand any of this. What are you going to do and which cowboy?'

'We know someone,' I explained. 'Someone who knows the country and has transport.'

'What about the police car outside the door?'

'We're not going out of the front,' I grinned.

'Then how?'

I explained about the back door and about Waldo and his van. She wasn't convinced.

'You can't do this,' she said.

'Why not?' Hisham asked, a little incensed. 'We're perfectly capable of taking care of this ourselves.'

'No, I mean, you can't do it by yourselves, not without us.'

'Why not?' I protested.

'This is about all of us. We all have an interest in finding Gandoury. So we all have to go, or nobody goes.' She folded her arms in a way that told me we had little choice in the matter. Also, what she was saying made sense. It just seemed impractical. Hisham voiced my thoughts.

'Are you serious?' he said. 'Can you imagine trying to travel with the old bird?'

Shadia clearly didn't like her aunt being referred to that way. 'Don't even try to think of doing it without her. She's seen worse than either of you ever have. She'll manage fine.'

I set down my trumpet case. I couldn't understand why it was so difficult arguing with her. 'I'm sorry, it's just not going to work. It's the two of us or nothing.'

'The three of us then,' she said.

I looked at Hisham. He gave a quick nod. Even he could see there was no point in trying to argue with her.

'Okay, then you need to get out of here so that I can get dressed.'

'We'll meet you at the fire escape in ten minutes.'

'Make it fifteen.'

'I'm not so sure this is such a great idea,' Hisham grumbled when we were back in our room.

'She'll be fine, so long as she doesn't bring too many clothes with her.'

Fifteen minutes later it was dark outside. We left the room and walked along towards the fire escape door at the end of the corridor. I was glad to see that Shadia was there ready and waiting. Also, she seemed to have taken the point about travelling light. She had what looked like a vanity case and a large shopping bag with her clothes in it. When I pushed open the door, I let out a yelp. To my astonishment they were all there, crowded into the darkened stairwell.

'What the hell?'

'I couldn't help it,' Shadia explained. 'I had to tell my aunt, then she insisted on telling your uncle, and . . . well, they all wanted to come.'

Suddenly everything seemed a lot more complicated. Uncle Maher spoke up, his deep voice rumbling out of the gloom.

'No point in trying to talk us out of it, boy. Our good name is at stake.'

I stared at them all, with their coats on and their bags clutched underneath their arms. I could have been looking at a photograph of a lost tribe seeking shelter. In the green glow of the emergency lighting the staircase itself seemed to take on another aspect, like a shaft leading down into a world beneath the one that we knew. I turned to Shadia, then raised my voice so that all of them could hear.

'You do realise that the moment we step out of this hotel we'll be breaking the law?'

Everyone chimed in. Nothing was going to talk them out of it; they were in agreement. It was decided that Shadia and I would go ahead. If all went well, we could come back with Waldo and the van to pick everyone up. We went down the stairs and out of the rear exit that delivered us into an icy wind on a dark street.

'Is that all you're taking?' She nodded at the trumpet case I was carrying.

'The rest can be replaced.'

'Maybe for you, but I'm not taking any chances.'

Fifteen minutes later we were standing on the leafy, tree-lined street by the river.

Shadia squinted through the dark. 'What is that thing?'

'A 1976 Birchaven,' I said authoritatively.

'A what?'

I leaned up and knocked on the door. Waldo Tucker answered the door wearing a tee-shirt and a pair of bright red boxer shorts with Mickey Mouse on them. Shadia let out a gasp and turned her back.

'It's all right,' I told her. 'He's a friend.'

'Hey man.' He rubbed his eyes. 'What's happening?'

'Waldo, we need your help. It's an emergency.'

He stepped aside for us to enter. 'Are you guys eloping or something?'

'It's more serious than that.'

'What could be more serious than marriage?' Shadia asked. I ignored her. While Waldo put some trousers on and then made coffee, I explained the whole story and showed him the list. He nodded as he read his way down.

'Well, sure, I mean, some of these places I've heard of. Small town venues, you know.' He removed his reading glasses. 'What I don't get is why.'

'It's difficult to explain. We came here to your country because we were invited to play our music. To show the world that our country

179

is more than just poverty and corruption. We have to return home on those terms.'

'Sure, but this guy isn't even part of the group, right?'

'He's acting in our name,' Shadia broke in impulsively. 'He's making us look like asylum seekers when we are not. We're musicians.'

'She has a way of putting things,' said Waldo.

'Yes,' I agreed, feeling suddenly proud to know her. 'She does.'

'I think I understand,' he nodded solemnly.

'We don't have a lot of time, Waldo,' I said. For some reason, I had thought without really knowing him that he could be counted on, but now I had doubts. He had a distant look in his eyes and for a moment I wondered if perhaps I was wrong. Perhaps I had misjudged him. But then he grinned and threw out his arms.

'Well, hell, why not? What have I got to lose?'

What did any of us have to lose?

PART III

*   *   *

The Fugitives

'It's hard to get lost if you don't know where you're going.'

Jim Jarmusch

Chapter 24

Band on the Run

The storm washed us out of Washington like rats spooled from the deck of a sinking ship. It was no longer snowing. Instead, plump raindrops slapped heavily onto the windscreen. Everything had been turned upside down. One moment we were being feted and the next the city was casting us out. I read in a book that it was once common practice for besieged cities to make sacrifices by throwing one of their own over the wall to the attacking barbarians in the hope that this would buy their safety. In this case we were throwing ourselves over.

What was the purpose of all this, I wondered? We wanted to go down in history for our music, for bringing ourselves to the world. There was honour in that. We wanted to be respected as musicians and not remembered as opportunists who had come asking for favours.

We were driving into darkness, with no sense of where we were going or how we were going to get back. I felt responsible, as if we had betrayed not just the confidence of Ms DeHaviland, but of our entire country, of everyone who had been so proud of us and helped us to come here. We were in the hands of a stoned record producer of dubious reputation whom I had met less than twenty-four hours ago. Did I honestly believe that we could make things right?

I was stiff with dread, sitting up in front between a dozing Hisham and Waldo, who was staring straight ahead with the rapt expression of an incarcerated lunatic who suddenly, and against all expectations, found himself a free man. Had anyone spoken to me at that point I am quite sure I would have broken down and begged that we return to the hotel and turn ourselves in before it was too late. I was gripped with doubt, my fingers digging into the seat to stop myself from screaming.

'You should stop worrying.' I turned to look at Shadia, who was sitting behind me. 'You're feeling guilty.'

'How can you know that?'

'It's written all over you.'

'Well, I'm wondering what are we going to do when we find him.'

'*If* we find him,' she said. 'We'll have to deal with that when the time comes.' She nodded in the direction of Waldo. 'I'm more concerned about him.'

'He's our only choice. Without him we couldn't do this.'

'Well, if you ask me, he's a bit of a weirdo. He keeps *smiling* at me.'

'It's just an American thing, they do it all the time,' I reassured her.

When I glanced sideways at him, I saw that it was true he had a strange fixed grin on his face. What did I actually know about the man? How could I be sure we could trust him? For all I knew he might be taking us to a remote place to kill us.

It grew silent in the back. When I glanced over my shoulder, I saw that they were all asleep, slumped this way and that. Like fallen soldiers sprawled about the interior, occupying benches, lying on the fold-down table, reclining on the couch. Even on the floor, where John Wau was stretched out, his big head lolling back and forth with the motion of the vehicle. Uncle Maher and Wad Mazaj occupied the swivel chairs while Kadugli was flat on his back on the sofa behind the table, hands clasped together. He looked ridiculously at peace, like an ancient king resting in his tomb. Alkanary had been allocated the big bedroom at the back of the Birchaven and Shadia was sitting behind me. Everywhere you looked there were instrument cases, stacked up, leaning against one another, stuffed on top of cupboards. It was all that we had brought with us. The sound of gentle snores vibrated through the vehicle.

'You're sure about this, right?' Waldo asked softly.

'To be honest, Waldo, right now I'm not sure about anything.'

He chewed that over for a moment. 'I guess that makes as much sense as anything. You're running from the law, after all.'

'You're not helping, Waldo.'

'Yeah, sorry about that.'

I cleared my throat. 'It's very generous of you to do this for us, and not without risk.'

'Hey, don't sweat it. I always fancied myself as an outlaw.' He winked and pushed his hair back from his forehead. 'Maybe you should try to get some sleep.'

'Yes, perhaps you are right.'

I did try. I closed my eyes and managed in fits and starts. My head lolled against the window as I watched America roll by. The houses and intersections. The neon signs over supermarkets and strip malls. I was being introduced to a whole new lexicon of Americanese: Costco, Walgreens, Cracker Barrel, Chi-Chi's, Walmart, Popeyes, Dairy Queen. The names shot by, lit up in bright colours that made me feel as though I was travelling through a land of endless possibility.

I saw trees and buildings, rows of houses off in the distance. It was as if the whole country was in motion. All of it threaded together by the smooth black strip of tarmac held in place by white lines. We were totally unprepared for such a world. Where we came from the main road through the city was still known as Sharia al-Zalat, on account of the fact that it used to be the only asphalted road in town. Our roads came with added potholes and cracks to provide variety. Here, it felt as though we were zipping along a vast web. Around us, people moving north, south, east and west. Along the roadside there were places to eat, to sleep, to shop twenty-four hours a day. I was drowning, lost in absorbing what we were seeing.

'A penny for them. For your thoughts, I mean,' said Waldo.

'All we know about this country comes from films,' I said, watching the rain teem down the windscreen. 'We see your movies, television. We know all your heroes. Tarzan, Kojak, Columbo.'

Waldo grinned. 'You probably know them better than I do.'

'Yet you know nothing about us. We have no movies. We have no stories that mean anything to you.'

'It's a one-way street,' Waldo nodded. 'I get that.'

'That's why this is so important to us. We know your history and read your great writers. But this is our chance to show something of who we are.'

'Right.'

I wasn't sure he understood. I tried to go further. 'What I am trying to say, Waldo, is that by acquiring knowledge of you, of America, we inherited the sense that we are lacking in some fundamental way. Our history is lost in the dust while yours is written in neon lights. The Alamo, General Custer and Little Big Horn. You see? You have never even heard of the Mahdi.'

'The Mahdi?'

'He was like Crazy Horse, only different.'

The comparison didn't make much sense to him, or to me for that matter, but I was struggling to explain myself and it was all I could come up with at the moment.

'We have no faith in ourselves,' I said finally.

The truth is I had never really thought about these things, until now. Had I stayed at home, I realised, I might never have examined what I had taken for granted all my life.

'We had politics. We went left, we went right and when that failed, we turned to Islam. And now that we have exhausted that possibility, we have nothing, no way of moving forward. We must begin again.'

'You've been watching us all your lives.' Waldo chuckled to himself. 'I never thought of it like that.'

'Sure, except this is not a movie.'

'That's right, Toto, and this ain't Kansas.'

'Ah,' I nodded. 'The Wizard of Oz.'

'Have you ever heard of the *I Ching*?' Waldo asked after a time.

'*I Ching*?'

'*The Book of Changes*. Basically, it's the idea that the universe is ruled by change. It's all about the numbers. It's all written in the book.'

'You have a book in which everything is written in numbers?'

'Sure, kind of like your Quran, right?'

'The Quran is not written in numbers, Waldo. It's written in mystical words that nobody fully understands.'

'Right, well, it's kind of the same thing.'

'You can interpret what is written in the Quran one way, and someone else can see it in a totally different light. Some people believe we must understand it the way it was understood when it was written, fourteen centuries ago. Others believe we must try to understand it in the present: always new, always changing.'

'Well, there you go.' Waldo slapped the steering wheel. 'That's what I'm talking about.'

I wasn't quite sure we were talking about the same thing, but I appreciated the fact that he was trying to explain why he was helping us.

'Where I come from, Waldo, politics is a mess. Politicians are corrupt. They care only about making themselves rich. Nobody cares about the common people.'

'It's the same here. The big corporations fund the politicians so that once they get into congress they can change the laws to suit their friends. We're so dumb we can't see what they're doing. Our current president claims to be on the side of the working man, but he's basically only helping his rich friends.'

'Islam is not about change. It might have been once, but today it's

187

about transporting yourself back to the seventh century. You must live like the Prophet. You eat like the Prophet; you sleep like the Prophet. When you go to the bathroom, you go like the Prophet.'

'Sounds complicated. And what about music?'

'Oh no, no music. Take this *I Ching* of yours. If you worship a book, you would be stoned for idolatry.'

I stared out of the window. More signs proclaimed Welcome, Vacancies, Cheap Gas Next Exit. A huge red-and-green crucifix glowed bright against the night sky. It reminded me of the minarets back home. When you move out of the space you live in everything is pulled out from under you. You are an unknown quantity. Everything has to be explained.

'America was once a colony of Britain, right? That is also something we have in common,' I said. 'To free yourself from foreign rule, you must have something to believe in.'

'Well, I guess that makes sense.'

'In America, you made a new beginning. An empty slate on which to write. You made movies about yourselves. You invented your own history.'

'Sure, you could say that.'

'Our slate was not clean. After independence we could not decide if we should try to be little Englishmen, or big army generals. One day we had one and the next we had the other.'

Waldo looked over at me. 'You're saying you need something of yourself to believe in.'

'We never found it, that common cause, a belief in ourselves. Instead we traded one form of authority for another. Religion tells you this is bad, that is good. We lacked the confidence to trust in who we were.'

'Well, you certainly seem to know a lot about it.'

'I can talk, but I can't fix it.' I glanced over my shoulder to make sure the others were still sleeping. 'I'm just trying to explain why this is important to us. Does what we are doing make any sense to you?'

'Well, sure it does, I guess.'

'It's not about the money, you understand. Our integrity is at stake.'

'Right, I get that.' He glanced across. 'What you were just saying about taking control.'

'We need to tell our own story, on this matter as in everything.'

'Yeah,' he nodded. 'I see that.'

After that we were both silent for a time. Waldo drove with one hand on the wheel. The road ahead was empty. The speed of the vehicle felt comforting. Soon we would be far from Washington, and the Kennedy Center, far from everything. Somehow I found that thought pleasing.

Chapter 25

Pearly Gables

I must have slept some more. When I opened my eyes again the van had come to a halt. Dawn was breaking and we appeared to be in a small town, on a main street. There were fields on either side of us. Through the windscreen I could see Waldo talking to an old man in a chequered jacket who leaned to one side as if held in place by the wind. He had a drooping moustache and bulging eyes and he wore a cowboy hat that he grasped with one hand. With the other he was pointing along the road.

Waldo hopped back in behind the wheel. The van tilted as we swung around in the road eliciting a chorus of moans and groans from the back. We passed a school and then a church followed by an open field with strange-looking posts sticking up into the sky. On the far side of this was a large stone building. We turned and drove around the side. A huge American flag flew from a pole on the front lawn. Alongside this stood a painted wooden sign with gold lettering on a white background that proclaimed it as the 'Pearly Gables Retirement Home'. Over the front door hung a tall wooden cross. Little stone figures with wings and bows were set among flowerbeds either side of the entrance.

'Are we there already?' Hisham sat up and yawned. 'What is this place?'

'There must be some mistake. Waldo, are you sure about this?'

'As sure as I can tell.' Waldo checked the list and then peered through the window. 'Does look a little strange for a concert venue, I have to say.'

As I followed Waldo up the front path, I wondered how Gandoury could possibly have found such a place. When we rang the bell, a robust black woman dressed in a crisp white nurse's uniform appeared. She squinted past us at the bus parked at the end of the drive.

'Yes?' she asked, looking us up and down.

'Good afternoon, madam,' I said. 'We are the Kamanga Kings.'

She squinted at me. 'Come again?'

I repeated what I had just said. Her face remained blank.

'I have no understanding of what that means.' She turned to Waldo. 'What language is he speaking?'

'That would be English, ma'am.'

'Uh-uh, not where I come from.' She shook her head. Her hair was pinned tightly back under her cap. Everything about her seemed to be firmly fixed in place.

I was beginning to take this personally. I pulled myself up to my full height, threw my shoulders back and spoke in the best manner of Mr Micawber.

'My dear lady, I would have you know that by profession I am a teacher of the English language.' I spoke slowly and deliberately so as to avoid misunderstandings, since she was clearly either mentally deficient or hard of hearing. She clicked her tongue and rolled her head again.

'Ah-ah, still sounds like double Dutch to me.'

'He's a teacher,' Waldo said, trying to be helpful. 'In his country, he teaches English.'

'Well, it don't stand much chance of catching on, if you ask me.' She paused. 'An English teacher, you say? I have a nephew who was a teacher before they sent him up to Angola. Couldn't understand a damn word he said neither.'

'Angola.' I nodded, smiling, glad we were communicating finally. 'In Africa?'

'Africa?' she echoed, frowning again.

'It's a prison,' Waldo explained, before turning back to the woman. 'Ma'am, perhaps I should explain. We are looking for a friend of ours who may need our assistance.'

'You lost somebody?' The suspicious tone crept back into her voice as her eyes found me again. 'You don't mean one of those refugees trying to sneak into this country?'

'Not at all.' I rejected the description instinctively even though I realised, as I spoke, that we all qualified as such. What were we now if not refugees?

'I may be hard of hearing but I ain't stupid.' She folded her arms. 'What I want to know is what any of this has to do with me?'

Waldo stepped in again. 'We believe that you may have been contacted recently, with regard to a musical concert performance . . . ?'

'Music?' She reared back as if stung. 'Lordy, are these people musicians?'

'We are indeed, madam,' I said proudly.

'Well, I will have nothing to do with musicians.' She peered at me. 'Nothing on God's green earth lower than a musician. Never trust them.'

Waldo and I looked at one another, both of us taken aback. 'Well, we're trying to ascertain whether you have been subject to a fraudulent scheme instigated by someone claiming to represent this group of talented musicians.'

'A what? Oh dear, I shall have to call the director.'

'That might be advisable,' agreed Waldo with a glance at me.

'But before I do that, I'm calling the sheriff.'

'The sheriff?' echoed Waldo. 'Now hold on. I don't see why that should be necessary.'

She put her hands on her hips and squared up to him. 'Did you or did you not use the word fraudulent this very minute?'

'Well, I . . .' Waldo faltered. I tried to intervene but the woman reared backwards.

'Don't you come near me! I'm calling the sheriff right now!'

With that she began to close the door. Without thinking I leapt forward and managed to plant my foot in place to block it. She heaved the door back and slammed it again so hard I howled with pain. As I bent to soothe my injured foot, she repeated the action. This time the door hit me in the head. I staggered backwards into Waldo's arms.

At that moment, out of nowhere, a small, plump figure appeared underneath her elbow.

'Excuse me, Nurse Maxwell, did I hear you say music?'

The newcomer wore a pair of rumpled, striped pyjamas. He had a scruffy, dishevelled appearance. The few tufts of hair left on his head stuck out at all angles and his eyes were wide with wonder.

The woman glared down at the little man. 'Mr Siegel, you're blocking the door! And where are your slippers?'

The man continued to beam; a smile stretched from ear to ear across his moon face. 'Now, Nurse Maxwell, you did say music, didn't you? I distinctly heard you.'

'And what if I did? What business is it of yours?'

The funny little man gave a little whoop and yelled, 'They're here! The band is here!'

He then performed a kind of jig, laughing, skipping from one bare foot to the other as if the floorboards had suddenly caught fire. Waldo and I looked at one another. My first thought was to flee this madhouse, but I found myself transfixed.

'Mr Siegel, please!' Nurse Maxwell stamped her foot. The door, abandoned now, yawned open to reveal a procession of what appeared to be old and very infirm persons approaching us slowly. They were emerging from doorways on both sides of a wide corridor. Some seemed barely capable of moving, while others were possessed of a great deal of energy. Some walked of their own accord, others propped

193

themselves up with the aid of walking sticks and metal frames, yet others were in wheelchairs. They were all converging on us.

'Oh, my,' Nurse Maxwell sighed in dismay. 'Now look what you've started.'

With that she disappeared down a hallway to the left. I felt someone take hold of my hand and looked down to see the little man, Mr Siegel, smiling up at me.

'It's so wonderful you made it,' he said, enthusiastically pumping my hand up and down. 'This is dandy, just dandy. Everyone's been expecting you.'

I found myself being dragged into the house, down the hall, past the row of gathered onlookers. They were all pretty ancient, but they were nodding and smiling, one or two even clapped their hands.

'You did it, Ari.'

'I never believed you, but you proved us all wrong.'

'Oh, ye of little faith, eh, Cedric?' Mr Siegel lifted his chin.

'I stand corrected.' The tall, slim man wearing a dressing gown over his pyjamas gave a bow and snapped a folded ten-dollar bill from his pocket which he handed over. Mr Siegel made a show of straightening it out and running it under his nose in delight.

'They didn't believe I could do it, you see?' He winked at me, clinging to my arm as he led me on. 'But I told them. I promised them I would.'

'What exactly did you promise them?'

At the end of the corridor we came to a large hall. Emerging from the gloomy corridor we entered a large day room flooded with sunlight.

'This is it.' Mr Siegel threw his arms wide. 'Whadaya think?'

'What do I think?'

'Tonight is our annual ball, and you are going to play for us.'

'Annual ball?'

'Yeah, you know, guys and dolls?' Mr Siegel winked at me. 'It's romantic. The dames really dig it. I'm telling you, lots of promises are going to be delivered tonight.'

194

It was hard to imagine anywhere more unsuited to the idea of a celebration of any kind. The room was warm, airless and sedate. The furniture looked as though it belonged to another age. A soap opera played itself out on a television set in one corner. Most of those in the room were slumped with newspapers or books on their laps, dozing the day away. Others sat with blankets over their knees staring through the windows across the football field that stretched into the distance. There was something stately about the place. At one table four women played dominoes. None of them looked capable of even standing on their own two feet for very long, let alone attending a ball. I turned to Mr Siegel.

'I fear there has been some mistake.'

'Mistake? Where?' he echoed, eyes wide, shooting left and right. 'How? This is the room and you're the band. We even have a piano.' It was true. Buried under a heap of tattered magazines, blankets, an orange plastic trumpet and an empty jug. Mr Siegel tapped on the upright instrument pushed up against the wall as he, using a chair for leverage, hopped up to perch himself on the top of it and folded his arms. 'How could there possibly be a mistake?'

Waldo looked apologetically at Siegel. 'Sir, this is kind of difficult to explain, but we're actually here due to a crisis of management. We came here to try and locate one of our members who has gone missing.'

The little man's face darkened. 'Methinketh I smells a rat.'

'Thinketh?' I asked, confused again.

Waldo gave it another try. 'I am sure you can appreciate, sir, these folks came all the way from Africa.'

'Oh, sure I can, just as I'm sure you can appreciate that I paid a great deal of good American money for them.'

'How exactly did you pay this money, Mr Siegel?' I asked. 'I mean, did you speak to Mr Suleiman Gandoury?'

'I didn't speak to Sulayman or Sherazade. My lawyer did the deal.'

'Your lawyer?' I said.

'Am I not speaking English here, or what?' Mr Siegel closed his eyes and stretched himself to his full height. 'You may not be aware who you are speaking to. Given the circumstances and all, that's quite understandable, but you happen to be addressing Mr Ariel Siegel III, of Berger, Rothstein and Siegel?' He stared at our blank faces. 'I'm not seeing any lightbulbs. The point, gentlemen, is that for the purposes of this evening's entertainment, I contracted the services of an orchestra through the good agencies of my personal lawyer, Henry Siegel Junior, who also happens to be my nephew.'

'You contracted us through your nephew?' I asked.

'I believe that's what I just said.'

'Is there any way we can talk to this nephew of yours?' I enquired.

'Why certainly.' Siegel smiled sweetly. 'As soon as you default on our agreement, you're gonna meet him in court.'

He swung round as the door behind him was wrenched open and a man in a white coat rushed in. Tall, with a rigid back and thinning hair combed back over a narrow, prominent forehead, he was followed closely by Nurse Maxwell.

'Uh oh,' muttered Siegel.

'Would someone mind explaining the meaning of this outrage?'

'Here we go, Mr Law and Order has arrived. Everyone hold onto their wallets.' Siegel was rolling his eyes at us. The new arrival appeared to hold some position of authority. He turned his attention on the little man.

'Mr Siegel, can I assume that you are at the centre of this turmoil?'

'Assume what you want, Turkey, you're not going to be running this place for much longer anyway.'

The doctor's face grew rigid. 'Be that as it may, until that joyful day arrives, I believe that as director of this fine establishment I would be failing in my responsibilities if I did not step in when the harmony of Pearly Gables was being disrupted by pandemonium.'

'You use a lot of big words, Turkey.'

'That's Doctor Terkel, as you well know, Mr Siegel.'

'Gobble gobble. Once a turkey always a turkey, is what I say. Who's paying your wages, that's what I want to know.'

Doctor Terkel turned to us. 'I'm afraid I shall have to ask you to leave. This is most unbecoming of an institution dedicated to calm and repose. Nurse Maxwell, would you mind showing these gentlemen to the door?'

'There's really no need for that,' said Waldo. 'My friend and I were just leaving.'

'Hold it right there!' said Siegel, hopping down from the piano and running over to slam the door shut. He stood pressed against it, arms outstretched. 'Nobody goes nowhere. Not until I see my money or hear some music.'

'Mr Siegel, I strongly protest this manner of behaviour,' said Doctor Terkel.

'I would also like to protest,' I said, not sure what I had to protest about, apart from the way this whole affair had turned a corner into insanity.

'It's a free country. You can all protest all you want, but without my money, and the money of my good friends here,' Mr Siegel gestured at the onlookers, for by now he had the attention of the whole room. More were peering through the glass doors from the hallway outside.

'I can assure you,' Terkel began, but Siegel cut him off.

'Let me finish, Turkey.' There were giggles from his audience. 'We pay your salary and we pay for the upkeep of this place. Without us you would be back to peddling aspirin at two dollars a pop. Now, we have paid for this orchestra and they are going to play for us, and that is all there is to it.'

'When the board of directors hears about this . . .'

Mr Siegel beamed and took a little bow. 'They will thank me for taking the initiative and shining a ray of sunshine into the lives of a bunch of people who, let's face it, don't have a lot of sunshine to look forward to.'

'About your money, Mr Siegel,' I tried to explain. 'We are actually trying to locate the man responsible for this mess.'

'Forget about it, kid. I don't care about the money.' Siegel threw his arms out wide. 'The money means nothing to me. I have more than I can possibly spend in the time left to me. What I care about,' he said, stepping closer and poking me in the chest with a stubby forefinger, 'is whether or not you can play "Moonlight in Vermont".' He looked up at me. His big round eyes swam with desolation. 'Can you?'

'"Moonlight in Vermont"?' I repeated helplessly.

'That's all I'm asking. Just one song and I can forget the rest.'

Doctor Terkel was still shaking his head. 'I'm afraid this has gone far enough. I'm calling the police.'

Siegel cut him off sharply with an upraised hand. 'Let him answer.' He turned back to me. 'Will you do it? Will you play for us?'

All eyes were upon me. I suddenly felt sorry for this man. I realised that what he had been sold meant more to him than just a business transaction. I couldn't say no.

'I think that could be arranged, but I shall have to consult with the band,' I said finally.

'I can't ask fairer than that.' Siegel stepped aside and patted my shoulder enthusiastically. 'Go consult.'

As he walked us to the front door, the director thrust his hands into his white coat. 'I'm afraid you'll have to excuse Mr Siegel. He's been under a lot of stress.'

'Is he ill or something?' Waldo asked.

Doctor Terkel turned to face us. 'Pearly Gables is not simply a retirement home. It's a hospice. Our guests are terminal patients who have chosen to spend what remains of their life here with us.'

'They're dying!?' Hisham echoed, when we were all back in the bus.

'Ya Allah,' sighed Alkanary. 'This is where you bring me? I swear you won't be satisfied until the last breath leaves my body.' She slumped back in her chair.

'How did we become involved in this?' Wad Mazaj went on in his reedy, high-pitched voice. 'I thought we were supposed to be finding Gandoury?'

'Yeah,' I said. 'That's the part I don't understand.' I explained all about Siegel and his lawyer.

'It's so sad,' Shadia said. 'They're so excited. We can't just drive off.'

'Look, we're here, okay?' I said. 'It's not their fault. Siegel is trying to do something good for everyone in there.'

There were a few groans and mutterings. Then someone cleared his voice and everyone turned towards John Wau's deep baritone. 'What's wrong with making a few people happy?'

'He's right,' Kadugli agreed. 'We're here, we can't just turn our backs.'

'They were practically dancing on their walking sticks,' I said.

Hisham giggled.

'Growing old is no joke,' growled Alkanary.

'Well then, that's settled,' said Shadia. 'We have to do it.'

I liked the way she made things seem simpler rather than more complicated, unlike the rest of them.

'While we're playing, Gandoury is getting further away,' Hisham pointed out.

'True,' I agreed. 'But I think Siegel knows something about this whole deal. Perhaps he could arrange for us to speak to his lawyer, the one who made the deal.'

'That's all very well,' Shadia interjected. 'But right now, we need to make a decision. Do we play for them, or do we drive on?'

Uncle Maher stood up abruptly, bumping his head on the low ceiling. 'That scoundrel took money from those people in our name.'

'Sure, but *we* didn't take their money,' protested Hisham.

'It doesn't matter,' Uncle Maher went on. 'It was taken in our name.' He looked around at us. 'Even if we never catch him and never see our money again, this is how people will remember the Kamanga

Kings, as a bunch of charlatans, defrauding dying people out of their money.'

When he put it like that there didn't seem to be much choice. There was more mumbling, along with a few grudging nods, but the weight had tilted in favour of a performance. Even Hisham could see he was outvoted. The talk shifted to practical details.

'What kind of music are they expecting?' Kadugli asked.

'Well, that's the problem,' I said, explaining about 'Moonlight in Vermont'.

'We don't know those songs,' John Wau pointed out.

'Old jazz standards.' I looked at the blank faces. 'How difficult can it be?'

'Well, we used to know a few.' Uncle Maher rubbed his chin, glancing at Alkanary. 'We played some in the old days, remember? For embassy parties, that kind of thing.'

'Of course I remember,' Alkanary said quietly. 'My mind is not entirely gone yet.' She began to hum a few bars.

'"Night and Day",' said Shadia. We all turned to look at her. 'I used to accompany her on my keyboards.'

'What about sheet music?' asked John Wau.

'Oh, we can download what we need,' she said. 'Anyway, I have something better.' And with that she rushed off to the back of the bus to return a moment later with a USB stick.

'I used to have a load of cassette tapes. I transferred them. I take them everywhere I go. I've listened to these since I was a child. Ella Fitzgerald and Louis Armstrong, Cole Porter. It's all on here.'

'Amazing,' said Alkanary, reaching out to take the memory stick and turning it over in her hand. 'Where does the sound come out?'

Shadia explained that it had to be connected to a computer, or a device of some kind. 'Can we play this?' she asked Waldo.

'Certainly. I may have a fondness for the old ways, but I also have a fascination for the new.'

Shadia climbed over into the front seat and plugged it straight into the Birchaven's stereo console. She flipped through the menu and a moment later the sound of Sarah Vaughan filtered through speakers spread around the interior.

'Pretty good, huh?' grinned Waldo.

We sat in silence for a moment, then John Wau got out his guitar and started strumming along. Hisham began tapping the tabletop and then everyone was slowly reaching for their instruments. It was a little cramped but we quickly managed to start working on the tune in our own distinctive way. We played it again, then we moved on, spooling through the numbers until we came to a song that brought a murmur of recognition. 'In a Sentimental Mood'; 'It Don't Mean a Thing'; 'My Funny Valentine'. It turned out we actually knew the tunes; we simply didn't know what they were called. I stepped down from the bus to where Waldo was standing under a tree smoking a joint.

'How's it looking in there?'

'I think we might just get away with it.'

'So are we on, or what?'

We both turned to find Mr Siegel standing on the lawn, barefoot and still in his pyjamas, despite the cold. I smiled at him.

'Mr Siegel, it looks like you will be having your concert after all.'

'Oh, happy days!' he smiled. Nurse Maxwell appeared in the doorway behind him waving something in the air.

'Mr Siegel! Your slippers.'

'Uh oh, looks like they found me.' And with that he took off around the side of the building with Nurse Maxwell in pursuit.

'Who is that?' asked Shadia.

'He's the one who invited us here.'

'Oh,' she said slowly, as if the full impact of our undertaking had just dawned on her.

'What I'd like to know,' said Hisham as he came up, 'is how did Gandoury ever find this place? Maybe we should be talking to this lawyer in New York.'

201

'All in good time,' I said.

Hisham shook his head. 'Since when did you become the captain of this ship?' He wandered off without waiting for an answer.

'It's a wonderful thing you're doing,' Nurse Maxwell confided later, as we stood and watched the day room being converted into a concert hall. The residents were shuffling about, chattering excitedly amongst themselves. She seemed to have softened her tone.

'I'm surprised that they should be eager to have a ball and not wish to rest,' I said.

'You're still young,' she sighed. 'Life doesn't just stop when you get old. You'd be surprised about the things that go on in this place.'

I believed her. Seeing Mr Siegel, I would believe anything.

'It's a sad thing,' Nurse Maxwell went on, 'but nobody has any further use for these folk. Their families are happy to inherit their money but they don't want anything to do with them. Their friends have passed away. All they can do is wait.' She clucked her tongue in lament. 'Some of them can be a trial, Lord knows, but it's a sad reflection on the state of human compassion today.'

A group of orderlies was clearing the furniture out of the day room and setting up a stage made from wooden boxes fitted together.

'They used to have regular dances, back in the old days when I was just a little girl. My mother worked in the kitchen.' Her eyes had filled with a strange kind of light and she blew her nose loudly on a tiny handkerchief that she took from tucked inside her sleeve. Then she spun on her heels and marched from the room without another word.

As we made our way up towards the building that evening the sun was setting over the field behind the house leaving the sky a blaze of red. I found myself wondering what we were doing. Almost a day had gone by and we were no closer to finding Gandoury. We seemed to have found another purpose than the one we set out for.

Chapter 26

Old Songs/New Kings

We had spent the next few hours practising in the back of the Birchaven, feeling our way through the songs. We didn't rely too much on the sheet music, instead playing by ear. And here the skill and collective memory of the group kicked in. We found that we could get through a handful of songs with a little effort. Shadia's recordings were a great help, and we put together a repertoire that we guessed would be familiar to our audience and yet distinctive enough to be our own. There wasn't much we could do after that than hope it didn't cause too much offence.

The day room had been transformed almost beyond recognition. We were all amazed to see the stage, the covered tables, the coloured bunting that hung from the ceiling. It was as if they had been preparing for this moment for years. Paper chains and streamers hung in long arcs and the lights had been turned down low. They had even managed to get rid of the old sour smell of boiled socks that had permeated the place before, bringing with it a hint of imminent death.

The audience, too, had undergone a transformation in a few short hours. Instead of the pyjamas and dressing gowns we had seen them shuffling around in earlier, the men and women who began to file in slowly as we set up our instruments appeared to have stepped from another age. The ladies wore long dresses and the men dinner suits and ties. There were pearl necklaces and fancy earrings. Some of these outfits looked rather threadbare and ill-fitting, but despite this the formal clothes brought a sense of occasion and dignity to proceedings.

Mr Siegel bounced into the room, an impious figure clad in a perfectly fitted tailcoat and bow tie. An impresario, a man in his element. He was no longer barefoot, either, wearing not only socks but some very shiny shoes too.

I'd like to say that the Kamanga Kings' impromptu road tour of the United States of America got off to a resounding start, but that would require me to be somewhat imaginative with the truth. Most of us were playing those songs for the first time in our lives. The fact that a good deal of our audience was either partially or completely deaf no doubt helped our cause.

'Just follow my lead,' said Kadugli as he stepped up beside me. 'And watch her.'

He didn't need to tell me that. I had my eyes on Shadia from the moment she took centre stage. She was wearing a long dark blue dress that shimmered and sparkled, clinging to her form. This was to be her night. The others took up their positions around the stage, then, when he was ready, Uncle Maher lifted the violin and paused. We all waited. Then he drew his bow across the strings and Shadia led us off into 'Stars Fell on Alabama'. She sang the song perfectly. A testament to the years she had spent singing along to those old cassette tapes she had treasured since she was a child. She sang confidently and we trailed along in her wake, following cautiously, trying not to overstep our luck. She was radiant. Without the glasses and with her hair swept up and her wearing that dress I was reminded of the evening of our performance in Washington. I gazed at her with new eyes.

What we lacked in experience we made up in energy. There were false starts and missteps. At times we seemed to be playing against one another rather than together. It was a learning process, and a reminder of what seemed like a lifetime ago, when we were back on that abandoned steamer with the birds flying over our heads. But there was a joy to it and it was as clear to our audience as it was to ourselves that whatever our differences, we loved playing together.

Shadia sat down at the piano and took us through a lilting version of 'Blue Moon', then we were off again. There were difficult moments when we wandered off the path, and struggled to stay with the tune, but Kadugli would always wrestle us back in line, calling out commands left and right. He would nudge me and we'd start blowing harmonies to restore order. But if the evening belonged to anyone it was Shadia. Her voice was a golden thread guiding us through the darkness. As we fought our way through, she was the one who gave us our sense of direction.

To our surprise the audience loved it. They clapped their hands and cried out for more. They moved around the dance floor with cautious grace, some with assistance, so that it appeared almost as if time itself was slowly winding down around them.

It was over all too soon. Mr Siegel was dancing with Nurse Maxwell, who was twice as big as him any way you cared to measure. He leaped onto the stage and kissed Shadia on both cheeks before shaking hands with us one by one. Even Mr Terkel, wearing a tweed jacket with a purple scarf around his neck, stepped up onto the stage to thank us for our wonderful performance.

'That was amazing. You were amazing,' I said as I helped Shadia down off the stage. She clutched my hand. Without her glasses she could have walked off a cliff without noticing. A flower was pinned into her hair.

'I've dreamed of this moment all my life,' she grinned, still floating after her performance. 'I wanted to be Billie Holliday. As a child I used to sing those songs to myself over and over.' She gave a dismissive wave of her hand. 'Just one of those silly girl things. A way of escape.'

Someone was tugging at my jacket and I turned to see Mr Siegel beaming up at me.

'You're a genius, kid. I knew it the first time I set eyes on you.' He wagged a finger in my face. 'I said to myself, this kid gets it.'

'Well, I'm glad you liked it, Mr Siegel.'

Grabbing my arm in a remarkably fierce grip he steered me through the crowd towards the big double doors at the far end of the room and out into the terrace. The grassy fields stretched off into the night. The air was cold and crisp and the stars were as sharp as glass shards. Siegel reached into his jacket for a little silver flask. He unscrewed the top before holding it out. I declined the offer and watched as he lifted it to his lips and took a long swallow. Then he wiped his mouth with the back of his hand and made a noise like a horse as he slipped the flask back away.

'I can't tell you how much this means to me, kid. Did you see how lit up they all were? Amazing. You've made a lot of people very happy tonight.' He glanced back at the building. Inside, people were winding down, saying their goodnights. It was easy to see what he meant.

'In the end, it's the small things. The little moments when you feel alive. Those are the ones that stick with you. The night I met my wife. The day our first child was born.' He chuckled to himself. 'You're young, kid, but you'll understand what I mean one day. Don't get me wrong, I'm not complaining. I had my fair share of fun, you know? And now, well, it's all coming to an end. The truth is there isn't that much left for me to live for.'

'What about your wife?'

'Oh, she passed a few years back.' In the glow of light coming from within I could see his eyes were glistening. 'That knocked me out, I have to admit. To tell the truth, I didn't expect to get this far without her.' Siegel fell silent for a time. Then he gave a loud sniff before turning to me again. 'Look, kid, you didn't have to do this, I understand you were stiffed by your manager. Consider it a bonus.' He pressed a fat envelope into my hands. 'It's not much, but it's all I have left.'

'Thank you,' I said as I took the envelope. 'You mentioned that it was your nephew who had made the arrangements?'

'Sure, well, if you make it to New York, look him up.' He scribbled a number on the envelope. 'I'm sure he can help you. Just tell him I sent you. He'll take care of you. It'll be fine.'

He patted me on the arm and winked one last time. 'Goodnight, kid. I can't express my gratitude. Thank you for making an old man very happy.'

I watched him step inside and make his way through the crowd, pausing here and there to exchange a word with the last stragglers.

'He's right, you know,' said a voice out of the darkness. I turned to find Nurse Maxwell. She was off to one side, out of the light, smoking a cigarette by herself.

'How is that?'

'What you did this evening. You've no idea how happy you made them.'

'Well, it was really not that much.'

'You could have walked away, but you didn't.' She was staring at me intently. 'What you have is a gift. Most people would give an arm and a leg to have that even only for a minute.'

'Thank you.'

'Good luck, son,' she said. 'When life begins to fade, it's the bright moments that stand out.'

Gift it may have been, but you wouldn't think it to witness the scene I discovered when I got back to the Birchaven. I opened the door to find chaos.

'What's going on?'

'What are we doing here?' Wad Mazaj was pacing up and down. 'I mean, tell me, where are we and why are we playing this music for these old people?'

'They're not old,' Alkanary interjected.

'It's my fault,' said Uncle Maher, lowering his head. 'I agreed to this harebrained idea. I take full responsibility.'

'Ammu, please,' I said. 'We took a vote and it was decided that we should try and bring Gandoury back ourselves. And we are going to do that.'

'Maybe so,' grumbled Wad Mazaj, 'but we didn't agree to go around the country giving free concerts while we did it.'

'Who said anything about free?' I asked, tossing the envelope onto the table.

'They gave you this?' Uncle Maher looked inside and gasped. 'There's several thousand dollars here. I thought they had already paid?'

'It's a bonus. Mr Siegel wants you to know that he greatly appreciated our performance, although I personally think we could have been a little tighter.' I looked around the faces. 'I think we broke new ground.'

'Well, it was interesting,' mused Kadugli. 'We did manage to give those old classics something of our own flavour.'

'What do you mean, broke new ground?' Shadia asked.

'Just that.' I shrugged. 'We did something we'd never tried before and we found the flow between us.'

'Yes,' said Uncle Maher. 'That was interesting.'

Hisham handed back the envelope. 'There's over five thousand dollars in there. How much do you think Gandoury took?'

'No idea, but I have the lawyer's details, so we can ask him when we get to New York.'

'New York!' Shadia gave a whoop and punched the air. I couldn't help smiling. Not everyone was happy, of course. Wad Mazaj was sulking.

'I don't want to be in this van any more. I'm *hungry*.'

Waldo echoed this sentiment from the driving seat. 'Am I the only one here who's starving? What say we get something to eat?'

That brought a rallying cry and so we drove on until we came to a place on the outskirts of town where a number of brightly lit restaurants were set in a square around which there was a parking area. Vietnamese, Chinese, Korean, Mexican. We wandered from one

208

place to the next, peering through windows and scrutinising menus. Nobody could agree on what to eat. One place was noisy and full of screaming kids. Another served food we had never heard of.

'I heard they eat dog?' Wad Mazaj sniffed.

'Where did you hear that?' I asked. 'Here you are in a foreign country and the first thing you do is complain about people who are just like you, trying to get by.'

'Relax, will you?' said Hisham. I shook him off. I was growing more and more impatient with the lot of them. Finally, I broke out the envelope with the money and handed some out to everyone. We agreed to meet back at the Birchaven in an hour. We needed a break from each other.

I wandered around alone, wondering where Gandoury was and what he was up to. I had lost my appetite. I found a bench where I could sit and watch the cars rolling by. I saw families parking and heading excitedly towards the lighted windows. Their lives seemed so completely lacking in worry. They had everything they could possibly want right in front of them, all for the taking.

'It's not as wonderful as it looks.'

I looked up to see Kadugli.

'The life here. They have their own problems.' He lowered himself down alongside me, then rubbed both hands over his face. He looked older, more tired.

'What was it like then, in the old days?' I asked. 'It must have been different from this, touring with the greats.'

'Sure, a lot of big names. Miles, Sting, Dr John, Wynton Marsalis.' He breathed a long sigh. 'I was a backing musician. I wasn't playing my own music. There's a difference.'

'So why did you come home?'

'Why?' Kadugli took a deep breath and exhaled slowly. 'It was good while it lasted. Good money and a party every night. But you become separated from who you are and what you want to do. I lost my way, musically, and in other things.'

'That's why you came home?'

'In America you can be anything you like. The flip side of that is that you can wind up not knowing who you are.'

'You think that's going to happen to us?'

'Not while we have you to keep us in line.' Kadugli smiled. 'You did well today.'

'You think so?'

'We could have driven on. We didn't, and thanks to you we made a lot of people happy.'

'Well, it wasn't the most popular move.'

'No, but it was the right one. Your father would have been proud.' He got to his feet and stretched. 'The others will follow you. You just need to learn to trust yourself.'

I watched him walk away, dissolving in the shadows under the trees. There was something about him, I realised, that I had never really understood.

Chapter 27

Vanessa's Story

It was a freezing cold night. It was lucky in a way that there were so many of us inside that tin box Waldo called home. I woke the next morning stiff and in pain from sitting upright. In the back the mood was subdued. People sniffed and coughed. The men went outside to relieve themselves under the trees. By some unspoken agreement it was understood that the bathroom inside the Birchaven was reserved for the women. The rest of us would make do with stops along the way. I stood there yawning, a blanket around my shoulders, happy that the night was over.

'You sleep all right, buddy?' Waldo wandered over. 'Not too cold?'

He had slept in a room at the motel across the way. It was too risky for the rest of us to do the same. They would ask for identification and with the ICE no doubt looking for us by now, it made no sense to take chances.

'Fine, thank you. How about yourself?'

'Slept like a log, thank you very much. Need to let some fresh air into this place, though.'

After we had opened all the windows Waldo took the wheel and started the engine. There were moans and groans as everyone climbed aboard and then the big vehicle was swinging back onto the road. A few miles on we stopped for breakfast and sat shivering in the warmth of frying grease and percolating steam. They had green tinsel every-where and country and western music playing, steel guitars and violins humming softly over our heads. On a television screen at the far end of the room, a man with an orange face and crazy hair was shouting at an audience.

'Is that the president?' I asked Shadia.

'I think so.'

The caption along the bottom of the screen read Anti-Immigration Rally and the picture cut to images of people standing in the street holding up placards which read America First. I thought of Ms DeHaviland and of agents Baumgarten and Blanco. It felt almost as if the entire country was somehow hunting for us. The waitress leaned over as I was about to order.

'Cheer up, honey, it might not happen!'

'What might not happen?'

'Oh, you're a card!' she chuckled into her hand. I pointed to one of the pictures on the plastic menu and was rewarded with a huge plate covered in French fries and eggs and thick slabs of what I suspected was ham. I was too hungry to care.

'Are you really going to eat all that?' Shadia looked slightly appalled.

'Maybe it was a little ambitious,' I conceded. I looked up, but she was no longer listening. Instead, Shadia leaned towards me and whispered;

'It's you.'

'Me?' I felt my heart start to pound and then I realised that she wasn't actually looking at me, but at a spot somewhere above my head where a rather fleshy-looking face that looked vaguely familiar filled the television screen. 'Is that me?'

'Quiet everyone!' Shadia ordered. She didn't need to say it. They had already fallen silent. I twisted round. The screen was high up on the wall in the far corner. To my surprise I recognised the voice of the person speaking.

'That's Vanessa,' I said, aware that everyone was now staring at me.

212

'Who is Vanessa?' frowned Shadia.

'I can explain,' I sputtered.

The screen reverted to a newswoman. She was very excited about something, and that something appeared to be us. The image behind her changed as Vanessa shrank into a little box in the corner of the screen.

'Vanessa, just talk me through this. You say that this group are under persecution at home. Can you give us some idea of what exactly they are running from?'

The camera closed on the window. Vanessa looked somewhat more glamorous than the person I recalled meeting in the Kennedy Center.

'Who is she again?' Shadia asked. Something about the tone of her voice told me I needed to explain exactly what had happened. But as I started to speak, she cut me off. Vanessa was speaking again.

'Human rights organisations have documented the persecution of musicians in many parts of the Middle East, including Sudan.'

'Right,' said the studio host. 'Just to give us a picture, we're talking about zealots who believe that music goes against the teachings of Islam, right?'

'Right,' Vanessa confirmed. 'These guys literally take their life into their hands every time they pick up an instrument.'

'What is she talking about?' cried Wad Mazaj, clapping a hand to his forehead. He didn't understand a word.

'She's talking about us,' said Hisham.

The anchorwoman went on:

'Sudan is a highly complex country. We've all heard about Darfur, of course. The 2011 referendum divided the country into two parts. Is that significant?'

'I believe so. With the loss of the South went the country's oil reserves. That has hurt the economy, which in turn has meant hard times for the people, which is why there have been a number of demonstrations.'

'Do you think this crackdown on artists is some kind of distraction?'

'I believe it is, Wendy.'

The anchorwoman, Wendy, turned back to us. 'Now, one man who was very involved with South Sudan is a well-known Hollywood star who has become something of an expert on the country in recent years. George, tell us how things look from where you are.' The screen cut to a grey-haired man standing in the sun.

'Who is he again?' I asked. Everyone hissed for me to shut up.

'Well, Wendy, the situation has developed badly. There seems little doubt that the government in Khartoum has run out of ideas. Basically, time has been called on this regime and we need to see change.'

'What do you have to say to your critics, those who believe that we shouldn't be involving ourselves in the affairs of a country so far away?'

'Well, that's a fair point, Wendy, but, uh, look, I would say this; you can sit on the wall and pretend this doesn't concern you, right? That's your choice. But I believe we have an obligation, a duty, to try and help people less fortunate than ourselves. This is about saving lives.'

'So, let's be clear,' said Wendy, cutting back to address the camera. 'Basically, these guys are in danger. They can't go home.' Behind her a publicity picture of the group appeared, the same poster that had been hanging in the Kennedy Center. By now we had the attention of every single person in the diner. Even the cook was leaning out of his hatch to have a look. Wendy was summarising. 'A nationwide hunt is on for a group of Sudanese musicians, the Kamanga Kings. Let's go live now to the Kennedy Center in Washington D.C., where I believe we have the director . . . Mrs DeHaviland?'

'That's Ms, actually.'

'I'm sorry. Ms DeHaviland, we understand that the FBI has been drawn into this nationwide search. Can you tell us what the situation is right now?'

Ms DeHaviland, as I now tried to think of her, looked uncomfortable. 'Well, first let me emphasise that this is a highly unusual situation.'

'Okay, but you have lost *everyone* in this group, is that correct?'

'We don't believe they are lost.'

Wendy skipped past this. 'Did you have any idea when you invited them that they were planning to seek political asylum in the United States?'

'No, of course not.'

'Then how do you explain their disappearance?'

Ms DeHaviland looked tired and strained. 'Right now we are trying to clarify the details, and until we have all the facts it would be irresponsible of me to speculate.'

'Uh huh. So, given what we've heard about the dangers they face if they return home, do you believe they should be granted asylum in the United States?'

'Well, it's really not my place to say.'

'But since you invited them to this country you must have some sympathy for their cause.'

'We are an arts centre, that's what we do. We try not to let politics influence our judgement.'

Wendy had lost interest in Ms DeHaviland and was already turning to a politician with neatly coiffed hair. Behind him were the ICE agents, Baumgarten and Blanco. They stared grimly at the camera.

'Senator, do you believe these people constitute a threat?'

'I'm afraid we have no choice but to assume that to be the case. Homeland Security concerns are our primary interest here. Effectively, these people entered the country under false pretences. This case should serve to highlight what goes on every single day when people take advantage of our generosity.'

'We understand their lives might be in danger if they return home.'

'Well, I sympathise with that up to a certain point, but it's not

our job to police the world. People have to sort out their own problems. We can't solve things for them.'

'We invite artists to this country all the time and usually there's
no problem. Do you think we should treat this differently?'

'Not at all. Everyone must be treated equally. Now, as you know,
their country is on the list of states that sponsor terrorism.'

'Senator, you're not suggesting these musicians are terrorists, surely?'

'Don't go putting words into my mouth. What I'm saying is that
we need to have all the facts. There is a reason the president called
for a travel ban on people from their country.'

'You think the ban was justified?'

'I believe we have to be vigilant about who we let into this country
and, frankly, I think it is a mistake to lower our guard. We should
never allow people into this country until we know who they are and
what their intentions are.'

'So, there you have it,' announced Wendy triumphantly cutting
back to us. 'Band on the run. They are literally running for their lives.
We'll have more on that and other stories on the hour.'

The picture cut away to music and titles in bold, vibrating colours.
A little girl carrying a balloon ran across a lawn chased by a big white
dog. I turned back to find everyone staring at me.

'Who is she again?' Shadia folded her arms. 'Vanessa?'

'She interviewed me in Washington.'

'She interviewed you alone? Why was she interested in you?'

John Wau leaned forward, tapping a long finger on the table. 'The
question is, what exactly did you say to her?'

'I certainly didn't tell her we were seeking political asylum.'

'Maybe you just weren't thinking straight,' said Shadia.

'That's not fair,' I protested. 'You know how it is with journalists.'

'No,' she said with a rather strange smile. 'I don't. Why don't you
tell us?'

'Guys, guys, please tone it down!' Waldo implored urgently. 'We're
drawing a lot of heat.'

Nobody was listening.

'You've turned us into a bunch of fugitives, boy,' Uncle Maher muttered.

'Worse,' said Shadia. 'Thanks to his girlfriend we're all terrorists.'

'My girlfriend? What are you talking about?'

The waitress appeared. She leaned over the table and looked around us. 'Listen, I have nothing against you folks personally, but I'm going to have to ask you to leave.'

I turned my head slowly and realised everyone in the place was staring at us.

'She's right,' I said. 'We need to leave now, and we need to do it quietly and with no sign of panic.' I got to my feet and counted out notes into the waitress's hand. Shadia leaned over and plucked another twenty from my hand to add to the pile.

'Thank you,' said the waitress, jerking her head over her shoulder. 'Go out the back door.'

We slid out of the booth and moved down beside the counter to a door marked Exit that led past the kitchen to the rear of the building.

Once back in the Birchaven we began to feel safe again.

'We're wanted people,' Hisham said. He sounded shocked. We all were.

'It's as if we were criminals,' Alkanary said. 'We did nothing wrong.'

'We left our hotel when we were told not to.' Uncle Maher shrugged. 'It's obvious.'

'Look,' I began. 'This is my fault. I should never have suggested it.'

'Hold on,' Shadia lifted a hand. 'Before you do your martyr act. We all agreed to do this together, remember?' she looked around the assembled faces. 'Right?'

There were a few half-hearted mumbles in reply.

'Then we have nobody to blame but ourselves.'

There was silence after that. I think it would be fair to say that until the moment we saw ourselves on the news program it had never really dawned on us, the full impact of what we had done.

My superstitious side was asking whether we had broken some universal law. Was there a secret pact that we had transgressed that had led to us being lost, stuck in permanent flight? We might end up spending years like this, travelling from town to town, playing for the mad, the forgotten and the ones who had nowhere else to go.

Chapter 28

Over the Hills

Waldo sped us skimming through sleepy towns towards a range of hills that covered the horizon, rising up to meet the open sky. I wasn't sure where we were exactly or where our next destination was, apart from the fact that it was the next place on the list.

'Do you know where we are going?' Hisham asked, leaning over from the back seat.

'No, but Waldo has a machine that does.' I pointed at the dashboard. Hisham looked sceptical, but Waldo's face lit up.

'Nothing to worry about, man. Look, it's even offering us a short cut.' Waldo drew a finger across the map on the little screen. 'That should save us about four hours' driving.'

'That's good, no?'

'So, we have to go over those hills?' Hisham was not entirely convinced. 'They look rather high.'

'Well, it is somewhat late in the year, but hey, it wouldn't suggest it if it wasn't safe, right?'

Hisham and I exchanged glances but neither of us said anything. Around us the houses were already beginning to spread out more thinly until there were more trees than homes. The road narrowed as we started winding upwards. The squeaky female voice from the dashboard kept telling us what to do; turn left, turn right. Waldo ducked his head to peer up through the pines ahead of us. I followed his gaze and saw a thick band of cloud nestled above us, blocking out the sky. The world grew dark and cold as we climbed upwards into the mist.

'Are you sure about this, Waldo?'

'It'll be fine, buddy. Trust me.'

I glanced round and caught Shadia watching me. I had the feeling she still harboured suspicions about me and Vanessa.

'I'm sure he knows what he's doing.'

She clicked her tongue in annoyance. 'Why is it that men always feel they have to reassure women, even when it's obvious they themselves have no clue what they are talking about?'

I didn't have an answer for her. Perhaps better for me to keep quiet, I decided. She was right about one thing. I felt no degree of certainty about what we were doing. We seemed to have missed a turn. The little device on the dashboard kept repeating the same phrase over and over. 'Take the next exit on the right. Take the next exit on the right.' Waldo tapped it repeatedly with his finger which didn't seem to help.

The voice went into a high-pitched warble that sounded as if she was speaking Japanese. I realised that the noise of the others behind us had quietened down. The bus lurched across the narrow road as Waldo tried to knock some sense into the navigation device. He pulled the wheel sharply to straighten out.

'Sorry, folks!' he called over his shoulder.

The woman's voice was getting more insistent. By now she was quite incoherent. Then abruptly, the little screen flickered a couple of times and went dark. Waldo sat back and stared at it.

'Well, I'll be damned. I haven't seen that before.' He straightened up and grimaced at the road ahead. 'Looks like we're on our own now.'

I glanced back at Shadia but decided against speaking. I didn't need to. The silence that settled over us imposed its own sombre mood. Now we were seriously climbing into the mountains. It was clear that the Birchaven was struggling, the engine whining loudly at the steep gradient. At the tight corners, Waldo wrestled violently with the wheel. Cries of alarm sounded from the back as people were thrown from side to side. They would just about manage to settle down again before we reached the next hairpin bend. I dug my fingers into the foam of the armrest and clung on tightly.

'Perhaps we should consider another way, Waldo?' I whispered.

He winked at me. 'Have a little faith, man, all right? It'll be fine.'

I wasn't so sure. The clouds clamped over us tightly as a veil of mist drew itself over the pine trees, and the world became eerily silent. A strange light sank down to cover the world. And then, out of the clear air, a soft bright flurry of snow flew into our faces. We swept on, higher and higher into darkness.

We pulled over for a break and the men went scurrying left and right to find a quiet spot in which to relieve themselves. There was a smell of oil and burnt rubber, along with the clicking sound of cooling metal coming from the chassis. A glance over at the side of the road revealed a giddy drop. The mist cleared briefly and I caught a glimpse of the distant plain far below.

'Quite a sight, ain't it?' said Waldo, from further along.

'Waldo, er . . . how long do you suppose it will take us to get over these hills?'

'I understand you folks haven't seen weather like this before, but trust me, this is pretty normal.' He smiled, exhaling smoke into the frosty air. 'It's slow going because the old girl is carrying more than she's used to and she ain't as young as she was. Hell, none of us is. Have a little faith.' He walked back, zipping up his trousers. 'As soon as we are over the ridge, the road flattens out and it's plain sailing after that.'

Everyone bundled themselves eagerly back into the warm interior and then we were off again. The mountain that rose before us just seemed to keep going and I wondered just how much faith we would need to get over it. Between the treetrunks, buttresses of cold grey rock slid out of the mist like the prows of ancient warships. It seemed to be asking a lot.

I became aware that a discussion was taking place behind me.

'What's going on?' I asked, looking over my shoulder at the assembled faces.

'We've been talking,' Wad Mazaj began before tailing off, looking at Uncle Maher, who stared at the ceiling. I looked at Hisham, but he was fiddling with his headphones. 'There has been a suggestion that perhaps we should take advantage of our situation.'

'What does that mean?'

'It means that here we are, in America. Travelling, playing,' Wad Mazaj continued.

'I don't follow.' I looked to Shadia for an explanation.

'He's saying we should forget about Gandoury and just stay behind, apply for asylum.'

'What?' I couldn't believe what I was hearing.

'We may as well,' Hisham chimed in. 'I mean, we're already being chased for it, right? So why not go all the way?'

'We know how you feel,' I said. 'Maybe let the others speak for themselves.'

Wad Mazaj moved forward so that he was closer to me, falling into the chair behind me as we veered around another bend.

'You saw that on the TV back there. Everyone thinks we have a case. We are musicians, our lives are in danger if we return.'

'Except we all know that's not really true any more.'

He lifted a shoulder. 'It makes no sense to go home now. To what? This is an opportunity, for all of us.'

'What about your family, what about everyone waiting at home?'

'You don't think they would be better off if we were sending them money from here?' asked Hisham. There were murmurs of agreement from the back.

'That's not what we're doing. We can't.'

'Why not? What's to stop us?'

The bus lurched again. I felt like I was going to be sick.

'Can we talk about this later?' I looked around the faces, hoping for support. Nobody could meet my gaze except Shadia. They had obviously been talking about this when I wasn't around.

'Sure,' nodded Wad Mazaj. 'Let's leave it till later.'

He returned to his seat and Hisham slipped into his place.

'You should think about it. Maybe instead of wasting our time chasing Gandoury we should follow his example.'

'I know how you feel about it.'

'Why not? What's to stop us?' Hisham had a look of quiet satisfaction in his eye.

'We made a promise. To Ms DeHaviland.'

'Who cares about that?'

'I care. We should all care. When we entered this country, we made a deal. We are not breaking that.'

'Why not?'

'It's a matter of principle. We gave our word.'

I was looking for some sign of support, any sign whatsoever, but there was nothing.

'Okay, apart from people like yourself, who are still living in the nineteenth century, do you think anyone cares about that stuff?'

I would have said more but the van gave another hard lurch. I had to grab the seat and hold on for dear life. Through the windscreen the sky was growing blacker and the snow once more began to fly at us. It might have been my imagination, but it seemed heavier than we had seen before. Winged creatures floated towards us out of the gloom. I found myself mesmerised by the snowflakes. It felt as though I was being dragged into a bad dream. All daylight had been extinguished now and the headlights tunnelled into the wall of white that rushed at us out of the darkness. Trees flew by like outstretched skeletons, white sleeves on their bare branches.

The road twisted at such a sharp angle that we had to slow almost to a standstill with Waldo spinning the wheel as fast as he could without taking his foot off the accelerator. A terrible feeling of dread came over me, that we were all going to die here on this mountain. I turned my head to see Shadia staring intently ahead. Her hair had come loose and hung down one side of her face.

'We really should consider turning around,' I whispered to her. She nodded without speaking. She looked as queasy as I felt.

'The road is icing up,' said Waldo, who was frowning with concentration. He dared not slow down or speed up for fear of losing traction. I was trying not to think that he looked rather scared.

'Is there another way?' I suggested.

He answered without taking his eyes off the road. 'Too late for that, old buddy. No way to turn around here. We're just going to have to ride this baby out.'

I looked at Shadia. Words were no longer necessary. We were on a ship that was careering out of control, and now it was plain that even the captain was worried. Clearly, the road was so narrow as to make turning a complex and dangerous manoeuvre even in good conditions, in broad daylight, on a sunny day, but in the dark, with a precipitous drop on one side and a rocky incline on the other, it would have been suicidal. It occurred to me that if we got stuck up here we would, in all likelihood, freeze to death.

The front of the vehicle swept out wide over the void as we swung round another bend. The bottom of the bus scraped the road with a crunch, grating along as we went round another hairpin bend, sparks flying out from beneath us. I was hanging onto the armrest and trying to ignore the cries of alarm coming from behind me. Down below, through the trees, clusters of lights glowed warmly in the distance, advertising houses, roadside stops, filling stations, safety. They winked like bright pearls in an undersea world.

The windscreen wipers had slowed almost to a halt, weighted down by the heaps of snow that had built up, wafting slowly back and forth like ostrich feather fans. The tarmac had vanished, the lines dissolving into white as the edges of the road merged with the surrounding landscape. What had started as a brief flurry had thickened into an unbroken wave of white that obscured the way ahead. It felt as if we had lost all sense of gravity and were floating in a soup. We seemed to be sinking in the stuff. The Birchaven was big and unwieldy, but now, as the wheels crunched over the powdered snow, it felt as if the slightest error would send us flying off into the void.

'Just have to get over the top,' grunted Waldo.

Nobody spoke. We were all too frightened. I felt the wheels slip, losing their grip for a second, spinning as we slid backwards for a terrifying moment before they dug in again.

None of us had seen anything like this. Despite the whine of the heater my feet were frozen stiff. Oddly, I suddenly felt an absurd sense of freedom, as if, in the depths of my fear, despite the danger, I would not have changed where I was for anything in the world. I felt so close to death and yet more alive than ever. I was having trouble breathing and realised that Shadia's fingers were digging into my hand. I tried to think of something reassuring to say but couldn't.

'Ya Allah,' she whispered.

At that moment the vehicle gave a violent lurch. Waldo let out a cry of alarm. I felt the wheels spinning beneath us, heard the high-pitched whine of the engine. Then the world swung around before me until we were facing the void, sliding sideways towards the precipice. A collective howl went up as the vehicle struck something and spun around. Then everything was whirling. The trees rushed towards us. Beyond them was only darkness. We were dead. I saw the long fall down the cliff face to the earth far below.

We hit something side on, hard. The door in the back flew open to reveal the void below. I heard all the screaming and shouting around me. We weren't moving. Smoke and an acrid burning smell rose up between my legs from the engine. Waldo was saying something but I couldn't make out the words. There was a grating beneath me.

'Nobody move!' Waldo yelled.

Another cry went up as we slid another few metres. Then came a jarring thump as we hit something and came to a halt.

We sat in the dark. The engine had gone out. The only sound was the whistle of the wind outside, the creak of the trees overhead. Shadia and I slowly let go of one another. Waldo's unsteady voice reached out in the darkness.

'Okay, everybody stay calm. It's all cool.' There were groans from the back. 'I'm not sure just how firmly we're sitting. It may be an idea not to move around too much.'

Which is exactly what everyone in the back started doing. The bus creaked alarmingly and we felt the earth shift underneath us.

'Tell them I'm serious about not moving.' Waldo was trying to sound calm.

'Everyone listen!' I yelled. It came out in a hoarse croak. I didn't recognise my own voice. 'You must keep still!'

'I'm going to get out and check the vehicle is secure,' Waldo said quietly. 'We should be okay but stay put or we might just knock ourselves over the edge.'

'Nobody move!' I whispered in a low squeak.

'Where's he going?' Wad Mazaj's tremulous voice came as Waldo cracked the door open.

'He just told us,' hissed John Wau. 'Now keep still.'

'Is he leaving us here?'

'Everyone keep quiet!' Shadia yelled. This time they listened.

A gust of freezing wind blew into the vehicle as Waldo slipped to the ground. He struggled to close the door but eventually managed it. For a moment I glimpsed him in the side mirror, before he disappeared from sight around the back of the Birchaven. I didn't move. I don't think I even did much in the way of breathing. I listened to the creak of the metal around us and the moan of the wind as it flew against the sides. There was a banging from somewhere at the back and something thumped against the window next to me. I let out a scream. It was Waldo. I lowered the glass.

'I've secured the rear wheels with chocks, but I don't know how well they'll hold. The ground is iced up pretty bad. We need to get help.' His hair and beard were already thick with white flakes, as were his clothes. He was shivering as he pointed up through the trees. 'I thought I saw a light up there. I'm going to take a short cut and see if I can get help.'

'Wait, Waldo, I'll go with you . . .'

'No, you'd better stay here . . .' He said something else, but it was lost in the wind.

'What?'

'Just sit tight. I'll be back as fast as I can.'

I watched as he slid about trying to cross the icy road, barely able to stand up. Then he scrambled up the steep embankment and disappeared, the faint beam of his flashlight bobbing away into the trees.

'What if he doesn't come back?' asked Hisham after a time.

'He'll be back,' I said, although I'm not sure why I thought this was possible.

I heard Wad Mazaj reciting the 'Fatihah', the opening verse of the Quran. I had no objections. We needed all the help we could get. The others seemed to agree with my sentiments, until a voice from the back sounded.

'Will you stop that nonsense?' Alkanary called out. 'Do you really think your precious Lord will be able to find us all the way up here?'

Wad Mazaj fell silent. Nobody had the heart to argue with her. So much for religious conviction if one opinionated woman could put a stop to it.

There we were, trapped in a strange vehicle clinging to the side of a mountain in the dark in the middle of a storm of such icy fury that none of us had ever experienced before. How long we sat there I cannot say. I think we were too worried to talk. Then Shadia let out a cry of alarm. She was pointing forwards through the windscreen. I couldn't believe my eyes. A gigantic hand was scraping towards us.

A whole tree. Not a branch, but a whole tree, tumbling and sliding towards us.

'It's going to hit us!' yelled Hisham.

A collective cry went up as the tree struck the front of the vehicle, dislodging us. We began to slowly spin round. Everyone was screaming. Wad Mazaj was praying out loud. Alkanary was wailing, deaf to Shadia's efforts to calm her. When we came to a halt again, I looked back and saw John Wau crouched on the floor with his hands over his head.

'We have to do something,' said Shadia.

Sure, but do what? I tried to speak but managed only to croak something unintelligible. Finally, I heard myself say. 'I'm going to find him.'

'He told us to wait here, remember?' Hisham insisted.

'What if he doesn't come back? We'll die here,' Wad Mazaj wailed. 'Let the boy go.'

'That's easy for you to say,' Shadia said, rushing to my defence, which was nice.

'It's okay,' I said. 'I won't take long. I'll just go up the road a bit.'

'Are you mad, boy?' Uncle Maher demanded. 'In this storm, in this wilderness?'

'It's fine,' I said, looking into his sad brown eyes. 'Waldo said we were near the top.'

'You shouldn't go alone,' said Shadia. 'I'll come too.'

'No,' I assured her. 'That makes no sense.'

'This is no time for male pride.'

'I'm just being practical. I'll stick to the road. If Waldo comes back, you tell him which way I went.'

Having said my piece there wasn't much more for me to do but put my plan into action. I reached for the door handle and tried to open it. The wind outside was blowing so hard I had to lean all my weight into it. It suddenly flew out of my hand. I slipped and immediately fell over. The wind felt stronger than it had been earlier. The road was slippery and covered in snow and patches of ice. I struggled to stand firmly enough to force the door shut. My hands stung from the icy metal and I was already beginning to regret my plan.

I managed to stay upright, my feet threatening to fly in opposite directions, clinging to the side of the vehicle, wondering what to do next. Gradually, I dared to take one step and then another. Using awkward, flat-footed steps I made my way out into the middle of the road. I looked back and saw all their faces illuminated by the light inside the bus. They were watching me through the window as if they expected me to be swallowed up by a monster or something. I lifted my arm to wave and then thought better of it when I realised I was in danger of losing my balance. Instead I turned and put one foot carefully in front of the other and began to walk slowly away.

Every step seemed to reinforce the foolishness of my decision. The furious wind was freezing. I considered the idea of going back but decided that admitting defeat was probably worse than whatever I had to face out there in the darkness. I carried on, my feet sliding left and right. Above me the branches sawed back and forth against one another. The wind whistled fiercely through the trees.

How long I walked, I don't know. It felt like hours but I was so cold I was no longer thinking straight. Gradually, I felt the angle of the road ease and the wind drop. I was sheltered by the hill itself. Walking became a little easier. I could hardly feel my fingers. My face was numb. Then, all of a sudden, I glimpsed a chink in the black wall ahead of me. It disappeared, then reappeared again as I moved. It grew steady until I was sure it was a light. I began to hurry, afraid that if I didn't get there soon, it might just vanish.

The light was coming from a building off to the left. I began moving more quickly, eager to find out what it was and, in my haste, slipped to my knees a couple of times. A road sign appeared, half-buried in snow. *The Silver Cloud Bar & Lounge.* Another sign nailed across it flapped in the breeze. I pinned it back to read the word, *Closed.*

Closed? But how could that be? I could see a light. I stumbled off the road and plunged straight into a snow drift that came up to my waist. Gasping, I managed to drag myself back onto a path leading through a gap in the trees. The snow was thick and heavy and I lost my footing several times. Before I reached the entrance, I came to a halt. My teeth were chattering and I could no longer feel my hands or feet. But I could hear something. Music! I was losing my mind. I was convinced I could hear 'Lost in the Stars'.

Cautiously, I climbed the icy wooden steps across the front of the entrance to a porch that ran along the front of the building. Across large glass doors letters spelled out the word Hotel. I pressed my nose to the glass and peered through the letter O.

Chapter 29

The Silver Cloud

It was a long room, almost bare of furniture. Chairs and tables were stacked along one wall. In the middle stood a man who appeared to be dancing with a large double bass. He was twirling the instrument as if it was his partner, while revolving gracefully around the floor in wide, sweeping circles. The music I could hear through the door was an Argentine tango. A 1950s jukebox set against the wall emitted a warm yellow glow from its glass surface.

I wondered if the cold was causing me to hallucinate. The whole scene struck me as odd. But I pressed my nose closer to the glass as I caught the flicker coming from the open fire that burned halfway down the room. I hesitated about pushing my way inside only because of the sight of the man dancing.

He was a strange-looking fellow, rather large and shapeless. He wore shiny boots and a low pork-pie hat like the kind Lester Young used to wear. From his features I guessed he was a Latino. He looked like a young Caetano Veloso. He moved with remarkable grace for his height. His body turned so lightly as his feet glided gently over the varnished wood. I became so engrossed in watching him as he spun and weaved about the room that I forgot my teeth were chattering and my body was shaking.

As the song came to an end he opened his eyes, went over to the wall and gently set the instrument carefully down alongside the jukebox, bowing his head and tilting his hat, as if he had just taken his leave of the most beautiful lady at a fancy ball. Then a weariness seemed to pass through him and he leaned his weight over the jukebox, his face illuminated by the blue light emitted from within as he placed a cigarette between his lips. Without lighting it, he turned and wandered with a sigh towards the bar that ran along the far end of the room. I watched in wonder as he climbed rather unsteadily onto a chair. I hadn't noticed the rope that hung there until that moment, but now I watched him slip his head through the noose and draw the knot close to his neck. He still had the unlit cigarette in his mouth. He raised one shiny boot and placed it on the counter, his other foot on the chair. It dawned on me that he was about to push himself off.

I struggled to open the door, which appeared to be jammed. I pulled and pushed, wrestling with the handle, which was stuck, or perhaps frozen by the cold. Finally, I put my shoulder into it and threw my weight at it. Without warning it flew open and I tumbled inside to run a few steps and land face down in the middle of the room.

We remained like that, the two of us, me sprawled full length along the floor and he standing there on the chair, trying to maintain his balance.

'What the hell?' he muttered, the cigarette tumbling from his lips.

I tried to speak, but my face was frozen. He carefully removed the noose and climbed down. Then he came towards me, moving cautiously around me, as if he didn't quite believe I was real. He leaned over me.

'¿Qué coño? Where did you spring from?'

I was having trouble making my mouth work. It was like when you go to the dentist. The man was scratching his head as he helped me over to the fire.

'You speak English?'

'Eng-English, yes.'

'How did you get here?'

I pointed over my shoulder. 'Music. We're musicians.'

'We?' His eyebrows shot up. 'There's more of you?'

'Oh, yes, they are back in the RV.'

'RV?' I could see he was having trouble following me.

'Yes. A 1976 GMC Birchaven.'

'You mean like some kind of time-travel thing?' He cocked his head to one side.

'No, no, not time. Sudan? Africa?'

'Claro,' he nodded. He still didn't seem convinced.

'I was trying to find Waldo'

'Who or what is a Waldo?'

'He's our friend. He's lost, out there.' I pointed.

'Right.' The way he was staring worried me a little.

'We must get them. It is very cold.'

'It's usually like that in winter.' He shrugged.

'Maybe I could fetch them. They could stay here . . .?'

He rocked back on his heels. 'Well, we're actually closed right now. I mean, I'm just the caretaker. Officially I'm under strict orders not to let anyone in.'

I looked around. 'And there's nobody else here with you?'

'No, sir, not for a few weeks now. People will start to show up just around New Year.'

'So, then . . . nobody would know,' I said. He folded his arms and studied me for moment.

'Know?'

'That we were here, I mean?'

'I would know.' He pointed his thumb at his chest. 'And I would not be doing my job if I didn't report it.' Then he sniffed and thought for a moment. 'Africa, you said?'

'That's right. Musicians.' I paused. 'You are a very good dancer, by the way.'

This seemed to take him by surprise. 'Thank you,' he said.

'You are a fan of tango music.'

'I play, or used to play, the accordion.' He nodded at the double bass. 'I'm trying to diversify.'

'Right.'

'My name is Rudy, by the way.'

'Rushdy,' I smiled. 'Very close.'

'Sure.' We stood there for a moment. He was still undecided. Then he made a throwaway gesture with his hand. 'Joder. What the hell,' he sighed. 'I guess we'd better go find them.'

'Thank you, sir. So kind of you.'

'Just one moment.'

He went back over to the counter, climbed onto the chair to untie the rope which he tossed behind the bar. Then he led the way over to the front door. In an alcove he pulled on a big coat and found a flashlight before turning to me again.

'Are you illegals?'

'Illegals?'

'Aliens? Undocumented immigrants?'

'Oh no, not aliens.' I tried to assure him with a smile. 'We are the Kamanga Kings.'

'Sure you are. Look, you'd better put this on.' He handed me a heavy parka.

The wind had dropped somewhat as we tramped through the heavy snow, but I was grateful for the coat and the fur-lined hood. When we reached the road, I pointed down to the right and we set off in that direction. In what seemed like no time we saw the Birchaven in the distance, jammed up against a large tree.

'There it is!' I pointed. He drew to a halt.

Rudy stopped, cocking his head. 'What is that noise?'

I listened for a moment. 'They are singing, to keep their spirits up.'

'Sounds like they're murdering someone,' he muttered.

When I knocked on the door, they fell silent. I saw Wad Mazaj peering out.

'Who is it?'

'Who do you think it is?'

The door flew open and they all tried to lean out at the same time. We managed to fight our way inside and pull the door closed. They all fired questions at me at the same time.

'Where have you been?' asked Hisham. 'You've been gone for hours.'

'We were worried,' said Shadia.

'Who's this?' Wad Mazaj was staring at the man from the hotel. I switched to English.

'This is Rudy.'

'Rudolfo Jimenez Ventura,' said the man, lifting a hand. 'At your service.'

'Mr Ventura is the owner of the Silver Cloud Hotel. He says we can stay there.'

'Uh, no, that's not actually, strictly true,' Rudy corrected. 'I'm just the caretaker. But under the circumstances I guess it's all right for you to stay up there. Just for tonight, mind. You'll have to leave in the morning, or I'm in a ton of trouble.'

There was a cry from the back as Alkanary shoved her way forward. 'A hotel, you say? What are we waiting for?'

There was no stopping her. She jumped down and stalked off up the road with Shadia in tow, trying to stop her tripping over the hem of her coat. In itself that fur coat was a source of wonder, a reminder that Alkanary had a long history behind her. How many years had she kept that coat, stuffed away in the back of a wardrobe back home where you would literally die if you tried wearing something like that. It suggested that despite her despair she had never really given up on the world. She'd dampened down her feelings over the years with copious amounts of araqi, which had no doubt done untold damage to her health, but there was no sign of her slowing down now. Although I suspected her animated spirit was partly due to the secret supply of Scotch I knew she had in the back room of the van.

The others were still mooching around, debating the pros and cons of remaining in a freezing cold bus in the middle of a snow-storm or taking shelter in a hotel. It might have been obvious to the rest of the world, but they still had to have a discussion. Fifty years of independence and forty odd years of civil war and we asked ourselves why?

'What seems to be the problem in there?' Rudy asked.

'Oh, it's nothing. Politics.'

'Right,' he nodded warily. 'Stay away from that.'

'You don't like politics?'

'Either that or politics doesn't like me. I'm undecided.'

'But you are in the home of democracy.'

'That's what they keep saying,' he said, letting out a long sigh. 'It sure doesn't feel that way right now.'

They were still trying to decide whether or not to take their instruments with them. Surely it was better to have them with us, in case the Birchaven fell into the icy void? In the end Kadugli headed out with his saxophone case and promptly fell over, after which it was decided to leave the precious instruments behind. I left a note for Waldo on the dashboard before jumping down again. Up ahead the others were slipping and sliding. Rudy winced as Wad Mazaj flew into the air and landed with a thump.

'What about Waldo?' Shadia asked, as we caught up with them. 'Where is he?'

'I don't know. I didn't see him.' The wind was picking up again and flakes of snow slapped like cold insects against my face.

'I hope he turns up soon. This is going to get worse before it gets better.'

'You might be right.'

The group was strung along the road behind us like a wayward herd. Alkanary was up ahead. She stopped to call back.

'Come on, are you going to let an old girl like me beat you to it?'

'I don't know how she does it,' Shadia confessed, waving to her.

The snow was getting heavy again and the occasional gust of high wind was so strong it forced us to stop and turn our backs until it died down. What with one thing and another it took nearly an hour to get back to the shelter of the hotel. By then the snow was falling so thickly you couldn't even see the road from the front steps. We wrestled our way through the door and collapsed gasping into the first chairs we came upon.

'Al Hamdoulilah! We're saved!' Alkanary threw her arms around Rudy and kissed him on both cheeks so hard his face reddened. There was laughter and relief all round. Everyone was in high spirits.

Shadia was still worried about Waldo. 'What if he goes back to the car and we're not there?'

'I left him a note.'

'A note?' she echoed. 'Do you think that's enough?'

'Place looks like a damn refugee camp,' Rudy muttered as he stamped with an armful of firewood.

'Mr Rudy,' I said, stepping in front of him. 'We're worried about our friend, Waldo.'

'I understand that, but in this storm there's nothing you can do.' He saw the expressions on our faces. 'Okay, look, if you gotta go, you gotta go.'

'That is very kind of you, sir.'

'Look, kid, this is going to be heavy going if you're going to thank me for everything.'

'Yes, sir.'

'And cut out the sirs, for Christ's sakes! It reminds me of the army.'

When I stepped back outside, I immediately regretted my decision. Why was I always volunteering to go out? Where was Hisham in all this, or one of the others?

The snow was so thick that within less than a minute I was completely blinded. A moment ago, inside the warm hotel, it had seemed almost like a good idea. I was staggering down the road, gasping and stumbling, falling to my knees in deep drifts. I scanned the forest left and right. I saw shadows moving everywhere and the old superstitions came back. What was I doing out here?

'Waldo!' I wailed at the wind. 'Waldo!'

In the end I realised I would perish if I stayed out there much longer. The wind was at my back, pushing me down the road into the darkness below. What had possessed him to think we could make it over a mountain like this? He called it a hill. You needed a four-wheel drive monster with tyres like claws, not that soft plastic shell designed for summer trips to the beach. I felt bad for him, but I couldn't see where in the whirring blackness I could hope to find him. I was overcome by sadness at the thought of Waldo being out there somewhere, alone at the mercy of wolves or bears. I was sure they had bears around here. I struggled back up the incline, now with the wind in my face. For every step forward I took two steps back. I put my head down and gritted my teeth. Finally, I stamped up the steps and fought my way through the door.

'Ah, the wanderer returns,' chuckled Wad Mazaj.

Rudy was handing out mugs and pouring coffee from a large pot. 'We don't have the fuel to turn on the heating in the other wings, so we'll have to make do in here.'

'I'm sorry,' I said to Shadia. 'I couldn't find him.'

'At least we tried.'

By now the lounge did indeed resemble a refugee camp. Blankets had been found somewhere and everyone had made themselves comfortable on the floor, or wherever they could pitch a makeshift bed. The group appeared to have settled down. Uncle Maher stretched out on the wooden boards with a loud groan and closed his eyes. Shadia was combing out Alkanary's wispy hair at a table by the fire. The grand old lady had somehow managed to procure a tumbler containing a dark liquid that I assumed was whisky. John Wau and Kadugli were, as always, deep in conversation. Music, politics. They never seemed to tire of those subjects. Hisham was in a corner with his headphones on, lost in his own world. He gave me a wave and then went back to tapping his fingers on his knees.

'With this storm, nobody will be out trying to repair the phone masts, otherwise we could call for help,' Rudy said, surveying the scene.

'Maybe that's not such a bad thing,' I said quietly.

'Seriously, man?' He tilted his head to one side. 'I asked you if you were illegals, remember? You said no.'

'We're not. I mean, technically, we are not illegals . . . yet.'

'Yet?' Rudy folded his arms. 'What does that mean?'

'It means that there are people looking for us because they think we are illegals, but we're not.'

'Okay, I don't understand a word.'

'Well, we're just looking for someone, one of our group who went missing.'

'And he is illegal?'

'No. Well, I don't know. And actually, he's not really part of our group. He lent us some money and then stole some more.'

'Vaya historia,' said Rudy. He threw up his hands as he walked away. 'I knew it. This is going to cost me my job.'

After that, I went over to join Hisham, who was sitting at the upright piano in the corner of the room. He ran his fingers along the keys in an anxious, distracted way.

'What's up with him?'

'He's worried we're going to get him into trouble.'

'Well, he's probably right about that.'

I watched as he pulled out his tobacco and began rolling a joint. 'That thing earlier, about the others wanting to stay behind. How serious do you think they are?'

Hisham looked at me out of the corner of his eye. 'Of course they're serious. Anybody can see that they can make a better life for themselves here.'

'But that was never the deal. We came here to play, not to stay indefinitely.'

'Get real. It's the opportunity of a lifetime.' Hisham gave a shake of his head. 'It's obvious to everyone except you.'

'They think their lives would be easier here, I get that, but never going home?'

'It's funny, when you think about it.'

'What's funny?'

'I don't know, this whole dream we're chasing. The old Kings, like a symbol of some other time when we had dignity and respect.'

'What's so funny about that?'

'Well, it's all long gone, if it ever existed.'

'I don't get it. What are you doing here, if you don't believe in it?'

'What are we going back to? Tell me that. We could have a life here, as a band. We could make money, play for audiences. This is a chance to do what we've always wanted to do.'

'Living here is not as easy as you think.'

'So that's it, you're afraid?'

'I'm not afraid,' I said, glancing over my shoulder at the others, although this wasn't entirely true. 'It's just that we don't belong here.'

'Come on,' he laughed. 'Where does anyone belong? We all have to stay where we belong?' He struck a match and held it to the tip of the joint. 'We're chasing a dream, a myth, and there's nothing wrong with that, but it's an escape, just like everything else.' The smoke turned his voice into a dry croak. He held out the joint. I shook my head. 'We should be living in the present, thinking of now, and of the future, not tying ourselves to a dream our parents had. Independence, what did that ever bring us?'

'So, what? You're saying we should just forget it and pretend to be Americans?'

Hisham was shaking his head again. 'You don't get it. People like you never do.'

240

'If you want to stay, that's up to you,' I said, raising my voice, aware that everyone else had been listening to us. 'And that goes for the rest of you too. You're free to do whatever you want, but first we're going to straighten out this mess Gandoury has made. After that, I don't care what you do.'

I got up and walked away, out through the front door to the porch. It was cold, but I needed to clear my head after the fug of the interior. My eyes adjusted slowly to the light until I could see stars peeking through little gaps in the clouds. I heard the door open and Alkanary came out. She had a blanket wrapped around her shoulders. She stood for a moment before coming over to stand by me.

'You know, you shouldn't judge your friend too harshly,' she said.

'It just makes me angry to think that the only reason he came along is because he wanted a chance to start a life for himself here. It feels like a betrayal.' I gripped the railing in front of me.

'You feel he took advantage of you, coming on this trip?'

'I can't believe I didn't see that.'

'It's not true, and you know that.'

Her face was deep in shadow. 'That evening when you came to my house, remember? After you left me, I was so upset. I was crying. Life is unfair. Getting old is cruel. I felt as though I had wasted so many years.'

Her voice came out of the darkness, deep and low. Her eyes were lost in the shadows

'But then I thought about you and Hisham and how excited you were about something that I thought had died years ago.' She stepped closer and put her hand over mine. 'You gave me back something I thought I'd lost for ever.'

'But he's ruining it all,' I said.

'Your father was like that,' she said softly. 'It had to be everything or nothing. He prized loyalty above everything else and he never forgave anyone he thought had betrayed him, even when he was wrong.'

She looked me in the eye. 'We're not all perfect. We can't live like that. We have to forgive.'

With that she turned and disappeared inside. I stood there lost in my thoughts. Maybe she was right. Maybe Hisham was just as confused as the rest of us. He was trying to work things out.

I'm not sure how long I stood there, but I can remember being startled by something that was out there in the trees. My first thought was a bear. I was sure they had bears around here. What did you do when you encountered a bear? I had no idea. As I stared at the spot the shadow moved again. I took a step backwards. Something was moving towards me over the snow. A shadow seemed to be trying to extricate itself from the trees. Then, out of the darkness, a figure shrouded in white stumbled into view.

'Waldo? Is that you?'

I rushed down into the snow and dragged him up the steps and through the doors into the room. Everyone just stared in amazement. He was all but unrecognisable. His eyebrows were fat white caterpillars. Long trails of ice extended from his nostrils down around the sides of his mouth to the beard that had turned itself into a snowy wasteland. His features were bloodless and tinged with blue. Waldo stood there looking like a creature that had been buried for hundreds of years in the mountainside, then he made a bleating sound like a sheep having its throat cut, his legs collapsed and he fell to the floor in a heap.

Chapter 30

Off the Map

Waldo proved to be heavier than expected, but together we managed to lift him up and carry him to one of the long benches next to the fire.

'He's not going to die, is he?' Shadia asked. I had no idea. Death sounded altogether too dramatic but considering the events of the day pretty much anything was possible. Leaning over him, I slapped Waldo's face gently a few times until he stirred and lay there gasping and groaning to himself. After a time, he opened his eyes and looked around. Rudy handed Shadia a mug of coffee into which he had poured a liberal dose of rum. She cradled Waldo's head and held the mug to his lips. It seemed to revive him somewhat.

'Trees, all I saw was trees.' Waldo was trembling and Shadia tucked the blankets more tightly around him. 'I must have lost my bearings. I was walking round in circles. I was too tired to go on but I knew that if I stopped I would freeze to death.'

'You could have died,' gasped Shadia.

Waldo gazed up at her in wonder. I saw curiosity in his eyes, as well as gratitude. His hand closed around hers.

'Thank you,' he murmured. 'I thought I was done for, and then I heard a piano. I thought I was going mad, I tell you.'

'That was Hisham,' I said, happy to break up their little moment.

Waldo smiled. 'Well, you may just have saved my life, my friend. I couldn't see any lights. It was pitch black.'

'You must have gone way over to the north side,' Rudy mused. 'All the windows on that side are shuttered.'

'Always a drama!' muttered Alkanary as she wandered by carrying a bottle of rum she had picked up from somewhere. 'I'm supposed to be the old woman here.'

As Waldo settled down everyone began to relax and people returned to their makeshift beds. Blankets and improvised mattresses were scattered around the floor. Finally, I lay down and listened to the wail of the wind outside. I turned on my side on the uncomfortable pool table that was my bed for the night and thought about the life that awaited me when I returned home. Assuming I could beg for my old job back, or find another school that would take me, I would return to the regular tedium of classes, the crush and heat of the market place, the crowded buses, the noise and dust of the city. Was that what I wanted?

As I drifted off, I recalled Mr Siegel's joy as we played those old songs that brought back sweet memories. The strange delight on the faces of those people dancing before me. That little improvised performance had been more satisfying even than our show at the Kennedy Center. The air had been charged with a kind of sorcery. I wondered if we could ever get that back again.

I awoke to a bird singing outside the window. I rolled off the pool table and stood up, my limbs stiff from the cold and the hard surface. The fire had gone out. Pulling the blanket round my shoulders, I staggered over to the door and pushed it open. The air was cold and crisp, the sky bright blue. The ground was the most brilliant white, dotted here and there with large black boulders. To the right a parting in the trees revealed the valley out of which we had struggled. Everything was so calm that the previous night's storm felt like a fantastical tale, one that I only half believed.

'It's beautiful, isn't it?'

I hadn't noticed her, but Shadia was sitting on a wooden bench set up against the wall. She had a shawl of some kind wrapped around her with strange geometrical markings on it. Her hair was tousled and her face looked soft and puffy from sleep.

'Yes, it is,' I agreed.

'Whatever happens, at least we'll have this.'

We stayed out there for a time, neither of us feeling the need to break the silence. I couldn't remember why I was feeling jealous the night before.

Inside, Waldo had woken up and appeared to have recovered from his ordeal. All around people were stretching and yawning, getting to their feet. I thanked Rudy again.

'It's very kind of you,' I said.

'It's what it is,' he shrugged. 'Where I come from you help people if you can.'

Everyone set about restoring the room to some kind of order while Rudy disappeared into the kitchen to see what there was to eat. He emerged with mountains of toast, eggs and pancakes. It was a feast and we were all famished. After that, three of us decided to set off and check on the condition of the Birchaven. The sun glinted on the damp road as the ice melted. The sky was a brilliant blue. It all looked quite different from the previous night. The van was a forlorn sight. There was a dent in one side where it had wrapped around a tree and probably saved itself, and us, from falling down the mountain.

'Well, at least she's in one piece,' said Waldo, wandering around the vehicle. 'I guess that's a good thing.'

'You seriously drove up the mountain in this thing?' Rudy asked.

Waldo patted the side of the Birchaven. 'Nothing wrong with her. I had the whole thing rebuilt from the ground up.'

Rudy stared at him. 'Well, the obvious question is why?'

The question seemed to confound Waldo. 'Well, just because, man. You know?'

Rudy and I exchanged looks as Waldo got in behind the wheel.

'He loves his van,' I said.

'I guess he does.'

The engine started with some difficulty and we managed to manoeuvre it carefully back to the car park area in front of the hotel where we cleared a space with snow shovels. Everyone was overjoyed to see our transport was still intact and they rushed out to check on their instruments. Rudy watched us.

'So, you guys are touring, or what?'

'It's a little more complicated than that,' I said, going on to explain what had happened.

'And you think you're going to find this guy?'

I sighed, catching Shadia's eye. 'It's a bit of a long shot, but we're determined, yes.'

'Well, good for you.'

At some point Rudy went over to the upright piano and lifted the lid. He sat down and ran his fingers across the keys.

'If I don't play the old thing every couple of days or so it gets real mean. I'm afraid it will come after me, trap me in the hallway and beat me up or something.'

I don't think anyone, including myself, really knew what he was talking about. It didn't really matter. Rudy's fingers danced lightly back and forth along the keys.

'"Lush Life,"' nodded Kadugli.

'That's right. Duke Ellington and Billy Strayhorn.' Rudy switched to another number without blinking. 'Why don't you try one?'

So Kadugli sat down and had a go. Rudy nodded his approval.

'Monk. "Ruby, My Dear".'

They went on like this for a while, running through Monk and Mingus and then on, up and down the alphabet of jazz. They started out with familiar classics, but soon veered off into less well-known territory. We sat back and watched, occasionally contributing a thought, or a guess, sometimes right, usually wrong. I'd never seen

Kadugli enjoy himself so much. It was as if he had found some strange connection with this character that was Rudy Ventura.

'Not bad. Not bad at all,' grinned Rudy, looking around the room at us. 'So what do you play when you're not covering the classics?'

I became aware that everyone was looking at me to come up with some kind of explanation.

'Well, there are a range of influences on our music,' I began. 'In fact, you might say that we represent many of the traditions from different parts of our country. From Nubian chants going back thousands of years, to Merdoum, to Khashif wedding music. Love songs.'

'That's just the traditional stuff,' Hisham chipped in. 'But we listen to other music, of course. Arabic, African, Latin, jazz.'

'It's all connected,' said Kadugli. 'We just tap into it.'

'Let's just play something,' said John Wau impatiently. He set his guitar on his knee and began strumming away. Wad Mazaj picked up the dellouka and beat out a rhythm to accompany him. Then Rudy took his double bass from its case.

'Can I join in?'

'Sure,' everyone said.

The next couple of hours were some of the most extraordinary I have ever experienced. Rudy's range was vast. He seemed to be able to follow us without difficulty. He did a turn on the double bass, then produced an accordion that he strapped on and which began to wheeze and bellow and whine in his long, bony hands. We started to come together as, by turns, we chased after him and then he followed us. It was a curious and torturous route we created between us, but it also felt completely natural, not forced at all. The morning passed in a flash. We covered everything, from traditional old Sufi chants to blues and even rock and roll with a rendition of 'Dizzy Miss Lizzy'. We stopped for coffee and since there was a general consensus on the issue of hunger, Waldo volunteered to make sand-wiches. Shadia offered to help him. I tried to join in but ended up simply acting as waiter, carrying out plates while they laughed together like teenagers in the kitchen. The sun was still shining. I pulled out Gandoury's slip of paper and examined it. The others gathered round.

'When's the next date?'

'Tomorrow afternoon.' I handed the paper to Waldo. 'No way we can make that.'

We had already missed one venue thanks to the storm, so it seemed to make sense to cut along to the next on the list. Waldo pored over some maps on the counter.

'You know,' said Rudy, 'this break in the weather might not last. Probably makes sense to try and get off the mountain before night-fall.' He grinned, holding up his hands. 'Not that I'm trying to get rid of you or anything. This was fun.'

'You should come with us,' said Kadugli.

'But he's not one of us,' protested Wad Mazaj. 'He knows nothing about our tradition, our history. He's not one of the Kings.'

'You're talking about the old kings,' laughed Kadugli. 'This is something new. This is about music, not history. We're off the map. We're free. This is about us now.'

The discussion went back and forth, between the traditionalists and those who thought such things no longer mattered. Wad Mazaj snorted his disapproval, but John Wau was in favour. Two opposite poles. Rudy, who was a little lost once we switched to Arabic, watched us with a bemused look on his face.

'Look, guys, seriously. It's not a problem.'

'You should come,' said Shadia, deciding the issue. Nobody really objected. 'After all,' she went on, 'it's only for a couple of days.'

'Actually . . .' Waldo cleared his throat. 'Rudy and I were talking earlier. He knows a studio we could use in Baltimore.'

'A studio?' I said.

'Sure, we talked about it, remember? A chance to get this band down on tape.'

'But we don't have time,' I began. 'I mean, we would need days.'

'No, man.' Rudy was shaking his head. 'I mean, listen to you, you guys are the real deal. You can play. All you need is a few hours.'

'He has a point,' said Waldo. 'Some of the great jazz albums were cut in a couple of days.'

We looked at each other. I turned to Rudy.

'This studio is an actual possibility? I mean, we could use it?'

'Sure,' he nodded. 'They're friends of mine.'

'What about money? I mean, we don't have much.'

'We can figure that out. It's not a problem.'

'If we're going to try and get off this mountain we should get going,' said Waldo.

'You mean, we're leaving this beautiful paradise?' Alkanary sighed, looking around. 'Just as I was getting used to it.'

Chapter 31

At the Mall

The Roosevelt Diner was a brightly lit place with yellow walls and shiny red seats. Outside, the sky was streaked with purple and blue. The journey downhill had gone more smoothly than we had feared. A few hair-raising turns, but nothing too bad. Still, it was a relief to be back on flat ground, though nevertheless a shock to find ourselves in the real world again. I had no idea of the name of the town we were in. It felt as if we had been swallowed whole by the vastness of America. All the places had begun to look the same.

We gravitated towards a couple of booths close to the back that seemed to promise some shelter from curious eyes. We had already acquired the habits of fugitives: looking for exits, keeping our heads down, trying to appear inconspicuous, which, under the circumstances, was an absurd idea. We stood out like a herd of giraffes. The woman behind the counter had clearly seen her share of oddballs. Her eyes ranged over us as we settled down, but her face remained impassive. Through the serving hatch in the wall I could see the kitchen. The cook was a scruffy, unshaven man with large black hoops in his ears and a narrow beard that was knotted like a piece of string dangling from his chin. He looked big and muscular, and worried. He peered through the hatch at us, a cleaver in one hand.

'What'll it be?' the waitress asked, tapping her pencil against her pad. She had a faraway look in her eyes as though she saw right through us. I had a feeling we had chosen the wrong place.

'Does the special include bacon?' I asked.

She gave an audible hiss. 'We can take it off, but I can't lower the price.'

'I'll take it anyway.'

'Why not?' grumbled Wad Mazaj. 'You're already damned.'

'Stop it, both of you,' hissed Shadia. We had agreed to try not to speak Arabic to avoid drawing attention to ourselves. True enough, the waitress was now looking at us with renewed suspicion.

'I'll take the grilled cheese sandwich,' Shadia said quickly.

The others hummed and hawed, unable to make their minds up.

'This food is playing havoc with my digestion,' mumbled Uncle Maher. He wasn't the only one. The travelling and irregular hours seemed to be having a general effect. Everyone was tired and irritable. To prove the point, Wad Mazaj started voicing his doubts almost as soon as the waitress had left the table.

'What is happening to us?' he protested. 'I mean, what exactly are we doing, chasing around the country? For what?'

'What are you talking about?' I asked. 'I thought we were all agreed?'

'Yes but look at us.' He had a pained expression on his face. 'I'm tired of sleeping on the floor of a van. I'm not young. I can't deal with this. We have to give ourselves up,' he said. 'Before someone gets hurt.'

'If that's how you feel then perhaps we should take a vote,' I suggested.

'Always the democrat, teacher,' said John Wau.

'Well, you should know,' grumbled Wad Mazaj. 'You and your people voted yourselves out of the country.'

'It was a referendum,' sighed John. 'And we would not have voted out if *your* people had shown the slightest indication they wanted us to remain as equal citizens.'

'Oh, so it's our fault? We are to blame for you abandoning us?' Wad Mazaj was furious.

'Hey, hey! Cool it,' said Waldo. 'We don't need the attention, fellers.'

'Now is not the time for this,' I whispered.

'I just want to go home,' said Wad Mazaj. 'I want to go back to my life.'

'I thought you wanted to stay here,' I said.

'Not any more.' He shook his head. 'I'm just tired.'

'We're all tired,' said Uncle Maher. 'But we need to put things right.'

'We represent something,' Shadia said. 'We mean something to a lot of people. We have to remember that.'

'Good for you, girl,' muttered Alkanary.

'It's about pride, who we are and where we come from,' said John Wau.

'You think anyone cares about all that any more?' Wad Mazaj countered.

I tried to moderate.

'Is there something else you'd rather do?'

Wad Mazaj looked unsure of himself. 'Well, I just mean this wasn't what I had in mind. I mean, I just mean this isn't the America I expected.'

'What did you expect?'

'I don't know. I suppose, you know, things like Disneyland.'

This was greeted by a chuckle from Alkanary. 'Now the truth comes out.'

'You want to go to Disneyland?' Shadia asked.

'I'm just saying I heard about it.' Wad Mazaj looked a little sheepish. Shadia and I looked at one another.

'Is that alcohol?' As she passed by our table the waitress's sharp eyes had fixed on the miniature bottle of rum Alkanary was nursing. She seemed to have a secret store of them, no doubt taken from the hotel back in Washington. 'You're not allowed to drink in here. We don't have a licence.'

'Well, that solves one problem.' Alkanary struggled to get to her feet.

'You have to eat something, Aunty.'

'I'm fine, child. I'm not hungry anyway. I'll just go back to the bus and sleep.'

As she made her way uncertainly towards the door, Shadia turned to me.

'I'm worried about her. She's not complaining but I think all of this moving about is tough on her.'

'She'll be fine,' I said, trying to reassure Shadia. After all, there were other, more pressing things to worry about. Over her shoulder I watched the waitress lean through the serving hatch to consult with the cook, both of them staring in our direction. I just wanted to eat and get out of there. The others went back to arguing about the purpose of what we were doing. As it started to heat up I tried to tune out. I just wanted to be somewhere else, but people around us were beginning to take notice.

'Hey, fellers,' Waldo said in a low voice. 'Come on.'

'He's right,' I said. 'Now is not the time for this.' Other diners were already glancing at our table, nodding in our direction. As if to underline the point, when the waitress returned with our food she lingered after setting down the plates. An awkward smile transformed her heavily made up face into a garish mask.

'What language is that you're speaking?'

'It's Esperanto,' Rudy said brightly. 'We're in town for a convention.'

'What is that, some kind of Spanish?'

Rudy tried to explain, but she clearly didn't believe him. As the others began to eat, I turned to watch her. She walked past the serving hatch and disappeared through the doorway to the bathrooms.

When she came out the waitress straightened her uniform, glancing briefly in our direction before lowering her head and heading past us.

'I have a bad feeling about this place,' I said.

'What kind of bad feeling?' Shadia asked.

Before I could answer the swing door to the kitchen squeaked open and the cook appeared. He looked bigger somehow. His arms were muscular and covered in ink. There was a tattoo of a tear under his left eye. He nodded a greeting at Rudy.

'Hermano.' Rudy nodded back as the chef placed his big hands on the table and leaned forwards. 'I don't know what you've done. You don't look like terrorists to me. But esa perra has called the federales, so you better get lost.' He jerked his head in the direction of the bathroom door. 'There's an exit round the back. Use it.'

We all stared at him intently, trying to understand his words, partly in Spanish and the rest with a heavy accent. The cook rapped his knuckles on the table and then disappeared back inside the kitchen. We turned to Rudy for explanation.

'We need to move.'

'We should do this quietly,' Shadia said. 'Not everyone at once.'

No sooner had she spoken than everyone was on their feet, all moving in different directions at the same time.

'Just stay calm. Try to act naturally,' Shadia urged. Nobody was listening. Over her shoulder I could see the elderly couple in the next booth glancing back at us.

Shadia and I headed for the bathroom door. It led us into a dark corridor. I pushed open the door to my right and overheard a voice speaking in a low whisper.

'They're here! I'm telling you. All of them. The terrorists. Which ones? The ones on television, of course.'

Shadia dragged me backwards by my arm. 'This way.'

At the end of the corridor there was an emergency exit. I pushed the bar slowly, half expecting to hear an alarm, then we were out into an alleyway behind the diner. We walked along to the end. In the street ahead I saw flashing lights passing by. There were sirens in the distance.

'We can't stay here,' Shadia said, grabbing my hand and tugging me along. We ran across to the other side and went around the corner.

'Try to walk slowly,' said Shadia. 'And stop looking back, you're drawing attention to us.'

I kept quiet and did as I was told. My thoughts were in turmoil. Half of me longed to go back and confront the police. To tell them they were mistaken and explain that we had done nothing wrong. The other half wanted to just disappear in a puff of smoke.

'In here.' Shadia led me through an open doorway into a blast of warm air. I heard soft music playing lightly all around. There were birds singing somewhere and what looked like trees.

'What is this place?' Suddenly everything in America seemed filled with menace.

'This is good,' she reassured me.

'Yes, but what is it?' The bird sounds were coming from small speakers hanging in the air. I looked up and saw people rising and falling, gliding through the air on escalators. Glass-sided lifts shot up and down, left and right. There were people everywhere.

'It's a shopping mall.' Shadia cocked her head. 'What's the matter with you?'

'Nothing. I just never saw anything like it.'

'Seriously?' She rolled her eyes and marched ahead. I hurried along behind, trying to take it all in.

People were laughing and talking, carrying parcels and bags. Some dragged reluctant children along. They wandered by in streams, in bunches, in waves, as if in the grip of some kind of fever, or trapped in a dream. We came down a short ramp to a large open area. In the middle of this a huge tree had been placed. It rose up through the middle of the building and was decorated with all kinds of shiny coloured strips of flashing coloured lights. At the top of it was a huge glowing star. The branches were draped with shiny tinsel and glowing figures. There were deer and jolly round men in red. I knew what Christmas was, in principle, but I'd just never seen it celebrated like this.

'Just try to act naturally,' said Shadia, tucking her arm through mine. 'Pretend we are shopping like everyone else.'

'I can't think of anything more unnatural.'

'Ya Allah, have you been living in a cave?' She squinted at me. 'Just play along. You'll be fine.' She gave my arm a squeeze.

'People really come here to enjoy themselves?'

'Don't get high and mighty about it. It's a shopping mall. People come here to shop.'

Well, there was no doubting that. There were shops selling everything: clothes and brightly coloured toys, sports equipment, appliances, watches, shoes, spectacles. Above all, food. I saw ice cream and pizza, tacos and burgers. A lady handed me a paper, offering me a massage in a chair. I began to see why people seemed to be in a state of anxiety; so many decisions to make, so many possibilities. I couldn't remember ever having gone shopping as such. I mean, obviously, if I needed a new shirt I would go and find one, but that wasn't quite the same. This was shopping as an Olympic sport.

'Your problem is that you've never been shopping for something that you didn't need.'

'Why would I shop for something I didn't need?'

'There doesn't always have to be a reason for everything.'

'Then why do it?'

'Because it makes you feel good.' She spoke as if explaining the concept of gravity to a child.

We arrived at a large open space; a circular platform suspended between floors. The whole thing, top and bottom, gleamed with glass and light. There was an enormous waterfall that cascaded down two floors from high up close to the glass dome overhead.

'Amazing,' I murmured.

'There is a mall in Dubai where they have penguins.'

'What for?' I asked, mystified.

'No reason,' she shrugged. 'It's just funny.'

'How do the penguins feel about it?'

'I don't know,' she laughed. 'I never asked them.' She was shaking her head. 'Did anyone ever tell you that you take things too seriously?'

'I do?'

'You need to relax. Life is about here and now, not about whatever lessons you can learn from some stuffy book by an old Englishman who would not even know of your existence if you had lived in the same time.'

'You can learn a lot from literature.' I sniffed, trying to rally my own defence.

'Really, like what? Give me an example.'

'Well, just things. You know, about life, about love.'

'Love, really?' She stopped laughing.

'Why? What did I say?'

'Maalish, it's not important.' She dismissed the idea. 'Let's get a coffee or something.'

'How long do you think we should stay in here?' I asked, as we stepped onto an escalator and rose smoothly up to the next level. Looking around me, I wondered if this was what my life would be like if I stayed on here.

'Just until we're sure nobody is following us. What are you smiling about?'

I hesitated. 'I was thinking that if we lived here, we could do this every week.'

'We?'

Shadia turned away and I followed her around the mezzanine trying to look inconspicuous. It was easy to be lulled into a sense of ease by such places. It was like a dream, where everything was within reach, and available, only of course it wasn't. A girl in a bright red jacket and hat with matching short skirt held out a basket full of chocolates shaped like deer.

'Happy Christmas!' she smiled.

'And to you!' I said, helping myself before Shadia dragged me away. 'What? What is it?'

'You're enjoying yourself too much.'

'It's just chocolate. Here, I took one for you.'

'It's not the chocolate.'

'I really don't think I'll ever understand you.'

'Nobody asked you to. Understand me, I mean.' She held out a hand. 'Give me some money.' She nodded over her shoulder at a coffee stand.

Drinking coffee from paper cups, leaning on the railing, looking down at the centre of the mall, I felt as if we were in a movie of our own making. For a brief moment I felt I was an American.

There were three different levels and we were on the uppermost. From up there the mall felt like a place of pilgrimage, a temple to which people came to worship. On one side was a bank of lifts with glass walls. People inside pointed out excitedly as they were shot smoothly and silently through the air. Down below the crowds milled about like small insects. It seemed so incredible. So many strangers. That's when I saw her. It was only the briefest of glimpses. An upturned face. I knew instinctively that I had seen it before. I just couldn't remember where.

Then it came to me. I was frozen in place, watching the figure rising to the top of the escalator just below us. I grabbed Shadia's arm and tugged.

'What is it?'

'That woman.'

'Haven't you had enough of staring at women today?' she frowned.

'No, no, not a woman. *That* woman.' She followed my finger. 'I've seen her before.'

'I don't see anybody.'

The woman had stepped off the escalator and disappeared, vanishing into the crowd. I moved left and right. I couldn't see her any more.

'There.' I pointed.

The woman had reappeared, circling around the floor below. A tall, striking woman with Latin American features, wearing a lime green jumpsuit and high heels.

'Don't you recognise her? She was at the hotel in Washington. She worked there.'

Shadia reared back. 'Are you serious?'

'Don't you remember? She was always in the lobby.'

'I don't know, maybe I just don't spend as much time as you do studying women.'

I ignored that. 'I'm sure of it,' I said. Pushing in front of a large family, I dragged Shadia onto the escalator going down. 'Sorry,' I apologised. 'Sorry.' They glared at me and said something I couldn't catch that I think might have been Spanish, but we were moving down the stairs at a fast pace.

'You must be mistaken.' Shadia was trying to drag me back. 'It makes no sense. Why would she be here?'

'Come on, we're going to lose her.' I urged her to move.

'What if you're wrong?'

'I'm not wrong.'

Ahead of us the woman was walking with purpose along the upper level just ahead of us. At the end of the corridor the floor opened onto a circle of restaurants and cafés. We held back to observe as the woman approached a figure seated at one of the tables. At first, we could not see who it was because he had his back to us and there was another large Christmas tree in the way. It was only when we edged around that we saw who it was.

'Is that who I think it is?' Shadia asked.

'It's Suleiman Gandoury,' I whispered. 'We've found him.'

'What's he doing with that woman?'

'I don't know. They must be in this together somehow, but it would explain the phone call. Ms DeHaviland and the ICE agents told us the caller was a woman.'

'We need to speak to him, right now.' Shadia moved to step forward. I put out a hand to stop her.

'Wait!'

'What?'

'We should follow him, find out where he's staying, and then we should get the others.'

Shadia was shaking her head. 'We don't have time for that. And the others might already be captured, remember?'

I was still in shock. I could hardly believe that Suleiman Gandoury was sitting there as clear as day. He was wearing a tracksuit and eating a hamburger. The woman sat down opposite him and the two began to talk. They looked like any other couple out for a day's shopping.

'I don't know,' I said. 'What if he makes a run for it?'

'Are you serious?' Shadia stared at me. 'After everything that's happened? I want to hear what he's got to say for himself. We came all this way because of him. He needs to know that what he did was wrong.'

All of which was true, of course, but it didn't make me feel any better about the idea.

'We can do this, Rushdy. Trust me. We can do it.'

Gandoury didn't see us at first because we approached from the other side. I kept the tree between us for as long as I could. When we emerged, it was into the gaze of the woman. Now that I saw her close up, I saw that she had dyed her hair. Now she had long blonde streaks in it. I saw her eyes widen as she recognised us and she leaned forward to touch Gandoury on the arm. It was too late. He looked up as I stepped in front of him.

Chapter 32

¡Ayúdame!

'Hello, Suleiman,' I said.

The round table was made of some kind of plastic designed to look like wood. It was strewn with the remains of a meal in Styrofoam boxes and bright paper. To give him credit, Gandoury didn't bat an eyelid.

'Ah, ahlan, our young friends. Marhaba, welcome.' He stretched his arms expansively. 'Please, join us.'

'You don't seem surprised to see us,' I said, slipping onto the seat opposite him.

'Well, I suppose I knew there was always a possibility we might run into one another.'

'How can you sit there so calmly?' Shadia had remained standing. She leaned down to thump the table. 'You stole our money. You tarnished our reputation.'

Gandoury smiled at that. 'That sounds very grand. Please, I'm just a humble servant.'

'What?' Shadia retorted. 'Who gave you the right to set up a tour for us?'

'Everything I've done, I've done for you.' Gandoury's smile broadened. 'It may not seem that way, but when I explain, you'll see I was right.'

'Oh, please!' Shadia snorted.

'This was never about us,' I said. 'You planned this all along. It was about the money.'

Gandoury waved the suggestion aside. 'No, no. Please. There are groups that would kill for this kind of exposure.'

'You're saying what, that this was some kind of publicity stunt?' Shadia asked.

'You have to admit, it's working pretty well.' Gandoury was all smiles.

'You're forgetting something,' I reminded him. 'Nobody gave you permission to set up a tour. Uncle Maher turned down your offer. I was there.'

'People change their minds. All the time. He accepted my offer of financial support for outfits and instruments, remember? I thought he would come around. And once you were here, what's the harm?'

'I can't believe we're listening to this,' Shadia said.

'Admit it, Gandoury, you had no intention of getting us to play. We wouldn't even know where you had booked us if I hadn't kept that sheet of paper.'

'An oversight on my part.' Gandoury shrugged his shoulders. 'But now that you're here, it's even better.'

'I can't believe this. What about her?' Shadia pointed at the woman.

'Esmeralda?' He stretched out a hand towards the woman. 'She and I, well, love is a mystery, is it not? You can understand. We plan to start a life together.'

'Together?' echoed Shadia. 'Excuse me while I vomit. You set these venues up. You took money from them in our name.' Her voice was growing louder. We were beginning to draw attention from the people around us.

'If you're talking about me, I think we should speak English,' said the woman named Esmeralda. Her eyelids were painted the colour of pistachios, perhaps to match her jumpsuit.

'Now, Esmeralda, please,' Gandoury smiled. 'Let me deal with this.

Look,' he said, studying us both for a moment. 'The fact is I can't go home. I'm too close to the men who have been in power all these years, and their time is up.' He chose his words cautiously, watching us closely. 'The president is wanted by the International Criminal Court.' The thin mouth twisted in distaste. 'I don't want to be there when it ends.'

'So that's what all this is about?' I said. 'You running from a sinking ship?'

'I'm just trying to do the best I can.' Gandoury spread his hands wide. A paragon of humility. You had to give him his due, he could talk his way out of anything. 'Look at me. Does it look as though I am living in luxury? Of course not. I am eating simple food in a humble place. Money is not everything. We have to make sacrifices for the things we believe in.'

'You're a crook,' Shadia shouted. 'You betrayed our trust. You should be ashamed!'

'Me?' Gandoury looked confused. 'All I'm trying to do is make a fresh start,' he said. 'What I don't understand is you. You're young. This is a chance to begin anew. The two of you. People back home would kill for this opportunity.'

'I've heard enough,' I said. 'We should get moving. You too.'

'Come on, it's not all that bad,' he smiled. 'Look at this big charity concert they are planning for you. Such a line-up of celebrities. I admit, I'm a little envious I can't be there myself.'

Now I was confused. 'What are you talking about? What concert?'

'I've heard enough,' Shadia said. 'Let's go.'

'Really? Where are we going?' Gandoury asked.

'We're going to find the others, and then we're going to give ourselves up to the authorities.'

'Well, forgive me, but I don't think so.' Gandoury was smiling as he got to his feet. 'It's been nice talking to you, my youthful friends, but I am afraid Esmeralda and I must be going. Good luck with your sad lives over there. I shall think of you. Not often, but once in a while.'

'Now, hold on. You're not going anywhere.'

As I stood up to block his path, Esmeralda, to my surprise, threw herself over me and began screaming. Some of it was in Spanish and all of it was in a very high-pitched voice and quite unintelligible. We stumbled back and fell against a table.

'¡Maldita sea! Help me somebody! He's trying to steal my purse!'

Around us people leapt to their feet as we thumped into a large trash container that tipped over, taking both of us down with it.

'¡Ayudame, por favor!' she wailed. She carried on screaming in Spanish very loudly. Two large Latino men dressed in workmen's clothes started coming towards us.

'Hold him till the guards arrive,' someone shouted.

'Someone call the cops!' a white-haired lady yelled.

Shadia rushed in and managed to drag me to my feet, giving Esmarelda a shove that sent her sprawling into the arms of the two workmen. I looked around for Gandoury, but in the confusion he had vanished.

'We have to go,' Shadia yelled, grabbing my arm to pull me along. Across the other side of the rotunda I could see more men in uniform coming in our direction. Since we had no real idea of the orientation of this mall or even a proper sense of where we were running to, the next few minutes passed in a blur. We ran through stores, up and down moving staircases and along corridors. There seemed to be guards approaching from every direction. In the end we found an emergency exit tucked into a corner behind a stand shaped like a giant hotdog and we crashed through it without hesitation. Then we were down the stairs and into a freezing cold alleyway with ice hanging down the walls in sheets. We ran to the end of it. I looked left and saw guards outside the mall entrance talking into their radios. I grabbed Shadia's hand, turned right, and ran.

Chapter 33

Doctor John

It was dark by the time we managed to get back to the Birchaven. Somehow the police had moved on and clearly didn't know what kind of vehicle we were travelling in. The others jumped when I opened the door.

'Where have you been?' Hisham asked. They were all on edge, sitting there in the shadows.

'Good to see you, man.' Waldo greeted me with a hug. 'Everyone's a little jumpy. This place was crawling with cops.'

By some miracle they had all avoided being captured, but the experience had scared them.

'This is crazy,' Wad Mazaj said. 'Running around like criminals.'

'I'm too old for this,' agreed Uncle Maher.

'We are lucky nobody was hurt,' summarised John Wau soberly.

Waldo tapped me on the shoulder. 'You'd better take a peek at the old lady; she's not looking too good.'

Shadia rushed through to the back with the rest of us close behind. Alkanary was sitting up on the bed, her back propped against the wall. She was moaning softly; her eyes were closed and she looked terrible. Small and frail, she seemed to have shrunk even more. Shadia sat down beside her.

'Is that you?' she groaned. 'Where have you been?'

'It's me, Aunty. I'm here now,' she said, before turning to me. 'We have to get her to a doctor,' she said, patting her hand.

'A doctor?' John Wau was hovering in the doorway. 'What's wrong with her?' The others were crowding into the narrow space behind him.

'Please,' I said, trying to urge them back. 'She needs air. There's no sense in everyone being in here.'

'How are we going to find a doctor?' Shadia asked. I turned to Waldo.

'Is there any way we can get her to a doctor without alerting the authorities?'

'I don't know,' said Waldo, stroking his beard. 'It's going to be risky.'

'Maybe I can help,' said John Wau, who kept getting in the way. I ignored him.

'I used to know a doctor,' said Rudy from further down, 'but that was way back.'

'Where?' I asked. 'I mean, maybe there's a chance.'

'Well, actually, it was in prison in New Mexico.'

'How does that help?'

'I didn't say it would help.' Rudy was studying the ceiling. 'I just, you know, said I knew a doctor. Whatever.' He shrugged and wandered off. I bumped into John Wau again as I turned.

'Please, John, we have to give her room. She needs a doctor.'

'That's what I'm trying to tell you.' He was staring at me as if I was an idiot. 'I am a doctor.'

'What are you talking about? You mean, a doctor, doctor?'

'Unless you know of some other kind.' He rolled his eyes. 'Oh, you're thinking what, witch doctor? Leopard skins and potions? Animal sacrifices, that sort of thing?'

'How can you be a doctor?'

'I don't know, I think it might have something to do with the years I spent in medical school.'

266

'Sure, okay, I get it. What I mean is, why did I not know that? Why didn't you say?'

'What was I supposed to say?' John Wau shrugged. 'Some people are uncomfortable with the idea, for some reason. I can't think why. So, do you mind?'

I stepped aside and he edged past me into the room. He leaned over the bed and started doing exactly what a doctor would do, taking her pulse, examining her pupils. I was still trying to get used to the idea.

'Is she on any kind of medication?'

Shadia produced a bag full of pills and John Wau went through them carefully.

'Okay. Any idea how much she has been drinking?'

'You know how she is.' Shadia shook her head helplessly. 'It's impossible to keep track.'

'Well, that has to stop. And she should eat something.' He straightened up and turned to face me. I was still staring at him in awe. 'You can close your mouth now.'

'Just tell us what you need,' I said.

'Can we stop at a pharmacy? In the meantime, get her to drink something without alcohol in it,' he said to Shadia. 'You should stay with her. Let me know if there is any change.'

We helped to make Alkanary comfortable and then moved out of the bedroom into the living area. I turned to John Wau.

'Look, I'm sorry. I really didn't know.'

'It's all right. I understand.' He sat down at the table and produced a pair of reading glasses from his pocket. Also something I hadn't seen before. He spoke without looking up. 'You were brought up that way, to look down on people like me. I get that.' He looked up at me for a moment before waving the subject aside. 'It's not important.'

Rudy leaned over and tapped the paper John was writing on.

'You're not going to get those things without a prescription.'

'No?' John Wau looked up at him.

'No.' Rudy shook his head adamantly. 'But hey, this is America. We're addicted to opiates. You can get anything you need in any major city.'

'Okay,' nodded John Wau. 'America.'

'You'd better believe it, buddy. Just hand it to me.'

I handed Rudy some of our rapidly diminishing cash and he disappeared out through the door without another word. We sat there for almost an hour before he returned bearing, to our surprise, everything we had asked for.

Waldo whistled in admiration. 'Without so much as a prescription to show for it.'

It didn't take us long to get out of town, racing along a slick wet road. In the distance the sun was setting. A red band of light stretched across the horizon ahead. While Waldo drove, we squeezed around the table in the back to reassess our situation.

'We have something to tell you,' Shadia began. She glanced at me and I nodded for her to continue. 'When we were in the mall, we saw someone.'

'Who?' asked Uncle Maher. 'Who did you see?'

'Suleiman Gandoury.' I sat down beside Shadia. She shifted over to give me room.

'Gandoury, here? So, it's true?' Uncle Maher was shocked. 'I can't actually believe he would do such a thing.'

'That's why we're here, remember?' Hisham said, with his usual tact.

'I know, but it's one thing to entertain an idea, but quite another to have it confirmed. He was always so courteous to me.'

I signalled to Hisham to keep quiet, and to his credit he did.

'We saw him in the mall,' I went on. 'We went after him but he escaped.'

'How?' Wad Mazaj was outraged.

'He had a woman with him,' Shadia explained. 'From the hotel. She made a scene and we had to leave quickly.'

'So, this is good, right?' said Rudy, when it had been explained. 'I mean, you're on his trail.'

Which was true. The question was, what would he do now? Where would he go?

Uncle Maher was still having trouble taking it in. 'Why would he do that?'

'It looks like he has his own plan,' Shadia said. 'He intends to stay in this country, and this is his way of picking up some extra cash.'

'I have to admit,' Uncle Maher said, 'I never really liked the man.'

'Well, he's been going around picking up money on our behalf,' said Hisham, who had remained silent for as long as he could. 'This is our chance. We have to catch him.'

'I agree,' I said. 'We're close now.'

Uncle Maher sounded his frustration in a string of obscenities the like of which none of us had ever heard from him before. 'All the stress he's caused us. If I ever get my hands on him I will personally strangle the son of a bitch myself.' He sat back, oblivious to the look of shock on our faces. 'Take us to the next venue. The sooner we get our hands on him, the better.'

'We still have a recording to make,' John Wau pointed out. 'Right, Rudy?'

Rudy bobbed his head. 'Sure, not a problem. Just got to make a few calls.'

'There's one other thing,' I said, glancing at Shadia. 'Gandoury mentioned a concert. Some kind of charity event. He said it was big.'

'He said we were involved,' Shadia added.

'That can't be right,' frowned Uncle Maher. 'We know nothing about such a thing.'

'I was going to look online,' said Shadia. 'I just haven't had a moment.'

'Okay, then that's agreed. We go on to the next venue, catch Gandoury and then make the recording.' There were no objections and so we drove on. It took a while to find the venue, which was quite far out of town. I thought of how, just a short while ago, all I knew of the world was gleaned from books and films. Now I felt I was truly inside it, seeing more than I could possibly take in. I felt the urge to describe what I saw, to write it down and give my own account of the world the way the old travellers and writers of geographies once did. Al Kindi, Al Idrisi and all the other dead voyagers who had left their mark on history. All my life I had lived under the tyranny of the words of others. Perhaps it was my turn at last.

Chapter 34

The Girl in the White Dress

A large woman with purple lipstick appeared alongside the driver's window. She wore a baseball cap that was balanced on top of her afro and was waving an American flag frantically.

'You can't park here, sir,' she said, peering past Waldo at the rest of us in the back. 'This is a private function.'

'We're the band,' I said brightly.

'Yeah, man,' Waldo chimed in. 'We're the band.'

'The band?' For a second she glared at Waldo as if he were mad then the darkness lifted and a gap-toothed smile snapped her features up like a sunblind. 'Ohmygod, we've been waiting for you!' She started flapping the flag frantically, as if it had just caught fire. 'It's the band! The band! We have to clear a way through. And someone call Shakeela. Tell her she can stop having a heart attack.' Then the Birchaven was surrounded by smiling people waving us through.

'What's the matter with them?' asked Shadia.

'I don't know,' I replied, as mystified as she was.

Our escort followed along, hands on the sides of the vehicle, guiding us to a spot behind an enormous pyramid-shaped building. The roof was made of glass that came together against a sky split by bands of turquoise and red. At the apex stood an enormous golden cross that glinted in the last rays of the setting sun. A large open doorway beckoned, beneath a sign that read; 'Welcome to the Buttercup Multifaith Community Center – Where All Faiths Are Respected.'

'Is this a church?' Wad Mazaj asked suspiciously.

'No,' Shadia and I said together. 'It's not a church.'

He settled back but looked unconvinced.

We were led into the building through a side entrance and found ourselves in a huge hall where about a hundred tables were spread out. An army of helpers was busy covering the tables with cloths and setting out plates and glasses, knives and forks, decorating them with paper bunting and flowers.

'That must be the happy couple,' said John Wau, pointing. 'He looks like one of us.'

The banner strung high on one wall read, Congratulations, Mattie and Tiberius. Beneath the banner were two enormous photographs. The first showed a white woman with a round face and prominent front teeth. She looked around ten years older than the man next to her who must have been in his twenties and looked very much like he could have been from South Sudan.

'I don't get it,' Waldo said. 'Is this a Jewish wedding?'

'Jewish?' echoed Uncle Maher. 'Did he say Jewish?'

'Ya Allah,' sighed Wad Mazaj. 'Can this get any worse?'

'Why do you say that?' I didn't quite follow. Waldo pointed out some men wearing hats and boys with skullcaps on.

'We're playing for Jews now?' Uncle Maher went on, still in the dark.

'It's all right, Ammu, I'm sure there's an explanation.'

'Actually, I think I'm half-Jewish,' said Waldo.

'Which half?' Hisham asked.

'I'm not sure.'

'Has it come to this?' Uncle Maher seemed beside himself.

'There's nothing wrong with playing for Jews,' Shadia explained. 'It's no different than playing for any other kind of American.' Uncle Maher looked unconvinced.

'Accept it, Ammu,' I said, patting him on the back. 'We're displaced now. We have to accept one another.'

A girl of about eleven stepped into my path. She was wearing a long white dress and her hair had flowers in it. She stared accusingly at us.

'You're the ones on television, right?'

'On television?' I asked.

'The ones the FBI are looking for?'

'No,' I said, trying to move past her. 'That's not us.'

'Yes, it is.' She sidestepped to block me again.

'You're mistaken,' I smiled. 'We're the Jewish band.'

'Nice one,' murmured Shadia in my ear.

'Thank god you arrived.' The girl was swept aside as a large man came towards us arms outstretched. 'You are a sight for sore eyes. I am Samuel Isaacson. Welcome, welcome!' A woman walked behind him. A little younger than him, she was in her forties. Her face was stretched taut with fatigue and an uncomfortable smile.

'My wife, Judith. My dear,' he turned to her, clutching her by shoulders with excitement. 'These are our Falasha musicians.'

'Falasha?' Uncle Maher almost choked on his tongue. 'Did he say, Falasha?'

'Actually . . .' I began, but Shadia elbowed me in the side. I grasped the man's hand in both of mine and pumped it up and down. 'We are honoured to be here, sir.'

'I don't understand anything any more,' Uncle Maher muttered to himself. 'Are we Jewish?'

'We were getting worried.' Mr Isaacson was wearing a long-sleeved shirt with a frilly front that was drenched with sweat. 'Your manager came by earlier to collect the final fee, but then he had to leave in a hurry. It's a bit confusing.'

'Yes, it is,' I said.

'Who's the handsome groom?' asked Shadia, nodding at the portraits.

Isaacson turned to look up. 'Tiberius is a wonderful young man. It has been a huge challenge for him. His story is one of courage in the face of adversity. Well, I don't need to lecture you on that.' He broke off, shaking his head in incomprehension. 'That he has survived at all is a miracle. Now he is in America and he has chosen to take the huge step of converting to our faith. I can't tell you how much I admire him.'

'Is he saying we have to convert?' Uncle Maher cupped a hand to his ear. Shadia tried to reassure him.

I caught sight of the little girl in the white dress again. She was standing on the far side of the hall talking to somebody wearing a uniform and pointing in our direction.

'I have a bad feeling about her,' I said.

Shadia looked over and frowned at me. 'She's just a little girl.'

'Where should we go?' I asked. Mr Isaacson had paused to attend to his phone. He waved someone forward.

'He'll take care of you.'

A tall boy of about seventeen with hair and a wispy beard the colour of a carrot, over which a yarmulke rested, had come over.

'Hi,' he said, raising a hand. 'I'm Kermit. Follow me.'

'Do we have to play?' Wad Mazaj asked. 'Can't we just get on our way?'

'We can't just leave now,' John Wau said.

'Why not?'

'Because he's one of us. Tiberius. That's why we're here.'

We brought in our instruments and did microphone checks. Then Kermit took us down below the stage to a room where we could wait our turn. A long table covered in food and drink lifted everyone's spirits.

'Ah, good,' said Uncle Maher. 'I'm starving.'

'It's all Kosher,' said Kermit with a smile.

Uncle Maher muttered to himself. But hunger overcame his reluctance, and he and Wad Mazaj went over to examine the food. Kermit was still there, smiling.

'So, you're like Falashas, right?' I smiled back at him but said nothing. 'Really cool, that whole Ethiopian connection? Solomon and Sheba.' He would have continued in this vein, I feared, but thankfully his telephone rang and he disappeared out through the doorway. Exhausted, I sank down onto an orange sofa and closed my eyes.

'Do you think Gandoury planned this just to torture us?' Hisham asked.

'I wouldn't put it past him,' I sighed.

'Here,' Shadia held out a sandwich.

'What is it?'

'No idea, but it tastes all right.' She shrugged her shoulders. 'Kosher and halal is more or less the same, right?'

I squinted at her. 'I'm not sure you'll get away with that.'

'Well, that's what I told them.' She jerked a thumb in the direction of Uncle Maher and the others, who were now tucking in enthusiastically.

'If it's meant well . . .'

She laughed. A ripple of joyous, liberated sound.

There was a television set high on the wall of the room and Kadugli was pointing at it.

'Isn't that us?'

We all turned our attention to the little screen. It was fairly old and the image on it was rather fuzzy, but I could make out the publicity photo from the brochure at the Kennedy Center.

'They're talking about the concert,' said Kadugli. 'Quiet everyone.'

On the little screen a new series of images had appeared, of people, some of whom looked familiar, others not. The headline along the bottom read, 'Charity Concert for Asylum-Seeking Musicians'.

'That's Beyoncé,' said John Wau. And he was right, it was. Someone managed to find a way of turning up the volume. A man who looked vaguely familiar, wearing sunglasses, was also addressing the issue.

'These are artists whose lives are in danger. We have to ask ourselves what we stand for.'

'John Legend,' murmured Shadia behind me. 'And that's Cardi B.'

We cut back to the studio and the presenters, a blonde woman and a very excited young man with dreadlocks. 'Musicians have come together to raise support not just for the Kamanga Kings, but for artists everywhere.'

'It's true, Jason. This has to be seen as some kind of reaction to the current administration, whose hard line on migration has been the focus of a lot of debate.'

'Right,' agreed Jason. 'This is the artists taking a stand. And what an incredible line-up. Everyone who is anyone is going to be there.' He rattled off a series of names, some of which were familiar, before making his final point. 'The one question on everyone's minds is, where are the Kamanga Kings?'

The sound faded as we tried to take stock. 'It's what Gandoury was talking about,' Shadia said. 'A concert for our benefit.'

'But why?' Uncle Maher wanted to know. 'Why should they care about us?'

'Maybe it's a trap,' said Wad Mazaj.

That started another discussion. I moved away from the group and went over to sit down in the corner by myself. I had to clear my head.

'What do we do?' I asked, thinking aloud. 'If we go there we'll be surrendering ourselves.'

'Maybe it's genuine,' said Hisham. 'They could just like our music.'

'It doesn't matter. They'll never let us play,' said John Wau.

'They believe in us,' Hisham went on. 'This is a proper chance at hitting the big time.'

'Maybe this is our best way of bringing an end to this.'

Kadugli had been silent so far and was sitting by himself in another corner, drinking from a plastic cup. I saw him reach for the bottle of Jack Daniels that was standing on the table next to him. I was surprised. I had never seen him drink. Neither had anyone else, apparently, judging by the silence that fell over the group.

'We go out in a blaze of glory. One final concert, this time for all the world to see.'

I looked at Shadia. She too was mystified by this change in character. I got up and went over to him. His eyes were bloodshot and unfocussed. I wondered how much he had had to drink.

'What's going on?' I asked Kadugli.

'Everything has to come to an end, right?' he laughed, before tilting the cup and drinking deeply.

I was trying to think what to do when a man appeared in the doorway.

'Look who's here,' said John Wau. 'It's the lucky man.'

We all turned to stare at the newcomer. He was tall and handsome in a smart grey suit, with long tails at the back and a top hat, which he held under his arm. He looked rather like an extra who had stepped from a production of *David Copperfield*. We stared at him until he gave an awkward little wave.

'Salaam aleikum.'

'Tiberius,' said Shadia, going up and shaking his hand. 'Congratulations,' she said in English.

'Thanks.' He bowed his head and smiled. 'This is a really big day. I don't know how to explain it.' He looked around at us. 'I'm happy you could be here. Also, my apologies, I may have twisted your story a little bit to fit the family's interests.' He grinned, displaying the kind of charm that had no doubt led him to where he was today.

'Don't worry about it,' said Hisham. 'We're proud to be here.'

'Thank you,' said Tiberius again.

'How long have you been in this country?' I asked.

His eyes darted round wildly. 'About five years. They saved me, you know. I was just a kid in a refugee camp, trying to survive. I had lost my family. The whole village was destroyed, razed to the ground by those bastards in Khartoum.' He looked me in the eye. 'I don't mean any offence. When I landed here I knew nothing. The Isaacsons picked me up from the dirt and gave me a life. It's a dream come true.'

The way his voice wavered suggested he wasn't quite sure what kind of a dream he was in, nor whether he was going to wake up. He kept switching to English, which he spoke in a stilted, self-conscious way. His story was a reminder of how neglectful we had been. The war in the South had gone on for years and we never gave it a thought. People had lost their lives, their homes, their loved ones. We in the north never saw it, save for those who were unlucky enough to be drafted into the army. It had been too far away to affect us. We stood in respectful silence as Tiberius carried on with his testimony to a broken nation.

'They bombed us. I was ten years old. How we survived I don't know. We walked for weeks, living off berries and roots, anything we could find. Many of us died. Eventually we crossed the border to Ethiopia and for the next seven years that's where I stayed. Hell on earth. Then one day Ruben turns up. I didn't know who he was, but he's about to become my brother-in-law now.'

'Mabrouk.' Shadia reached out to squeeze his arm. 'Congratulations.'

'You know the funny thing? I could do so much for my people, they said. So now I travel up and down the country, telling my story. Sometimes there are hundreds, thousands of people, listening to me. When we were walking, all those years ago, sleeping at night listening to the sounds of the animals, we thought the world had forgotten us, but now, can you imagine? They are all listening to my story.'

'I'm happy for you,' I said. Even as I spoke the words I realised how they clashed with the sadness in him. I had the feeling that a part of him had been lost.

'I became a messiah. It sounds strange, but it's true. People wanted to touch me, just to see if I was real. They showered me with money, as if by giving it to me they would become better people. I became a reflection of their own goodness.'

It sounded like a confession. It was as though in us he had finally found people who could understand him. He hadn't come here to tell us his story, he had come for our approval.

'And now you're getting married. You have a new family.'

'Yes.' He sighed heavily. 'Mattie is a good woman and very coura-geous. They tell me I am one of them.' His eyes came up to meet mine. 'Even though we all know that's not true.'

John Wau clapped him on the back. 'Be strong, brother.'

I wanted to ask him about Gandoury, and how he had set up the concert, but just at that moment the door flew open and Waldo stood there shaking.

'Guys! Uh, we have to go, right now!'

'What is happening?' Uncle Maher asked, still holding a plate of food. I could already hear the sirens. The little girl in the white dress. I suspected she had managed to convince someone she had seen us before.

'What's going on?' Tiberius asked.

'We have to leave,' Shadia said. 'Unfortunately, I don't think we'll be able to play for you.'

'Is there another way out of here?' John Wau asked.

'I can show you,' said Tiberius.

As we started for the stage door, Uncle Maher grabbed my arm. 'Our instruments are still on stage.'

'We have to leave them,' I said.

His fingers dug into my flesh. 'Leave them? Are you mad?'

I felt torn. 'We can't risk it.' I hustled him along ahead of me.

'I'm getting too old for all this running about,' Uncle Maher groaned.

We followed Tiberius out of the room and down a corridor through the basement. I guessed we were underneath the great hall. Above our heads, heating and water pipes snaked through the building. I could hear the rumble of voices and the croak of an announcement being made over a microphone, followed by more clamour. We finally reached a wide double door that led to a ramp and a loading bay.

'Wait a second.' Shadia clutched my arm. 'Where's Wad Mazaj?'

We looked back. I remembered him wandering off to look for a toilet. Now he was nowhere to be seen.

'We can't wait,' I said. 'We have to go.'

Tiberius looked a little lost when I shook his hand. The stiff collar had broken free and now stuck awkwardly up under his chin like the wing of a bird he had stuffed down his shirt. I wanted to say something, but I couldn't really think what. I held out my hand.

'Good luck with everything.'

'Come with us,' John Wau said. 'Just leave all of this behind and come.'

'I can't,' Tiberius smiled. 'I'd love to, but it would be wrong.'

'You'll be all right,' Shadia said, touching his shoulder. He smiled and nodded as though he didn't quite believe it.

Then he was gone and we were moving up the ramp. Waldo and Rudy had gone to bring the Birchaven round. When they arrived we climbed in quickly and Waldo reversed slowly round the side of the building and into the main street. All we saw of the squad cars and the FBI was the limpid pulsations of their red and blue lights in the night air.

Chapter 35

Celebrities

We drove on late into the night, in almost total silence, trying to put as much distance as possible between ourselves and that place. It felt as though we had turned a corner. We now had the police literally chasing us. The loss of our instruments and of Wad Mazaj was a shock to all of us.

I leaned my head against the window and tried to tune out the sound of the radio that Waldo said he needed when he was driving. I found myself thinking back to the euphoria we had all felt at the outset of this venture. Our night of triumph at the Kennedy Center now seemed so far away, like something I had once dreamed. There was a tap on my shoulder and Shadia leaned over.

'How are things back there?' I asked.

'Oh, not so good,' she whispered. 'I have to admit, it all feels a little hopeless. Poor Wad Mazaj. What will happen to him?' She glanced over her shoulder. 'I'm worried about the older ones. Uncle Maher and my aunt. They're tired, Rushdy, they just want to go home.'

In the brief flashes of amber street light that fell through the window, I saw the others sprawled about the interior. It was a portrait of despair. The only thing that we had left was Rudy's double bass that had been lodged in the little bathroom. It was blocking the corridor and had to be moved whenever you wanted to get by. His accordion was back on stage at the Buttercup Center.

'How is she doing?'

'John took another look and he thinks she should be in hospital.'

I stared ahead through the windscreen. The night seemed to be closing in on us. It had started to rain again and all I could see was a blur of lights washing through sheets of water.

Before I came here I had known nothing of what America was. The most powerful nation on earth, it had always been up there, floating above us. As distant as the gardens of paradise. Even if we caught up with Gandoury again there was no guarantee that we would get any satisfaction out of that. He would deny everything and claim it had all been done for our benefit. It was hard to see how we could win.

But now it occurred to me this was no longer about Gandoury, or his plans, or even about the money. It was about us. To end this odyssey, we had to find our own conclusion. It wasn't about finding justice or proving our innocence. It was about this moment, about establishing our name in the world. For everything the Kamanga Kings had ever stood for, standing up for the things they came to symbolise, for what we believed in, our own history, for all of those before us who had devoted their lives not only to music, but to speaking freely, to expressing themselves against those who would silence us for their own benefit. It was about all the Gandourys in the world. This was our chance to change that, to put us and all the others on the map.

'We have to play this concert,' I said out loud.

'What?' Shadia leaned forward again. 'What did you say?'

'I said we have to do it.'

'But how? I mean, we don't have any instruments. We don't even know where it is or how we get there.'

I didn't know how. I just knew we had to do it. I stared straight ahead through the windscreen at the darkened road ahead, the headlights carving a bright tunnel through the surrounding gloom. I asked Waldo how long it would take us to get to New York. Waldo pulled off the road into the forecourt of a service station. It was closed. A neon sign threw a red glow over the wet, glistening tarmac. Waldo traced a finger across the map, following a trail that led onwards and upwards along branches and bifurcations.

'We'd have to drive all night to get there by tomorrow.'

'Can we do that?'

Waldo looked at his watch. 'We could. The problem is I'm kind of beat. Can you drive?'

'Me? No, I . . . I never learned.'

'I can,' said Shadia. We both turned to look at her. Waldo shrugged.

'It works for me. If you could spell me just for a few hours I'd appreciate it.'

'Wait a minute,' I said. 'Are you sure?'

'Do you have a problem with me driving?' Shadia shot me a searching look.

'Not when you put it like that, no.'

Shadia climbed in behind the wheel and Waldo explained various things about the Birchaven as well as marking the route on the map. Then he got into the back and room was made for him to lie down. We edged out onto the road.

'Why are you watching me?' Shadia asked, her eyes on the road.

'I'm not watching you.'

'Yes, you are.'

'I trust you, okay?'

'I'm glad to hear it.' She looked round at me. 'Actually, I've never driven anything this big before.' The van lurched forward as her foot slipped and she let out a whoop. 'It's fun!' she grinned. I said nothing. Better to leave her to it, I thought.

Everyone settled down. They lay on the carpet, draped themselves over the table. It was more and more like a travelling circus, a caravan. I was too tense to sleep. I sat in the passenger seat and watched Shadia's profile as she drove, her eyes fixed intently on the narrow beams of light that ploughed through the darkness ahead of us.

'Why don't you sleep?' she asked. 'Or do you feel you have to watch me.'

'No, there's just too much going on in my head.'

She nodded. For a time there was silence between us. I watched the rows of orange sidelights on the big trucks as they slid by.

'It's funny,' I said, after a time.

'What's funny?'

'This. You and me, driving across America.'

She laughed lightly. 'Yes, it is pretty funny.'

'Whatever happens, I'll always remember this.'

'Me too.'

Despite everything, at some stage I must have fallen asleep. When I opened my eyes the night had lifted. It was still raining and through the speckled glass I glimpsed grey sky. I felt cold and stiff. Waldo was behind the wheel once more and Shadia was curled up next to me with a blanket round her. She felt soft and warm. I did my best not to move so as to avoid disturbing her.

We pulled off the road and onto the concourse of a service station. Waldo filled the tank while the rest of us shook ourselves into life and waited while Shadia checked that Alkanary was all right, before going over to the diner alongside us. We made ourselves comfortable in a couple of adjoining booths and took turns going to the bathroom to freshen up. The waitress was a grey-haired lady with a stony face. She snapped up the menus and scribbled down our orders and thumped the bell on the counter to hand in the slips to the cook. On the wall at the end there was yet another television that brought news of disasters around the world. A train wreck, a flood somewhere muddy and distant, and the president making a speech. None of us paid much attention. We were hungry and still half asleep.

'I long for your mother's food,' Uncle Maher grumbled. He put down his fork and looked at me. I saw the years weighing down the corners of his eyes. 'I understand that we must see this through . . .' He broke into a fit of harsh coughing. He pushed aside his plate.

'But I am tired of this travelling. The truth is I just want to go home.'

I reached across the table and patted his hand. 'We're almost there. As soon as we get to New York we will turn ourselves in.'

Shadia nudged me. 'Look, it's us again.'

I looked round at the screen. It was true. Underneath that picture of us onstage at the Kennedy Center ran the headline, Band On The Run.

'The extraordinary power of social networking,' the announcer was saying. 'A week ago it's safe to say you could count on one hand the number of people who had heard of the Kamanga Kings. Now there are literally hundreds of thousands of supporters adding their names to an online petition.'

The speaker was a plastic-looking figure with a silver mane of perfectly arranged hair. He leaned forwards, speaking earnestly to the camera. American television was full of such people. They spoke like preachers addressing their flock.

'Rock star Bono and guitarist the Edge both count themselves as fans.' The image cut to a shot of two men in leather jackets and sunglasses. 'Just two of the latest celebrities to attach their names to a movement that is pledging support for a group of musicians from one of Africa's most troubled nations.'

'Oh no!' Uncle Maher's chin sagged in dismay. 'Haven't we had enough of this already?'

Shadia was waving for us to be quiet. Another person had appeared on the screen.

'It's her,' Hisham cried. I looked again and this time I recognised her from the pamphlet he had shown me. The name echoed from the television in almost the same moment.

'Performance poet Zenobia,' the anchorman announced chirpily, 'has emerged as one of the leading lights in this campaign and she's in our New York studio. Tell us what all the excitement is about.'

'Well, Ted,' Zenobia began. 'I grew up with the legend of the Kamanga Kings. In Sudan they were huge. Time and again they have brought people together. For decades they symbolised the breaking down of barriers, whether they be of race, ethnicity or religion.'

'Yet music was banned for a time, and musicians became an endangered species.'

'That's correct, but the legend of the Kings lived on in contraband recordings, cassette tapes and so on. As the country enters a new phase of turmoil it is no coincidence that the Kamanga Kings are once more emerging as the embodiment of the spirit of the nation.'

'Okay, tell us about this benefit concert.'

'Well, Ted, we have seen a rallying of the artistic community around this issue. It's no coincidence that as this country is witnessing the hardship caused by travel bans, the demonisation of migrants and the separation of children on the borders, people feel a need to express their opposition to those politics.'

'The response has been pretty amazing. It seems everyone wants to get involved.'

'It's a pretty wild line-up so far. John Legend and Herbie Hancock are going to be there, I understand, along with Kamasi Washington, Lizzo and Kendrick Lamar.'

She spoke clearly and concisely. Watching her I had a vague recollection of a little girl who lived down the road from Hisham. More importantly, I could see how he might be enchanted by her. It was also clear that she completely outclassed him. She was on another level. I glanced at him, but he was busy watching her. He would never see it until it was too late.

Ted thanked Zenobia and they cut to a grey, angry man in a suit standing on the steps of the Capitol building in Washington.

'Senator Brock, what's your take on this situation?'

'Well, it's clearly quite unacceptable. Our immigration system is broken. We cannot allow people to simply come into our country and run amok. These people must be brought to account.'

'Are you saying they should be made an example of?'

'Well, that's not for me to say. We have procedures and protocols in this country for a reason. It makes us a laughing stock and sends the wrong signal. Holding a concert in the honour of fugitives from the law is frankly unacceptable. We must bring this farce to an end, and before others are encouraged to do the same.'

'Thank you, Senator. Well, there you have it, a star-studded concert tomorrow night at the Apollo Theater in Harlem, for the benefit of refugees everywhere and one particular group of musicians who are as we speak on the run from the authorities. Stay tuned for more on that story.'

The gleaming white teeth of the presenter were replaced by what looked like a smiling orange bouncing across a street. We huddled together.

'But we can't possibly go there,' said Uncle Maher. 'They would catch us.'

'That's exactly why we have to do it,' I said. 'The whole world will be watching.'

'He's right,' said Hisham.

'It's a trap,' said Kadugli, still in a sombre mood. 'They'll pick us up before we can play.'

'What about some of your friends from the old days, can't they help?'

'That was a long time ago. You can't just call people up like that.' He shook his head and turned away. I didn't get it. I tried appealing to the others.

'They've all come out in our support. We owe it to them.'

'Rushdy's right,' Shadia said. 'People are counting on us.'

'Do you think we can get through?' John Wau asked.

'They won't have a choice,' I said. 'Not if the whole world is watching.'

'A chance to restore our dignity,' nodded Uncle Maher. 'Maybe the last one we'll get.'

Hisham got up. 'I'm going to try and call Zenobia again.'

I watched him go. As he passed by the counter I noticed the two waitresses were whispering together. The older one was staring at us in a way I didn't like.

'I think it might be time to leave,' I said.

Shadia tugged my arm and nodded at the screen.

'A further development in that story,' Ted the anchorman was back. 'There are reports that Homeland Security have arrested a man whom they believe is one of the fugitive African band seeking asylum in this country.' A night scene bathed in flashing red and blue lights showed a slight figure being led towards a car; his hands were bound behind his back and he was bowed forward, the image of a broken spirit.

'Wad Mazaj!' cried Uncle Maher, speaking our thoughts aloud. We caught only a fleeting glimpse before he was ducked inside the car and the flashbulbs went off around him.

'Oh, no,' whispered Shadia.

'We have to finish this,' said Uncle Maher, suddenly resolved. 'For him, for all of us. We have to prove there was a reason for this.'

By now other diners were turning to look at us. The older waitress appeared. She had dyed-pink hair and wore narrow framed glasses that made her eyes look bigger.

'I'm going to have to ask to see some ID.'

'ID?' I echoed.

'Folks are getting nervous.' She gestured over her shoulder. 'They can hear you talking and whatever that is, it ain't English.'

'Is that a crime now,' asked Rudy, 'not to speak English?'

'I'm sorry?'

'No,' insisted Rudy, 'I'm sorry. Let me ask you, lady, have you ever heard of a place called Restrepo?'

'Where is that?' she queried. 'Somewhere in Mexico?'

We were all silent, watching a side of Rudy none of us had ever seen before. He was shaking his head.

'No, it's not in Mexico. It's in Afghanistan. One of the toughest postings you could have the misfortune to get.' He leaned forward, causing her to lean back. 'I didn't watch my buddies die over there to come home and be accused of being an illegal. I put in my time. I served these United States. What did you do?'

'What did I . . .?' She looked around the table as if wondering if she could have made a mistake. 'Okay, I'm going to have to ask you all to leave.'

'That's fine,' Rudy said, getting to his feet. 'But I want you to remember this moment. Next time you see that flag waving proudly in the wind, you remember what happened here.'

With that he headed for the door. We all stood and followed him out, aware that the other diners were watching us with a mixture of confusion and, unexpectedly, respect.

The rain was coming down in waves as we ran across the puddles to jump inside the Birchaven. Somehow, and despite the weather, the mood among the group was upbeat. Everyone wanted to talk about the benefit concert in New York. Could we really pull it off and avoid getting arrested?

'The whole world will be watching,' Shadia said.

'I can get us instruments,' Rudy said. Hisham hopped in behind him.

'Did you get through to her?' I asked. He shook his head.

'Maybe Mr Siegel's lawyer can help,' I said, turning to Shadia.

'Of course. His nephew.'

'We have to do this. We have to see it through.'

Shadia was staring at me in an odd way.

'What? What did I say?'

'It's not what you said, you fool.'

Getting to her feet, she began to make her way to the back of the bus to check on Alkanary. I looked at Rudy and he just winked at me.

Outside, it looked dark and industrial. I could see that Waldo was not happy and I suspected we might be lost. Then Shadia came rushing back.

'She's gone!'

Chapter 36

A Submarine on Wheels

Waldo stamped on the brakes and pulled over, then we all trooped back to the bedroom to confirm that there was no sign of Alkanary. She must have left while we were in the diner. But why? And where did she go?

'We have to find her,' said Shadia. 'She might be in trouble.'

'She can't have gone far,' I said.

Waldo jumped in behind the wheel and swung the Birchaven around.

'We'll circle a few blocks. Keep your eyes peeled.'

How far could an infirm old lady get in a city she didn't know? The answer seemed to be quite far, or at least far enough for us to have trouble tracking her down. We drove in circles until we were pretty much lost, going deeper into run-down areas with abandoned shops, rolled down shutters, broken glass glistening on the pavements. There was still no sign of her. How could she have possibly disappeared so completely?

'We're never going to find her,' said Hisham.

'We can't just leave her in this godforsaken place,' said Uncle Maher, peering out through the windows. 'Ya Allah.'

'We have to split up,' I said. 'It's the only way.'

Waldo pulled off the road into an empty lot. Hemmed in by a

chain-link fence and flanked on both sides by burnt out buildings, the broken concrete was crisscrossed by weeds, twisted wire and abandoned furniture; a charred sofa, a refrigerator, a smashed television. It looked like a war had played out here not so long ago. As we stood there trying to decide what to do a car rolled slowly by along the street, the air shuddering to the heavy bass beat. Three men inside studied us as they cruised slowly by.

'Puro Azteca.' Rudy read the graffiti painted on the side. 'This is gang territory. Not a good place to be.'

'We're not going to stay,' I said. 'We just have to find her quickly and get out of here.'

'I'm really not too happy about parking the old girl here,' said Waldo.

'We're not leaving until we find my aunt,' insisted Shadia.

'We must split up and go in different directions,' I said. 'Let's meet back here in half an hour no matter what.'

Everyone else seemed to agree. Kadugli and Hisham went one way, John and Uncle Maher another, while Rudy was all right being alone. Waldo insisted on staying with the Birchaven. Shadia and I made up the last pairing. I was trying to hide my annoyance at this delay. We didn't have time to waste and it felt as if with every step we were getting side-tracked away from our objective. I was afraid we would all become lost in this country. I looked back and Waldo waved reassuringly.

The street was dark and deserted. There were sirens in the distance. The houses around us looked as though they had been ripped apart. Windows were covered with plywood sheets that in turn had been painted over with graffiti messages. It was hard to believe anyone actually lived here. Many were nothing more than empty shells. The walls streaked with black above the windows where smoke had once billowed. A dog was barking nearby. I kept looking over my shoulder to catch shadows jumping around behind my back. If not for Shadia, I'm not sure I would have stayed a second longer. The wind blew

291

along the street, sending a chill down my spine. On either side of us the weeds grew high, and the pavement was littered with broken glass and all kinds of rubbish.

'Where could she possibly have gone?'

'She can't have gone far,' I said, trying to sound a positive note.

A car rolled slowly up behind us. I couldn't decide if it was the same one I had seen earlier. It was black and had a red stripe along the side that looked like flames. The driver glared at us through slitted eyes as they slid up to us.

'Don't look at them!' I hissed, suddenly feeling an old-fashioned urge to be protective. Shadia said nothing. We hurried along, with the car moving alongside.

'What do we do?' Shadia asked.

I had no idea. The only thing preventing me from running off was pride. I didn't want to look like a coward. The car accelerated, rolling past us to turn a corner and disappear.

'What's that?' I pointed. There was a faint glow coming from the far end of the street up ahead. It looked like a neon sign.

'Bar,' she read. We looked at one another, thinking the same thought. Instinctively we began hurrying towards it. The sign was on the inside of the window. The glass was protected by wire mesh. Despite this, it had been splintered into a spider's web mosaic that sparkled and glittered by turns. The door was reinforced with metal braces and cracked down the middle.

'This has to be it,' I said. 'Where else would she go?'

Inside, we were hit by a heavy gust of stale air and beer. The interior was so dark and gloomy I could barely see where to put my feet. The linoleum was sticky and with every step the soles of my shoes made a ripping sound as though coming unstuck.

The man behind the bar was as big and broad as a house. His head was shaved and his shirt was open, revealing a dirty vest and a complex tangle of gold and silver chains, medallions and crosses. Indigo tattoos rose up his neck in tiers of indecipherable script in what might have been Mandarin or Sanskrit. A scar ran from the corner of his mouth up to his right ear, which appeared to be missing a sizeable chunk.

'What'll it be?' His voice sounded as though he had been gargling nails.

'Maybe this wasn't such a good idea,' I whispered.

'Just give them a chance,' she said. She pointed. 'We'll have two of those.'

'That's beer, you know,' I explained.

Shadia flipped her hands up. 'It's a bar, what did you expect?'

The place was small and dark. The floor and ceiling were painted black. A string of coloured lights was draped over the shelves behind the bar, providing almost all the lighting. It was almost empty. Scattered around the place were men and women clinging to the walls. No more than eight in all. A couple of them glanced over at us, but the rest just ignored us. There was Motown music playing lightly over the speakers, which was about the only good thing I could say about the place. Down at the far end was a kind of low stage with a chrome-plated bar running vertically up to the ceiling in the middle.

'Pardon me,' said a voice, 'but you folks seem to have lost your way.'

The speaker was a man I had not noticed, partly because he was painted in shadows by the wall. The brown suit was several sizes too large for him and the colour matched the stained wallpaper behind him. He looked rather like an ageing turtle coming out of its shell. His eyes swelled out from his head like bloodshot eggs. A gold tooth glinted in the dark. With the suit and the hat perched on his head, he looked like someone had just left him behind there, sleeping on the bar counter, for about thirty years.

'We're looking for a friend,' I said.

'Ah, then you will need help.'

'Help?'

'I am happy to offer my services, in exchange for . . .' He held up his empty glass.

'Okay.' I turned to look at the barman, but he was already refilling the man's glass.

Two bottles of beer had appeared on the counter in front of us.

'That'll be twenty dollars,' said the barman.

'Thank you, kind sir.' Our new friend raised his glass in salute. Shadia did the same.

'I didn't know you drank beer.'

'I don't,' she said, lifting the bottle to her lips. 'But this seems as good a time to start as any.'

Whatever I was about to say died on my lips as the door to the bathroom opened and Alkanary stepped out. It took me a moment to recognise her. The way she strolled across the room as if she didn't have a care in the world. Hanging from her left hand was her old fur coat that smelled of moth balls and decades of hanging in a wardrobe. It dragged behind her along the floor like a dead animal. She let it fall as she climbed back onto the stool alongside the old man with the head like a turtle. She held up her empty glass to the barman.

'We have a new benefactor,' Turtle Man nodded at me. Alkanary turned towards us.

'Aunty!' cried Shadia.

'Twenty dollars,' said the barman. It seemed to be the only number he knew. I wasn't in a position to argue. I handed over the money as he set more beer in front of us, even though we had hardly touched the first ones.

'We were worried about you,' Shadia said.

'Well, here I am. Isn't this a wonderful place?' Alkanary sighed softly.

'You shouldn't be here. You should be resting.'

'I know,' said the old lady. 'But I woke up and I was bored, and also terribly thirsty. I got out of the van. I had no idea where I was so I just started walking. Luckily I found this place.' She looked around her. She seemed distracted, as though she still wasn't really sure where she was.

'That's wonderful,' I said, 'but we really have to go.'

'Go, go, go!' She shooed me away. 'These people are very friendly. I didn't have any money and look, they've all been buying me drinks.'

I looked at Shadia and saw the same concern on her face that I felt.

'The problem with you,' Alkanary went on, addressing me, 'is that you are always in a hurry. When you get to my age you want to enjoy every moment because you know that you don't have that many left.' She raised her glass to Turtle Man. I watched Alkanary tip the neat whisky down her throat. As she set her glass down, Turtle Man waved for it to be refilled.

'Maybe we should take it easy,' I suggested gently.

'I'll take it easy when I'm dead.' Alkanary tutted impatiently. 'What's the point? We're all lost. Still, I want to thank you, my boy.'

I was puzzled. 'Thank me for what?'

'For what? For this great adventure.' She waved a hand expansively. 'I thought my life was over, but it turned out there was still one more journey in me.' She chuckled, swaying dangerously on her stool. I put a hand out to balance her and as she loomed closer, the overpowering reek of the alcohol made my eyes water. She banged her glass on the counter.

'Whisky,' she growled. 'On the rocks.' Never a word of English, and now she was ordering drinks like a pro. She was wearing long black gloves that came up to her elbows. The ones she wore on stage. She peeled these off carefully and placed them on the counter in front of her. Turtle Man whistled his approval. 'I like that. A lady with style.'

'Twenty dollars,' said the barman flatly.

'I'm not paying for any more drinks,' I protested.

'We have to get her out of here,' said Shadia, throwing a hand out to stop Alkanary tipping off the barstool. She and her new admirer were laughing like jackals.

'We should really be going,' I said.

'Sit down,' said Turtle Man. 'Relax.'

'You don't understand,' Shadia said. 'The FBI are after us.'

Everything in the room seemed to stop.

'The FBI?' The barman cracked up. He was bent over wiping tears from his eyes. 'Whatchado? How many people you waste?'

'No,' I began. 'It's not like that.' But Turtle Man was ahead of us. 'Don't you get it? They're the ones on the TV.'

'No shit?' the bartender said. 'That was you?'

'Yes,' I admitted, feeling a certain degree of pride. 'That was us.'

'Whyn't you say so? Drinks are on the house. What'll you have?'

'No, thank you, really.' I tried to catch Alkanary's eye, but all of her attention was fixed, like a medieval poet studying the stars, on the glittering array of bottles on the glass shelves behind the bar. 'We really have to be going.'

'We need to get to New York,' Shadia said.

'Right,' nodded the barman.

'Before the Feds get you,' added Turtle Man.

Then there was a cry from behind us. We all turned. Someone over by the window was pointing outside. We all moved over to take a look.

'What in hell is that?'

'It looks like something out of Star Trek, you know, on TV?'

'Star Trek? How old are you again?'

'Well, I don't know. A submarine then.'

'Shit! You ever seen a submarine with wheels on it?'

I was trying to peer out over their shoulders. A wall of light was floating along the street. A long silver wall with wheels on, lots of wheels and orange lights along the sides. It had a kind of bulbous shape at the front and back and did in fact look like some kind of unearthly craft. I'd never seen the Birchaven lit up like that before. It

296

rolled slowly by. In the glow of the dashboard I could make out a familiar face inside the cab.

'It's Waldo!' cried Shadia.

'Damn! You mean, that's your ride?'

'Man, I wouldn't be seen dead in that thing.'

'Be careful what you wish for.'

'You all going back to Africa in that thing?'

'No, man, they going back to their planet. Don't you see the little green wires sticking out their asses?'

There was laughter all round as Shadia and I said our goodbyes and finally managed to steer our rather inebriated diva out through the door. Alkanary was blowing kisses to everyone.

'Come back soon, honey,' called the Turtle Man. 'I'll be waiting.'

'Oh, my God, is she hurt?' Waldo asked, looking at Alkanary as we waved him down.

'She'll survive,' I said. Considering the amount of alcohol she had consumed it was a miracle she was conscious. He rushed forwards to open the side door. Alkanary had some difficulty negotiating the steps, but with a little help she made it. Shadia led her through to the back. Inside, the others were sitting around.

'We lost Kadugli,' said Uncle Maher.

'Lost him how?'

He shook his head sadly. 'I don't know, he just never came back. We were searching for him when we saw you.'

We spent some time driving round in circles looking for Kadugli, but it was as if he had vanished into thin air. I couldn't believe it. We were being whittled slowly down. Kadugli was such a vital part of our sound I couldn't imagine what we would do without him.

It was clear that we couldn't stay here forever. We sat sullenly in silence as Waldo swung the big vehicle back onto the main road. In a short space of time the rows of buildings gave way to a post-industrial landscape of abandoned warehouses and factories, all in a similar state of decay. A tangle of overpasses and curling flyovers led up and out into the grey, foggy air. It felt as though we were in the middle of an urban landscape that had no end to it. Huge lorries squeezed by us, buses and cars, pick-ups and speeding vans. Everybody in a hurry to get out of this place, it seemed, to get to somewhere new, somewhere clean.

Chapter 37

Life Happens

I dreamed I was back home. The sun was shining and a warm wind blew across the yard. My mother was there. It was the same as I remembered, only different, as if the world had changed. Then, in that slow realisation that comes only in dreams, I understood that it wasn't the world that had changed, but myself. There was something else, too. Something, or someone, I just couldn't put my finger on.

I opened my eyes to find Shadia leaning over me, tugging at my sleeve. I wanted to ask her what she was doing there in my home, but I couldn't speak. Slowly it struck me that the Birchaven was no longer moving and it wasn't a dream at all. Shadia really was there nagging at my sleeve. I struggled to sit up, finding a crick in my neck.

'What? What is it?'

'Can you come back here for a moment?' she whispered.

I struggled upright. She looked sombre. Her hair was a mess. Through the side window I saw early morning commuters walking purposefully towards what looked like a railway station. The others in the Birchaven were still asleep or rubbing their eyes and turning over, trying to get comfortable. Hisham was curled up in one of the big chairs. Uncle Maher was on the sofa. John Wau slept upright on the table with his head on his hands. There was a limit to how long we could go on like this and it was drawing closer.

Shadia ushered me through the narrow connecting space to the bedroom at the back.

'What is it?' I asked. Her eyes were shining. Then I looked past her into the gloom and saw Alkanary lying face up on the bed. I could see immediately that something was wrong. I moved past Shadia. The old lady seemed very still. Indeed, she didn't appear to be breathing. I glanced back at Shadia standing in the doorway. She had her hand to her mouth. I leaned over the bed with the idea of shaking her, but the moment my hand touched hers I knew it was too late. I drew back. Behind me I heard Shadia give a little sob.

'Ya Allah,' I said quietly.

'When I woke up she was just . . . I knew something was wrong.' Shadia sniffed and stifled a cry. 'Is she . . .?'

I sank down onto the side of the bed and we sat there together, suddenly at a loss.

'It must have been last night,' said Shadia. 'It was just too much for her.'

We stared down at the frail little figure.

'I've never seen her happier, though.'

'No.' Shadia smiled through her tears. 'She was flying, as she liked to say.'

I went to wake John Wau. Lost for words, I closed the door behind him and gestured at the bed.

'Can you check?' I asked. 'Is she really gone?'

It only took him a moment. He placed her hands carefully across her chest and stood up.

'We must get her to a morgue.'

'A morgue? How? I mean, we can't.'

'We have to,' said John Wau. 'We can't keep her like this.'

'It's over, Rushdy,' said Shadia softly. 'We have to turn ourselves in.'

She was right. I knew she was. The door flew open behind me, thumping into my back.

'They have a description of the van,' Rudy said, breathlessly. 'It was on the radio.' He fell silent, stopping and looking around. 'What's up? Is she . . .? ¿Que pasó? What happened?'

'Life happened,' said John Wau, looking down at the bed.

'I'll be back in a moment,' I said to Shadia. I walked forwards, shaking Hisham awake as I went and leaned over the front seat to Waldo. Through the windscreen I saw the tumult of people going by. Waldo looked round at me.

'I can't believe it,' he said softly when I gave him the news. 'Shit, man. I'm sorry to hear that.'

'What have they been saying on the radio?' I asked.

'They have a description of the vehicle.'

'Okay, so what do we do now?' I stared out through the windscreen.

'Well, first order of the day has to be to ditch the old girl,' Waldo said.

'The old girl?' said Hisham yawning. 'What did I miss?'

Waldo tapped the wheel affectionately. 'Sticks out like a sore thumb.'

'Yes, of course.' I cleared my throat. 'We need to make a decision.'

Hisham frowned at me, realising that something was wrong. He looked towards the rear of the van.

'I'll get the others,' he said quietly.

We all gathered around the kitchen table in the back. Uncle Maher couldn't stop crying.

'The best thing is for Waldo to take her to a hospital,' I suggested.

John Wau objected. 'Technically, the hospital is for people who are living. You cannot just deliver a person there once they are deceased.'

'Then what?' I asked.

Shadia stifled a sob. 'We can't just leave her with strangers.'

I went back down to the rear to take another look. The strange thing was that Alkanary actually looked quite peaceful. She even seemed to have a smile on her face. I remembered her last night in the bar. You couldn't argue that she hadn't enjoyed her life up to the very end.

301

'We have to take her with us,' Shadia said as she came up behind me.

'Take her with us?' I gave an involuntary laugh. 'How? Don't you think we might draw some attention to ourselves? And how easy do you think that's going to be?'

'It doesn't matter.' Shadia sobbed, pressing a handkerchief to her nose. 'We're not leaving her.'

We went back to join the others. Nobody had any idea of how to proceed. From time to time a sob would come from Shadia, or a sniffle from Uncle Maher. It felt very sad. One thing was certain, we couldn't just stay here indefinitely. Every time we went through from front to back, we had to lift the top of Rudy's double bass out of the way. It was a huge case, made of fibreglass and with wheels on the bottom. Propped inside the toilet, it stuck out blocking the hallway. Most of the time it was just an inconvenience, but now an idea began to surface.

'She's not that big,' I said.

'What did you say?' Shadia was leaning in the bedroom doorway. Her look told me she was wondering if I had lost my mind.

'She's small. I mean, in size. She's tiny, in fact.'

'Maybe you need to sit down for a moment?'

'No, no, I'm fine.' I was trying to get the courage to say what was on my mind. Instead I pointed. She followed my eyes.

'You're mad!' she said.

'It's big enough,' I suggested.

'You are insane. We are not putting my aunt in that thing . . . even if she could fit.'

'I think she might fit,' Hisham offered helpfully, drawing a fierce glare from Shadia. 'I mean, if she was curled up.'

'Curled up?' Shadia made it sound like we wanted to cut Alkanary into pieces.

'She sleeps like that, on her side, curled up. It would be like she was sleeping,' I said.

'Except that she's not. She's dead and you should have some respect.'

'These are desperate times, and they call for desperate measures.'

'What is that, another line from one of your precious novels?' She looked pained when I didn't respond. 'How would we carry it anyway?'

'It has wheels on it,' I pointed out.

'Guys, I don't want to push you,' Waldo called from the front. 'But there's a cop wandering around out here and I think we should make a move.'

I went forward to join him. I nodded at the station. 'Where do the trains from here go?'

'First in to Baltimore centre. You'll have to change. From there take a train straight to Penn Station, New York City, man. The Big Apple.'

Back in the rear, I found Shadia waiting. 'We have to make a decision. Either we leave her here, or we take her with us.'

Finally, she gave the briefest of nods. She wiped her nose on a handkerchief.

'We have to take her.'

'You think it can be done?' I asked John Wau.

'Well, if rigor mortis hasn't set in yet.' John Wau heaved a deep breath. 'But I cannot sanction this. It goes against all the ethics of my profession.'

'We're not asking you to do anything,' I said. 'So, you wouldn't be breaking any oath or anything.'

He still wasn't happy. 'Well, you need to consider this; the deterioration of the body starts immediately when life ceases.' He glanced towards Shadia and lowered his voice. 'In a few hours she is going to start to smell.'

I looked down at the slight figure in the bed and wondered once more how we had managed to get ourselves into such a predicament. I glanced over at Rudy, who stood by the bedroom door. Shadia had refused to come with us.

'We don't have a choice,' he shrugged. 'It's not for long.'

'She'd want to see this through,' said Hisham.

'I'm not here,' said John Wau, stepping out of the room.

Rudy and I gazed down at the sad figure curled up on the bed.

'You think this is wrong?' I asked.

'No sé, hombre. My army training didn't cover this.'

'Perhaps we could wrap her up in a sheet,' Hisham said.

I agreed. That way it would at least be a bit like the way we bury people at home.

'Okay,' nodded Rudy. 'That makes sense.'

It wasn't easy. You don't realise just how uncooperative a corpse can be until you have to move one. The sheet made the task a little less unpleasant. She became nothing more than an unwieldy burden and could have been a sheep for that matter, though I could never have said that to Shadia.

'You sure you're okay with this?' I asked.

Rudy nodded. 'Sure, man, wouldn't be right to leave her behind.'

When we finally managed to get her curled up inside the case, Rudy sat on the lid to help get it closed and finally I managed to snap the clasps shut. We stood and admired our handiwork. It felt as though we were performing a ritual.

'Maybe we should say a prayer, or something?' Rudy suggested.

'She wasn't actually very religious,' I pointed out.

'That's true,' said Hisham.

We managed, without too much difficulty, to get the case into the living area, where Shadia stared at it with a look of horror. She glanced up at me and the only thing she said was, 'I don't want to know.'

We lowered the case carefully down the steps and leant it up against the side of the Birchaven while we said our goodbyes. Waldo stuck his hands in his pockets and stared at the ground.

'This has been one of the greatest experiences of my life and I want to thank you for that.'

'Come on, Waldo, you're going to meet us in New York.'

'Well, yeah, I mean, I'm going to try, but let's be honest. There's a chance I won't make it, or you won't, or whatever.'

'Whatever happens, we'll see you before we go back.'

'I hope so. I mean, I was really starting to get a feel for this fugitive thing,' he said wistfully.

'You have to make it to the concert,' I said as he gave each of the others a hug. Then it was my turn. I realised I was going to miss him.

'You have my number. I'll try to get up there if I don't get stopped. Just don't get caught, man.'

'I'll try my best,' I promised him.

We shook hands and then embraced and he gave Shadia a hug and then we were off, crossing the darkened forecourt, Hisham and I steering the instrument case. Waldo was going to drop Rudy, Uncle Maher and John Wau at the bus station. If all went well we would meet up again in New York at the benefit concert venue for one last performance. Over my shoulder I caught a final glimpse of Waldo standing there alongside his beloved Birchaven. I knew I would remember that image forever.

Chapter 38

End of the Line

The station was small and had only two platforms. Through the glass I could see the Birchaven pulling out of the parking place and turning left. Shadia couldn't stop crying. I held the case upright while Rudy went to buy the tickets. I couldn't let go of it. I felt bad about treating Alkanary in such an undignified fashion, but it was only for a day or so, and we had no choice. I told myself this over and over again. Once things were settled we could make the appropriate arrangements to have her flown home. As we joined the passengers waiting to board, I took Shadia's hand and squeezed.

'It's what she would have wanted, to stay with us, to see this through.'

Shadia was too upset to speak. Hisham leaned over.

'Speak English, remember? People get upset about that kind of thing nowadays.'

'Right.'

We sat in silence and tried to look as if we did this all the time. The instrument case brought a few odd looks, but nothing more. Hisham helped to make the transfer when we reached Baltimore's main station. We carried it together up and down the stairs. Shadia went to buy tickets. Finally, we got onto the train for New York. Between us Hisham and I managed to prop the big case upright beside one of the luggage racks.

'You think that will do?' he asked, stepping back to survey our handiwork.

'She'll be fine,' I said, quickly correcting myself. '*It'll* be fine.'

Shadia and I sat together while Hisham moved down the carriage, far enough away not to raise suspicions, but close enough to be able to come to my aid if I needed help moving the case. There was no sign of any police officers either in the station or on the train. I spotted a conductor entering the carriage at the far end and the other passengers started searching for tickets.

'That should really travel in the special car, which has space for bicycles and such-like,' he said, indicating the double bass. He was an elderly man with grey hair sticking out of his ears. I tried to smile.

'We don't like it to be out of our sight.'

'I can understand that. Double bass, is it?'

'Yes,' I answered cautiously. 'That is correct.'

'A fine instrument. Well, the train's pretty empty today, so I suppose it's all right. Just watch out you don't obstruct the passageway.'

'No, sir, I shall endeavour to prevent that eventuality.'

He frowned at me for a moment, before grunting and moving on. I sat back in my seat with a sigh.

'You think he recognised us?' Shadia whispered.

'I don't know. I was expecting him to ask me to open it up so he could have a look.' My hands were damp with sweat. 'I keep thinking, if Hisham and I hadn't gone to her house that night, perhaps she would have been better off. If we had left her there she might still be alive.'

'Don't think that,' Shadia said quietly. 'It was the right thing to do. This tour, it brought her back to herself, to who she once was. It's sad to say, but this is how she would have wanted to go.'

I wanted to agree, but I couldn't help but wonder. I don't think anyone would choose to die in a stranger's van in a foreign country.

'She once told me that before you came to see her she thought her life was over. You gave her hope back. You allowed her to dream again.'

I sat back and tried to relax. I looked out of the window at America flying by. Slowly we began to leave behind the dark fields and trees through which the low sunlight flickered. Then we entered an area of urban desolation. Old industrial buildings that were abandoned. I saw houses with their windows boarded up, and factories with broken windows, some with strange metal panels on the sides and one with a tower that looked like a bottle with the word 'milk' written on it. It was like looking at the ruins of another era. Railway tracks overgrown with grass, chimney stacks, more houses, abandoned cars standing on bricks with their wheels removed.

'It's good that you insisted we take her with us,' Shadia said at one point. 'We couldn't possibly have left her behind.'

'Yes, but . . .' It still felt a little disrespectful to be carrying her around in an instrument case.

'She's my aunt, I have to look after her.' Then she looked thoughtful. 'Aren't you supposed to bury the dead within three days?'

'Yes, but I think that rule can be suspended if you are travelling.'

'Convenient.' She looked as if she didn't quite believe me.

Suddenly feeling an unusual sense of responsibility towards the Almighty, I tried to think of any similar case to draw a parallel, but there aren't many examples in Islamic history of people transporting bodies in instrument cases. If Allah was all wise and all knowing then surely he could see into our hearts and know that we meant no disrespect. And if he couldn't, well, there wasn't much we could do about that now.

An hour went by then Shadia coughed and leaned towards me. 'You don't think she is beginning to smell, do you?'

'What? No. Not at all.'

I sniffed the air cautiously, seized by a terrible fear that she might be right. There was a strange smell in the air. Was that what I thought it was, or was it just the unfamiliarity of the train? I tried to look further down the carriage towards Hisham, but he appeared to be asleep.

'I think it's too warm in here.' Shadia was beginning to grow frantic, looking up and down the carriage, which was almost empty. 'Perhaps we could open a window?'

'It's not that kind of a train.' The windows were all sealed.

'Okay, I know.' She fumbled in her bag. 'I have some perfume.'

Without waiting she began spraying the stuff in the air all around us. A woman seated further down scrunched up her nose as she looked back at us.

'Maybe that's enough,' I suggested.

'You're right. Enough.' She smiled at the woman, who turned her nose back to her magazine.

'We're trying not to draw attention to ourselves,' I reminded Shadia.

'Sorry.'

As we sat there in silence, looking at the world through the windows of a speeding train destined for New York, I wouldn't have chosen to be anywhere else in the world. This whole adventure had come to be about much more than just us. I didn't know about Hisham's plans, or what he would do when we got through all of this. Maybe he belonged here, among all the millions of people chasing the American dream. All I knew was that it wasn't for me. I felt Shadia's hand squeezing mine.

'What are you thinking?'

I looked at her. 'I was thinking . . . that I'm actually looking forward to going home.'

'Yes,' she nodded. 'Me too.'

After that we fell silent again, each lost in our own thoughts. We were both exhausted and managed to fall asleep for a time. I opened my eyes as the conductor announced over the PA system that we were pulling into Penn Station. Hisham came over and helped me to get the case off the train. Then, when I could manage to roll it alone, he moved forward to walk a few paces ahead of us.

The station was crowded, and bigger than we had imagined. Crowds milled about us, all trying to go in different directions at the same time. The case proved cumbersome and awkward as we negotiated it onto a narrow escalator that brought us up to a concourse. People rushed about left and right. It was hard to see which way to go. We went one way and then another. I caught a glimpse of Hisham over by a corner. He seemed to be waiting.

The station felt claustrophobic and stifling. The ceiling was low over our heads and voices came over the loudspeakers barking words that we could not fully understand. Trains arriving and leaving, warnings about terrorists. Be alert. See Something, Say Something. There were men and women in uniform. Men with guns. We kept changing our direction in order to avoid them. It was hard to be inconspicuous when carrying a large instrument case. And people kept bumping into it, tripping over. They would turn to yell curses back at us as they went on their way.

We reached Hisham and together turned a corner into another tunnel. People seemed to keep walking straight into us. We struggled on, past brightly lit shops and cafés, snack bars and what have you. I was sweating and feeling completely disorientated.

At the end of the tunnel was a set of stairs that would take us up to the street. And there we found ourselves faced with another problem. The escalator was being repaired. They had put up an awning around the bottom and the top. The only alternative was the stairs.

'Maybe there's another way,' Shadia suggested. 'There must be a lift somewhere.' I felt her stiffen and turned to follow her gaze.

Two armed soldiers were coming towards us. One was talking into a radio strapped to his shoulder. The other was looking directly at us. They were both fingering their guns. I turned to look at Hisham. He was already on the stairs and had turned to come back towards us. When he saw the soldiers he stopped and started back up.

'No time,' I said. 'We have to move.'

'But . . .'

'We just take it slowly.'

310

As we started up, dragging the case one step at a time, Shadia explained that this wasn't the station she had expected.

'If you see pictures of the old station, it used to be a really grand place, with high ceilings, like a cathedral. So beautiful.'

'What happened?' I was moving backwards up the stairs, pulling the case behind me up each step.

'I don't know. Someone must have decided they didn't need such places any more, that they could make a profit by tearing it down.'

'An accountant,' I suggested. Shadia smiled. We laughed together as I paused to take a break and wipe the sweat from my brow.

It was precisely at that moment, as the case rested against my side, that a businessman hurrying down, carrying a briefcase in one hand and talking into his mobile, chose to push past us. In his haste he brushed by a woman wearing high heels who was level with Shadia. The woman was knocked off balance. She fell sideways, her ankle twisting as her heel snapped off. She staggered into Shadia, who in turn knocked the case sideways as she tried to right herself.

If I had been holding the case firmly, I might have been able to prevent what happened next. As it was I saw all of this, as if in slow motion: Shadia falling, the case twisting out of my grip. I felt the weight inside the case shift as it came away from me and began to fall. I watched it tip over and slide away, bouncing down the stairs, gaining speed. People leapt out of the way. There were screams and shouts of outrage and warning. It carried on down, thumping hard into the wall on one side before careering back. I was frozen in disbelief as the disaster unfolded before me. There were so many people, coming up, going down, waiting at the bottom. All of them potential victims. Women, children, pushchairs. Old folks with sticks, young people laden with rucksacks and bags. They looked up and screamed. They jumped aside, leapt out of the way. Through all of this the case banged its way down as if it had a life of its own, a black torpedo that was impossible to stop.

On the concourse below people were turning to look up, others pointed. The two soldiers were grabbing their guns and radios, yelling orders left and right. By the time the case reached the bottom it was travelling at such a speed that it came off the stairs and careened away across the shiny floor. Then it spun round and rammed straight into a concrete pillar. The clasps must have been worn, or badly fixed. Whatever. They snapped open and I watched in horror as the lid rose up to reveal the contents.

There was a moment of stunned silence as events came to an end. The soldiers were pointing their guns at us.

'On the ground now!'

'Hands where we can see them!'

Shadia's fingers were digging painfully into my arm. Someone else was screaming. A woman, one hand to her mouth, the other pointing into the case.

'Ya Allah!' Shadia wailed. 'It's over.' And she sank down to the steps and began to cry.

Chapter 39

Ms DeHavilland's Predicament

The next few hours were a nightmare. I recall only fragments. Being surrounded by police officers and men waving guns. We were handcuffed and separated, pinned to the ground. I watched helplessly as Shadia was dragged away. A group of specialists arrived clad in white suits and helmets. They looked like astronauts. They examined Alkanary's body before sealing it inside a casket and taking it away. All of this under the gaze of an incredulous audience. The onlookers were held back behind lines of tape. The station was shut down. They escorted me up the stairs and into the back of a police car. I caught sight of Shadia alongside me in another car. Hisham was nowhere to be seen. At least he had managed to slip away.

Now I was treated to my first real glimpse of New York City. Despite my situation it felt like something of a miracle to be here. I pressed my nose to the glass and marvelled at the high buildings, the big shops, the boutiques. I saw people going around their daily business. This was their home. It looked like a film, exactly as I had imagined it. The only part I hadn't counted on was being handcuffed in the back of a police car.

They took us to an unremarkable building on a side street. It looked like an old warehouse with brick walls and long strips of small glass window panels. The sign in the lobby said it was the offices of Homeland Security Investigations. Everything took a long time. I was passed from one group to another, through countless security barriers, until, finally, I wound up in a small room with a table and no windows except for a narrow strip of glass high on one wall. I had plenty to think about. Our journey was at an end. It wasn't so bad. We had put the band back together and we had been invited to play at one of the most prestigious venues in the world. It would have been nice if things had ended on a high note, but you can't have everything. I sometimes think that life is about all the obstacles that fall in your path.

When the door finally opened it was to reveal two familiar figures: Agents Baumgarten and Blanco.

'Well, that was some ride you took us on,' said the woman. Agent Baumgarten stood in a corner, hands in the pockets of her grey suit, her jaws chewing steadily.

'Do you have any idea of the diplomatic crisis your escapade provoked?' asked Agent Blanco. They went back and forth between themselves, talking as if I wasn't really there.

'Okay, so, which one of you killed the old lady?'

'What? No, nobody killed her,' I protested. 'She just died.'

They looked at one another. 'You expect us to believe that?'

'It's the truth. The excitement. It was just too much for her.'

Blanco leaned across the table. 'So, you killed her.'

'Not like that. Not the way you're suggesting.'

'But you know I'm right,' he insisted. 'If you hadn't gone running off like that she would still be fine.'

He had a point, though I didn't need him to tell me. I already knew it.

'Did you find everyone? I mean, are they all here?'

'We haven't got all of them yet, but we will.' Blaumgarten's face was blotchy, bags under her eyes; she looked both unhappy and unhealthy.

'What happens now?'

'Oh, now the fun begins. The prosecutors are just adding up how many violations they can charge you with.'

I swallowed. 'Then what?'

'Then you go to prison for a looong time.'

The two of them looked at one another and chuckled before sauntering towards the door.

'Better make yourself comfortable, amigo,' said Blanco. 'Because these four walls are all you're going to see for a long time.'

The door closed behind them. I heard the snap of the bolt being shot into place.

I don't know how much time went by after that. The strip of sky that I could see through the narrow window that ran along the top of the outer wall began to change colour, signalling the end of the day. I wondered how Shadia was doing as I began to resign myself to spending the night here.

The door opened again and Ms DeHaviland appeared. She looked tired. Her hair was out of place and she was clearly stressed. She sat down in the chair opposite me and placed her hands flat on the table. Closing her eyes for a second she said;

'If I had ever imagined anything like this happening I would never have invited you.' She paused and opened her eyes. 'This has gotten completely out of hand. I just don't understand, Rushdy. You should have put a stop to this right at the start. People have suffered. I don't have to tell you that.'

'Ms DeHaviland, it's hard for you to understand, but we were trying to put things right. Perhaps we went about it the wrong way, but our reputation was at stake.'

'Well, that's very sweet, but I hardly think it's worth the price, do you?'

I didn't have an answer for her. I just wanted this to be over. Ms DeHaviland took a deep breath.

'Rushdy, we have a problem, and I'm afraid there is no easy solution to it. This whole thing has been blown out of proportion. The president is tweeting about it. They are making jokes about it on the late night talk shows.' The look on my face told her I didn't quite understand the meaning of all this. 'To put it simply, the whole world is now watching. You've become celebrities.'

'We never intended that,' I began, but she cut me off.

'It no longer matters what you or I want. This is beyond that. Do you understand? We are now in the midst of a media storm.'

'A media storm,' I repeated. I leaned forwards. 'Ms DeHaviland, how is Shadia?'

'She's fine. You don't need to worry about her. What you need to do is help me find a way out of this predicament.'

'Predicament?'

'Let me try to explain.' She tapped a long red fingernail on the tabletop. 'You are going to do exactly what I tell you. Is that understood?'

I thought for a moment. I had a feeling I had been here before. I knew what I had to do. I had seen it a thousand times. 'Ms DeHaviland, I would like to consult with my lawyer?'

'I'm sorry, what did you say?' Her jaw hung open.

I repeated my words, just as they did in every legal drama I had watched for years. I produced from my pocket the business card of Mr Siegel's nephew and placed it on the table.

'Mr Henry Siegel Jr. He has key information relating to our case. He will also ensure that everything is done properly.'

Ms DeHaviland sat back in her chair and folded her arms. 'Well, I never would have guessed.'

Mr Henry Siegel Jr turned out to be a larger, rounder version of his uncle. He arranged our cooperation in return for immunity from all charges and safe passage out of the country. He also provided information about his contact with Gandoury. When and how he had contacted him and how the tour venues were arranged. He even knew his current whereabouts.

And so it was that as the day was coming to a close, Shadia and I found ourselves in an unmarked car being driven by our two favourite FBI agents, Baumgarten and Blanco.

Chapter 40

One Last Time

Despite our circumstances, it was still quite incredible to see New York by night. The lights up and down Broadway. The huge buildings towering over us. It seemed to have taken a lifetime to get to this place that I already knew, that I had constructed in my imagination for years. The films and books, but most of all the music. Somewhere inside this hazy labyrinth of sound and light, streets like canyons, hooting car horns, yellow taxi cabs and the distant wail of sirens, there was a hidden beat, a sound that rippled down through the ages, back to the time of legends, when Dizzy and Monk and Mingus and Coltrane had all walked these streets, chasing their own dreams.

Shadia and I were silent. It was all so overwhelming. We held hands like children lost in the woods, hoping only that we would find a way out.

I read everything I could; signs over hotdog stands and pizza places, coloured lights announcing shows and basement bars. Street signs that read Broadway, Central Park and Times Square. It was all there, within our grasp. Turn left, turn right. Walk. Don't walk.

'There's so much to see, it feels as if you could spend years and not see all of it.'

Then Shadia was tugging my hand and pointing. There ahead of us, above a brightly lit entrance, stood our name spelled out in lights on the marquee: The Kamanga Kings Benefit Concert. One Night Only! Sold Out!

'That's us,' I said. We looked at one another, then Agent Blanco's gruff voice sounded from the driver's seat.

'This is your stop,' he said, lifting his chin to watch us in the mirror. 'Looks like you're getting a lucky break, but don't think we're taking our eye off you. We've got all the exits covered.'

'You don't have to worry about us,' I said.

They drove past the theatre and turned left at the next street and then left again to bring us into a narrow alleyway. We drove along until we came to a brick building with an iron fire escape attaching to the outside.

'Okay, this is you. Take the stairs up and someone will meet you. We'll be right here when you're done.' Agent Baumgarten twisted round in her seat to look back at us. 'Well, go on, what are you waiting for?'

Shadia and I climbed out of the car and paused for a moment.

'You realise this is *the* Apollo Theater?' she said. 'I can't believe it.'

'Me neither.'

As we crossed the street a familiar figure stepped from the shadows. 'Kadugli!' cried Shadia. And it was him, looking tired and somewhat shamefaced.

'Are you all right?'

Never one to dwell on his own troubles, Kadugli waved the question aside.

'I didn't know if anyone would turn up.'

'I knew you wouldn't let us down,' I said.

'What choice did I have? This was fated to happen.' He gave a kind of laugh. At that moment the door opened and we were ushered inside.

'I'm glad you're back,' I said, patting his back. 'It wouldn't be the same without you.'

We climbed a steep iron staircase into darkness out of which a band of light fell as a door opened at the top. I stepped inside to find the others waiting for us. Everyone had made it. Uncle Maher was sitting on a sofa in the corner with a despondent look on his face. He leapt to his feet when he caught sight of us.

'Dear boy, I thought you were lost!'

We embraced. It felt good to be back together again. Wad Mazaj was explaining how the police had simply released him.

'Fools, they had nothing to charge me with. They even drove me up here.'

Shadia and I exchanged glances but said nothing.

'But where have you been? And what did you do with Alkanary?'

'She's in good hands, uncle. I'll explain everything.'

Before we had time to go further Rudy appeared in the doorway accompanied by a woman wearing a set of headphones around her neck.

'Guys, this is Nanda, she's our stage manager.'

Nanda explained everything we needed to know about the sound-check and microphones. There was a bathroom where we could freshen up and our stage outfits had been brought in.

'Wait a second,' I interrupted. 'What about our instruments?'

Nanda shrugged as if this was not a problem. 'They were delivered to the back entrance about an hour ago.'

We went through to another room where, sure enough, our instruments were waiting for us. I rushed over to check on my trumpet.

'How about that for coincidence,' Wad Mazaj laughed.

'It's no coincidence,' I said quietly. I looked around at them.

'You'd better explain,' Uncle Maher said, sitting down.

So we explained, Shadia and I, what had happened to us.

'So they're letting us play because it would be too embarrassing not to?' John Wau summarised.

'That's about the size of it,' I nodded.

'It's time,' said Uncle Maher after a while. 'We could not have kept running forever. We needed this to end. This is as good a way as any.'

The others agreed.

'Has anybody seen Hisham?' I asked. There were shakes of the head. He apparently had decided that he was done with us. I must admit I felt a little disappointed.

'Okay, how are we going to do this?' I asked. Just as we gathered around to plan, Rudy walked in.

'Guys, you have any idea who's out there?'

He ran through a list of artists, some known to us, others not.

'But are they all going to play?' Uncle Maher asked.

'Yes, of course. That's why they are here. They want to play with us.' Rudy pointed. 'With you. We should go down and meet them.'

So we followed him down to another area backstage. As we walked in there was a spontaneous round of applause. It was quite unexpected. Then I was surrounded by people who wanted to shake my hand and congratulate me. I couldn't quite believe it. Some of the faces I recognised, others were new to me, but their names were familiar.

'Isn't that Herbie Hancock?' Shadia whispered to me. I looked. It might have been. It just seemed so unlikely. I don't really recall who I met, or what I said over the next hour. I was quite overwhelmed by the fact that so many well known artists seemed to want to know me, to know us, I should say, for this was about the Kamanga Kings.

'Didn't you play with Wynton Marsalis?' I asked Kadugli, nodding across the room towards the man himself.

'It was a long time ago,' he said, modest as always.

'You should say hello.'

'When the time comes.' He shrugged it off and moved away. Rudy was beside himself with excitement.

'Do you have any idea how big this is?'

'It's one last concert, Rudy. Whatever happens, we have to go out there and play our best.'

A large curtain separated us from the auditorium but we could hear the sound of people out there talking and moving around, finding their seats. A small man wearing shorts and a baseball cap appeared.

'That's Pharell Williams!' Rudy whispered as the man came over and shook all our hands very earnestly.

'This is tremendous. What you're doing. Your bravery is a shining beacon for the world. A reminder to us all of the words that stand on that statue of liberty.'

It sounded like he was practising a speech, which turned out to be the case as later I heard him speak the same words when he went out to introduce us. In the meantime, I could sense the others beginning to grow nervous as we started to discuss what numbers to include in our set.

'Let's stick to what we know. A couple of our own numbers and then some standards that we can bring some of the others in on.'

This was quickly agreed on and Rudy was soon busy going around coordinating what we could play and with whom. Several acts were scheduled to perform before we came on. We would play a short set, no more than four numbers, then we would be joined by a selection of the stars who had come to join us. There was a house band consisting of a very famous bass player, drums and keyboards that would remain on stage and would keep us all in line. Rudy explained they were all very well known and highly respected. He went on to outline the running order.

'The concert is for the Kings, but of course the audience expects to hear all these special guests.'

He ran through a list of who would play before us. It sounded like a lot, but apparently there was plenty of time.

'Then you come on and start playing. Then some of the others will come on and join you.'

I relayed all of this to the others. There were objections of course. It wouldn't have been the Kamanga Kings without some disagreement. I didn't mind. I was just glad to see that everyone was there. I felt a hand tugging at my sleeve. I turned towards Shadia. She didn't speak.

She didn't have to. Over her shoulder I saw what she wanted me to see.

Standing in the wings at the edge of the stage were two figures. The woman wore a colourful wrap around her head and large spectacles. She looked taller and thinner than on television. In the shadows next to her stood an even more familiar figure.

'This is Zenobia,' Hisham said, pushing his hands into his pockets.

'I thought you weren't going to make it.'

'I'm sorry,' he said, looking down. 'When I saw what happened, I just took off.'

'You didn't have a choice,' I said. Although I'm not sure I would have done the same. 'But at least you're here.' Shadia said nothing. Before either of us could say more Zenobia intervened.

'You guys are amazing. This thing has just become so huge.' She threw her arms around Shadia to give her a hug. 'You've reminded people of why our values matter. Freedom, democracy, tolerance, all the things this country prides itself on.'

Shadia looked a little overwhelmed, but managed to hold it in. 'We were just trying to put things right,' she said.

Zenobia, too, spoke as if she was practising a speech. When Shadia managed to extricate herself she stepped back next to me. Hisham smiled.

'So you guys finally got together?'

Shadia and I looked at one another. We had never acknowledged it openly, but something had happened. We both laughed. Zenobia excused herself.

Hisham tilted his head to look at me. 'You've changed, you know? You're not the same. You're more sure of yourself.'

'Don't do that. Don't try to flatter me.'

'It's true,' Shadia said. 'He's right. You're the leader now.'

'Have you seen who's in there?' he said, pointing towards the backstage area. 'It's unbelievable. Every star you can think of. I have to try and talk to Kendrick.'

As Hisham moved away Shadia turned to me.

'Is he still going to stay behind?'

'I don't know,' I said. Somehow I could already feel the distance between us growing. Rudy appeared, out of breath: things were starting up. I could hear a drum roll.

'Okay, that's Omar Hakim with the house band. They will warm up the crowd, then Erykah comes out and does her number. Then Pharrell. After that, it's you.'

He went on. I listened. The sound of the names and the numbers we would perform together lodged in some part of my brain, while another part seemed to be observing events from a distance. I knew this was an important moment in my life, one that wouldn't come again, and that took me back to the beginning, to how all of this started, to the very idea of the Kings.

When I was a child I learned to live with the fact that my father's life was bigger and brighter and more colourful than mine ever would be. I accepted that, also the fact that since he had died before I was old enough to address him as an adult, he would always be an absent observer, watching over me, judging my life in a way that I could never challenge. Yet, here we were. For the first time I felt that I was finally coming to terms with that loss. I was myself. I would never be him, just as he could never have been me.

I came out of this reverie to hear Shadia speaking to me.

'Are you all right?'

'Yes,' I smiled. 'I think I am.'

*　　*　　*

The concert went by in a blur. It seemed to last forever and it also felt like it was over in a matter of minutes. I can remember particular moments that stand out with shining crystal clarity; an exchange, a silence, a glance. It's impossible to convey in words what I felt that night.

As the others were preparing to go on stage. Rudy patted me on the back.

'Hermano, this is huge. You've done something people will not forget for a long time.'

'Thanks, Rudy, for helping us to get here.'

'No problem, man, I'm just sorry that we didn't get a chance to get you into a studio, but hey, this concert is going out live. Millions of people are going to hear you! And we'll have a record of that.'

I thanked him again. Next to me John Wau was running his hands nervously up and down the frets of his guitar.

'Slow down,' I said. 'You'll wear yourself out.'

'You're right. I can't believe this is happening.'

'We'll be fine,' I said. 'We've prepared all our lives for this.'

I crept forwards to peer through the curtain. The house band was in full swing. The whole building seemed to reverberate with sound. The audience was cheering and applauding.

'Woah!' Hisham was standing next to me. 'You know who that is?' A technician hissed at him to be quiet. Someone was making a speech. I couldn't really hear the words, but they were clearly appreciated. People were filing past us, many stopping to shake our hands as if we were celebrities ourselves.

'Listen,' Hisham said, turning to me. 'I just want to . . .'

Whatever he was about to say was silenced as there was a brief pause in the applause and then I heard our name.

'The Kamanga Kings!'

We were led out onto the raised platform that ran along the rear of the stage. The audience clapped and whistled and cheered as we came on. I could hardly believe what I saw. Beyond the stage rows and rows of seats rose up in circles towards the sky. Every one of them was occupied, although most people were on their feet clapping and cheering. It felt as if the whole building might just take off and launch itself into space.

'I don't believe this,' I murmured, turning to find Shadia. When she looked back at me, I could see she too was overcome.

Uncle Maher counted us in and we launched ourselves off. We played four numbers back to back, then the lead celebrity in the yellow glasses bounced on to join us. He whispered something to Shadia and she smiled and nodded. Then they launched into a duet of 'I've Got You Under My Skin'. Then, 'Let's Call the Whole Thing Off'. Once again her knowledge of Ella Fitzgerald's repertoire saved all of us. We provided background. It was a little shaky at times, but we held it together.

Herbie Hancock came out to wild applause and went over to the keyboards. I didn't recognise what he was playing at first and then realised it was one of Kadugli's compositions, 'Kings of Kush'. I had no idea how he knew that number, but we came in behind him and followed it through. After that we switched to a jazz standard, 'Strasbourg/St Denis'.

At one point I looked across at Hisham on the keyboards and it felt like the old days, as if the rift had been healed. Then all the celebrities came on stage to join us and the crowd were on their feet going wild. A well-dressed couple took to centre stage.

'That's Beyoncé and Jay-Z,' Shadia whispered.

The man raised a hand for silence and then began to speak.

'We want to take a moment right now to remember all the men, women and children who are out there in the darkness, facing death and hardship, people who see this country as a burning beacon of hope. Their fate hangs in the balance as this administration plays with people's lives.' He paused to take his wife's hand. 'So let us thank our brave friends for making this journey, for lighting up this land with their sound and their soul, and for reminding us that we are all wanderers in this world.'

It was all over before we knew it and we were milling around backstage where a party was in progress. There was plenty to eat and drink. At one point I found myself standing next to a rather odd-looking man wearing a woollen hat and lots of gold chains around his neck.

'Congratulations, man,' he said, holding out his hand.

I thanked him and asked him who he was. It turned out he was a road manager for Wynton Marsalis.

'How long have you done that?'

'Oh, man, years. I mean, really, like decades.'

'Then you must know Adam Kadugli. He used to play with you.'

'Oh, yeah.' The man squinted across the room. 'But he never played with Wynton. He did roadie work for us for a time. Sure, I remember.'

I understood everything now. When he had returned home it had not been in a moment of triumph, it had been a man seeking refuge. He came home to hide from the world.

There was another shout from the door and I saw Waldo had appeared.

'You did it, man, what an amazing show.'

As the celebrations continued, I realised that someone was missing.

'Have you seen Hisham?' I asked John Wau.

'He was here a moment ago. I think he just went out.'

I stepped out into the corridor and walked down it. At the far end I saw him, his silhouette dark against the light coming up the stairs from outside. I was about to call out to him, but I stopped myself. I stood there and watched. He seemed to be thinking. Then he took a deep breath and started down the stairs. He never looked back.

I turned around to find Ms DeHaviland standing behind me.

'It's time,' was all she said.

Epilogue

A soft wind blows across the hosh, bringing with it that familiar blend of dust and sunlight that makes me breathe easy, knowing that I am home, where I belong. I can hear Shadia singing to herself as she hangs the laundry up to dry.

Writing this story down has been something of a relentless obsession these past months. The details come back, sometimes with ease, at other times not. I have found myself trying to make sense of everything that happened. What it meant to us and to me personally. Also, in the bigger picture, the sense of why this was so important at the time. We felt as if we were bringing not just ourselves, but our history, our nation, the people who for so long have lived in the shadows of rulers who speak for us but act only for themselves.

After our hour of triumph on stage, the final journey was conducted mostly in shadows and silence. We were allowed one final trip in the Birchaven, accompanied in front and behind by police vehicles. Our celebrity entourage had melted into the dark and the lights of Broadway faded behind us as we sped down the darkened parkway following the signs to JFK airport. A discreet exit. The Kamanga Kings were literally going to disappear into thin air.

The airport's name brought back the memory of the statue I recalled floating over the dimly lit lobby of the Kennedy Center, what felt like a lifetime ago. We said goodbye to the Birchaven and to Waldo.

'You'll have to come and visit us,' I said to him.

'I'll do that,' he laughed.

Then we were ferried through a service entrance and along corridors that led us round and round until finally we reached a white room with windows along one side, through which we could see the aircraft parked on the tarmac. A door opened and a group of men and women wearing uniforms with the letters ICE emblazoned on them came in. At the head of the group were agents Baumgarten and Blanco. They seemed to be happy this was coming to an end.

We stood in line and were each reunited with our luggage. We identified our cases and then watched as the ICE crew went through our belongings with their blue rubber gloves. I was too tired to care. I just wanted it all to be over.

'One person is missing.' A pair of them were consulting a list. The man holding the clipboard looked down, looked up again, picked us out with his ballpoint pen, asked us to step aside when our names were called, then resigned himself to shaking his head.

'We have a problem.'

I stepped forwards. 'He's not coming. We have no idea where he is.'

There was a groan from the others as they anticipated further delay. Everyone was tired, but there was nothing to be done. We waited. Finally another door opened and Ms DeHaviland appeared. She waved me over.

'Can you tell me, hand on heart, that you have no idea where Hisham is?'

I could have given her Zenobia's name, but I suppose I felt I owed him one last favour. I didn't think that I would ever see him again. Despite everything, I wished him well. I looked into her eyes and shook my head.

'I'm sorry,' I said.

'It's all right, Rushdy. I believe you.'

With a long sigh, Ms DeHaviland nodded. She handed me an envelope. Gandoury had been detained and our money confiscated.

'This has been an extraordinary experience,' she said in parting. 'But I pray I never have to deal with a group like you again.'

With that she stepped back and indicated that the embarkation could continue. Through the glass I could see the steel coffin bearing Alkanary's remains being lifted into the cargo hold. I heard a sob from beside me and looked round at Shadia.

'It's time to take her home,' I said, squeezing her hand. She nodded, and together we walked down the jet bridge towards the plane. At the end, I paused for a second to turn and look back, but Ms DeHaviland had already gone.

I hope one day that these words will find their way out into the world, so that people can read the story of the Kamanga Kings, but there are more immediate concerns to hand. As I write this, I can look out through the doorway of my room to the open yard. The wind is blowing in circles, little eddies that stir up the ground. Everything is changing.

Our adventures abroad seem to have triggered something far more significant. A revolution is under way. People came out to occupy the squares and demand the end to the regime. It feels like the beginning of a new era. Of course, we can't really claim responsibility, but I'd like to think that the Kamanga Kings provided at least a tiny bit of inspiration. At night our music can be heard in the impromptu camps. Kadugli has been seen down there playing for the crowds. The final outcome is still uncertain and we must be strong and united if we are to succeed. But nothing worthwhile is ever achieved without struggle.

I was offered a teaching post at a rather fancy private school. I only have to work a couple of times a week, teaching the kids about music, which comes easier to me than literature. Thinking back now to the beginning, to when this idea first dawned, I imagined that, if we were lucky, we might manage to spark a brief, fleeting moment that would flare across the sky like a comet. And just like those celestial bodies, it would soon burn out, extinguished by the infinite darkness of eternity. Some things are destined to remain shrouded in the mystery of legend, and I supposed the Kamanga Kings was one of them.

Yet it wasn't to be. The kings did not fade once more into obscurity. Instead we began receiving offers to play abroad. This summer we shall travel to play at festivals all over Europe. The line-up has changed a little. Wad Mazaj went back to driving his taxi. He said the excitement was too much for him. Uncle Maher is still going strong. I have a feeling that he will outlast us all. John Wau and Kadugli are still the backbone of the ensemble. We have a new keyboard player, a woman this time. Shadia remains our lead singer, and will return to full duties in a few months – or as soon as she feels like it after the baby arrives.

I know that somehow, no matter how hard I try, I will never do justice to that trip. We were lost and America helped us to find ourselves. Now, as I sit here listening to my wife singing in the kitchen across the yard, I think how lucky I am, and how I hardly seem to have deserved such good fortune. And maybe that is the nature of luck, that we cannot know it, or expect it, and that all too often it comes in a form that we could never have predicted. We are not rich, nor I imagine will we ever be, but we have something more, something that cannot be quantified, something that is true.

There are moments, some of them recorded in history books, but many of them not, which remind us that miracles are possible. They are come and gone in the blinking of an eye. We snatch eternity from a brief encounter that allows us to rise together to the heavens, lifting our spirits, up into the deep, dark unfathomable night that sooner or later will cover us all. If that is not the essence of music, I don't know what is.

Acknowledgements

Books seem to emerge from a point of inflection at which two ideas converge. The first was less of an idea than a longstanding desire to write about the uniqueness of Sudanese music and of the plight of musicians who have suffered so much over the years. This book is dedicated to them, and to all persecuted musicians everywhere.

The second line of inspiration came during a trip to Washington DC, and here my thanks go out to Alicia Adams and everyone at The John F. Kennedy Center For The Performing Arts for inviting me to their Arabesques festival back in 2009 – that's how long this book has taken. More specifically, I'd like to thank my friends Ahdaf Soueif and Omar R. Hamilton for our conversation one evening in which the story came up about two Sudanese athletes who had just run off and were seeking asylum. I'm sorry this took so long.

More indirectly, this book also owes a debt to the anonymous woman who knocked on our front door when I was a child offering music lessons. My mother's response, that 'none of my children are musical', left me with a lifelong sense of frustration. To my regret, I never proved her wrong by learning to play an instrument. It has come down to my children, Aisha and Louis, to disprove our genetic lack of musical talent. My thanks to Louis Rustum in particular for taking the time to read the manuscript and offer suggestions.

A dedication also goes out to my father, for the oud I still have, for introducing us to the music of Hassan Attiya, and for the record he always claimed to have cut in one of HMV's recording booths in Oxford Street, many years ago — never heard but still a source of wonder.

My thanks also to Ellah Wakatama for her enthusiasm and faith in my work, which I hope one day to repay. With that go my thanks to everyone at Cannongate who has worked so hard to make this book ready. Thanks also to Euan Thorneycroft and his team at A.M. Heath in London.

And finally, to Jannah Loontjens for being a constant source of support and inspiration.